ROWAN

ANNE GREGOR

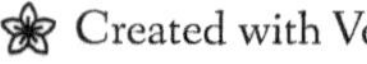 Created with Vellum

PREFACE

Phytophthora infestans is a water mold—a fungus-like microorganism—and the cause of Ireland's potato blight. The Irish Potato Famine began in 1845 and hung on through 1852, killing a million men, women, and children—losing at least another million to emigration.

Many emigrants seeking cheap passage to America found themselves on overcrowded 'coffin' ships that had no regard for passenger safety. Little food and water during the six-week to three-month voyage. Squalid, close quarters below deck caused thousands to die during the journey, with more perishing from typhus once in port.

Countless Irish immigrants during the famine years landed in America poor, malnourished, lacking a trade, and speaking little English. They set up small ghetto communities on the eastern seaboard where the ships' passengers disembarked at the Boston and New York ports.

Their lack of skills and literacy forced the Irish into accepting the worst jobs. Working long hours and receiving little pay. America's expansion push called for cheap labor, and

Irish immigrants fit the bill. They built roads, canals, bridges, and laid track for railroads.

It was after the Civil War that the Irish began pushing westward alongside the railroad companies, helping the transcontinental crossing lay track across America. Many of these same Irish settled along the track, bringing their culture and religion with them. Atoka, Oklahoma, is one such place.

In 1852, Joseph Byrne, barely out of nappies, survived the eight-week voyage from his family's beloved Ireland to America's coast. Starting out in his young teens, Joseph survived working the transcontinental railroad line for eight years. By 1872, the Missouri—Kansas—Texas Railway, or Katy, reached Atoka, and Joseph found his home. In 1873, the twenty-three-year-old Irish railroader met the love of his life, Neakita, a Choctaw native. His wild Rose.

THE IRISH WOLVES TRILOGY FOLLOWS THE LEGACY AND DESCENDANTS OF JOSEPH BYRNE.

ROWAN

S he had become a cliché. She was the woman standing outside the restaurant's window, in the dark, in the rain, her long black hair swimming in rivulets down her back, lashes dripping, rain cutting paths across the planes of her face. Her cold, wet misery—her tithe to watch the warm scene inside. Everyone was smiling and laughing, eating and drinking, kisses to cheeks and hands touching beneath the table.

For the ones inside, it was family. It was love.

For her, the woman outside, it was lonely. It was cold. A recurring, waking nightmare.

Raven and River. Rowan's beloved sisters. They were the ones she was watching through the window—with the men they loved.

Rowan's problem—she didn't want a bright-haired fairytale prince. No, she wanted the dark king.

A man who did not want her.

Outside looking in. Wishes that don't come true.

1

NEW YEAR'S DAY—EARLY MORNING

"What in the hell do you think you're doing?" Hugh bellowed, startling Rowan and almost making her tumble from her precarious perch.

She was currently stretched atop one of the highest rungs on Hugh's library ladder. Flustered and annoyed, her usual feelings around the retired oil billionaire, she stopped reaching for the book that had caught her eye. Technically, a book hadn't caught her eye, but an exquisitely crafted archival box and her curiosity about what it might hold got the best of her. It was placed on the *highest* bookshelf, mocking her short frame, which was why she found herself on the ladder in the first place.

Rowan swung her head around, ready to growl back a response, the only language the man seemed to understand, and remind Hugh the Harasser that he had, in fact, *given* her permission to be here not three hours ago at Irish Wolves Pub & Eatery.

Wolves was the O'Faolains' first experimental step as restaurateurs and where she'd spent New Year's Eve with her two sisters and their significant others, Bran and Patrick, Hugh's sons...*and* Hugh. Both of their families had been staying at the

O'Faolain compound in Muskogee, Oklahoma, during the holiday season and for Raven and Bran's wedding.

Before she could shut down the Master of Moodiness, Rowan lost her balance. One moment, she was all easy elegance —*à la* Belle swinging on her hometown bookstore's ladder, carefree and smiling. Then one foot slipped, the arm previously reaching for the treasure above her head flailing, which shifted her weight and momentum. A ballet choreographed in disaster, and unlike the bibliophilic Beauty, there was no singing and certainly no grace.

She felt her remaining hand slip, which allowed her upper body to slow-fall backward. The only purchase left was one foot, five little toes, gripping a step. For a single heartbeat, Rowan thought she might tip her body back toward the ladder's safety. Unfortunately, her windmilling arms had no effect on gravity.

Rowan had a moment to consider what a header to the stone library floor might feel like—on her face—when a warm hand slid beneath Rowan's pajama shorts. Beast to the rescue. Large fingers gripped her bare ass, stopping the inevitable fall. Rowan's body halted abruptly, arched backward at an awkward angle like a stringless marionette.

However, with Hugh's hand hidden beneath her shorts, a risqué sculpture in freefall might be a better description. Visualize Atlas holding up the heavens and then replace the Titan with Hugh holding her ass.

His warm grip was the architectural keystone suspending disaster and injury. It also created a shocking level of intimacy.

As Rowan slightly twisted toward the O'Faolain patriarch, she witnessed the widening of his eyes and the complete stillness of his body as his fingertips found their resting places, touching her most intimate...nooks and crannies.

Hugh might not be a Greek god, but the man was huge and

mouthwateringly gorgeous. No matter how undignified her current position, she prayed he'd keep touching her.

Rowan was afraid to move. First, she didn't want him to take his fingers away, and second, if he moved his fingers, she was afraid a moan might slip out.

And then...his fingers flexed—barely—and, oh God, she moan-squeaked. *Kill me.*

Squeaking was so not sexy.

Hugh's eyes flew to hers. He was the most intense man Rowan had ever met, and right now, she wanted all that pent-up, growling, testosterone-fueled intensity sinking into her body. His dark brown eyes looked almost black as they stared at one another.

Hugh inhaled deeply before reaching his free hand toward her and placing it against her side closest to the rungs. Rowan shivered as his heat radiated through the thin material of her sleep tank, then inhaled sharply as his grip tightened and his thumb pressed below her right breast.

It was Hugh's turn to moan. Rowan watched him close his eyes and swallow. He was *always* rigidly in control of himself. At that moment, he looked a hairsbreadth away from pulling Rowan into his arms and finally, *finally*, touching her the way she'd dreamed of him doing—the way his face always said he wanted to.

Opening his eyes, Hugh easily lifted her from the ladder, setting her carefully in front of him. As he slowly pulled his fingers from inside her shorts, Rowan knew he must have felt her damp heat. When he muttered "Christ" under his breath, she was sure of it.

He hadn't removed his hand from her side yet. From his much greater height, Hugh was 6'4" to her 5'4", his thumb rested snugly under her breast, pushing her boob slightly higher than the other. He *had* to know where he was touching her.

When his thumb slowly swiped right, the nail's tip edging her painfully erect nipple, Rowan *knew* he knew what he was touching.

As Rowan took a tentative half step forward to close the gap between their bodies, Hugh's breath exploded, and he practically tripped over his feet as he released her and jumped back. Rowan could only blink in wonderment at the man's mercurial moods. She was tired of him looking at her like he wanted her close while putting up walls to keep her far away. It was confusing and frustrating—and had been going on for months.

Tired of the mixed signals, Rowan took a step toward him. "Hugh," she began softly, "Will you ki—." Before she could finish asking him to kiss her, he cut her off.

"Why are you here?" he demanded.

So, they were playing the Ignore What Just Happened game. Typical. He stood there, looking furious and devastatingly handsome, damn it. He still wore his slacks and white button-up from Wolves. The blazer was gone, and his sleeves were rolled up, showing off the ridges of his muscular forearms and their dusting of dark hair. God, Rowan wished she could explore his body. For days.

"If you'll recall, you told me when we got home that you were headed to your office to make sure our flight to Dublin was finalized for the morning, and you also wanted to answer some emails." When he continued to stare with his unblinking stoney expression, Rowan got even more pissed. "*You* told *me* that I could use your library for about an hour while you worked. And that's what I did after I changed!" Rowan shouted. "I've only been in here, like thirty minutes."

"That was two hours ago."

Shit. Rowan could feel her cheeks heat. Damn. Damn. Damn. Clearing the stutter of embarrassment from her throat, she calmly replied, "Time obviously got away from me." This was true. There were so many books to see and touch and a million more still in boxes to discover. How could he blame her for that?

"It's late, and I don't have time to waste playing librarian with you," Hugh snarled. "I'm going to bed. Please shut the door on your way out."

Rowan's whole body was combustably hot. Scorching. Initially, the heat had come from the object of her deepest desire, Hugh Darcy O'Faolain, having his hands on her body. Finally. The heat running lava tracks through her veins now was all fury as Hugh's bedroom door clicked closed behind him. *Asshole.*

Rowan knew he desired her. He'd done nothing but visually stalk her for months. He'd practically torn Ciaran Murphy's head from his shoulders when the Irish pub owner had dared put his arm around her. Hugh's behavior wasn't fatherly, at all, but the stubborn man refused to make a move on her! It had to be their age difference, but Jesus, get over it.

Her two older sisters were married to or dating his sons. Rowan *was* the youngest of the lot, but still, again, he needed to let it go. She was a woman who knew exactly what she wanted and who she wanted doing it to her.

She was sick of his heated looks and possessive behavior if he *never* planned on *acting* on one damn thing. Only a few hours earlier at Wolves, she and Hugh had spent time alone together looking at the memorial she'd helped design for his late father. There had been a moment where he'd rested his heavy hand on her lower back. It felt like he had been branding her, staking his claim.

Then they'd danced together as the clock struck midnight. He'd pulled her tight to his body. The new year had started with the two of them holding each other. It had seemed a portent for things to come. A beginning. And then...*Why are you here? It's late, and I don't have time to waste playing librarian with you. I'm going to bed. Please shut the door on your way out.*

Screw that. Rowan had had enough of his bullshit. Mind made up, she opened the door Hugh had disappeared through and found herself in an all-white paradise. Rowan wasn't sure what she'd expected of Hugh's bedroom, his inner sanctum, but breezy white linens and warm woods weren't it. But then, black silk sheets and red roses didn't match him either. The more she looked around her, she decided the simplicity in the room was beautiful and peaceful.

Unfortunately, the aesthetics hadn't rubbed off on the killjoy.

Hugh's bedroom included an open lavatory. She heard the shower running, but surely, he hadn't gotten in yet. He'd only stormed off a few minutes ago. More lovely white met her eyes; counters, braided rugs covered warm wood floors, white-framed family photos. Rowan momentarily got sucked into looking at the candid pictures of Hugh and his mother and father and Hugh with his sons. They were so and heart-warming that Rowan almost forgot she was in Hugh's personal, really personal, space.

Her favorite was a candid photo of Hugh holding Bran to his side, his chubby legs and white blonde hair unmistakable. His other arm held a baby. Patrick. The absolute joy of Hugh's smile made Rowan's heart pound. An answering joy spread along her nerves. Hugh was an exceptional father. She wished desperately that her own father could have met him.

Rowan rounded the wooden partition to find— Oh. My. God. —Solid glass walls. Hugh naked behind the glass. One hand plastered above his bowed head, water beaded off his short hair, running tracks through his long dark beard, highlighting the white and silver streaks. His broad back blocked most of the spray, giving Rowan an unimpeded view of Hugh's magnificent body. His other hand...Christ, her mouth was dry. His other hand was stroking his extremely large, extremely erect sex.

He was masturbating. Rowan was watching Hugh O'Faolain masturbate.

She backed up a step until her back hit the wood slats of the dividing wall. She could only stare in wonder at his body. Knowing a man is big and fit isn't the same as seeing that man naked...and aroused. His body was art, all ropey muscles, furrows, and valleys. Abdominal ridges highlighted by the perfect vee of his hips. A Spartan warrior—one she wanted to touch and taste. Rowan felt her nipples harden and her sex clench with every stroke of his palm. She should run.

Running wasn't her style.

His fingers had brushed between Rowan's legs, Jesus. He'd felt everything from her core to between her cheeks. It had taken everything he had, all his determination, not to let his fingers sink in everywhere they could. He was still imagining doing just that, which is why he was currently jacking off, but fuck him, he knew from multiple other attempts that his hand would never relieve the ache he felt deep in his body for that woman.

He groaned as he remembered his fingertips barely sliding against the lips of her sex. She'd been feverishly hot. Wet. For him.

He hated himself for wanting her. He was even more furious with himself for getting off to thoughts of her, but at that moment, he couldn't stop. Knowing she was younger than his sons didn't force his hand to cease.

He could not, would not, touch her. More than he had only moments ago, he supposed. Hugh stroked a little faster thinking of her plump breasts and hard nipples. That top she'd been wearing left little to the imagination, and where Rowan was concerned, his imagination was poetic.

Hugh froze as movement caught his attention. His head jerked up and...he had an audience. Rowan was there. She was leaning against the opposite wall, her eyes wide. God, her nipples were hard, and her mouth was parted, panting. She'd been watching him. She was turned on. *That* almost had him coming, but...

He let go of his hard flesh, taking a small step away from the glass, about to grab a towel and demand answers as to why she was there.

She held her hand out to him and shook her head. Through the shower's mist, Hugh watched her mouth move, heard the words her lips formed, and knew he was in trouble.

"Don't stop."

That's all she said. Her eyes never wavered. She only stood straighter, and Hugh watched Rowan's hands pinch the thin hem of her tank and tug it over her head. Hugh's hand landed flat against the glass wall of his shower. He hadn't even been aware of stepping close to the partition again. Her breasts were perfection. Full. He ached to cup them in his hands.

There was a tattoo on the side of her right breast. What the fuck was it? Hugh didn't care, he only wanted to suck and bite the mark—cover her mark with his.

"Rowan," he groaned. "I'm not touching you." It was all he wanted.

"I'll touch myself and wish it was you," she replied, her voice husky with desire.

He'd done so well at pretending for months that she could never want him this way. That his obsession was one-sided. Sure, Hugh had seen her watching him, but he assumed it was because he constantly made an ass out of himself around her. He'd felt like a pervert for wanting such a young woman. He hadn't dared entertain her wanting him. Jesus, it still didn't change things. She was too young to recognize he wasn't what she needed.

He had to be stronger. Why, then, was he not stopping this?

She leaned back against the wall, arching her back slightly to make her breasts stand out even more. No matter the number of chastisements heaped upon his conscience, he couldn't look away. He could not pull his gaze from her body. Then she shocked the hell out of him. Rowan looked him in the eye and slowly ran the fingers of her right hand across her breasts, ripping a groan from his throat when she squeezed her nipples before sliding down the flat plain of her stomach, slipping beneath her shorts. She was bare beneath, he knew personally. Was she...was she going to touch herself? Make herself come? While he fucking watched?

Rowan only continued to consider him as her fingers slipped lower. She widened her stance. Hugh saw her hand moving side to side, then up and down, in and out. Her pants roared in his ears. The bathroom could be burning down around his head, and he wouldn't have looked away. His right hand drifted toward his swollen flesh, pinching the head once. He was about to release himself, but Rowan was watching him intently. She moaned, "Yes, Hugh."

As her movements became more frantic, Hugh couldn't stop from pumping himself in return. They never stopped watching each other. Rowan's mouth had curved in an almost painful expression. She was close, so close. Hugh stroked faster and faster. His balls were tight, and he could feel himself tipping over the edge. As Rowan screamed his name, Hugh painted the glass walls in streams of white. His body bowed in a perfect pain, his legs shook, barely holding his weight. That was the most erotic moment of his life, and he'd only touched himself.

His most sensual experience was with a woman younger

than—*Damn it!* He stood straight, ashamed about what he'd done. Hugh flinched at seeing Rowan's perfect breasts still on full display, swearing as she slowly pulled her hand from between her legs, wishing simultaneously that she was completely naked and thankful it was one less visual he had to endure during his sleepless nights.

Rowan never said another word. She bent down to retrieve her top from the floor, her breasts swaying with the movement, and slipped it easily over her head. He saw her tattoo clearly then. A triskelion disk and a tree, probably to represent her name. She gave him a smile, small but enough to show off her gorgeous dimples.

Dimples that he only wanted her to show him. If she were his alone, Hugh would demand she only smile for him.

It was painful to remember that she would never be his, and he would never be hers.

She turned and left. His cum still marked this moment of folly.

2

DUBLIN, IRELAND—MAY

Rowan's thoughts were all jumbled. She thought she was dreaming, but she also thought she was awake. Her eyes wouldn't open. Asleep. Her mom and dad just hugged her. Dreaming. Her parents were dead. A car wreck. Reality.

She would do anything to have them back. To run her fingers through her mother's long black hair, a testament to her proud Native American heritage—just like Rowan's. To see her hazel eyes crinkle at the corners when she laughed, teasing her Irish dad about his brilliantly white skin hurting her eyes—just like Rowan's.

She really should try to wake up, but Mom and Dad were holding her hands now.

"I love you, my sweet little Rowan tree," her mother whispered, clasping Row's hand to her chest.

"M'iníon. Mothaím uaim thú," her father spoke as he kissed the knuckles of her other hand. *My daughter. I miss you.*

"I'm glad you're here. Raven, River, and I miss you so much. Can you stay longer? So they can see you too?

Rowan knew this was a dream, but even so, she'd never want her sisters, her best friends, not to see their parents again. The three remained strong after the death of their parents because they chose to. They chose not to allow depressing shadows to linger. They expected each other to share when one of them was going through a rough patch. To catch one another when they stumbled.

Rowan focused again on her parents. They were now standing against the far wall in whatever room this was. She felt hot tears leak from the corners of her eyes, knowing they were leaving. Of course, they couldn't stay. This was only a dream. They smiled once more before disappearing.

Damn it. Rowan hated how alone she felt. Even in her dreams, she ended up alone.

She sighed, feeling sorry for herself. But...there was *some* reason Rowan needed to wake up. A meeting? Hair appointment?

She stopped trying to pry her eyes open when she remembered a story her mother used to tell her at night sometimes. The story of why she and Dad chose Rowan as her name. Mom said it was because rowan trees have deep roots and are resistant to frost and wind. They are slender but hearty. Small but mighty. Dependable. Just like Rowan was, she'd said. Another tear slipped free, tracking down her temple. She loved that story.

Finally, the warmth of too many blankets forced Rowan to open her eyes. Unfortunately, that small victory only led to confusion. She was in the white room from her dream—the lovely one with her parents. She loved dreaming about them. She and her sisters believed it was Mom and Dad's way of sending their love.

This was not her bed.

"Rowan, oh God, Rowan!" Raven was crying and holding Row's right hand to her chest, red-eyed and hiccupping in her distress.

"Oh, God, Row. I love you. I love you. I love you. We've been so scared," River wailed, her sister's hands clasped tight to her thighs.

There was rustling and what sounded like a door opening before someone shouted, "I need a doctor in here now!" Rowan couldn't see the speaker through the black curtains of her sisters' hair, but there was no doubt that the voice belonged to Hugh.

Rowan realized her left arm was in a sling, and she had all sorts of wires and gadgets taped to her body.

Her confusion must have shown on her face because Raven explained between sniffles, "It was Sam Delton. He shot you." At Rowan's gasp, her sister assured her that she'd been very lucky and would make a full recovery. "Thank God the bullet missed anything...vital, but it was close, Row."

"So damn close," River finished. "You've been sedated and asleep since surgery. Two days."

River choked on the 'two.' They must have been so worried. Rowan thought back to her last memories. She remembered going to the bakery, walking with...Rowan stiffened and tried to sit up, only to moan in pain and fall back.

"Where is the fucking doctor?" Hugh bellowed out the door as Jo and her grandma, Nan, rushed in. One worry down then, Jo was safe.

"Thomas? Peter?" Peter had been her guard that day. The Byrnes, O'Faolains, and Jo and James O'Connor had been guarded by Thomas MacGregor's security for months. Once the Oklahoma authorities discovered that a deranged psychopath was hell-bent on hurting their families, they'd gone nowhere without a guard. Delton's warped reasoning and delusions had made their lives increasingly difficult, especially when it was discovered he'd followed them to Ireland.

"Peter was shot twice," Jo explained. "In his leg, which

caused considerable damage, and his arm. With rest and physical therapy, he will be okay. Thomas is with him now."

Nan scooched in on Raven's side and kissed her face about forty times, tears falling down Rowan's neck. "My sweet baby. Oh, Rowan, my love, my love. Tell me what you need. Anything."

"I'll be fine, Nan. I swear. I'm sorry I worried everyone so much." Rowan was still trying to process that their stalker had actually shot her. "Is he still...out there?" Rowan swallowed the fear clogging her throat at the thought.

Bran and Patrick stepped toward the bed then, each putting hands on her sisters' shoulders. "The extra men MacGregor hired to patrol the neighborhood caught a reflection from the roof of a nearby building. They all had walkies and MacGregor sent out orders as soon as the shooting stopped," Bran explained.

"They knew where to concentrate their efforts. Once Delton realized he was surrounded, it was over."

"Enough, boys. Rowan doesn't need every detail," Hugh growled at his sons.

Rowan dismissed the Guru of Denial's comment. She needed to learn how to become an expert on ignoring him if she hoped to ever control her feelings for the man. He'd made it abundantly clear, more than once to her chagrin, that he would never be romantically attached to her.

"What do you mean by, 'it was over?' Did he surrender?" Rowan queried.

Nan was the one to answer while she finger-combed Rowan's hair. "He jumped. Killed himself, and good fecking riddance, I say."

"Nan!" River gasped. "Language," she teased, trying to lighten the mood.

"I said what I said, and I won't apologize. That despicable

human hurt one of my girls and so he was more than welcome to die at his own hand."

Rowan could only shake her head. It was crazy to wake up, find out she'd been shot, and then find out the shooter was dead.

"Since the shooting, the FBI has gotten much further into Delton's online sexual predator presence. They believe many of the women in his videos can be identified and contacted. Delton is dead, but he had a lot of money in several accounts that they've discovered since getting a hold of his phone and laptop," Patrick explained.

"He was wearing a uniform shirt from that coffee shop we loved," River added. "When they searched the store, the FBI found his luggage in the back, including his laptop. He must have been planning on leaving Dublin after he shot you, Row." River finished, touching a napkin to her eyes, tearing up again.

"He was in contact with several 'people of interest,'" Bran air quoted. "Which means they have solid leads in taking down several nasty predators. Delton, at least, won't be hurting or terrorizing anymore women. Also, our families are finally free to live our lives openly again."

"No more buddy system," Rowan said, attempting a smile.

"The accounts of money Pat mentioned are probably not all of them," Raven explained. "The FBI believe they'll uncover more. That money can be used to help the women that Delton abused. For counseling or anything else they might need."

"It's probably the same money his father stole from the O'Faolains, right?" Rowan asked.

"Most likely," Jo answered. "But Hugh said he didn't want a dime of it back. He is relinquishing all claim to the embezzled funds to help the women that were hurt."

At this, Rowan looked at Hugh, who, shocker, remained silent. Christ, that man was the most...the most irritating human being.

"You cried before you woke up. Are you hurting?"

Ahh, he speaks. Observant and direct. His dark hair, barely long enough to lay over, was shaved close on both sides. His beard was a ridiculous source of fantasy-laden daydreams, and his broad shoulders and muscular thighs were beacons shouting "touch me" beneath his gray tee and jeans. The t-shirt hid ripped abs. She would know, after all, she'd seen him naked.

But oh, God. He looked wrecked.

Rowan cleared her throat, darting glances at Raven and River. They immediately sat up straighter. "I'm sore, but it's bearable."

"What made you cry? You were talking in your sleep."

Good Lord, no wonder the man was so successful. His motto had to be "Let Nothing Go. Ever."

When her sisters touched her legs, questioning, Rowan couldn't lie. "Mom and Dad. I dreamed they were here. I promise to tell you guys about it later. Okay?" They both nodded. "You too, Nan." Her grandma nodded, equally as moved.

A harried-looking doctor entered her room before Rowan could ask any more questions. He was handsome in a mid-forties, vacation needed ASAP, kind of way. His nurse was an older woman who followed the doctor into the room. One more body, and the walls would pop at the seams.

Her sisters and Nan backed away from the bed so that the doctor could approach. "Miss Byrne," he smiled. "I'm Dr. Trenton, and this is my favorite nurse, Terese."

Terese grinned, patting her salt and pepper bun "I'm only his favorite, because I bring him donuts every week."

"Hey, not true, T," Dr. Trenton denied. In a stage whisper, he added, "But if I were to be bribed, donuts are the way to go. I'm the one who took care of you in surgery, by the way."

"Thank you, Doctor. Hopefully, I'm well enough to get out of your hair sooner rather than later."

"I want to take a look at your incision and poke about your chest in a painful way to check that everything is healing as it should," he chuckled. "Seriously, though, you'll probably want to hit me before this is over."

Rowan didn't laugh because her chest and shoulder area were starting to fuss at her. Laughing would have been a big no-no. "I don't mind. The sooner you say I'm okay, the sooner I can check out of this lovely white box."

Dr. Trenton began to untie her gown, and her sisters crowded the bed, uncaring that the doctor might need room to do his job.

"Boys, leave the room. Now." Hugh demanded.

What in the hell was Hugh going on about now? It's not like Bran and Patrick would try to sneak peeks at her breast. Jesus! Raven and River raised their brows at Rowan and then told their spouses that they would call them back when the doctor had finished his exam. Bran and Patrick smiled at Rowan before leaving the room.

Hugh was still staring at Rowan, or more specifically, the doctor currently peeling her gown aside to get to her bandages. Most of her left breast was exposed now. Dr. Trenton immediately started removing the tape and gauze.

"Luckily, the bullet passed between the ribs below your breast here," The doctor explained as he touched a spot below her breast that she couldn't see. "It got hung up between the bones in your back. One rib in the front was cracked and two in the back. With patience, you should feel fine in a few months with only a bit of lingering tenderness."

Hugh came closer to the bed, standing directly behind the doctor. If Dr. Trenton was uncomfortable with a berserker breathing down his neck, he never let on.

. . .

Trenton was all business as he discarded the bandages on a tray the nurse had placed next to him on the bed. All Hugh could think about was how close he'd come to losing Rowan, and now, how close another man was to Rowan. Doctor or not, he didn't like it. He was irrationally obsessed with the need to hold her and assure himself that she truly was going to be okay.

He hadn't slept or left her side since she'd gotten out of surgery. None of them had, except when Bran and Raven would take moments to spend time with their son, and Patrick would force River to take a quick nap on his lap in the waiting room. Even Devlen, Bébhinn's fiancé, insisted she sleep at her apartment last night.

Getting that call, Christ. He went mad with rage. He wanted to hug her gently to his chest and tell her...he couldn't tell her how he felt, but fuck him, he wanted to.

"Hey, Row," River began, "at least your boob tattoo was on the other side."

He'd seen that particular tattoo and a lot more than that.

Jo, Nan, and Raven all laughed at River's joke. He wanted to laugh too. He wanted to pretend he wasn't falling apart. He couldn't. His chest felt tight every time he relived MacGregor's call, telling him that Rowan had been shot. Had she not made it...Hugh wasn't sure if he could have recovered.

Jo excused herself to check on MacGregor and his man, Peter. Rowan's gaze met his. Something in his face must have alerted her to his distress because she raised her brow in question. Hugh could only shrug and shake his head. He crossed his arms over his chest and tried to pay attention to what Dr. Trenton said about her recovery and eventual physical therapy.

"Hugh. Come here, please."

His head jerked to Rowan's face. She was holding her right hand out toward him.

"Rave, make room for Hugh, please."

He wanted to go to her. He wanted to only go to her. He needed to touch her and assure himself she was whole. Raven stood and moved back, giving him room to walk up and take Rowan's hand. Clasp her delicate fingers between his own, much larger ones.

He could take her hand in front of her family.

He could claim her as his.

He took one step forward, his eyes never wavering from hers. He stopped.

She was still too young for him.

"I wish..." Hugh couldn't finish. He knew he was about to break both their hearts. Hugh saw the moment Rowan realized he wouldn't take her hand—his rejection. Her hand fell to her side. God, the pain in his chest was debilitating.

"If my wishes were wants granted, I'd be yours, and you'd be mine, Hugh."

She'd said that—out loud and in front of her sisters. In front of her grandmother, the doctor, and a nurse. Courageous. An action Hugh could not claim at that moment. He felt his face burn with shame. Regret. He spun on his heel and yanked the door open. Before the click sounded at his back, he heard Rowan speak once more.

"Goodbye, Hugh."

He ignored the alarmed looks on his sons' faces as he burst out of Rowan's room. He couldn't leave the hospital fast enough. The last look he'd seen on Rowan's face would forever be etched in his memory. Disappointment. Defeat.

Hugh knew he was doing the right thing. Why, then, did he feel like the dumbest man in the world?

In twenty years, hell, even in ten years, Rowan would thank

him for not allowing her to be shackled to an old man. Hugh had also proven that relationships and marriage weren't for him. He knew his ex-wife was a horrible woman, the opposite of everything Rowan Byrne encompassed, but the truth was, he'd still failed. He hadn't made Helen happy. Ever. There was a possibility he couldn't make any woman happy.

There had been women over the years that he'd liked well enough. Women who wanted more than casual sex. He'd never been tempted. Not one time.

Hugh shook his head as he stepped through the hospital's automatic doors. He'd never been tempted, but that was before Rowan, and she deserved better than an angry older man dimming the very qualities that drew him to her.

3

———

Raven, River, and Rowan took a moment away from Nan's wedding reception to catch their breath and rest their feet next to the giant metal wolf sculpture a local Dublin metalsmith and their good friend, Josh Ryan, created for the O Building's lobby. The four-story building where she, her sisters, and their husbands and Hugh lived—stood next to Triskelion Territory Designs, the sisters' business. The O'Faolain Wolves, as they were known in Oklahoma where both families had grown up, had managed to create a complicated family dynamic with the Byrne sisters that crossed pretty much every personal and professional boundary.

Case in point, the two blended families lived together, ate together, shopped together, went on dates together, did business together, made babies together, and had sex...well, not Rowan and Hugh. Since this was a private, mental conversation, Rowan would admit that she and Hugh had watched each other masturbate. Once. *Okay, damn it.* Rowan would not sink to the low level of lying to herself. Twice.

Unfortunately, Hugh managed to snuff out each minuscule particle of feelings from the encounters, pretending he wanted

23

nothing to do with her—the youngest Byrne sister and his family by marriage.

The second 'show and don't tell' encounter between them happened in Scotland three months ago. It was the awful night that her sister River had received a photo album of her husband, fiancé at the time, cheating on her. It had been sent from that pathetic excuse of molecules, Samuel Delton. Rowan took a deep breath, thankful yet again that he was now deceased. The world was a better place without that horrible man breathing the same air.

Rowan, Hugh, and Patrick had flown immediately to Inverness from Dublin to comfort her sister. Hugh called Rowan on his way to the airport to let her know what had happened and that he was picking her up. River was not only upset by the pictures, but Delton had covered the album pages in a type of fiberglass powder that burned her skin and created a horrible rash.

Of course, Rowan had gone. Raven hadn't been able to go. She'd been too close to giving birth. Rowan had told herself being in close proximity to Hugh wouldn't be a problem for her. She was just as capable of pretending that they were not desperately attracted to one another as he was.

That evening, after she'd spent time comforting her sister, MacGregor had offered his room to her and Hugh. Thomas said there was a couch bed for Hugh. Between the emotional talk with River and pent-up feelings for Hugh, Rowan had felt like her skin was tight and sensitive to the point that a light touch might make her scream. She wanted relief from River's tears and Hugh's confusing interested indifference.

She had tried to talk to him once after their shower moment. It was the night River and Patrick had gotten back together. They'd been partying at Murphy's bar with Josh Ryan and his girlfriend, Sadhbh, the younger sister of Saoirse Kennedy, Jo's good friend from college. Saoirse was also a close friend of the Byrne sisters and a Dublin real estate powerhouse. The evening had been a lot of fun until Hugh and Patrick walked in.

Hugh had gotten so jealous when Ciaran Murphy had hugged Rowan that Patrick had to physically restrain him. He'd gone home after the incident at Pat's request. Rowan had gone back to their table while River spoke to Patrick. Twenty minutes later, she'd received a text from River that she was leaving with Pat. Rowan didn't blame her sister for giving in. Even after he'd screwed up the relationship, it was clear that Hugh's youngest son would move mountains to get her back...and it didn't hurt his cause that he loved River desperately.

Rowan only lasted another hour at Murphy's. Her anger over Hugh's behavior had soured the pleasure she'd found earlier with her friends. He shouldn't be allowed to get away with that. He shouldn't be allowed to non-verbally mark his territory when he'd never once admitted out loud that he wanted her.

She'd taken one more shot of Slane before saying her good-byes. Rowan remembered being thankful for the liquid courage when she'd stood outside Hugh's door. After all, bearding a lion in his own den is not for the faint of heart or the sober.

The "conversation" that night had been a colossal letdown. He'd answered his door shirtless and in sweats that rode danger-ously low on his hips. He'd looked so beautifully masculine it had almost shut down all cognitive thought. Hugh hadn't even let her through the door. So, standing in the hallway, she'd point blank asked him why he wouldn't acknowledge that he wanted her. Why he wouldn't date her. Fuck her.

Rowan wasn't super proud of her behavior.

"Why won't you let another man have me if you don't want me?" She could tell that question had rocked him.

And what had Rowan gotten for her trouble? What had she

earned for putting her feelings out there? Hugh at his worst. Unemotional. Cordial. Stiff.

"I apologize for making things awkward between us. It wasn't my intention. I'll work at moving past," and there, he clenched his fist that held the door open, *"...this. You are way too young for me to ever consider a true relationship. New Year's...it was a mistake that never should have happened."*

And then the motherfucker said, *"Goodnight, Rowan."* And closed the door gently. In her face.

A mistake. Those words had crushed her. She'd played that conversation on repeat for weeks until she vowed to take a page out of River's book. *Fake it until you make it.* Hugh would no longer control their narrative. She would say what she wanted, do what she wanted, and date whom she wanted. He didn't get to make her feel like a mistake to be forgotten. Not anymore.

She'd made promises to herself that night, promises she hadn't kept. Rowan never spoke her mind to Hugh again, pressed him for more, dated someone, or created her own story. She'd been so, angry at herself, and angry at him, she'd had felt like pushing Hugh that night.

She wasn't even sure why, only...he still watched her. Always. His eyes would follow her wherever she walked, whoever she was speaking to...he watched her. If that was his idea of *"moving past...this,"* he was doing a piss poor job of it. That night they shared the room had definitely been the perfect opportunity to make Mr. O'Faolain uncomfortable.

Perhaps, rethink his stance?

*W*HILE *R*OWAN SORTED *through her bag, she'd told Hugh to take a shower first in the en suite bathroom. He was out in fifteen, and Rowan took his place. When she emerged from the bathroom's steamy environs, she was barely able to make out the* bedroom's features. The only light came from the soft glow of the wall's plug-in night light. When she approached the couch, which sat on the wall next to the bed, she noted that Hugh hadn't pulled the bed out, choosing to curl his large frame to fit the loveseat.

Ridiculous. He probably wanted to pretend to be asleep before she finished showering. As if she would throw herself at him in some sort of uncontrollable lust lunge. Rolling her eyes, she ignored Hugh and climbed onto her king-sized, plush, comfy mattress. After all, she had plans. She moaned at the soft, crisp sheets and pillow top at her back. She moaned again when her head had pressed into a lavender-infused down pillow.

Hugh stayed completely still. Not a single breath or shift. Clearly, he was hoping she would fall asleep quickly so he could relax. Tough shit. She was going to win at least one round against the stubborn bastard. Her time in the bathroom hadn't been just about washing the day's stress and dirt away; no, it had been a board meeting of one. Rowan knocked out a very simple plan to take Hugh down.

This confrontation was long overdue.

Rowan sat up and began by taking her hair out of the clip where she'd put it up to keep her hair dry, then shook it out so the black tresses would fall across the white sheets once she was laid out. Before she could change her mind, she whipped off her t-shirt, sleep pants, and panties.

Hmm, was there a slight rustle to the right of the bed? Coming from the couch? Rowan didn't bother to cover her naked body. She needed to be able to touch herself unimpeded and give Hugh complete optical access.

Rowan laid back, making sure her hair was spread all around her body and over the side of the bed—part of her "look at me" plan. She then surreptitiously pulled the blanket and comforter close so she could tuck some of the material behind her back and hip. Just enough to tilt her body slightly up, giving Hugh a better viewing experience...IMAX—no special glasses required.

Satisfied with her prep, she began by massaging her breasts, which were extra sensitive, squeezing the heavy mounds and rolling and pinching her nipples. Within moments, Rowan felt an answering tug in her core. She was breathing heavily. Hugh had to hear her pants in the still room. She soon forgot about revenge, concentrating on what it might feel like if it were Hugh's hands on her body.

She glanced toward the couch and a thrill zinged through her nerves. She could definitely make out an outline of broad shoulders...he was sitting up. Watching.

Rowan let her legs fall open as she ran her fingers over her body, getting closer and closer to her center. Hugh was panting with her now, his heavy breath setting off mini spasms deep inside. Her eyes had adjusted to the dim room, and Rowan could make out movement on the couch. He had to be touching himself. Stroking. She moaned louder as her fingers swept her wet seam, collecting moisture to circle her sensitive flesh.

Her eyes slid shut as she slipped two of her fingers inside, slowly pumping, slowly building toward release. Her breath whooshed out of her when her eyes opened to Hugh standing next to her, the Grim Reaper; reaper of her soul. He was naked and pumping his length as he watched her fingers disappear, in and out, in and out.

"Rowan. Christ, Rowan." Hugh was beyond pretense. Finally.

Rowan spread her legs wider, she was so wet, her fingers found no resistance. Her hips began to quiver and jerk. Hugh pumped faster and faster.

"I'm going to come, Hugh," Rowan hissed.

"That's it, baby, come for me," Hugh demanded in his deep gravelly voice. He was leaning half over her body, his gaze locked *on her body. As she felt herself tip over the edge, she clamped her lips together to tamp down the keening release that wanted to escape her throat. Hugh wasn't nearly so quiet as he groaned, shooting streams of cum all over her belly.*

"I like you on my skin, Hugh," she whispered, still trying to catch her breath.

Rowan might die from how satisfied she felt. She flung her hands above her head and stretched languorously. Hugh didn't speak; he only stared at her body as if he couldn't believe what had just happened. He shook his head and stepped back from the bed. His still semi-hard sex hanging between his thick, muscular thighs. When Rowan chanced a look at his face, she knew their moment was over.

Hugh looked stricken as if they'd just done something wrong. Regretful.

He turned his back to her then and reached for his clothes. Without even glancing her way, he said, "Please, Rowan. This can't happen again. We will never be anything more." He pulled on his sweats and t-shirt, still facing away. "I don't want to hurt you, but I do not want a relationship with you. Ever."

And then he walked out of the bedroom and shut the door.

So, Rowan had won. And lost. Everything.

Rowan had been released from the hospital six weeks ago, and with massage and PT, she barely felt a twinge where she'd been shot. A small scar marred her smooth skin, just under her left breast. Her sisters told her not to worry about explaining the scar to a lover, that they'd never look past her tits anyway. They were amazingly supportive, as usual.

She still had nightmares, but those were getting fewer and further between. Probably because Samuel Delton was dead. Thankfully, a few weeks ago, her ex-guard Peter was able to fly back to Louisiana to be with his family to finish his convalescence and PT. The O'Faolains, Byrnes, and O'Connors were enjoying their freedom to move about unguarded and in smaller groups after months on high alert. Since Delton was gone, MacGregor's security guards were no longer needed, and their lives were a whole lot less complicated.

Their business was booming. Thank you, Jesus, for their office manager, Dom. The older gentleman was an ex-butler Bran had convinced to leave his position at the posh Dublin hotel, The Fitzwilliam, to work for them. He managed to keep them all on task and schedule. Her sisters were happy. They loved their husbands, and their husbands loved them. Now, Nan was married and extraordinarily happy and about to leave the O Building and fly to Morcote, Switzerland for her honeymoon—Jo's wedding present to Nan and Devlen. She'd rented them a fully staffed, small villa for two weeks. Nan had fallen in love with the picturesque village when Rowan and her sisters had taken their grandma there last summer for vacation.

Taking a sip of her Bushmills Black Bush, Raven sighed. "Nan literally died over her present. Seriously, River, that rocking chair you found in Scotland is...I don't even have the words, and neither does Nan. It is a stunner. I could run my fingers over the carved flowers for days and find new hidden blooms."

"Dougal Donaldson may have been the world's biggest Scottish ass, but that man is a master woodworker." River smiled. "I'm thankful that Thomas was with Jo and me that day. He saved the whole meeting. The day the head of our security detail became a curmudgeon whisperer was my gain."

"Speaking of Thomas MacGregor," Raven began, "Jo mentioned she was leaving tomorrow for Oklahoma. She said she had a meeting with her folks to discuss a few new clients and to hammer out her schedule for the next several months.

James will be there as well. He and Jane are back from their extended honeymoon. Jo seemed strained when she mentioned the trip." Raven tapped her lip thoughtfully while her other hand was busy rocking her son, Daniel. The uber fancy rocking pram was a gift from Hugh's mother, Matilda.

"Thomas told Pat that he was taking an extended leave from his security firm to visit his family in Scotland. One of his best friends, a man named Johnny, who's been in France for the past several months on a job, is going to take over Thomas' duties for the next few months," River offered. "He also mentioned that he hadn't spent near enough time with his little sister. Apparently, she's "hiding something," River added with air quotes.

Jo hadn't revealed that she and Thomas would be parting ways. Strange. Rowan would corner her tomorrow. "Surely, those two will meet back up once their schedules allow." Rowan hoped so, anyway. Speaking of separation, Rowan had to tell her sisters about her plans. She was about to put her thoughts into words when Raven placed a trembling hand over Rowan's knee.

"Have you found someone to talk to?"

Her sister didn't have to explain. Raven and River had asked her to consider speaking to a therapist when she was recovering in the hospital from the gunshot. Even before getting shot, they knew that finding out her picture had been posted on Delton's dark website affected her sense of safety. How many people knew her face? Her name? Could there be someone worse than Delton waiting in the shadows even now, biding their time?

Of course, the site had been taken down and even security expert Thomas MacGregor believed she was safe. There were still moments when Rowan caught herself looking over her shoulder as she walked down a sidewalk. After being shot, she admitted to herself and her sisters that she did need to speak to someone outside of the family. She didn't want fear to take an even firmer foothold than it already had.

"I did. I think I'll really like her. I have my first appointment next week." Rowan inwardly grimaced when River and Raven looked so relieved and happy. Unfortunately, once they knew where her appointment was...

Taking a deep breath, Rowan cleared her throat. A disgusting habit she had to have picked up from Raven. She started with, "So..."

Raven and River immediately focused on their youngest sister, brows raised in high alert. Here it goes, Rowan thought. "I'm leaving in the morning with Jo."

"The fuck you are," River shot back immediately.

"River," Raven admonished. "What's this all about, Row? You never mentioned going anywhere."

Rowan shrugged sheepishly. She'd known her sisters would be upset that she'd waited 'til the last moment to tell them. "Nan and Dom know. I just made them stay quiet. I took a job in Tulsa."

Blink. Blink. Blinking. Oh, God. Blink. Sniffle. More sniffles.

Fuck. Glassy eyes. Tears.

"But..." River couldn't finish. Her lips were wobbling. "The baby—October..."

"Riv," Rowan grabbed her sister's hand and squeezed. "It's only mid-June now. I'll be home in three months or less. Plenty of time for auntie duties, I promise."

Raven only stared at her. Her one reaction was a small pat to River's knee. Otherwise, she was still. Still and, if her white knuckles were any indication, struggling.

"You're running."

That wasn't a question. Raven knew why Rowan was leaving, and she wasn't happy. "Yes," Row answered honestly.

River's hormonal tears dried when she realized what was actually happening...and why. "I will fucking kill him for this,

Rowan! Why does that King Ding-a-ling get to stay with all of us when my baby sister is being run out of town?"

Phew! River's pregnancy hormones were as unpredictable as Raven's had been. Except River's were much more *Godfather*. Rowan almost lost a finger last week when she'd taken a bite of River's toast during breakfast.

"It isn't Hugh's fault." At both sisters' looks of disbelief, Rowan added, "Seriously, he has been keeping his distance. We rarely see each other and when we do, we rarely interact." Rowan refused to admit that she'd sworn Hugh had followed her and Ciaran Murphy on a dinner date two weeks ago. He'd sworn it was an 'I'm glad you didn't die' offer of food, which was kind, but Rowan could tell the younger Murphy wanted more. A lot more than Rowan was willing to give.

River disagreed. "He still watches you in his broody, silent, annoying way."

Yes, he did, but Rowan had gotten much better at pretending not to notice. *Fake it until you make it.*

"Row," Raven began, pursing her lips, obviously reluctant to push, "you are running. Right?"

Rowan sighed. Defeated. Worn down from months upon months of watching the people she loved most get their happy. They would never, not in a million years, make her feel like the odd one out, but she felt that way, nonetheless. She would never tell her sisters, but she'd stood outside a pub one evening in the rain, watching the foursome smile and laugh over dinner. It had hollowed her.

Then there was watching the man she loved, and yes, damn it, she did love Hugh O'Faolain, drift further and further away from her grasp.

They had shared intimate moments, yes, but they also, at least Rowan had believed they had, shared a bond, one born of respect. She wasn't what he wanted or needed, though. She had to leave. Had to.

Some of her thoughts must have passed over her features because Raven and River placed their fingertips on each of her cheeks.

Love. Only love. Always.

"I understand."

"I support your decision."

"Thank you," Rowan gulped back tears, desperately relieved they were letting her go. "I would never ask for you guys to keep anything from your husbands, but would you mind asking them not to mention my leaving to...to their father?"

"Of course. Bran will not offer the information."

"Patrick tells, he dies."

Christ, poor Patrick, Rowan thought with an inner laugh. The first real humor she'd felt in weeks. She'd miss her sisters. She'd miss her nephew. She'd miss Dublin and Triskelion.

She would miss Hugh.

4

Patrick, River, Bran, Raven, and little Daniel were making a day of looking over the new property. Hugh and his sons had bought the bankrupt distillery that Patrick had found. His youngest son had been working on this particular deal for several months, and it was now theirs.

Only thirty minutes outside of Dublin, the vast acreage had the potential for more ventures besides making good whiskey. His daughters-in-law mentioned that it could easily become a wedding destination or a high-end corporate weekend retreat. He adjusted his grandson, Daniel, in his arms. The little guy had fallen asleep during the initial walk-through and hadn't stirred since.

Rowan hadn't come. He was disappointed but not surprised that she'd opted out of participating in the outing. She opted out of every occasion Hugh was a part of. He hadn't seen even a glimpse of Rowan since Bébhinn and Devlen's wedding reception. Rowan had moved into Bébhinn's place once they left for their honeymoon until she found her own place. That was the last bit of information he'd been given.

That was almost four weeks ago.

Hugh wasn't a fool. She was avoiding him, and it was killing him. He wanted to ask his boys what she'd been up to, but his damnable pride forced his silence. He just pretended every day that he didn't notice her absence. That he didn't care.

He'd been desperate for even a crumb of information, but it was like his boys and Rowan's sisters had made a pact to pretend Rowan didn't exist. Raven and River did not smile as often as they used to. They didn't seem as happy. Hugh was devastated because he couldn't deny that he was the root cause of everyone's discontent. He was only shocked his sons hadn't asked him to leave town.

Hugh sighed. He was flying to Tulsa as soon as they got back to Dublin. Bobby was already at the airport readying the jet and locking in their flight plan. He needed to give his family a break and hopefully allow Rowan to enjoy her family again. He spoke with his mother every day, and she mentioned last week that she and Diana, his mother's best friend and all-around wealthy busybody, were returning to Oklahoma. She'd been home for a few days now. It would be less uncomfortable if he used his mom as an excuse when he told Bran and Patrick. They would believe he wanted to make sure their grandmother had settled back in, and he did want to check on the Muskogee compound.

His mother mentioned that she was excited to get home and check in with her house guest. Hugh hadn't known she'd allowed someone to live in her apartment while she'd been traveling. When he asked who, she got flustered and said they'd been taking care of things for her, promptly changing the subject to complaining about Diana swimming nude the night before. Hugh couldn't hang up fast enough, which, thinking about it now, must have been his mother's intention. He'd get to the bottom of his mother's evasions soon enough.

Rowan. His thoughts always came back to her. He was

desperate and so damn lonely. Even when he just watched her, there was a small amount of comfort knowing she was at least close. Now, it was silent. He felt cold, directionless, rudderless. One missed turn, and he might lose himself. He'd already lost his way. Even during family excursions like this one, everything felt wrong. Rowan was the missing link, and yet he couldn't fathom how they could ever fit together again.

He'd considered giving in to what they both wanted at least a thousand times every day—and then he would remember the sole reason he'd pushed her out of his life. When Rowan was thirty, Hugh would be fifty-nine, forty to sixty-nine, and the rest...it didn't even bear considering.

She would regret it. She would regret him. Eventually.

Rowan's complete absence, however, was intolerable. Daniel stretched, his long legs pushed against Hugh's forearm. Hugh absently kissed the babe's head, where only the barest of white hair covered his scalp. Raven lied to herself daily about how her son's hair was getting so long. Hugh chose not to enlighten her. The boys barely had two strands to rub together until they were at least eighteen months. God, but Daniel looked the spitting image of Bran and Patrick. Hugh couldn't say he missed his children being this age because, honestly, he cherished every age, including now.

His boys had made him a better man when they'd been born, and they still made him a better man thirty years later. Love did that to a person.

Hugh had decided not to tell the kids that he was leaving in a few hours. He'd already written an email explaining his plans and itinerary. It would be auto-delivered to them both tomorrow morning. The four of them, and probably Rowan since he wasn't going, were meeting Saoirse Kennedy and her fiancé, Timothy Daniels tonight for dinner, which was when he planned on leaving.

Hugh never regretted investing in Tim's construction company. The man did excellent work on the O Building, as everyone called the damn building that housed their apartments. Tim would be heading up the facelift on the distillery and all the other buildings that would be added as well.

Raven's assistant and part-time nanny, Bre, was watching Daniel tonight, so Hugh knew they'd stay out much later than normal. He had a driver scheduled to take him to the airport at seven. He'd sleep on the plane and be in Tulsa around one in the morning with the time difference. He planned on going to his hotel penthouse so he could visit his mother for a few days before heading on to Muskogee.

Pulling Daniel just a little tighter to his chest, he breathed through his emotions. He hated leaving his family while so many amazing changes were taking place. He hated missing a single moment, but he'd created this mess with Rowan. This divide. He needed to fix it.

Hugh had hoped to catch even a glimpse of Row before he left town. It wasn't to be.

5

Boys-

I'll be in Oklahoma for the foreseeable future. Flew out last night. I want to check on Mom and spend some time at our Muskogee property. I've accepted several invitations to golf tournaments and a four-day hunt at a lodge in Kansas.

I scheduled a meeting for you boys next week with Tay Withe. He's been a master distiller for thirty years. If you think he's as talented as his resume suggests, you two might want to take him out to see the site. Keep me in the loop. See attachment.

**Consider the name Three Wolves for the whiskey.*
I would like to see a presentation on potential builds for the property. Give Triskelion four weeks to submit their ideas. I will sign off on whatever you two decide. Raven and River had several suggestions yesterday that held promise. Once the initial plans are given a green light, send to Daniels for quoting. He needs to see the property as well. He may have ideas of his own.

There is dock slip in Dublin's harbor, large enough to hold a good-sized yacht that I'm interested in purchasing. Ask Miss Kennedy to see to that. Slips are hard to come by of that size and I want this one. Also, Naas Canal can handle good sized boats and is a short drive from the distillery. See attachment. Please give my apologies to Raven and River. I never wanted to create an environment that made the girls feel as though they couldn't be themselves...together with their sister. I hope my absence solves this problem.

I would appreciate news from both of you. I dislike being gone from you boys for so long. And Daniel.
You both know that I love our Muskogee compound. I think perhaps it's best that I make Oklahoma my permanent residence again. Pat, I will come back in October to see my newest grandchild.

I will come the moment either of you need me.

Dad

6

––––––

"Oh, Rowan!" Matilda gasped, hands going to her chest as she took in the hours and hours of painstaking progress Rowan had achieved on the armoire memory cabinet. Hugh had shipped the cabinet here after River had found it in Scotland, sitting in a talented woodworker's shop. It was a sumptuous American black oak, but the real jewel of the piece was the tree of life carved in the doors.

Rowan had been living in Matilda's hotel suite—penthouse or luxury apartment was a better description—for a little over three weeks, working on her design job for a boutique during the day and this cabinet in the evenings. When Rowan had reached out to Tilly, as the older woman preferred to be called, and asked if she might consider letting Rowan stay at her place until she and Diana returned, Tilly had been thrilled.

When Rowan had asked that she keep the small detail of Rowan living there from her son, she'd gone silent, hesitating. Matilda had to be curious why Rowan would ask for the favor, but she was circumspect enough not to ask. *"Of course, dear. I'll let Tina, my assistant, know to expect you and have a key made."*

And that was that. Rowan had been here almost a month

and enjoyed every moment of working on this cabinet. Tina had given her enough photographs and boxes and folders of memorabilia treasures to fill four armoires. It took her seven days to sort the trove into what would eventually make up the individual 'rooms' inside the cabinet. Vignettes that explored a small part of O'Faolain history through arts and crafts—high-end arts and crafts.

Rowan grinned up at Matilda from her kneeling position in front of the cabinet. "I should be done in no time, but still, I'm stoked with the progress." Tilly had only gotten back to Oklahoma the night before, and she couldn't wait to see her reaction.

Matilda looked stunned, her eyes taking on a sheen as she tried to take in all the family bits at once. Standing, Rowan said, "Here, Tilly, let me take you through the rooms that are done, and I can also describe my ideas for the remaining space."

At Matilda's nod, Rowan started at the top. "Jo found a lovely shop in Dublin that sold a lot of antique textiles, painted silk wallpaper, and things like that. Before I left the city, I visited the shop and found this lovely French toile and striped silk paper. I can tell you," Rowan laughed, "it felt like sacrilege to cut that fabric into tiny bits, but once I saw how perfect it was as a backdrop, I got over it."

"Stunning. Absolutely stunning, sweetheart. You must take Diana and me to the shop the next time we visit. Perhaps in October when River and Patrick have their baby."

"Oh, I will. I didn't know Diana would be coming for the birth. That's awfully nice." Diana Gaines was Matilda's oldest best friend, exorbitantly wealthy, sharp, witty, and a fire-breathing dragon. Rowan and her sisters adored Diana now, but it took a moment to get used to her prickly nature. Her acerbic wit was entertaining, like watching a practiced thespian on her personal stage. It was also amusing that Bran, Patrick, and Hugh shuddered in terror at the mere mention of her name.

"Of course, she will. She didn't make it to see Daniel because she had managed to get a small cold right before we were to fly out and she didn't want to chance being around a newborn or the family. Diana's poor secretary, who accompanied us while we traveled, looked as though she'd been through the wringer when I got back from Dublin. Diana was upset about not being there and made sure everyone was miserable right along with her." Matilda chuckled at the memory.

"She loves the boys, and Hugh as well. She just doesn't show it very well." Matilda shrugged. "Enough of that woman. We decided to take a two-month break from one another. We were both getting on each other's nerves by the end of our trip. However, fifteen minutes ago, Diana's secretary emailed me dinner reservations at the Country Club. Her brother and his son will be in town," Matilda sighed.

"So, two months meant two days?" She only smiled and shrugged at Rowan's question.

"Tina accepted the invitation. I had her add a plus one for you, and Tina is picking up several dresses for you to choose from. Diana will expect us all to dressed to the nines." Rowan didn't bother to decline. The O'Faolain matriarch could be just as stubborn as her son.

"Okay, give me the rest of the tour," Matilda gestured toward the armoire.

Rowan took her time explaining the piece. Why she'd chosen one item over another. Why she'd picked specific color themes. Matilda laughed when she spied the hand-drawn cards from her grandsons, oohed, and aahed over Hugh's handmade shell necklace when he was only five. He'd collected the shells himself during a family vacation in Greece.

"What are these spaces going to be?"

Matilda was referring to the paper placeholders that Rowan had tacked around the open spaces between the shelves and cubbies. Rowan felt her cheeks pinken. Damn her Irish complexion. She'd taken a chance on her skill as an artist. She was second-guessing that choice hardcore now.

"Well, some of the pictures I wanted to use didn't have duplicates. Not that I've found, anyway. And, well...dang, you might not want to use what I've done, which," Rowan threw her hands up, waving them to and fro, "is completely fine. You will not hurt my feelings, Tilly, I swear."

"What in the world, Rowan? Everything you've done is so exceptional, so thoughtful and one of a kind. How can you think I wouldn't like it?"

Perfect. Rowan managed to drum up extra anxiety by drawing more attention to her project. Taking a deep breath, she started walking to the guest room where she'd been sleeping. "Okay. I've been working on some pieces. One of them is done. I did it while I was still in Dublin with this project in mind." The other two are almost done. They just need extra time to dry. I did them in oil, and it takes a while."

Rowan flipped the light on, illuminating the bedroom and the three pictures on stands that stood near the floor-to-ceiling windows. Rowan stopped speaking as Matilda walked to the first picture. Rowan painted one of Jonathan and Matilda's wedding photos. The album held the normal, traditional wedding pictures, but the photographer had taken a few candid photos of the newlyweds. One in particular had caught Rowan's eye.

Jonathan and Matilda looked like they'd just walked onto the dancefloor. No one was near them. They weren't dancing, only staring into each other's eyes. As though they couldn't believe they actually belonged to one another. Jon was holding one of his wife's tiny hands to his chest. He was looking at her in awe. Matilda cupped her husband's jaw, her thumb laid across his lips. It was intimate. Private.

"If I were to name the picture, I would call it *Forever*," Rowan spoke quietly, the older woman still studying the painting.

Matilda swayed. Rowan wrapped her arm around her waist, gently backing the older woman until her legs met with the bed. She sat without being asked. Never taking her eyes from the painting.

Rowan hesitated before sitting next to Matilda on the bed. No one spoke. The only movement were the tears tracking down Tilly's cheeks.

Rowan understood loss. Sometimes a person needed silence when it hit. Sometimes, like now, they might need to know they weren't alone.

Rowan wasn't sure how much time passed before Matilda took a shuddering breath. She still looked at the painting, but her body had straightened. She had come back to herself. "It's hard to be the one still alive." She looked at Rowan, who was still sitting beside her. "I imagine you and your sisters know something about that."

"Yes." An understanding of each other's loss passed between them. "Would you rather have kept this picture private, Tilly? I can choose another for the installation."

"Absolutely not! I never want to forget what kind of love Jon and I shared. I want my son, my grandchildren, and my great-grandchildren to see what love looks like. Bran and Patrick have certainly found it with Raven and River."

Before Matilda could query Rowan if she'd found anyone special, Rowen hopped up and said, "Let me show you the other two. Though if they affect you as strongly as the first, we're going to need whiskey first," she teased, making Matilda smile.

"You can show me and then you and I are ordering room service and working on getting three sheets to the wind. How's that sound?"

"Like my best night ever. We should invite Jo. She leaves for Tokyo day after next and then Switzerland."

"I would love to see Josephine. Let's invite her over. Your Nan's been hounding me to get information on Honey Bunny. This will kill two birds, so to speak."

Poor Jo, Rowan thought, smiling. She led Matilda to the second painting. It was a small five-by-seven landscape of Matilda walking across a shallow rock bed stream. She was holding hands with two precious towheaded boys who were smiling up at their grandmother.

"Rowan, damn it! I'm not one to curse, but you are making me an emotional wreck," Matilda complained as she dabbed her eyes with a tissue Rowan handed her. "That was the year I decided to be an adventurer," she laughed, remembering. "I told Jon and Hugh that I was taking the boys camping, and they weren't coming with us. We went Devil's Den State Park in Arkansas. It was so beautiful. We went in the fall, and I remember the boys and I were in awe at the changing leaves."

"Do not tell me you slept in a tent. I won't believe you."

Matilda rolled her eyes, making Rowan giggle. "I did buy a tent and probably two thousand dollars' worth of stuff that I didn't even know how to use. The boys were beside themselves with excitement. They'd camped with Hugh before, so they knew more than me. Bran helped me unzip the tent, and when I saw the twelve pages of instructions, I promptly called the park ranger station. I asked the kind woman who answered if there were any furnished cabins.

"They only had the biggest one left. It slept eight, had beds, linens, heat and air, and a full kitchen. I booked it immediately, packed up the tent and all the other bags of crap, and found our cabin. It felt as luxurious as a five-star hotel after the near miss with the tent. The boys and I proceeded to have the best weekend of our lives. I swore them to secrecy, of course. Jon and

Hugh were forced to be impressed with my outdoor skills, and to this day, as far as I know, they never told on me.

"In my defense, I did start a fire and cook over it. I burnt everything, but my sweet grandsons never complained. Probably because I gave them each their own bag of marshmallows."

Rowan was laughing so hard by the time Matilda finished recounting her adventure she was wheezing. The thought of the well-to-do Mrs. O'Faolain in flannel, hiking and starting fires was a visual she would never forget.

"I can't believe you chose to paint this picture out of all the ones in those boxes. Rowan," Matilda started, shaking her head, "you have made me remember two of the best moments of my life."

"I'm beyond thrilled. I was nervous. I'm a novice artist at best, but your photos are a true inspiration. There weren't copies so I didn't want to use the originals, and I thought oil paintings would give an old-world whimsy to your memory closet. Now that I have most of your pictures sorted, Tina plans on putting the rest in chronological order in photo albums."

"A novice? Rowan, surely you jest. You are a true talent. As fine an artist as any painter with works hanging in museums. You and your sisters have proven that you're all talented designers, but darling girl, you are an artist. A painter. Your focus should be," Matilda waved her hand at the stands holding the paintings, "this."

Rowan blushed at the praise. She was thrilled that Matilda liked what she'd done so far. That was enough recognition for her. "Okay, one more," Rowan announced while handing another tissue over. She walked to the last easel and turned the stand around. It was a teenage, beardless Hugh, grinning and shaking hands with his father.

Jonathan looked so much like Hugh did now, minus the beard, that Rowan's heart had squeezed with emotion. There was a new silver Porsche in the background. The back of the picture was inscribed, *Hugh's 16th Birthday.*

Rowan swallowed. She missed her family. Her sisters. Bran and Patrick. Hugh.

Matilda studied the painting for several minutes. "I was so mad at Jon that day."

Oh shit, Rowan cringed. "Oh, geez, really."

"Buying my baby boy a sports car that I knew very well he would drive too fast in. I was furious but then, Hugh shook his dad's hand with that big grin, and Jon grinned back. Those two always melted my heart, and damn if I could stay mad at that husband of mine for longer than an hour," Matilda huffed, clearly still amazed at her husband's charm.

"I was relieved when Jon took hold of the back of Hugh's neck like he was a pup and growled into his ear that if he broke one single law in that car, one speed limit, the consequences would be severe. Whether Hugh listened is anyone's guess. I would say no, but he was never in an accident or arrested, so..."

"Then, do I have your approval to use these in the cabinet?"

"Of course. You captured all of our expressions even better than the original pictures. You do realize that if I were to show anyone your paintings, you would be booked out for years." Matilda took Rowan's hands into hers, "please tell me that you'll consider pursuing your art."

Rowan wouldn't promise anything. She was, however, very pleased that her work had touched another person as it had her. "I'll think about it."

"Hmm," was her only response. "Tell me, how are you coping without seeing your sisters and nephew?"

Rowan was thankful for the change in subject. "I'm desperate for nephew snuggles. Desperate," Rowan whined. "Auntie Row facetimes him every night, so he doesn't forget me, but it isn't the same. I miss my sisters too," she admitted.

"Why don't you fly home for a week? Surely, your job here won't go up in flames if you take a week off."

One month hadn't dimmed her thoughts of Hugh. In fact, her nighttime dreams were almost constantly X-rated if Hugh joined them. Going home and seeing him so soon again would be torture. She had to get over wanting him. It was unhealthy and it was causing issues in the family.

Her sisters told Raven two weeks ago that Hugh was practically unbearable. He thought he was hiding his feelings. They said it was painful to watch. He was too stubborn to ask after Rowan's absence, and so he didn't even know she was gone. He probably still thought she was avoiding him.

God, she missed that stubborn asshole.

To answer Matilda's question, Rowan reminded her that she was way ahead of schedule. The boutique was shaping up fast. "So far, this job has been a breeze, and my client is hands-on. It's kind of a dream job. I get to choose what I like and see my vision metamorphosize from the ground up. Plus, I missed Oklahoma, as crazy as that sounds. It's July, so that's like saying I missed high heat, humidity, and bugs," Rowan laughed, shrugging her shoulders.

"I never asked what you did to celebrate the Fourth of July. Diana and I were still in France, so not a holiday there."

"Oh, I had a great night. I went to Jo's. Her family had a big cookout and set up lawn chairs for the neighborhood's fireworks display. I sent pictures and videos to Raven and River. They were so jealous."

"I imagine they were. I know you girls were raised here and Ireland, but the United States has some pretty great holidays— and we know how to celebrate them."

"Food!" Rowan grinned.

"Which reminds me, find out what Jo wants to eat, and Tina

will order everything. We can celebrate your masterpiece," Matilda said, smiling softly at Rowan.

"Sounds amazing. I'll text Jo while I pour us a drink. We need whiskey after our tear fest."

"I like that plan, and while we wait for Jo, you can tell me why you're avoiding my son."

7

____

Bran

"Should we tell Dad?" Bran asked Patrick. Pat and River had come to speak with him and Raven this morning. It was eleven. He and Patrick had received the email from their dad an hour ago. Everyone decided to meet and discuss what should or could, be done about the shitstorm on the horizon.

"River and I need to decide if we call Rowan or not as well."

Bran gripped Raven's hand tighter. They were sitting in the living room. It was a beautiful day, with sunlight shining on part of Daniel's playmat. His son was currently grabbing his toes while he watched a mobile swing above his head. Bran smiled. His son always made him smile. Becoming a father had given him some insight into his own parent. Dad cared more about his sons' happiness than his own. He always had, and that's why the stubborn sonofabitch left them without a word of warning.

Sighing and rubbing a hand over his face, Patrick answered Bran. "Honestly, I don't know. I don't want him in Oklahoma by himself, and I know he supposedly has all these plans, but none of us believe him. He's running. He's never run from anything."

River snorted. "Yeah, he's running alright, straight into the arms of the person he was running from."

"There is some poetic justice in that," Raven acknowledged.

"I don't disagree, babe, but we still need to figure out what to do." Bran was slightly embarrassed about the tears that had pricked his eyes when he'd read the email and Raven's hug of comfort that followed.

Of course, she understood what it felt like. Raven and River missed Rowan. They hated the separation. His dad had only just left, and he felt the empty space he should have been filling already. Of course, only Dad would give his sons to-do lists on his way out. Damn it. He'd known he and Pat would try to talk him out of leaving. He wasn't wrong.

River looked at Raven for a moment, almost like they were communicating in some secret, silent sister language. Raven nodded. They'd decided on *something*.

River smiled at Patrick before sitting up straighter to address the room. "Raven and I think we shouldn't tell either of them anything. They made this mess, and they can damn well figure out how to fix their mess together."

"Dad doesn't do well with surprises, Riv," Patrick ventured.

Raven laughed then. "Your father doesn't like a lot of shit, Pat."

"True," Patrick chuckled.

"So, we do—nothing?" Bran asked.

"For now," River confirmed. "Both of them will be calling us by this afternoon to chew our asses, but again, that's a *them* problem. Also, Row has been staying in your grandmother's penthouse for weeks. Rowan asked Tilly not to tell Hugh. She agreed, which means your grandma may not know what's going on, but she's no fool. She chose not to tell her son for a reason. We'll have her support."

"I think we should check in on them in a few weeks. A

surprise visit," Raven's eyes twinkled in mischief. "Riv, you'll only be sixish months along, so flying shouldn't be a problem. Perhaps we can invade the compound and force a family get together. We can judge whether a few weeks of fighting have sorted them out or not."

"Or whether more drastic measures are needed," River added.

"Fine, Rave," Bran said, "but if this whole plan blows up in our faces, Pat and I will be pointing all our fingers in your direction."

8

———————

Rowan survived a Matilda O'Faolain inquisition. She would survive dinner with Diana Gaines. Her sisters laughed hysterically when Rowan told them that Tina had picked out Diana approved evening wear for her to try on. During their daily video chat, where the sisters told each other the minutia of their days and Rowan got to tell her nephew how much Auntie Row loved him, she also tried on the outfits.

Raven and River both chose a simple black silk wrap dress. It boasted long flowy sleeves with buttons to the elbow. The skirt was above the knee with a slit up the right leg. If conservative sexy was the goal—winning. River voted heels. Raven voted for strappy sandals. Sandals won. Hair down and wavy, a silver comb with three silver triskelia decorating the top held one side back.

Rowan exited her Uber at the Country Club's grand entrance. The meeting with the boutique's contractor had run over because Rowan wasn't happy with the dressing room lighting. Seriously though, was there a woman alive that wanted fluorescent lighting beaming across their bodies while they're stripped down?

She told the contractor, and the owner who showed up before the meeting ended, that the store would be hard pressed to sell an outfit if the woman was confronted with every wrinkle, dimple, and roll before they slipped the clothes on.

Her client gasped in horror. The contractor groaned. Rowan smiled.

Winning aside, she was late for dinner. It didn't matter if her excuse was valid or if it was one minute or one hour, DG had a zero-tolerance policy. For everything.

Rowan knew to avoid eye contact and order whiskey straight away. In this instance, Diana wasn't the biggest trap to avoid. That award went to Matilda O'Faolain.

Rowan's face still burned from embarrassment over their... "talk."

"You love my son?"

No foreplay. Noted. "Yes. I do."

"And my son is being an idiot?"

"I believe so."

"I know his feelings are engaged. They have been for quite some time. He has tried to hide them, but concealing something from his mother is an exercise in futility." Matilda shook her head in annoyance at her son.

"It's fine, Tilly. He has made his feelings toward me, or his lack of feelings, I suppose, more than clear and on more than one occasion."

"Will you tell me...I mean...can you explain his reasons?"

"Our age gap. Nothing trumps our ages in his mind—not our attraction to one another, not our similar tastes, not even the fact that he knows me better than anyone in the world, possibly even my sisters, and I know him. I know he loves his family, his mother and sons, and his grandson and daughters-in-

law. He is protective, opinionated, passionate, and stubborn as a mule.

"He sees me, and I see him, but it isn't enough. Not for Hugh anyway." Rowan took a deep, shaky breath, embarrassed that she'd shared all that with Hugh's mother but too far in to pull back. "It's enough for me. Hugh is enough for me."

Matilda pulled Rowan into a deep, maternal hug, where her aches were smoothed, and her tears could disappear onto her shoulder. Rowan didn't believe she'd ever opened up about Hugh that much to her own sisters, but damn it, she was tired of hiding.

"Why did you leave Dublin then?" Matilda asked while she walked them slowly to two comfortable swivel chairs in the living room.

Rowan sat down, wiping her eyes across her sleeves. "A woman can only take being told 'no' or 'it will never happen' or 'leave me alone' so many times before self-preservation kicks in. So, I left. I hope to gain a modicum of control over my emotions before I have to see him again."

"That makes sense. Do you think all hope is lost? Truly?"

"It took a while, but yes, I have accepted we aren't to be. Our story is about loving the same group of people, just not one another. He...he hurt me too many times, Tilly. I know he's your son, and I wholly admit he's one of the most honorable men I've ever known, but he threw me away and what we could have had together too many times.

"It is over."

"Never say never, my dear. That bull-headed Neanderthal may surprise you."

THE HOSTESS LED Rowan to Mrs. Gaines table where Matilda and Diana were sitting with two gentlemen. Clearly father and son if genetics were to be believed. They both stood at Rowan's approach, causing her cheeks to pinken at the fuss, but she'd been to enough fancy soirees since meeting the O'Faolains, she wasn't completely thrown.

Rowan smiled and held her hand out to the older man first. "You needn't have stood on my account. I'm Rowan Byrne."

He smiled at Rowan's introduction. "Even though I'm older, if I didn't stand for a woman while my sister is here to witness it, she'd whack my head with the champagne bottle."

Diana actually laughed. "Hush, brother, you have always been the biggest liar."

Her brother grinned again and took Rowan's hand to shake. "I'm Owen Stanton. I've heard many good things about your family from Di." Rowan internally giggled at Owen's nickname for his sister. "And this is my son, William. We call Houston home."

Rowan turned to the...the extremely handsome man beside him, taking in the chiseled cheekbones, tall, athletic build, and sandy blonde hair shot with grey. Jesus, Rowan thought, she must have a 'type.' Taking William's hand and smiling through her blush, Rowan said, "Very nice to meet you, Mr. Stanton."

"William. Will, please. It's nice to put a face to your name, Miss Byrne."

"Rowan. Or Row, please." She extended the same level of kindness that Owen and Will had. Who could have guessed that Diana Gaines was related to *these* men?

Dinner was a nice surprise. Rowan couldn't remember a night that she'd enjoyed that much. Before Hugh, certainly. And if she wasn't mistaken, Owen was attempting to throw a smidge of flirt Matilda's way. Rowan could not wait to tease her when she got her alone. Who'd be in the hotseat then?

"My son and his wife have one daughter, Samantha. She's turning four next week."

William seemed so thrilled by this that Rowan couldn't help

but grin. "Four, huh? I imagine she has quite a detailed birthday list for her grandpa."

"She sent me a voicemail from my son's phone. Sam's mom sent me a list later that I could make sense of. Samantha is *very* particular. The voicemail was thirty minutes long. She went over what she wanted as well as alternate gifts, brands that she won't accept and a reminder that I could ship directly to her house."

Rowan leaned closer to William's side and pretended to whisper, "Does your granddaughter spend very much time with her Great-Auntie Di?"

Diana tried to huff and puff as though she was offended, but once the whole table burst out laughing, she joined in good-naturedly. All in all, a lovely evening and totally unexpected. As the group moved to the lobby to wait for their cars to be brought around, Willaim asked Rowan if she'd like to catch lunch next week. It was a casual, friendly invitation, or it would have been, except William was fidgeting with his watch and his cheeks held a distinct tinge of blush.

The invite took Rowan by surprise. Her personal, intimate feelings had been tied up with Hugh for so long. She'd told herself, more than once, that she would move on. She would find a man who wanted her. Who wasn't embarrassed to date her. She just hadn't gotten around to that 'moving forward' step.

Before Rowan could overthink, she answered, "Sure, that sounds great. I'll probably be working at the boutique I'm decorating. Wallpaper is going up tomorrow, which is one of my favorite parts. They should be all but done by noon. I'll send you the address, and we can meet there. If that works for you, that is." Now, she was blushing. Too much information. Rowan despised word-vomiting, and she'd just puked. A lot.

Thankfully, he smiled, seeming to relax. "Great. If you could give me your number, I'll text you so you can have mine."

And that was that. Rowan had a lunch date with a man who wasn't Hugh.

HUGH WOKE up to his phone playing The Lonely Island's *I Just Had Sex*—the irony. Try a yearlong stint of abstinence. Fucking Patrick changed his alarm tone again. How did the little shit keep doing that without getting caught? Groaning, Hugh grappled with his phone before finally ripping the charging cord out so he could look at the screen and turn the alarm off. Eight a.m.

Christ, he'd only gotten a few hours' sleep. Once he'd reached the hotel and the staff got his bags hauled up, it'd been four in the morning. He rubbed a hand over his face and chest, trying to think why he'd even set an alarm. Then he realized he must have accidentally toggled one of his many alarms when he was checking the weather. It was probably time to get his eyes checked.

A workout would help energize his body. He had a small home gym in house, so he didn't have to use the hotel's. Hugh found that a person risked two things at public gyms—getting hit on or contracting a staph infection. Getting hit on by random women had lost its appeal about thirty years ago, and he'd rather stay staph-free.

As Hugh slipped on gym shorts and a t-shirt, he studiously avoided looking at his emails and texts. He knew Bran and Patrick had gotten the email hours ago with the time difference, and he wasn't looking forward to those conversations. Hugh knew he'd made the right decision to leave Dublin. He would miss everyone, but it was a small price to pay to stop hurting Rowan. And he had hurt her. Several times. His very presence after he'd basically told her that he didn't want her—would never have a relationship with her—that her feelings didn't matter to him...hurt her. It killed him.

The lies had felt like acid on his tongue, but Hugh had always been good at staying the course. He'd been so successful in business because the men and women who made deals with him learned quickly that if Hugh O'Faolain said it, he'd do it without fail.

Walking out of Rowan's hospital room when she'd offered him another chance, offered her trust, a future, herself. He'd thrown that away too. He'd walked out of that hospital knowing he was doing the right thing. He would not date a woman so young.

It was funny, the more he repeated his stance, his reasoning for rejecting Rowan, sounded weaker and weaker. He was weakening with his want. Had he stayed in Dublin...Christ, had he stayed in the same city as Rowan Byrne he would have thrown his choices, his rejection in the garbage.

He would have gone to Rowan and begged her forgiveness.

Hugh threw himself into his workout, turning the music up to drown out his thoughts. His body was warm, a light sheen of sweat covered him, and his muscles were swelling with the repeated reps.

He almost made it through the last set when thoughts of Rowan snuck past his defenses. Rowan smiling and laughing. Rowan conspiring with her sisters or whispering to Daniel as she rocked him to sleep. Touching hishand or leg. Turning to him for reassurance. How she looked when her back arched right before she came.

"Damn it!" He yelled, replacing the barbell in its cradle. Shaking his head in annoyance, he castigated himself. "Pretty difficult to do chest presses with a Goddamn hard-on, Hugh." Add talking to himself to his List of Lows.

He sat on the bench, staring at himself in the mirror. Jesus, he looked defeated. He picked his phone up, anything to postpone digging any deeper into his depression and scanned through his emails. None were from the boys. He had several text messages. One from Patrick. *Call when you get up. Bran's with me.*

He dragged himself to the shower. He'd at least be clean for his ass chewing.

Twenty minutes later, he was showered, dressed, and sitting at his desk dialing up Pat. It only rang twice before his son picked up.

"Hang on, let me put you on speaker. Bran and I are just getting drinks at the Lobby bar." He heard crystal glasses clink, and then Pat said, "Okay. Bran's here."

Hugh didn't say anything, he'd learned years ago that silence usually moved conversations along. He could hear muffled whispering. They were probably arguing with who would say what first. He heard the word 'oldest' and then a fist meeting flesh followed by a groan. Patrick must have pulled the 'you're the oldest card,' and Bran punched him. Their antics might have made him teary-eyed if he weren't irritated at having to discuss his decisions.

"Dad, are you still there?" Bran asked.

"Obviously."

"We got your email, and...and we *both* think it's absolute bullshit that you left without talking to us in person."

"It was." Silence. The kids must have thought he would argue. He didn't want to argue, which was why he'd left without a goodbye.

"But," Patrick began, sounding exasperated, "we agreed last year, less actually, that we were sticking together."

"I know you didn't forget the conversation, Dad. You don't forget a fucking thing." Bran sounded frustrated. "I get making a run to Oklahoma, of course. We both get that, but you're leaving us for who knows how long."

"It's always been the three of us together. Bran and I aren't fucking toddlers, I get that, but since we've been adults, you've been our dad *and* our best friend."

Okay, Hugh wasn't expecting the boys to make this conversation so hard. His body burned with excess emotion. The truth was, they were his best friends too. Hugh pinched the bridge of his nose to stem the strong emotions attempting an escape.

"I explained my reasons in the email."

"There's only one real reason. At least be honest about that," Bran pushed.

"Fine. One reason."

"Dad, I think there's something you should—"

Whatever Patrick was about to say was cut off by more thuds and groans. Good Lord, his sons could try a saint's patience, and Hugh was no fucking saint. Hearing a glass break was the last straw.

"Boys!" Hugh barked over the speaker. Silence reigned. Good. "I have better things to do with my time than listening to your ridiculous tantrums. I might reconsider how long I'll be staying, but I won't be pushed. Is that clear?"

"Yes."

"Yes."

"Fine. Now clean up the fucking glass from the bar before one of your wives gets cut. And boys, that better not have been one of my Rene Lalique's."

"Oh shit."

"Fuck."

Sighing, Hugh hung up and went in search of his mother. He was smiling, though. Bran and Patrick. "Jesus," he muttered, shaking his head in exasperation as he shut the door behind him.

9

____

Hugh rang the doorbell of his mother's suite and was about to lightly knock when the door was pulled open. Tina, his mother's assistant, answered with a wide smile. She must have known it was Hugh from the security camera. She was loaded down with dresses and dress bags.

"Good morning, Tina." He reached for some of the dresses to relieve the weight from her arm. "Let me take some of these for you before you fall under the weight of my mom's excessive shopping."

Tina laughed and allowed him to take several. "Thank you, Hugh. Just lay them on the dining room table. That's where I was headed when you rang the bell and, in my rush, I brought them with me to greet you," she laughed at herself. "Matilda will be out as soon as she's dressed. A warning, Hugh," Tina laughed, "expect an earful about not calling before stopping by *and* for not warning her that you were back home."

"I'm smart enough to let mom have her say. She always forgives me," Hugh smiled at the older woman. Tina had been with his mom for years. She had been an accountant for O'Faolain, and when she'd put in her resignation, Hugh had called her in and asked her if she was unhappy with their company.

She admitted that she and her husband had just gotten a divorce. He'd cheated on her, and she wanted a fresh start. Her children were grown with homes of their own, and she wanted something for herself that didn't hold any reminders of her life before the divorce. He'd offered a position as his mother's assistant, without asking his mother first, but once the two women met, his mom forgave him his 'presumption,' and Tina never regretted the career change.

"Why is mom getting rid of these clothes?"

"These clothes, you fashion ogre, are evening dresses that I chose for Rowan to try on. I admit, her tastes are much more conservative for someone her age. Though the ones she did end up keeping are stunning. But anything would look lovely on..."

Hugh could no longer hear Tina through the roaring in his ears. Did she mean Rowan Byrne? *His* Rowan? What was going on here? Before he could start demanding answers, his mother walked in. Looked at the table of dresses, then Hugh, and finally Tina, who was still, presumably, waxing on about how good Rowan looked in the dresses she'd picked.

"Mom," Hugh growled. "Why is Tina picking clothes out for Rowan?" He didn't bother to ascertain if it was *the* Rowan. Bits and pieces of conversations from the past few weeks started clicking into place.

When Raven reminded River that they needed to hurry if they weren't going to miss Row's call. The wide-eyed guilt after she realized Hugh had heard. River asking Raven if Rowan had sent any pictures of the boutique she was working on. As if the girls didn't all visit each other's design sites. And the most damning...his mother's *houseguest* that she'd successfully evaded giving him the name of.

Recovering her poise, Mom asked Tina if she would mind

bringing her and Hugh sandwiches and salads for lunch after she finished her errands. "I believe Rowan's sundress alterations are complete. Would you mind swinging in and grabbing that from Maisy?"

"No problem." Tina's smile was more of a grimace, clearly picking up on the tension between mother and son.

Once Tina finished zipping the garment bags and left, his mom placed her hand on one hip and turned to Hugh. "You," she pointed at her son, "would do well to not take that tone with me, young man."

What kind of fresh hell had Hugh managed to step in? First, the call with his boys, then finding out the woman he'd been running away from was already here and ending with pissing his mother off. Diana Gaines walking in and telling Hugh he was being dramatic would honestly be the cherry on top.

"I'm sorry for the...tone," Hugh gritted out.

His mother stared at him for a solid minute, probably trying to gauge whether he was sincere before saying, "Fine." Her sniff at the end indicated she wasn't *fine* yet.

"Is Rowan staying here? Is she the houseguest you mentioned?"

"Yes, and yes."

My God, was he going to need to ask a hundred and fifty questions to find out a drop of the story? "How long has she been here?"

"Umm, almost five weeks, I think."

Hugh exploded. "Five weeks? Are you fucking kidding me?"

"Control yourself, Hugh. For crying out loud, Son. How did you not know she wasn't in Dublin all these weeks?"

Her lifted eyebrow sent a flush of embarrassment across his cheekbones. "I never asked...that is, I thought she was—" Hugh cut himself off, but his mother finished the thought for him.

"You thought she was avoiding you. Yes, I'm aware."

Aware? Of fucking what, he wanted to shout. Hugh crossed his arms over his chest and only stared at his mother, waiting for her to explain. She crossed her own arms over her chest and stared back. Unblinking.

Sighing in defeat, he asked, "What are you aware of?" He regretted the question before it even left his mouth. Sweat started to prickle along his skin. He despised being embarrassed.

"I'm aware that Rowan was in love with you for months, and you wanted nothing to do with her. She chose to remove herself from the equation to...How did she put it?" Mom paused, tapping her lips in thought. "Stop humiliating herself. I believe that's how she worded it."

She *was* in love. Past tense. Hugh's knees buckled. He barely got his ass in a dining room chair. Rowan never humiliated herself. Ever. She was brilliant and brave in every aspect of her life.

His mom had moved to his side, patting his shoulder, and making tsking noises. Not even Mom's sympathy could fix how bad he'd screwed up—and not just between him and Rowan, but her sisters and his own sons. He'd been making everyone's life difficult for months.

Hugh looked up to find his mom dabbing her eyes. "Don't berate me for sniffling. You know I've never been able to stand seeing you or Bran or Pat upset. I don't care how old any of you boys get," she said quietly. She took a few deep breaths and blotted her eyes once more.

"Sorry for upsetting you, Mom." Hugh leaned his head against the back of his chair, studying the chandelier hanging above the table. His mom had bought the ugly thing when he was in high school and had hung it in every home since.

Hugh had been shocked when his parents had fought over it. His dad thought it was a ridiculous expense and gaudy to boot. He told her to *"Take the damn thing back!"* Hugh remembered his mom looked stricken by her husband's anger. She hadn't said a word, just started wrapping up the light so she could place it back into its box.

A single tear had run down her face before she could wipe it away. When dad saw the tear, he swayed, like her pain was a physical blow to him. He moved the light gently from his wife's hands and set it aside. *"Forgive me, Tilly. I had a stressful meeting today, and I took it out on you."* He hugged her tightly and asked her again to forgive him. That he loved the light and would hang it himself.

Dad did hang it...eventually. He and Hugh spent a considerable amount of time repairing a hole in the ceiling that Dad accidentally punched through, but true to his word, he hung it and Mom had been thrilled. Dad never complained once. He may have cursed under his breath, but he didn't do it where Mom could hear. His father had been the best example of honor and love. Dad had honored his wife.

Hugh exhaled, picking his head up. He hadn't honored Rowan. He should have honored her whether they were in a romantic relationship or not. His father would be disappointed in his behavior, and that crushed Hugh.

Meeting his mother's gaze, Hugh pointed up to the light, "I can't believe you lugged that old chandelier here. I never noticed before now, and I should have it's so godawful. I was just recalling how you and Dad had a disagreement about it and the disaster he made hanging it himself."

"Stubborn man and all on account of the ugliest chandelier in existence," she laughed at his look of surprise. "What? I realized when I got it home that I'd made a mistake, but then your dad got sideways, which made me dig in my heels. I would have returned it and gladly, but he had hurt my feelings, and he admitted it.

"Watching him make amends to hang that damn light felt the same as if he'd carved J + M in a tree trunk. I've lugged that eyesore to every home we've ever had because it reminded me of that day. Of how much your father loved me...and his ability to apologize."

"I miss him."

"He would be so proud of you, Hugh."

"Somehow, Mom, I doubt that."

"You're being too hard on yourself."

"I haven't been hard enough. I allowed my—"

His mother cut him off. "...fear of commitment?"

"...fear of the future to sway my decisions," He finished, ignoring his mom's interruption.

"You know your happiness is my happiness. Your sadness is mine as well. I believe you are accustomed to how parenting works by now."

"I am."

"Do you care for Rowan as only a friend or family member, or is it more?"

"More."

His mom stayed quiet for a time before asking perhaps the most dreaded of questions. "Would you tell me why, then, that you pushed Rowan away?"

Hugh covered his face with his hands, elbows propped on his knees. He needed a moment to digest the fact that he was discussing...this with his mother. "I'm too old for her, Mom. Way too old. Twenty-nine years too old!" Hugh pounded his fist on the table to emphasize the discrepancy. "I never wanted her to regret her choice. Waking up next to an old man while she's still the most beautiful woman in the world."

"Hugh Darcy O'Faolain, if only your father were here to box your ears! Did he or I raise you to believe, to ever consider, that love is so fleeting? That love is skin deep?"

"No."

"Do you think your father loved me less as I aged? When I no longer had a tight ass and perky boobs?"

Hugh cringed at that unneeded description. "Of course not."

His mother was on a tirade now, and sugarcoating wasn't on the menu. "Exactly. He loved me more, as I loved him more. Every year we had, we loved each other more." She placed her hands on his knees. "You underestimated yourself, and I believe you underestimated Rowan. I also don't believe turning Rowan away had anything to do with your age or at least, it wasn't the only reason.

"That woman you were married to made you afraid to take a chance again, and you knew that Rowan was all or nothing. You're still letting that poor excuse of a wife and mother color your decisions. She was horrible, Hugh. It was never your fault. She had something horribly wrong with her long before you came along. She was just a good enough actress that she fooled everyone. Everyone, Son, not just you."

This was a lot for Hugh to take in, and it certainly was not what he'd expected would happen when he returned to Oklahoma. Jesus, he felt wrung out, and it was only ten in the morning.

"Where is she?"

His mom sighed, clearly expecting the question and clearly not looking forward to giving him the answer. "She's been working on a new designer boutique downtown. It's a gorgeous space, and it's not far from Wolves, actually. Rowan has worked tirelessly on the space, and she thinks she should be able to wrap things up soon. Very exciting," his mom added in a decidedly unexcited way. She was rambling. His mother wasn't a rambler.

"Where is she now? Right now," Hugh thought to add in case his mother chose to misinterpret his question. Again.

"She's at the boutique, of course."

She was not telling him something important, but before he could poke further, she got up and told him she had something to show him. Swallowing his agitation, he trailed after his mother into the living room. She went to the armoire that he'd gifted her. River found it in Scotland from some artist outside Inverness.

She opened the doors, and Hugh almost lost his fucking legs again. "Rowan's been working on it for weeks. She says it isn't near done, but I can't believe it isn't close. It couldn't be more stunning. She only hung the oil paintings in yesterday."

Hugh couldn't even speak. No words could explain the scope of Rowan's talent. All the details, letters, homemade gifts, and knickknacks were special enough on their own, but the paintings...

"Did she paint these?" he asked with a sizable lump in his throat, taking in the painting of him and his father. It was his sixteenth birthday, and Dad had gotten him a Porche. This picture showed both of them grinning at each other. It was taken right after his dad had whispered in Hugh's ear that he'd rip Hugh's nuts off if he had an accident and scared his mother. Not even the threat of castration could dim the thrill of his first car.

Unbeknownst to his mother, the two of them had snuck out that night and took it for a rip on Highway 169. It was one of his favorite memories. And Rowan had painted it.

"I had no idea Rowan was such a talented artist," Hugh admitted as he examined the paintings of his parent's wedding and of Mom and the boys. There was so much to look at it would take hours to study each inch to find the hidden treasures.

"She could make a living off her art alone," Mom agreed.

"Yes, she could," Hugh agreed. "When will she get home?"

He would like to see her. He'd like to do a lot more than that. He'd like to beg her forgiveness, apologize for being the world's biggest idiot...ask for one more chance.

He would settle for being near her again.

"Hmm, I'm not sure. When I see her, though, I can tell her you're in town and would like to see her. Maybe?"

Hugh knew when he was being put off. "When does she usually get home?"

"Well, that depends on if she has a date."

THIS WAS Rowan and William's third lunch date. She had to continually remind herself to not compare him to...another man —there were times when those negative thoughts slipped through the cracks—but otherwise, she was enjoying Will's company.

Her sisters found it hilarious that she was seeing Diana Gaines' nephew. Rowan kind of found it funny, too, but she and Will never ran out of things to talk about. He was very close to his family, which was important, and he was clearly a tech genius, totally impressing Rowan. River would love him for sure.

It didn't matter that he wasn't a giant. Most men weren't, for heaven's sake. And it didn't matter that he didn't have a luxurious beard. Rowan was able to see his smile even better. And it certainly didn't matter that when Will held her hand or touched her lower back that her body didn't sizzle like a livewire.

No, it didn't matter at all.

Because it couldn't matter.

Refocusing on her date, Rowan asked, "Tilly seems excited about dinner tomorrow night." Owen Stanton had asked if Matilda and Rowan would like to join him and William for a charity cocktail party at the gorgeous Philbrook Museum.

Rowan's parents had gone to all the exhibits and shows at Philbrook. She was thrilled with the invitation and even more thrilled that Matilda blushed every time they discussed what to wear.

"Dad's been a nervous wreck for days. Whether anything comes of it, I'm just pleased that my father has found something besides financial projections to pique his interest."

"I think it's great they discovered ththey enjoyed each other's company when we met for dinner at the Club. I think they both would enjoy just having a friend to do things with. It's not as though they didn't know who the other was before that dinner, but I don't think they ever looked at one another before that as anything other than a connection of Diana's."

"Seriously though, I never thought my father would ever try to move on from my mother, even for female friendship. She passed away so long ago, I'd given up hope that Dad might find a life after Mom."

"Do you mind me asking how she died?" Rowan was always careful not to pry into another person's loss. It was so personal, and everyone handled the death of a loved one in different ways.

"Breast cancer. She was sixty-five. The doctors believed it had been growing for quite a while before they caught it. She stopped getting mammograms at sixty. That choice killed her. I was so angry for years that if my mother had made different choices, she'd still be here—with my father and with me."

Rowan reached across the table and took William's hand, squeezing in comfort and support. "I get it, Will. My sisters and I lost both our parents to a car accident when we were in college. There's always a hole left in a child's heart, but I don't know...If your father loved your mother like my parents loved one another—sometimes I don't mind that they went together.

To not be the one left behind. I can think of them as always standing side by side in my thoughts and dreams.

"Your father is very brave to step out of his widowed comfort zone, as is Matilda. I'm proud of them both." Thank goodness she and Will were tucked away in a corner at the sandwich shop where they were dining that day. They were discussing some weighty topics over soups and salads.

Rowan let go of Will's hand and sat back in her seat again. He looked pensive, and when he spoke, she understood why.

"I do not want to come across as presumptuous, assuming things..." he trailed off with a slight wave between them. "If you were to ever agree to date me, seriously date me, would our age gap be an issue for you?"

Rowan tried to control her eyes from rounding. If he only knew how little of a problem that was. She shuddered as Hugh's face popped between her and Will. Damn that interfering man, even when Hugh wasn't present, he could ruin a mood. Another reminder of why she was in Oklahoma.

Will was still waiting for an answer. He really did have a model's looks and build. If she were only concerned about a man's appearance, he would certainly tick every box, but more than that, William Stanton was a genuinely nice man.

Rowan didn't want to rush anything, but there was no viable reason not to see if there could be something between the two of them. "Age has never been an issue for me. I have...my last..." Rowan cut herself off. Lord have mercy. Why bring that up? "What I meant to say, Will, is that our age difference is not an issue."

Will looked at her, his scientific mind probably trying to fill in the missing strings of data from her foolish past relationship blunder. To make matters worse, the 'relationship' had only ever been one-sided.

"I have wanted to ask you about your ex-wife. I don't need to know why you aren't together anymore, but I would like to know if you two have managed to keep a friendship." At his look of surprise, she added, "It's just that family is obviously very important to you, as it is to me, and it would be lovely if you guys had been able to maintain...something. For your children's and grandchildren's sake at the very least." From their first lunch, she knew he'd been divorced for a couple of years, but he'd offered no other information.

Will cleared his throat, clearly not comfortable with the subject matter. Rowan didn't regret asking. A lot could be learned by how a person handled divorce.

"Katy is always invited to family functions, and we attend my granddaughter's school functions as a family."

He did not like speaking of his ex. Perhaps there were still feelings on one or both of their parts. It would be understandable and certainly something to address if she and William continued to see each other for long.

"I'm glad to hear it," she said, taking his hand once more and smiling. The slight tension melted between them instantly.

"So then, would you be my date at the Philbrook? We would go separate from Dad and Matilda."

"I will definitely be your date," Rowan smiled. She felt warmth blossom in her chest. Will smiled, clearly excited about an evening date after their lunches.

The fact that her kneejerk reaction was to say no was the impetus to accept.

Moving on was a real bitch.

Since it was a beautiful day, Will walked Rowan back to the boutique after lunch. She had a few more hours of work before she could call it a day. Will surprised her by sliding his hand down her bare arm and twining their fingers together. That sped her heart rate up. Rowan could feel his gaze, and she looked up and smiled slowly.

It looked like their dating status triggered Will's need to mark his territory, which in this case was her. She was well aware of the varying methods a man might take to show others what they considered theirs; an arm around the shoulder, hand-holding, and her favorite, a hand pressed against the small of a woman's back—subtle but effective.

Hugh had made her an expert on alpha attitudes. He didn't need to physically touch her to warn off possible competition. It was all in his dark stare. She shivered, remembering how it felt when he turned his intense eyes on her.

Rowan cringed. Damn her wandering mind.

She was walking hand in hand with a man that might one day hold boyfriend status in her life. She led him to the back of the shop, where there was a small, covered pergola with seating for future clients who, weather permitting, wanted to comfortably wait for their rides after spending an exorbitant amount of money inside.

Rowan walked them under the shaded pergola to the left of the back entrance. She could hear men and women working inside, but even if any of them stepped out to gather more tools or materials, they wouldn't notice her and Will. Once they stopped walking, Rowan let go of his hand so she could position her body in front of his.

"Thank you for lunch." Rowan could see Will was considering his chances of whether or not Rowan would allow him to kiss her.

If Hugh wanted to kiss a woman, he would simply say, "I want to kiss you." Damn. Damn. Double damn.

She started mentally ticking the pros and cons of hypnotherapy when Will gently placed his hands on her hips. His palms were warm through the light cotton of her rusty orange sundress. The material was lined but thin enough Rowan knew he could feel the thin bands of her panties. She didn't say a word as he used the purchase to move their bodies just that little bit closer.

"I won't see you until I pick you up for our date tomorrow night. I have meetings all day tomorrow with an up-and-coming tech firm. They believe our company might be interested in buying them out. Supposedly, they have some genius new tech they think Dad and I won't be able to pass up." Will smirked, probably having heard that line a million times before.

"We didn't make the trip from Houston to specifically meet with them, but since we were in town, we decided to give them some time. Dad loves dissecting any new technology and its potential pitfalls and usefulness."

Rowan laughed, imagining Owen looking at boring data and prototypes like a child at a toy store. "Are your children involved in the family business?"

"They are," he grinned proudly. He paused before asking, "Would you let me kiss you?"

Rowan was green but she'd known this was coming, and she would be lying if she said she wasn't curious. "Yes." He ran one of his hands gently up her back until his fingers slid up her nape to tangle in her hair, essentially holding her head steady while he bent low enough to breathe against her lips.

Rowan's stomach was doing somersaults. He didn't care that they were in public. He didn't care if the world knew he was interested in a younger woman. He only cared, at this moment, that they shared the intimacy of kissing.

"I've wanted to taste you since the first night we met," he admitted against her lips.

Rowan's toes curled at how good it felt. "Taste me then," she urged as she slid her hands up his chest to his firm pecs and hardened nipples. He took her mouth on a groan, her own moan mingling with his tongue.

Rowan wasn't sure how long they kissed, but when Will

finally broke away, her body was flush with his. Both were out of breath.

"That...that was...meant to be a small kiss," he admitted with a sheepish look on his face.

"Would you say it was the best kiss you have to offer?" Rowan raised her brows in question.

"Not even close."

"Thank God, you didn't give it your all then. I would have burst into flames if you'd put some effort into it," Rowan laughed, a husky note in her voice that immediately had Will focusing on her mouth again.

"If you let me kiss you again, I'm afraid you won't make it back to work."

Rowan touched her tongue to her bottom lip, feeling its fullness. She liked how that felt. A man wanting her like that felt delicious.

"I'm letting you go now." Putting action to his words, he let his hands fall from her body and took two steps back. "Go while the getting's good, Miss Byrne. Friday night can't come soon enough."

Rowan grinned as she backed up, turned, and started walking toward the boutique entrance.

When the door closed behind her, Rowan realized she hadn't thought of Hugh once while Will had kissed her.

She was thinking of him now, though. Damn.

10

Hugh had been pacing his mother's home for what felt like hours. His mood became darker at every turn. He'd studied the armoire. Rowan had created a masterpiece. Mom said she planned on leaving it open so that every time she glanced its way, she would find a memory to smile about. His mother would enjoy showing it off to company too.

Mom left for Diana's an hour ago, claiming the dark cloud hanging over his head was giving her a headache. Recalling their conversation before she'd left had Hugh clenching his fists.

"Who is she dating?"

"I know you're angry, but you caused this mess, and though I wish I could help you dig your way out of it. Raven and River believe it's best to let you two figure it out between you. That's why they didn't tell you Rowan was in Oklahoma and why they asked me not to give Rowan a head's up that you're lying in wait to pounce on her the moment she walks through that door." Mom thrust her finger toward the front door.

Ignoring how infuriating his family was currently being, he focused on the most pressing matter. "Who is he?" She ignored him and instead started sorting her embroidery floss.

"Do you even know who this man is? She was shot a few months ago by a psychopath. Maybe you've forgotten," he seethed, wanting to roar and shout and throw things. He wanted to run out that front door and track down Rowan himself.

"I know who he is and his family."

Somehow, that made him more furious. Who the fuck did the O'Faolains know that had men Rowan's age that weren't complete jackass layabouts?

"We've been over this. You don't have the right to be angry. You've admitted to turning her away. You've also admitted to hurting her feelings when you did it. What were you hoping would happen? That she'd stay single forever."

"Yes!" Hugh did shout then. He stared out the window for a moment, amazed at his selfish admission. He would like to retract his answer and say "No!" instead, but he wouldn't lie to his mother even though it was quite apparent that he'd been lying to himself for months.

She continued to sort floss while he moved through the rooms like an angry, caged beast until she'd stood in a huff and left.

The one room he hadn't entered was the guest room Rowan currently occupied. He'd stood outside the door several times already, never giving himself permission to invade her privacy. The sixth time of telling himself not to do it didn't work. He twisted the knob and walked into her bedroom.

His first thought, it smelled like her. He'd heard her tell Josephine O'Connor once that she wore perfume made from nude roses. Hugh had never thought that a rose's scent changed depending on the color.

He loved smelling her. Rowan had only been staying here a few weeks, but the room felt like her.

There were pretty dresses hanging on a screen in one

corner. A makeup table with all her feminine things: brushes, barrettes, hair ties, a pale-yellow ceramic dish with rings and earrings, necklaces and bracelets. He had seen all of them adorn her body at one time or another.

The walk-in closet was neat and tidy. Rowan was an extremely organized woman. All three Byrne sisters excelled in design and knew just the right spot for the smallest of items. The O Building in Dublin reflected their expertise. Each of the flats was stamped with the girls' touch. Bran's flat screamed Raven. Patrick's flat was all River. And because Hugh was not a complete ignoramus, his flat had clearly been designed by Rowan. Each time he walked through the door of his apartment, it felt like sunshine warmed him from the inside out.

He'd dreamed of he and Rowan sharing the space a million times.

He continued to walk around the bedroom, stopping next to the perfectly made bed. The mounds of white linen begged a person to sink into its pillow softness. Her nightstand caught his attention then and beckoned. He told himself not to open the drawer. That was an invasion of privacy he definitely balked at. With seemingly no willpower, Hugh watched as his hand reached for the glass knob.

"Don't you dare open that fucking drawer, Hugh O'Faolain!" Rowan had just gotten home and wanted to change out of her work clothes into something more arts and crafts comfy. She almost screamed when she saw a man standing in her bedroom. He was facing away, looking toward her bed.

Hugh, oh Lord, it was Hugh. Had she not been so startled, she would have known him immediately. She knew every line and curve of his big body. Rowan instantly felt hot and shaky.

Not nearly as impervious to him as she'd hoped she'd be after their separation.

Not impervious at all.

When Rowan saw him about to open the drawer in her nightstand, the horror of what he'd find inside killed her initial elation. Hugh jerked around, startled and probably embarrassed at being caught. She tried to control her features so that the man who tossed her away wouldn't know how his mere presence affected her.

His hair was still shaved tight to his scalp. He taken to the style a couple of months ago. Hugh had gorgeous hair. Thick with a slight wave, all shades of coffee and cocoa. The shaved look suited him just as well, making his dark eyes shine brighter and his cheekbones sharper. He still had his beard and mustache, thank God, he hadn't shaved them off. It was thick and wavy, brown shot with silver.

He'd always reminded Rowan of the actor Travis Fimmel, only Hugh was bigger, darker, and sexier—in her eyes anyway. One hundred percent beautiful man. "Why are you here?"

He crossed his arms over his chest, Hugh's tried-and-true defensive maneuver. It wouldn't save him from her questions. "Well?" she asked when he remained silent. Rowan would also like to ask her sisters and Matilda why they didn't tell her of Hugh's arrival.

"Why am I in Oklahoma? Why am I in my mother's home? Or why am I in your bedroom?"

Unimpressed with his non-answer, she simply said, "All of the above." Rowan knew he didn't have to answer the first two, but he did owe her an explanation for being in her private space.

"I'm in Oklahoma to check on my properties, take care of some business, attend a few golf tournaments that I was invited to, and attend a fancy game shoot in Kansas. I'm in this suite because I was visiting Mom after her months of traveling."

"And my room?" Rowan prompted.

Hugh uncrossed his arms letting them fall uneasily to his sides. He brushed his palms against the sides of his jeans. Hugh was nervous. Impossible. He was the most self-assured man she knew. He had a trademark legendary aloofness, which managed to madden almost everyone he encountered. *That* confident man was squirming!

Rowan crossed her arms over her chest and leaned nonchalantly against her doorframe. Waiting. *Take a dose of your own medicine, Mr. O'Faolain.*

He lasted another two minutes and then he shocked the hell and breath right out of her. "I missed you." He ruined it by cringing like he hadn't meant to admit his feelings.

What was Rowan supposed to say to that? He missed her. What in the hell did that even mean? She could not let this omission derail her 'moving on' efforts. She'd found a man who took her out on dates. Held her hand in public no less. Who had kissed her only a few hours ago. A man she'd agreed to date.

"Did you miss telling me to leave you alone? Seriously, Hugh, you might have just texted me." If Rowan weren't half a minute from a full-blown anxiety melt down, she might have felt bad for the look of anguish that passed over Hugh's beloved features, but she had to have tough love if she were to survive Hugh's inevitable guilt and push back after one of his 'slip of feelings' episodes.

"I'm sorry, Row. I was wrong. Will you just talk to me?"

Hugh's gravelly voice sent shivers up and down Rowan's body. He moved closer to the door—closer to where she was standing. He'd never initiated contact, so when he didn't stop until his feet stood in front of hers, where his body heat touched her skin, she stiffened in surprise. When Hugh placed his hands on each side of the door frame, she began hearing 911 emergency sirens.

She could run or stand her ground. Byrnes weren't runners, but in that moment, it felt like the safest course. Rowan was just taking a breath to tell Hugh to back off when they both heard the front door open and heard Matilda's voice ring out that she was home.

"Fuck."

Hugh's muttered expletive had her eyes meeting his. Direct. There was no hiding what they were feeling from one another. Rowan's emotions were easy. Embarrassment, hurt, and confusion. Hugh's body language was all demanding, aggression, and possession. There was also regret and longing.

Before his mom caught them in Rowan's bedroom, she went ahead and put the nail in their coffin before he could beat her to it. "Don't come into my room again. I will move out if I must, but you are not welcome in my space."

He tried to argue, but Rowan held her hand up, stopping his rebuttal. "The moment you left me in that hospital room was the day I stopped believing that something could exist between us. It's over, Hugh. I've moved on, and I can assure you that I will not embarrass either of us by ever pursuing you again."

Rowan saw Matilda walking down the hallway toward her bedroom, before she stopped, looked at Rowan with her son looming over her in the bedroom doorway like a harbinger of The Black Death, spun on her Louis Vuitton flats, and vacated the area.

Unfortunately, Hugh was still intent on conversation. "I fucked up, Row. I know I did. Please just let me explain."

Tears were starting to prick her eyes. All her hard work... No, she would not go back to that day, those feelings, again. Waking up to hear your family's stalker had shot you, sore, in pain, and with permanent scars to commemorate the day didn't hurt her as much as Hugh turning his back on her outstretched hand.

Not again.

"No more. I'm going to go finish the armoire for your mother and then I will pack and move. I cannot allow myself to be open to the type of hurt you are capable of putting me through. Don't ask me to, Hugh. It's cruel. I imagine you heard I'm dating someone, and you're here to mark your territory."

"That isn't true. I just found out you were in Oklahoma this morning. I just found out you were dating someone this afternoon."

"You didn't even know I'd left Dublin. Did you?"

He hesitated, but he answered honestly. "No."

"Were you still trying to run from me?"

"Yes."

"And ran right to me instead."

"Correct."

HUGH FELT his first breath of hope wheeze and wither. Christ, how could he ever try to fix things if she refused to hear him? He didn't blame her. She had a million reasons to mistrust and despise him. They might not have touched one another, but they had been intimate, twice, and he'd run away from her both times.

The idea that his mom might be right about why he'd fought against his feelings for Rowan was galling. The fact that he might have been running scared because of his ex-wife disgusted him. He didn't run from anything. Helen was a shit wife and a worse mother. He'd never been so thankful and relieved as the day the divorce was finalized. The weight he had intended to endure for a lifetime had been lifted. That freedom had been a gift.

He had felt considerable guilt that he'd chosen a woman who hurt his boys. He was growing his company and quite aware that he probably knew less than half of the hell she put Bran and Patrick through. It killed him that he'd allowed that woman's vitriol to touch them. He'd always loved his sons, but he worked a lot in those days.

Was Hugh to believe that a bad relationship that had been over for years still affected him? It seemed impossible, but he promised himself to explore the possibility. He still believed Rowan was too young for him, but he also admitted that he was past the point of caring. There was no living without her.

Watching her now, he could see that Rowan was trying to hide her hurt and anger, but her blank stare hid little from him. He'd done nothing but watch and study this woman for months on end. Changing the subject, he asked, "Do you have any lingering pain?" He gestured under his left pectoral in case she didn't know he was asking about the gunshot wound.

"I still have to be careful of running too many miles."

"Should you see a doctor? For a checkup."

Rowan's eyes narrowed. She probably thought he was trying to manage her, but that wasn't it at all. He woke up panicked at least once a night, reliving the nightmare of finding out she'd been shot.

Rowan took a deep breath, choosing not to answer him, she confessed, "Listen, Hugh, I've found a man who isn't embarrassed to be seen with me. I want to see where it goes, and I want you to stay out of my way."

Rowan stepped aside and motioned for him to leave her room. As soon as he was in the hallway, she stepped back into the bedroom and shut the door in his face.

I've found a man who isn't embarrassed to be seen with me. Is that how he'd made her feel? Like an embarrassment? Jesus, how could she not see that she was the one who should have been embarrassed to be seen with him?

Hugh walked silently to the front door, needing to put some

space between him and Rowan. "Hugh. A moment, please," his mother said from behind him.

He paused with his hand on the door. "Did Jonathan and I raise a quitter?"

Hugh felt his shoulders stiffen. "No."

"I didn't think so. Goodnight, Son."

11

———

Matilda was waiting for her in the living room where Rowan worked on the armoire. It had taken her a bit to get her emotions under control from the Hugh skirmish. A shower and comfy pajamas had done wonders, as did the refreshment table. A bottle of Glenmorangie 25 set on the sideboard for Rowan. The luxe copper label of Matilda's Absolut Elyx made a showy statement beside it, and a pitcher of ice-cold lemon water finished the trio. She explained that lemon water was so they could pretend they were health conscious while pickling their livers.

An hour passed in companionable silence. Rowan finished the last side panel in a cobalt fabric that had tiny white flowers sprinkled on the surface. She gave it a puffy quilted look using the batting she'd picked up from the hobby store earlier.

Once that was finished, Rowan started adjusting this bit and that bauble. Tilting photographs until they were perfect. Securing a Christmas ornament that Hugh had made his mother in the second grade. Another hour passed before she made the last paint touch-up. Rowan sat back on her heels to admire her work.

While she fiddled with one last wire, she told Matilda, "The boutique is definitely ahead of schedule if you can believe it. Two of the contractors are working all weekend because they have other jobs they want to get to, which works great for my client and for me. It's going to be stunning when it's finished. I took a ton of before pictures. The after pictures will make a hell of an impression on our website. River is dying to get her hands on them." Rowan laughed.

Her tech-savvy sister lived for website updates, posts, and generating interest in their designs on social media. Eventually, River would have to slow down as her pregnancy progresses, as Raven did, which would mean more work for Raven and Rowan. A new niece or nephew was so worth it, though.

"I'm thrilled because that means I can wrap things up faster than I initially planned and get home to my precious Daniel," she laughed. "Oh, and my sisters too."

Raven had asked her and River once if they minded her son being named after their late father. Rowan had understood her hesitation. Thinking about a name and saying that name out loud were two very different things. However, they all agreed that it would have been an honor for their dad. He would have been thrilled, which meant his daughters were thrilled.

"Your sweet nephew will be so happy to have his Auntie back. After all that Delton business and traveling for so many months, I'd like to take a moment to relax here at home, but I plan to move to my apartment in Dublin by mid-September. That way, I can attend River's baby shower and have a few weeks to help get anything else Patrick and your sister might need before the birth. Diana will come by the end of October. She told me her plans this afternoon.

"What is going on that wall?" Matilda walked up behind Rowan with a fresh glass of lemon water and pointed to the blue cloth with its sprinkling of flowers. "It's a lovely pattern."

Matilda had a very similar aesthetic to her older sister, River. Simple lines with hints of blue, and Rowan found it had been easy to create the pleasing palette for the armoire.

"That," Rowan smiled as she accepted the glass, "Is a space for great-grandchildren. I used the batting to make it easy for you to tack pictures. I even bought pretty jewel-tipped tacks for you. The loose wire is so you can use tiny clips to hang things. Like a laundry clothesline," Rowan explained.

"You've got to stop making me so emotional all the time, or I'll have to kick you out," Matilda laughed.

Rowan hopped up and went over to search through her 'bags of bits,' as her mother used to call the overflow from her daughters' projects, and found the pins, tacks, and clips. She dug out a mini clothespin and handed it to Matilda, along with a picture of her holding her great-grandson, Daniel.

"You hang the first one. I'm sure this space will fill up sooner than you think, but the great thing is you can change things around because it isn't permanent," Rowan explained.

"Oh, lovely. I would have never thought of adding something for new memories. Very clever, young lady," Matilda gleamed as she hung the first picture. "I wish Jon was here to see what you've done." Matilda kept her back to Rowan, staring at the memoryscape before her, running her hand around the wedding painting's frame.

"I miss you, my love," she whispered. "So damn much."

Rowan turned away quickly, surreptitiously dabbing her eyes while she picked up and set down a glue gun and bottle of paint. She turned around, though, when Matilda spoke.

"I'm unsure about going to dinner with Owen. I keep wondering what Jon would think."

Rowan leaned her behind against the table's top and regarded the older woman, who had turned around to regard Rowan in turn. "First, I'd like to point out that the goal is to enjoy good company. Owen is certainly that. We both know if he wasn't, his sister would have locked him away years ago in an asylum for the perpetually dull." Matilda snorted in amusement at Rowan's assessment of her best friend.

"Second, I'd like to remind you that my grandmother just got married. You both were lucky to have known what being truly in love feels like. Is it any wonder you might want something like that again? Nan was afraid too, you know. She thought of it like...like cheating, I guess. Except how is it cheating when the love that your husband bestowed upon you and that you bestowed on him is still honored? It isn't lessened or forgotten.

"It's a cherished memory. Always cherished. From what William has said, his father is extraordinarily nervous too. He loved his wife like you loved your husband. If you want my opinion, Owen might be seeking the same thing you are."

"And what is that?" Matilda asked, taking a seat at the table.

"A friend. A companion to do fun things like charity dinners. To have a plus one that you enjoy talking the night away with."

"Oh. Oh, I...yes, I think...that is right. I would like that." Matilda sighed, like a ton of tension was lifted from her shoulders.

"Will had planned for the four of us to drive separately, but why don't I text him that we would prefer to go together? I know he wouldn't mind, and I certainly wouldn't." Rowan wasn't lying either. Now that Hugh was in town, her budding romance with William seemed to be slipping through her fingers.

"I would prefer that, at least this first time, if you truly don't mind," Matilda admitted.

"I'll text him now." Honestly, it was a relief to have less

alone time with Will until she sorted through her feelings for Hugh. Feelings that she could not, for her life, shake.

"What will you do about my son? And before you get mad at me for not telling you he was coming, the family decided to stay out of your business."

Rowan paused in her texting to briefly squeeze her eyes closed. She may not be willing to show her anger to Matilda, but by God, her sisters would be hearing from her in the morning.

Rowan finished sending the text before answering. "What is there really to do about Hugh? He's here. He has every right to be here. We have never dated. We aren't currently dating. He's simply doing what he's always done."

"Which is what?" Hugh's mother asked.

"Circle me like a wolf. Mark his territory even though he never claims me. The normal. He doesn't want me, Matilda, but your son doesn't want anyone else to have me either." Rowan groaned in impatience. "It's frustrating."

"I'm sure it is, and you've done amazing at moving on despite his confusing behavior. I will preface what I'm about to impart by letting you know that I think Will is a wonderful man, and I believe his intentions toward you could not be more honest—but—yes, I know, there is always a but." She smiled, holding up her hand to stop Rowan from interrupting. "Hugh has had a bit of an epiphany. I will not break his trust, but...oh goodness," Matilda patted her eyes with a bit of leftover silk fabric folded on the table, "I would ask that you at least, at some point, let him explain himself."

Rowan looked at the painting she'd done of a smiling Hugh with his father. He used to know how to smile. "The only thing I can promise is that I'll think about it."

· · ·

"So, I guess we're keeping secrets from one another now?" Rowan asked Raven and River, completely furious with both of them for not telling her about Hugh. She was still in bed, having barely slept last night.

"I'm sorry, Row," Raven spoke in a quiet voice.

"If it makes you less mad at us, Bran and Patrick agreed, and they didn't tell Hugh you were in Oklahoma," River said, ratting out her and Raven's husbands.

Rowan heard a "Hey!" and a "What the hell, Riv?"

"River's always been the biggest tattler," Raven sighed, probably trying to get Rowan to laugh and lighten the tension.

It didn't work, which was a shame since Rowan hated being at odds with her sisters. She'd thrown herself into finishing the armoire last night, knowing she couldn't talk to her sisters until this morning because of the time. She only managed to sleep a handful of hours, thinking about what she was going to say to her sisters, but mostly about Hugh, damn him.

Her face burned when she pictured him opening her night-stand drawer. There were only two things to discover, neither of which she wanted him to find. A vibrator and a sketchbook.

A sketchbook of Hugh. She'd spent a year filling an entire book of the man. Every mood, every scowl. Part of the book was innocent. Family moments. When he looked at his sons with pride and love. Sitting at the bar, whiskey in hand. When he sat apart, loneliness dimming his eyes. When he held his grandson in his arms.

The second part...*weren't* family moments. His body, its strength and power. Muscles rippling. Erect and virile. Rowan had drawn the shower scene from memory, fist gripping his length. Hugh standing over her lying in bed. His face when he came. Some were pure fantasy. She'd taken to sketching her hottest dreams the moment she woke, sweating and trembling with need.

Hugh had embedded himself in her body. Her mind kept trying to picture a different path, a different ending to her story, but every damn day, her imagination placed Hugh in every scenario, dream, want, or need. William Stanton was the first man that came close to changing her story.

When Rowan didn't respond to her family's antics, silence stretched uncomfortably. She could imagine her sisters giving each other panicked looks. She broke the silence by repeating her question.

"*Are* we keeping secrets? I'm not talking about small things. You both knew this wasn't a small thing to me." Rowan felt tears prick her eyes. Hugh was the opposite of a small thing. To her. It didn't matter that he wasn't at fault, that he'd never broken promises, but he was the instrument in which all of her hopes and dreams had been erased. Picking up the pieces and trying to put them in a different order was painful. Raven and River knew how painful it had been.

"Let me take Daniel, babe," Rowan heard Bran say.

"Rowan," Patrick started, "Bran and I will leave you guys alone now, but before we go, I want to tell you what Bran and I were thinking when we didn't give you or Dad any warning. Dad isn't just our father, he's our best friend. And—"

Bran cut him off to finish. "...he's been upset and lonely for so long, we couldn't take it anymore. It's painful to see someone you love hurting."

"If there was even a snowball's chance in hell that this plan might work, the four of us were willing to take it. I imagine it's been just as hard for your sisters to see you unhappy." Pat finished.

Well, Rowan thought. Her brothers-in-law took the wind out of her sails. Tears slowly dribbled down her cheeks at the mess she and Hugh had made of everything.

"I...I'm sorry that—" Rowan began only for River to cut her off.

"Don't you dare apologize because of what they said, it is the truth, but it doesn't matter. We *were* wrong, and we hurt you when you're already hurting." River sounded furious with their part in all this, and Rowan hated that even more than them keeping secrets.

"No. I—"

Raven cut her off this time. "I panicked when you left us. Damn it, Rowan. Not sleeping in the same bed or not living in the same house is one thing, but you left the country. For weeks! We were desperate, but I realize now I was selfish. I thought *I* knew what was best for you. I do want you to have your heart's desire, and I was willing to be dishonest in the hopes of you getting it," Raven finished with a hiccup and a sniff.

"I might as well tell you, Row, the four of us planned on surprising you in Tulsa in a few weeks to see if our plan worked, and if it had, we planned on gloating. That's," River was hiccupping and sniffing now too, "how big of pieces of shit your sisters have become in your absence."

River's obnoxious mouth finally managed to break through Rowan's upset. She even felt her lips tip up in a small smile. How in the world could a person stay mad at those two? After all, Rowan had done her share of meddling. She'd tattled on Bran and Patrick more than once to Hugh, knowing he would always react. She'd also agreed to carry letters from Patrick and give them to River without consulting her sister and only telling Raven after the fact.

Rowan took a deep breath to clear her emotions from her throat. "Okay, you guys. Neither of you are pieces of shit. I recognize I've done my fair share of getting into your business. We've done this our whole lives with one sister or the other. Talked about what to do to help whichever of us was in trouble.

And since I wasn't there, you two concocted...whatever the hell this is."

"Are we good?" River asked.

"You completely forgive us?" Raven asked for extra clarity.

"We're good and you're completely forgiven," Rowan assured. "However, there is the situation with William, and I still want to see if there is potential for us."

"How were we to guess that you'd have your tongue down the man's throat after three lunch dates?" River demanded.

Rowan should not have texted them such a detailed account. But she'd walked into the boutique feeling all dreamy and wanted to share. It was an amazing kiss. Hubris Hugh never dared give into the temptation of sticking his tongue anywhere on or in her body!

The Byrne sisters were back in business. For them, forgiven really meant forgiven. Now it was all about damage control. "He and his father are picking Matilda and me up for a charity event at the Philbrook, the one I mentioned to you earlier in the week. That means, thank God, not as much alone time with Will. It's inevitable, though, that he wants to be alone with me."

"When do he and his dad head back to Houston?" River asked.

"Monday or Tuesday of next week, I believe. I also think he'll ask me to visit him there." Rowan cringed. She hadn't told her sisters every part of their lunch date. Christ, was it only yesterday?

"That seems a little fast. He can't expect you to drive all that way. It's almost eight hours!" Raven didn't love the idea of Rowan pursuing the relationship. That was evident.

"I told Will yesterday that I would date him. As in—I would be his girlfriend." Rowan blushed at the admission. What in the holy hell had she been thinking? Had the kiss been *that* good? It did make her feel things...she couldn't discount Will just because Hugh decided to rummage through her bedroom. Speaking of...

"You...what?" Raven was probably as confused as Rowan.

"You flipping agreed to what?" River practically shrieked.

Rowan was not above resorting to distraction. "I found Hugh in my bedroom snooping yesterday," she said. "He almost opened—*The Drawer.*"

"No!" Raven and River squealed at the same time.

"That would have been embarrassing," Raven laughed.

"Nah, he would have gotten a boner, and Row would have totally enjoyed the denim tent show." How did River come up with that crap?

Rowan heard Bran ask what would have been embarrassing. Patrick wanted to know who had a boner. Great. The boys were back. Her sisters weren't helping by laughing hysterically at their questions.

"Don't you dare tell them. I fucking mean it!" Rowan's cheeks were scorching.

So much for her repentant sisters. "Someone finding Row's sex toy drawer." Raven would pay for that.

"Potty mouth much, Rowan? The boner in question would be your dad's."

"Bre is watching Daniel while he naps. Pat and I are going to the Lobby for food until you three decide not to be disgusting. Do not ever, ever speak about toys and Rowan or discuss my dad's dick again. Seriously, for the love of God, babe," Bran said in exasperation.

"Row, tell us more about Hugh's—" Pat cut River off. Rowan heard him yell stop and then heard the door slam.

"You guys are so bad! Your husbands may never recover." Rowan giggled. "By the way, my job will be done early, so unless you guys are hankering for some Muskogee time, you needn't come to Oklahoma on my account."

. . .

River was still lying face down on her bed in her sleep tee and panties, thumbing through the new Interior Design magazine. She felt more lighthearted than she had in weeks. Listening to her sisters being ridiculous was excellent medicine.

"Oh, I don't know then," Raven said. "We'll talk to the guys about it today and see what they're feeling."

"If they're still talking to us, that is," River laughed.

"What in the hell is on your ass?"

Rowan almost peed her pants at Hugh's bellow. Twisting her upper body, she glared at…God, Hugh looked so good in a casual t-shirt and shorts. Her sisters asked, "What the hell?" at the same time.

"Get the hell out of my room, you asshole!" He didn't even react. His giant bear paw smacked down on Rowan's back, the other landed on her ass.

"When in the fuck did you let someone tattoo your bare ass?"

He wasn't roaring anymore. His voice was low and downright menacing. She heard "Oh Shit" coming through her speaker. An audience. Perfect.

"Hey guys, I have to get ready for work and kick a dickhead out of my room. I'll call you in a bit." Before they could reply, Rowan hung up and attempted to squirm out of Hugh's hold. "Let me go, Hugh, or I'll yell for your mom," she threatened.

Hugh ignored her, and honestly, Rowan ignored her own threat because Hugh's hand was no longer just holding her ass down. She felt his fingers move her sheer white cotton panties to the side of her cheek.

Her brain finally remembered what had caught his attention. The tattoo. Oh, God. Rowan redoubled her efforts to get out from under his hands. "Get off me, Hugh. For fuck's sake," she ground out. She felt the bed shaking where his knee had sunk into the mattress. She twisted her head to look at him.

His whole body was shaking in silent laughter. A tear, an actual tear, slipped from one of his black eyes, the bastard. Rowan let her head drop back on top of her magazine. Regret was sometimes a tediously embarrassing thing to endure.

"Christ, Row," his voice full of amusement, "you tattooed my initials on your ass."

"Shut up, Hugh, and *get out!*" Rowan moaned against the magazine's pages. "And in case you missed it, it means kiss my ass, Hugh Darcy O'Faolain." Rowan wasn't looking at him, but she would swear his body became as still as granite. She was about to risk a peek when she felt warm breath on her exposed backside—right before she felt Hugh's lips kiss the tattoo.

It was a brief press of his lips, but she felt that touch...everywhere. She may have moaned. He may have moaned.

"Would you like me to kiss your ass every day, Rowan?" He growled. "I will. Gladly."

What in the absolute twilight zone hell was going on with this man? He'd never ever initiated touching her. Ever. Rowan slowly rolled over now that his hands weren't holding her down and propped herself up with her elbows so she could watch him warily. Her usually sharp mind had deserted her.

Hugh towered over her, his eyes running the length of her body. Rowan had to stop her legs from rubbing together to relieve the sudden ache between them. And oh God, River's words were prophetic. Hugh was definitely turned on. He didn't even try to cover the evidence, but she supposed he wasn't embarrassed about any part of his body. Why would he be? The man was exceptional.

Finally, her wits came back online. Thank God Matilda was a late sleeper. Rowan would've died if she'd walked in on her son towering over her half-dressed houseguest in bed. "Get out of my room, Hugh."

He only stood there looking at her. God, he was infuriating. Rowan sat up slowly. Hugh's eyes clocked the sway of her breasts beneath her top. Sliding her legs over the side of the bed, she told Hugh to back up. He took one step back. When she stood, the difference in their sizes had never been more apparent.

Craning her neck back to see his face, Rowan told him once more to get out of her room. "I need to get ready for work."

"Will you let me see you tonight?"

Tempting, so very tempting but also the exact opposite of what she'd been working toward. She had to stop following Hugh around like a lost kitten. This was probably one more of Hugh's territory marking parties. Matilda admitted last night that she'd told her son that Rowan was dating someone but didn't tell him who it was. Hugh probably wanted to ruin her chances with Will and then move back to ignoring her.

The touching was new, Rowan admitted. Crazy to think their first, and surely only, kiss was on her ass. She would not, could not, allow him to keep, in essence, cockblocking her life.

"No," Rowan said, shutting down his 'let's talk' bologna.

"Why?"

Stubborn. Rowan started to move by him towards the en suite bathroom. He wrapped his fingers around her upper arm, stopping her from leaving.

"Why?"

Rowan blew out a weary breath. "I have a date. Now please leave my room and feel free to remember the common etiquette of not entering a person's private space without an invitation. Spoiler—you won't be getting one." Hugh pulled her back until her front was plastered to his. He looked furious. Good. She was furious.

"Who are you dating?"

"None of your business. It's never been your business. You made sure of that, Hugh," Rowan added. Knowing the dig would land.

It did, but he shook it off in record time. "It is my goddamn business. Who is it?" he demanded again.

"William Stanton. Diana Gaine's nephew." Rowan felt a moment of intense satisfaction at Hugh's shocked face.

"No. You're lying."

"I don't need to lie, Hugh. Christ! You've been running away from me in an embarrassing sprint for months. Why would you think I wouldn't seek a relationship with a man who isn't embarrassed to claim me?" Rowan demanded.

"A relationship?" Hugh roared.

Rowan yelped as Hugh spun her around, pressing her back against the wall next to the door. Leaning in close to her ear, he whispered, "And do you touch yourself at night thinking about *William?*"

The inference was clear—did she touch herself the way she'd touched herself thinking about Hugh. Rowan was furious. This! *This* behavior after a million rejections! She looked at his clenched jaw and furious eyes and stood on her tiptoes until he moved closer. Whispering in his ear, she lied.

"I don't need to use my own hand. Will knows how to use his just fine." She shoved his chest then, catching him off guard. He took two steps back and she ran to her bathroom and locked the door behind her.

12

___

After his confrontation with Rowan, he'd stormed down his mom's hallway intent on heading to his own place before he busted Rowan's bathroom door down. His mother had been sipping coffee in the kitchen, her soft silver curls wrapped in in a silk scarf and a matching robe cinched about her waist. It had been apparent to Hugh from the look on his mother's face, that she'd heard the argument.

"You're breaking into my home early today. Did you and Rowan have a nice chat?"

Great, Hugh thought, he'd pissed his mom off too. Quite a morning he was having. "I didn't break in. You gave me a key card years ago."

"My mistake, obviously."

Hugh wasn't sure if the mistake was not remembering or giving him a card in the first place. He chose option one. "No problem."

She clenched her jaw before having to release the pressure to take a sip of her coffee. "Do you know that last night I got Rowan to consider hearing you out at some point?"

"I didn't know that, no." Hugh was not enjoying this talk.

"I wonder if she'll still consider it after you barged into her bedroom at seven o'clock in the damn morning?" Mom shook her head in irritation. "Get out of your way, Hugh. You are your own worst enemy in this. Go home, Son. You both need to cool off and have cooler heads before you see each other again."

"She has a fucking date tonight. Am I supposed to just relax and watch some TV while another man...when..." Hugh couldn't even finish the thought.

"I heard her tell you she's seeing William Stanton. His father, Owen, Diana's brother, will be with William. We are going to the event together tonight. So, I doubt if there will be a lot of...bedroom things going on," his mom finally choked out, blushing.

Ignoring that his mother uttered *bedroom things* in his presence, he zeroed in on what she'd glossed over.

"Are you dating Owen Stanton?" Hugh refused to flinch at the thought of his mother seeing a man who wasn't his father. His father was no longer here. It's only that Hugh hadn't considered...hadn't pictured his mother moving on. It was selfish, but the young boy still lurking inside Hugh's grown body felt crushed on his father's account.

His father would beat his ass for having such uncharitable thoughts.

Mom blushed. He should have stayed in bed this morning—except he wouldn't have seen Rowan's tattoo. He wanted to laugh all over again. *Kiss my ass, Hugh.* My God, that woman surprised him in a thousand different ways.

"I am not dating Owen or anyone else, young man," Mom finally answered. Offended and rightly so.

Sighing, Hugh forced himself to say, "I wouldn't mind if you were, Mom. I only asked because you never said anything before." Oh, God. Was that moisture in her eyes? This was escalating.

Sniffing back what appeared to be actual tears, she busied herself with tidying the extra coasters. "It isn't a date, but I wouldn't mind having a male friend to do things with once in a while. To events like we're going to tonight. Rowan told me I was brave to get out and enjoy society with someone besides Diana."

Mom wasn't looking at him, still stacking and restacking the coasters. Hugh put his hand over his mother's, stilling her nervous fidgeting. "Rowan was right. I hope you and Owen have a great evening." She looked up and met his gaze, surprise lighting her dark amber eyes, the same color as his sons'. "I also hope William chokes on his fucking dinner and dies."

"Thank you, Will," Rowan smiled as he brought her another glass of ice water and a shot of Slane to their table. The evening was lovely and warm, but with a cool breeze moving through the flowers and topiaries. The Philbrook garden lights created lovely sparkles dancing in the deep striations of her crystal glass. For some reason, the golden whiskey, one of her favorite colors, made her miss her sisters terribly. Rowan could always enjoy herself without being part of the Byrne trio, but she also wouldn't deny that nights like this would have been better together.

She would be back in Dublin soon. She was working endless hours to ensure it.

She'd called Raven and River back on her way to the boutique that morning to meet with a William Sonoma representative who specialized in Breville products. The boutique would house a small coffee and pastry café. It had been Rowan's idea to turn the second floor, which had originally been earmarked for storage, into a chic, trendy café where shoppers would love to meet their friends. The bar would look over the boutique's wares, encouraging patrons to shop before or after relaxing.

Rowan's ears were still ringing from the shrill screams both her sisters belted out when Rowan recounted that morning's encounter with Hugh. She still couldn't believe he'd kissed her ass.

After discussing her options on how to handle dating Will and discovering what in the hell was going on with Hugh, Rowan hung up, promising to send pictures of her and Matilda in their evening dresses and to call them when she got up tomorrow morning, which was a Saturday, thank God.

William had been very appreciative of her dress choice. Admittedly, Rowan had felt special when he touched her lips with his and whispered how beautiful she looked. She chose a simple, nude slip dress, nude strappy sandals, and her favorite James Avery piece hung between her breasts, a silver filigreed Creation pendant—a birthday present from her parents. She left her hair long, with one side pulled back and secured with a simple silver comb.

While the guests this evening slowly made their way through the line of paparazzi who wanted to get pictures of socialites and politicians for blogs and social pages, an older woman told Rowan she looked just like Pocahontas. The woman's daughter literally almost died on the spot, but Rowan only laughed. It wasn't the first time she'd heard that. She and her sisters did kind of resemble the Disney princess. Raven was the only one who had those lovely lips, though.

Will sat beside her and grimaced when his phone dinged several times. Rowan could tell he wanted to check them, but he was too much of a gentleman. "Will, if you need to check your messages, I completely understand. Business doesn't stop for our convenience," she smiled to let him know she meant it.

Will looked sheepish. He reached for his phone and tapped

the back panel. "I would have loved to shut it off tonight, but there are some worrisome issues at work in regards to one of our newest jobs."

"I hope it's nothing too serious."

"Too early to tell, but we've had two security breaches in the part of our system that houses the specs. It shouldn't be possible. Our system knocked the hackers out, but...it's concerning. I wouldn't be so worried, but this new deal we're working on is a government contract and one of the biggest deals Stanton Industries has landed."

"I am perfectly content to sip my whiskey and listen to the orchestra. It's like being on a Bridgerton set. I'm in heaven and here come Tilly and your father so I won't be alone. Go, Will. Take care of business so that you can enjoy the rest of the evening."

He stood, looking down at Rowan with grateful appreciation. She was surprised when he bent, lightly cupping her jaw before kissing her. Speaking of Bridgerton romance, Rowan sighed and then inwardly cringed when she wished it were Hugh that had made such a romantic gesture.

"Thank you, Rowan. I will try to hurry," he said as he walked away from the table.

Will didn't make it back for dinner, which was a shame because it was beautifully served and delicious. She enjoyed Owen and Matilda's company. Rowan's presence didn't seem to put a damper on their lively conversation.

However, Rowan's lack of concern for William's absence was a definite red flag. She enjoyed his company, but she certainly didn't pine for it. When he finally rejoined their table, William looked slightly frazzled. Owen asked what he'd found out, and Will admitted that their top people were still attempting to find out how the breach had even occurred. He hoped to have more information by tomorrow.

"We'll need to visit Aunt Diana in the morning. I'm afraid, Dad, we'll need to head back to Houston directly after." William looked at Rowan then, taking her hand that rested on the table, an apologetic smile touched his lips.

Rowan wasn't glad Will's company was having trouble, but in truth, it would give her time to sort things out with Hugh. And there was the fact that she was returning to Dublin soon.

When she and Matilda were let off at the hotel, Owen and William walked them into the lobby. Rowan was pleased that Owen hugged Matilda before telling her that he'd had one of the best evenings he could remember. For her part, Matilda smiled, hugged the older Stanton goodnight, and said, "It was a lovely night, Owen. Thank you."

William stood before her, appearing a bit glum. "I hope I didn't completely wreck my chances. Tonight's interruption was unplanned and very unwelcome."

Rowan took both of his hand in hers, so he wouldn't get any ideas about kissing her in the lobby where a certain O'Faolain man might be lurking, and said, "Tonight was wonderful. I'm only sorry you missed so much of it. Do not think for a minute that I was put out. The situation sounds like a serious one. Please text or call me and let me know you got things sorted."

"I will, and I'll spend the next few days thinking of some way to make it up to you, and thank you for being so understanding."

Will leaned in to kiss her, and she had no valid reason not to. Surely, Hugh wasn't hiding behind a potted palm with a machete. He kept hold of one of her hands and placed the other on her lower back. He really was quite handsome. It was such a shame she was more attracted to the strong and silently angry type. William's mouth touched hers briefly, and then probably because he knew Matilda and Owen were waiting, he let her go with a promise to call tomorrow.

As she and Matilda stepped into the elevator to take them to the penthouse level, Rowan's phone dinged. A message from Hugh. Why in the hell did her heart begin thumping triple time?

I've thought about kissing your ass all day.

A strangled gasp escaped her lips. Matilda gave her a curious look. "Raven," was Rowan's explanation.

"My, she's up early. It's what, four in the morning there?" Matilda questioned.

"Daniel," she explained with a shrug.

I fixed the leg of your nightstand. It vibrated.

Rowan would flipping kill him if he invaded her privacy. Their floor dinged and the doors slid open. She half expected to see the taunting bastard waiting on her. All clear. She quickly squelched her disappointment.

He thought he'd won something with his cute little texts. A shame that. Hugh was about to get schooled.

Matilda spoke of the evening as they let themselves into the suite. It was obvious she'd enjoyed the night. Several friends and acquaintances were there.

"I'm exhausted though, sweetheart. I'm going to turn in, and hopefully, if my son can refrain from a dawn's early arrival, I'll be sleeping until noon." She laughed.

Rowan laughed, too, but her body also tingled at the thought of having Hugh's hands on her again. Wishing Matilda a good night, she entered her bedroom, and glanced at her nightstand. Rowan didn't really believe Hugh had done anything. He had to be guessing. Still, she would enjoy paying him back.

Rowan first dug through one of her bags until she found the camera remote to her phone. She propped her phone against the bathroom sink with the camera on so she could get the angle just right of the glass shower door. She quickly took her makeup off and got undressed, putting her hair in a bun so it wouldn't get wet in the shower.

It was easy from there. Turn the water on, produce a bit of steam, just enough to tease the glass with a hint of misty opaque. Rowan positioned her body in a similar pose to what she'd discovered Hugh in when she'd gone into his bathroom those many months ago. One lean arm stretched above her head; her hand wrapped around the remote to hide it. The other arm went low, the illusion that she was touching herself.

She clicked several photos. Satisfied one of them would work, she showered and, in great anticipation, looked at the pics. Selecting the most provocative where her head was tilted back, her mouth slightly open, on a moan perhaps, and her eyes looking at the camera. There was a hint of puckered nipple and a blurred hand below.

Hugh only thought he'd won something with his texts earlier.

She sent the photo with the caption, **Who's vibrating now?**

Rowan threw on a t-shirt and climbed into bed.

Goodnight, Hugh, she whispered before closing her eyes, a smile on her face.

13

───────

Rowan stretched, smiling at the light peeking through the window shades. She'd slept amazingly well. She needed to call her sisters. They'd be waiting for updates about last night's date. Her hand felt around her nightstand to grab her phone off the charger.

The nightstand recalled to mind what she'd done last night. Oh my God, Rowan still could not believe she'd sent that picture to Hugh. Served him right, but still. Raven and River would shit if Rowan confided in what she'd done.

Swiping up to open her phone, there were several texts. William, Nan, Raven, River, and...Hugh. She'd save Hughs for last. Her body tingled in anticipation of what he'd written. If he liked it.

Nan sent a picture of a new flower garden at her new home. Marrying Devlen had transformed Rowan's grandma. She seemed so full of life. It was heartwarming to see that Nan was adding flowers, making the new house her own. Nan texted her sisters and Rowan together. **Never worry. I am keeping the flower gardens at your place beautiful as well. You three had better come visit before my new**

great-grandbaby gets here. I mean it. They might be able to swing a weekend now that her job was wrapping up earlier than expected.

Her sisters used a joint thread to text Rowan this morning.

Row, you looked stunning at the charity. The Social Edition pics online are gorgeous! The one after the charity is smoking. Can't wait to hear how the night turned out for you and Will. Call soon.

Damn, Row, how many people asked you where your sidekick Flit was hiding? LOL Totally nailed Pocahontas—Will could have been your John Smith, I suppose. Call us already.

River, don't you remember. Rowan always hated that show because she wanted Pocahontas to choose Kocoum.

Oh, yeah. Moody and broody's always been her thing.

And big.

Dark hair.

Muscles.

Rolling her eyes at their teasing, she opened William's next.

Will apologized again for working last night. **I laid in bed for hours last night, regretting that I hadn't found a quiet corner so I could taste your mouth again. I've thought of little else. You are an incredible woman. I will miss you when I leave town today. Would you consider coming to Houston next weekend? I will send my plane to pick you up on Friday afternoon. Talk to you soon.**

Rowan sighed. He was wonderful, but she could already feel herself pulling back. He told her he'd thought of her for hours last night. Kissing her again. Rowan spent her time taking dirty pictures and sending them to another man before she happily fell into a deep sleep.

She wasn't ready to give up on them yet. She and Will could be...something.

Rowan's finger hovered over the last unread message. Hugh. Oh God. Rowan took a deep, shaky breath, let it out slowly, and opened the message.

Agree to see me tonight. Come to my place for drinks. You owe me.

Who in the hell was this new Hugh? Hugh 1.0 would never ask her over. Hugh 1.0 wouldn't have freely touched her body or put his lips to her skin either. What in the hell was he playing at? Her fingers hovered over the keypad. Agree or not? While Rowan thought about big girl issues like dating two men and the consequences, she propped herself up against the headboard and pulled her laptop close. She found the paper's Social Edition.

"Oh wow." She and Will were in several at the Philbrook charity. They looked good together. "Oh my." A photographer had gotten a closeup picture of Will leaning over her at their table. She was smiling as his lips touched hers. It had been a soft, sweet kiss. This picture made it look as though they were in love. Groaning, no wonder her sisters were so eager for her call.

Raven had mentioned a picture taken after the charity. Rowan clicked through the rest of the museum pictures before searching the main Social Edition page.

Stanton Tech Heir in Love. The bold description sat directly above a picture of her and Will kissing in the hotel lobby. Oh God, Oh God. Oh God. This was the reason her sisters wanted to talk to her, not the charity photos.

Matilda would see them as soon as she got up. Diana Gaines was an early riser. She would already have seen them, which means she would show Owen and Will when they visited her before they left town. *Staton Tech Heir in Love.* Christ Almighty, Hugh would see them.

Maybe he wouldn't see them. He didn't seem like a social media troller. Unless his sons tipped him off. She needed to call her sisters immediately and head *that* off.

She also needed to reply to Hugh's text from last night.

What do I owe you for?

Bubbles appeared immediately. **I stayed hard for hours.**

That mental picture dragged a moan from Rowan's throat. It amazed Rowan how comfortable she was with sexual discourse when it was with Hugh. They'd never even kissed, but they'd trusted each other to witness vulnerable moments.

Hugh knew her body and she knew his. Rowan would trust him with more than watching. She always had. He hadn't trusted her. Rowan kept asking herself the same question: What had changed?

She tapped her chin thoughtfully. Agree or not? Rowan could not let the image of Hugh's erection cloud her judgment.

How did you get it to go away?

You know how.

Christ have mercy. Lord have mercy. Pray for this sinner, Lord. Unfortunately, praying didn't stop her fingers from typing.

You'll only run. Why would I open myself to that? Again.

Bubbles for minutes. Hugh was either typing a novel or deleting and repeating.

I'll never run again. Give me one more chance. I want to explain.

There could only be one response. Rowan wanted answers. She hoped Hugh didn't let her down. **Okay.**

7. I'll have fruit, veg, and Slane.

She was in the deep end now. No returning to the ledge.

The last hurdle before she faced the day—a call to her sisters and maybe telling...probably telling them what kind of deep shit storm she'd willingly walked into.

They answered on the first ring.

"What's going on?" Raven asked.

"Spill," River demanded.

"The long or short"

"Long." Raven.

"Short." River.

"Medium it is," Rowan sighed. "Prepare yourselves. I had thought not to tell you everything, but I need your input and you have to know it all." Rowan swallowed her embarrassment and told her sisters a PG version of her and Hugh's previous sexual encounters. His rejection. His multiple rejections. Raven and River had witnessed the one in the hospital room.

Rowan detailed her time with William, short though it had been, and her feelings for the man. Trying to decide whether or not she could see herself with William long-term. Even though she'd told them some of what had happened the morning Hugh had seen her ass tat and the...touching that had followed, Rowan filled in the blanks of what he'd said and what she'd lied about.

"So, you made Hugh think you and William were intimate?" Raven asked for clarification.

"Yes, and I hate that I did it, but damn it, I didn't want him to know that I was still hoping he would want me back!" Rowan admitted.

"Let's be honest, Row," River started. "He always wanted you. He's just been a dumbass for months."

Rowan didn't disagree. She then told them about her date with William, that she did really enjoy his company, and she could see trying something more permanent with him. "But..." Rowan's reasoning petered off.

"But...you love Hugh, and you think you want to take the chance," Raven finished Rowan's thought.

"Exactly."

River asked about the pictures. Wondering why it looked like Rowan was super into William.

"I am into him, damn it! That's the problem, but less than thirty minutes after William kissed me in the lobby, I took a nude selfie in the shower and sent it to Hugh."

Turns out, her sisters could still be shocked. There was a lot of wha wha wha's and gasping. "In my defense, Hugh had egged me on by texting me ridiculous shit right before I got in. So, he got what he got."

"Okay, I'm swallowing my shock. For now. But...how...I mean, how did he respond?"

"Yeah," Raven seconded, "did he...make a surprise visit again?"

"He texted back, but I didn't get it until this morning. He asked me to come over tonight. He said I 'owed him.' I agreed to meet," Rowan revealed.

"I don't care if he wanted you to come over," River practically yelled. "Did he mention the picture?"

"And what did he mean you owed him?" Raven demanded.

"He said...well...he said I owed him because he was hard for hours after I sent him the pic." They had all the details now. Probably way too many details, but Rowan needed solutions fast, and that required oversharing.

"Sexy as fuck. Wow, my father-in-law has serious game," River teased.

"Game and hard dicks aside," Raven started her lecture, "I'm glad you're going tonight, but you have to set boundaries. Hugh's natural inclination will be to bulldoze all the obstacles between him and you. You know he had to have seen those pictures of you and Will. He'll be in damage control, and that may include damaging Will."

"I agree with Raven. Hear what he has to say about his past asswipe blunders, and then give yourself time to assess. You like William, but you love Hugh—though he doesn't deserve it after how badly he hurt you—so proceed with great caution," River advised.

"A great deal of caution," Raven seconded.

Hugh was tense. He'd changed clothes three times. He *never* second-guessed his first choice. He never gave a single shit what anyone thought of him. He said what he wanted, and the recipient either liked it or they didn't. He started out in a suit. Bad choice. A woman was coming to his place. He wasn't going to a board meeting for fuck's sake. He'd torn the suit off.

Next came jeans and a t-shirt. The jeans felt restrictive and irritating. He'd hated all the shoes and boots he'd tried on with it. He looked like he was running errands. Hugh stripped again.

Finally, he chose a pair of dark brown joggers and a soft, tan t-shirt. His feet were bare—no reason to tower over Rowan any more than he did naturally. This was a stay in casual date, well perhaps it wasn't a date, but it *felt* like it. He hadn't had a date in years, but he never remembered one feeling like this. Rowan would most likely choose comfortable. So, he would too. Clothes finalized; Hugh continued pacing through his apartment.

He'd missed Oklahoma. Not as much as he thought he would, but still, it was good to be back. His mother always lived in town. Hugh preferred living closer to nature. That's why the Muskogee compound suited him so well.

His sons loved living there as well, but they were married now, and their priorities were their wives—as they should be.

Hugh was excited about the distillery, so he knew he'd go back to Dublin sooner rather than later.

He did love Dublin. His sons were there, which meant Hugh would be there. He wondered if Rowan would spend part of her time in Oklahoma with him. She struggled to leave her sisters as much as he struggled to be away from his boys, and now his grandson—her nephew. Jesus, their family was convoluted.

Rowan did love the compound. She really loved the library. The unfinished library. Maybe he could draw her to his home using the library as a lure. Hugh groaned at his thoughts. He was getting ahead of himself. This was just a simple meet-up for drinks. He wasn't proposing for the love of God. It wasn't *that* big of a deal. It was a *very* big deal, he thought.

He also shouldn't be so bothered by the pictures of Rowan and William online. He *was*, though. Damn it, he was a lot more than bothered. Hugh had called the O'Faolain's head attorney that morning.

Interrupting the man on a Saturday had been thoughtless. Asking him to hire investigators to find any dirt he could on William Stanton was borderline out of control. Mom and Rowan would have Hugh's head if they knew he'd even considered it.

That's how crazed he'd been since seeing the woman he...a woman that was...of Rowan in Stanton's arms. He wanted to find anything that might destroy him. That William dared...If Hugh was being reasonable, he would admit that William couldn't have known she belonged to Hugh. Unfortunately for Stanton, Hugh wasn't in a reasonable headspace.

The photographs that hit the papers and online media this morning almost crippled him. He'd felt rage, despair, then denial. The way they looked at one another...Christ...there was a real possibility he'd screwed up any chance he'd once had of making Rowan his.

Did Rowan love William? It looked like she did.

She had agreed to meet Hugh. She'd agreed to hear him out. Rowan would walk through his door any minute and every speech he'd been practicing evaporated from memory. He was edgy and angry, and very, very panicked.

All of Rowan's favorite fruit and vegetables had been delivered on trays an hour ago. Chilled water and ice. Lemon wedges. Low ball glasses and whiskey. All her favorite things.

He'd golfed with a few friends and had lunch at the club today to waste several hours. He spent those hours surreptitiously staring at the picture Rowan had sent him. Naked and in the shower. He hadn't lied to Rowan. He'd been hard for hours. It had taken every ounce of his willpower to not let himself into his mother's place and into Rowan's bed.

He could barely make out her form, but he knew her body. Every naked inch and his memory was faultless. That bit of nipple he could make out had his mouth watering. He could see her eyes. They appeared to be staring right at him. Rowan had been playing with fire. He had instigated it with his initial text. He desperately wanted to know what she had nestled away in her side table.

Yesterday he'd had his mouth on her ass cheek. That had been the first bit of her skin that Hugh had ever tasted. He wanted more.

On the golf green, he was either adjusting his dick after looking at the shower pic or fuming over the pictures of William and Rowan. Had she sent William a naked picture too? No. Hugh wouldn't believe she'd do that. Her body belonged to Hugh. Or it used to.

When she'd been pissed at Hugh for coming into her bedroom, she'd admitted that William had had his hands on her body. Hugh didn't consider himself a violent man, but he'd had visions of beating the man to within an inch of death. He'd settled for attempting to ruin his reputation or his business. It was not nearly as satisfying, but he wouldn't end up arrested.

His anger was worse because he and William were friendly. He wasn't a stranger. Will was Diana Gaines nephew, so Hugh had been around the Stanton family several times over the years. Hugh and Helen had attended William's wedding thirty years ago.

That thought made Hugh pause. Hopefully the investigators would find out why Will and Katy got a divorce. Maybe he'd been a shit husband. Rowan wouldn't like that, he thought, grinning.

Hugh stopped his pacing when he heard his phone ringing. He'd left it by the whiskey bar and quickly moved there. He prayed it wasn't Rowan cancelling. He snatched the phone from the counter and saw that Bran was calling. Panic seared his chest. It was almost one in the morning in Dublin.

"Bran. What is it?" Hugh barely leashed his anxiety.

"Everything is fine, Dad. Seriously, I didn't mean to scare you."

"Then why in the fuck are you calling me at one o'clock in the morning? Are Raven and Daniel okay?" Hugh was taking deep breaths to calm his racing heart.

"Fine, fine. No worries. My son has decided sleeping at night just isn't his thing. For four nights," Bran chuckled softly. Probably hoping Daniel would change his mind about passing out. "Rave and I are taking turns."

Bran sounded exhausted. Parenthood...the great sleep depriver. Hugh's heart ached that he wasn't there to help too. "You pulled that shit with me. Did I never tell you?"

"No, you didn't, and I can only apologize for torturing you."

"Mom sorted me out. I called her late one night, waking her

and Dad, which she was pissed about until I told her you refused to sleep at night like a normal person, and I was losing my shit." The doorbell rang. Oh, God. Rowan.

Hugh walked over and opened the door. Rowan was in thin cotton shorts, a matching black t-shirt, and flip flops. Her hair was up in a bun, soft tendrils coming loose. Thank God. Casual. He waved her in and mouthed Bran, pointing at the phone. Her immediate concern soothed his earlier reaction. Anyone would have panicked. Christ, it was the middle of the damn night in Dublin. He mouthed, "It's fine."

"She told me to stop whining like a child." Hugh continued. "She also told me how Dad got me to sleep."

"Oh, Jesus. Tell me now. Please." Bran was desperate.

Rowan sat at the bar smiling. She loved their family as he did. He fixed her an ice water and a double of Slane, while he poured himself Glenmorangie 18. She loved Glen 18. Hugh had considered she might want to taste it on his tongue.

"Turn your air down so it's colder than the normal temperature. Then turn the television on, or music, but keep it low. Take your shirt off and lay on the couch. Strip Daniel to his diaper and lay him on your chest. Don't cover him up."

"Okay, I'm doing it all now. Give me a second."

Hugh could hear Bran murmuring to Daniel and moving about, following the instructions. Rowan took a sip of her whiskey and raised her brows in question.

"Daniel isn't sleeping at night," Hugh whispered. "Bran is up with him this time." Rowan nodded in understanding.

"Okay, I'm back. Who were you talking to?"

"None of your fucking bus—" Rowan was staring at Hugh, and he would swear that her look was a dare to tell the truth. Shit, he was fucking up already.

"Rowan."

"Oh, yeah," Bran said like he knew Rowan was coming over,

which he probably fucking did. "Tell Row hi. Okay. I'm on the couch and Daniel's on my chest, but he's squirming like he's cold and about ready to scream. Scream more that is. Maybe just a light blanket? Patty's blanket?" Hugh and Rowan grinned at each other then. Patty's blanket referred to Patrick's baby shower gift. He'd crocheted Bran and Raven's child a baby blanket and Raven put their son to bed every night with it.

"No. He gets his Patty when he stays asleep in his own bed like a big boy."

"Now what?" Bran sounded stressed. Daniel's fussing was becoming louder.

"Mom said to ignore you. She told me you'd eventually get tired of being ignored, which you did. She said the cold air would make you snuggle into my chest, which it did."

Bran spoke even quieter. "He's snuggling. Oh God, Dad, his eyes are getting heavy," Bran's voice was so low Hugh and Rowan could barely hear it. Hugh had turned the phone on speaker so Rowan could follow along.

"Ignore it all. No eye contact. Remember!" Hugh whispered back.

"If he goes out, let him sleep until six, then wake him up and do his normal routine, but Mom told me to give you two naps, not more than an hour to an hour and a half twice a day. No extra-long naps. In a day or two Daniel's clock should be adjusted."

"He's completely limp on my chest and sleeping."

"Try to sleep, too, Son. Call me tomorrow."

"Thanks, Dad. I love you."

Hugh had to blink his eyes rapidly to stop any moisture from escaping. "Love you too."

14
———

Rowan was in love. Okay, she'd already been in love but hearing Hugh talk his son through a parenting crisis... heart emojis were probably shooting from her eyes. *Calm down, Row. No jumping and leaping into anything yet.*

Hugh was barefoot. As if he needed to be any hotter. Good Lord, the man was a walking fantasy. And those joggers—hello, frontal outline. Rowan took another sip of her Slane hoping to cover any drool leaking out.

Hugh set his phone on the bar after he disconnected with Bran. Now that the call was over, he seemed unsure. Nervous. Did she unnerve the great Hugh O'Faolain? Rowan sat on a barstool. Hugh leaned two feet away. They said nothing, only watching one another. She wasn't sure what she thought might happen tonight, but silence hadn't been one of them.

"Your mom and I had lunch with Diana today," Rowan said, breaking the tension.

"Oh yeah?"

"Yeah." Conversation—o.

"Did she let you know all the ways you are losing at life?" Hugh asked, a small grin tilting his lips.

125

Rowan snorted at that. "Of course. Three main things for sure. Let me see," Rowan paused to take a sip of her whiskey. "I should have discussed the importance with my client that she needed to have a soft opening for 'certain people.' One can assume she meant 'affluent people' who weren't interested in rubbing elbows with, gasp, commoners."

"I'm unsurprised. What else are you doing wrong?" Hugh asked, moving one step closer.

Lord, Hugh was intense. His presence was nothing short of lightning, causing the small hairs on her arms to stand erect. "The second...I should focus on my painting. I'm apparently wasting my time in design."

He moved just that bit closer. He was still leaning against the bar, but now his leg was *so* very close to her own. "You've never wasted your time in design. You and your sisters are extremely talented. However," Hugh began, pausing to take a sip of his whisky, "she is right that you should focus more on your painting. Mom showed me what you painted for her, and, damn Row, your talent is breath-stealing. It stole mine," he admitted.

Hugh calling her by her nickname was...she didn't know, but she wanted to hear it pass his lips as often as possible, and at the same time, she was aware that they were skirting all the big issues.

Why did you push me away?

Did you like kissing my ass?

Did you like the picture of me naked in the shower?

Why are you touching me now?

Did you see the pictures of Will and me?

What changed...?

"The third?" Hugh asked.

Rowan froze. It was about the pictures of her and William, of course. And why had she ever admitted to *three* things? Damn. "My style," Rowan lied. "It's lacking, apparently."

Hugh set his glass next to Rowan's and moved to stand directly in front of her. Her knees touched the top of his drawstring. He placed his hands on either side of her body, palms flat on the marble top. "Your style is impeccable. Try again."

Rowan attempted to gauge his mood. Did he know about the pictures and assume, correctly, that Diana would bring them up. "Tell me, Hugh, what occupied your day?"

"Golf, picturing you naked, and you kissing William Stanton."

Not avoiding the big issues. Noted.

"Do you love him?"

Hugh's body appeared to double in size, swelling and surrounding her. Rowan inhaled, centering herself. She'd done nothing to be ashamed of and, in fact, she was the one who had everything to be pissed off about.

"Why do you care, Hugh? You told me, with all the clarity the English language allows, that "we" would never be a thing. So, why the sudden interest in my love life?"

"Love life?" Hugh growled.

Rowan held her ground, but Christ Almighty, the temptation to wrap her legs around Hugh's waist and pull him tight, was tempting.

She chose not to answer and gave the infuriating man a taste of his own medicine. Silence. Hugh placed his scorching hot palms on her thighs, giving each a squeeze. When he started rubbing his thumbs in circular motions, a gasp escaped.

"Are you in love with him? Please tell me," Hugh begged.

Rowan couldn't deny Hugh anything. Not really. Not ever. "No." A whoosh of breath escaped his mouth, his body pressed closer.

"Thank Christ," he whispered.

"Why, Hugh? Why now when I've finally started to move past you? Will wants to fly me to Houston next weekend. I'm considering it."

"No."

"You can't just tell me no and expect me to obey. You've tried to keep me all to yourself for as long as we've known one another. You've also left me incredibly lonely and sad," Rowen confessed.

Hugh's hands slid up her thighs to grasp her hips. "I know."

Rowan watched as Hugh's broad chest expanded as he took a deep, shuddering breath. Her truth was hard for him to hear, but he wasn't denying them. "You can't give me hope—you can't ask me to give up a man who might make me happy."

"I'm asking, damn it, Row, I'm asking," Hugh's deep voice boomed.

The pleading in his voice almost undid Rowan. Almost. He'd yet to explain...*anything*. "My answer will be no, and I'll walk out that door and not look back if you won't tell me why! Why are you pursuing me now? Why are you touching me?" Rowan felt near tears.

"Let go of me, Hugh. Let me stand. Give me space." Reluctantly, he dropped his hands from her waist and stepped back. She stood, and with a hand that was less than steady, Rowan picked up her drink, swallowing Slane before breathing out a fiery breath in relief. She'd needed a different type of warmth filling her chest.

Stoic Hugh was sexy. A trembling, emotional Hugh was destroying. He was clearly fighting a battle with himself. He'd asked her to come over so he could explain, but within a few minutes, he'd reverted to his trademark guttural grunts. At least he wasn't touching her. She couldn't think with his hands on her body.

Rowan finished her whiskey and set the empty glass down

with a finality that made Hugh flinch. Pushing away from the bar, she began to walk to the front door. Without looking back, she quietly said, "Goodnight, Hugh."

One second her hand was reaching for the door's handle, the next, a seething giant was pressed against her back, both of his hands reached above her head to ensure the door stayed closed, which proved how exhausting and unpredictable Hugh O'Faolain was.

Rowan didn't try to force the issue of leaving, nor did she ask him to explain himself. She would give him a few minutes to sort his thoughts and if he still wasn't capable of communicating them, she would leave, and she wouldn't allow him to stop her.

Taking his hands from the door, he gently placed them on her shoulders, making her body shiver from the contact. He turned her around. Ignoring his gaze was impossible. "Come to the living room and sit. I want to explain."

"Do you? Really?" Rowan raised her brows in question.

Hugh took one of Rowan's hands, leading her toward a soft looking white couch. He sat and pulled her down beside him. When she was situated, she was sitting at a slight angle from Hugh's body so she could give him all her attention.

He took her hand and placed it on his thigh. Briefly, she wondered if sitting this close was a mistake. Rowan could feel heat and muscle through the thin joggers. It was hard to not dig her fingers in.

"I *need* to talk because I *need* you. But do I *want* to? No."

Honesty. That was a good start. "Hugh, I've always wondered—" she stopped mid-sentence. No wonder Hugh was struggling. Rowan opened up with her sisters all the time, but even between the three of them, there were some topics they avoided.

"Wondered what?"

Hugh probably hoped by getting Rowan to talk, there would

be less limelight on himself—but...she did want to know. "I wondered if those times we, umm, watched each other, if you wanted me...before then. When did you start wanting me in a sexual way, I mean?" Rowan's face was beet red, and if the flexing of Hugh's leg muscles was any indication, he was discomfited as well.

"The day we met at Triskelion in Eufaula. The moment I saw you walk down the stairs. You were in that pretty yellow dress you love so much. I could only see you, never Raven or River. You." Hugh smiled, probably remembering the moment. "There was also the conversation I'd overheard between you and your sisters before you came down. Apparently, you weren't wearing any panties. Sitting so close to you at breakfast was uncomfortable because I couldn't stop myself from wondering what I'd see if I lifted your dress."

Well, that was...unexpected. And a total turn-on. "So, why then, Hugh? Was it truly all about our ages?"

Hugh absently placed his hand over Rowan's, tracing her fingers while he tried to find the right way to explain. "It was all about our age. Or I thought it was," he admitted. "I don't like that I'm so much older. I fear that you would come to regret tying yourself to me. That one day, you would only see an old man, and you would still be young and beautiful.

"And knowing you and your family, I knew you would never leave me because your honor and loyalty wouldn't let you. I just...I couldn't let you ruin your life."

Hugh watched Rowan's face carefully—watched as she let his truth settle. Speaking that out loud to Rowan made him realize that his initial feelings and reasons for keeping his distance were still very much valid. Maybe she'd never considered the long-term ramifications but now that he'd just painted a pretty good picture of what that would look like, she *must* be less enthusiastic about getting involved.

He took his hand from hers and crossed his arms over his chest. This whole night was a bad idea. Letting himself think the age issue was surmountable had been a big mistake.

"Oh no, you don't, Hugh," Rowan declared angrily. "You don't get to say your piece and then shut down again. You don't get to say you want me and shove me away."

She scooted closer to Hugh and shocked the hell out of him when she straddled his lap. She was so tiny compared to him that her knees couldn't reach the cushion. She poked his chest in her anger and continued her tirade.

"You told me your reason about our ages. Great, you got that off your chest. Why you couldn't have spoken to me months ago about your fears, I'll never understand." Hugh placed his hands on her hips. Having his obsession sitting on his lap was distracting the hell out of him.

"Had you talked it out with me, I would have told you that your concerns were noted, but they weren't my concerns. So, we could have moved on!"

Rowan was panting, she was so pissed. She was gorgeous in any mood, but angry Rowan might be her most stunning look, and since he pissed her off so often, he enjoyed it quite a bit.

"I did believe that you wanted me, Rowan, but I also believed you'd never studied all the ramifications of dating a man so much older. It has destroyed me to push you away, but if you look at all the cons, I think you'll change your mind. I won't deny I want you, but I struggle with the tomorrows, not the right nows."

"I would always be here for the tomorrows." Rowan looked defeated as if Hugh was being unfair.

Rowan's words were very similar to his mother's. Mom didn't think Hugh was giving Rowan enough credit to know her own mind. Still…"My concerns are valid whether you admit it or not," Hugh cleared his gravelly voice. Rowan shifted her legs, finding a more comfortable position. Her 'comfortable' meant that her sex was very close to Hugh's, and his concentration was unraveling.

"I'm done talking about your age drama. What's the other reason? You mentioned that you thought age was the only reason."

Age drama. Rowan had been spending way too much time with that old dragon, Diana Gaines. Everyone in the damn family knew how he felt about the age gap between him and Rowan. That was hard enough to talk about—the other reason… the other made him look weak. Hugh O'Faolain didn't do weak.

Rowan placed her hands on either side of Hugh's jaw before combing her fingers through his beard, which reached to his chest. Was Rowan into beards? That fucking William didn't have one. Her massaging fingers felt so good. It was reflex to tug Rowan closer. She sighed, allowing the move.

"This is off-topic, and don't worry, we'll get back on track, but I've wondered for weeks why you shaved off all your pretty hair." Rowan moved her fingers from his beard to massage and scratch her nails over his buzz cut. It was Hugh's turn to sigh. There surely wasn't a human alive that didn't like a scalp massage.

Hugh huffed out a laugh. "Something different. No great reason. Do you like it?"

"Asking for compliments, Mr. O'Faolain?" She grinned. Her dimples made him want to kiss her cheeks—before he took her mouth. "You're handsome no matter what style you choose."

"I've thought about shaving my beard. I've had it for years, and you never know, I could be hideous once all that hair is gone." Rowan's wide-eyed shock amused Hugh immensely. She liked his beard then.

"I wouldn't mind seeing you without it someday, but don't you dare shave it yet. You've never kissed me, and I've had too many fantasies about how it would feel against my skin."

Hugh leaned toward Rowan, his hands fisting her waist. "I could show you now," he whispered against her lips.

Rowan reared back. "Oh, no. We are talking. Only talking."

"For now?" Hugh needed clarification.

"For now," Rowan agreed. "Tell me the other reason you pushed me away."

Hugh rolled his hips against her body, creating friction. They both moaned. "I'm not pushing you away now. I'm pulling you toward me."

"You are," Rowan agreed breathlessly. "As good as that feels, I *will* walk out your door if you don't explain all the reasons why you kept hurting me and why you seem willing to...touch me now."

Hugh swallowed past his shame. "Christ, Row. You have to know I never wanted to hurt you." He leaned into her quickly and placed a kiss on the underside of her jaw. She stretched her neck to give him better access before catching herself and pulling back.

"Explain."

There was obviously no getting out of talking about his fucking feelings. "I didn't understand...or realize maybe, what else might be holding me back in...in taking what I wanted—you —until I came back to Oklahoma." Hugh could tell Rowan was biting her tongue so she wouldn't interrupt his explanation with questions. "It was Mom that helped me see what my problem might have been." At Rowan's smirk, Hugh added, "Yes, my mom. Don't be so smug about it."

Hugh took a deep breath and just said it. "I realized even before the ink was dry on my marriage license, that I'd made a huge mistake with Helen, but I'd never quit anything in my life.

So, I stayed the course. It's what my father had always taught me to do. I was young, twenty-three, your age actually, and I believed things would get better."

"Was she so different while you were dating?"

He chuckled, but there was little amusement in the sound. "Like night and day. She fooled all of us. When my parents realized how bad things were, they wanted me to divorce her immediately, but she was pregnant already. I didn't know it, but she was already pregnant when we wed. She didn't even tell me until our wedding night. It was her excuse not to have sex. It wasn't until that moment that I realized how truly deceived I'd been.

"She never desired me. She only consented for the sake of conceiving. Helen was a calculating bitch that I grew to despise —except when Bran was born, Christ," he began, shaking his head in wonder, "he was...I don't know how to describe it. He was my heart outside of my body. I would have done anything, tolerated everything that venomous woman threw my way, to create what I hoped was a perfect family for my son.

"I would say staying married was a mistake, but if I hadn't, I wouldn't have had Patrick."

"I thought she didn't want to...umm, have sex," Rowan wondered aloud.

"She didn't. Not with me, anyway. I can thank her parents for telling their daughter that she couldn't go back to her social life in Boston until she did her duty by giving me an heir *and* a spare.

"Helen was stunningly beautiful, and I hadn't had sex since before we were married. When Bran was probably about nine months old, she started coming to my bedroom late at night. I was young and desperate, and I didn't believe in cheating. If I wanted to have sex with anything other than my hand, she was it. Three weeks later, Helen was pregnant with Patrick, and I never touched her again.

"I know you're wondering if the boys are mine by blood. They are. I had DNA tests done after Patrick was born. It wouldn't have mattered to me. I loved them from their first breaths, but the O'Faolain attorney thought it was best to cover all our bases. If one of the boys wasn't mine, we could have ruined her and her family name by revealing it. It was for leverage only. I would have done anything to keep them. I'm sure she had affairs while we were married, but she must have taken precautions."

"I didn't wonder, actually. Bran and Patrick may have gotten their mother's white hair, but that's the only thing that horrible woman gave them. Seeing the three of you together... no, there was never a doubt as to who their father is."

Hugh liked the soft look on Rowan's face. He ran his thumbs over the ridges of her ribs. The barest inch from the underside of her breasts. "Are we done talking?" Hugh wasn't above begging. Rowan probably wasn't even aware that she'd arched her back. She also ignored his question.

"Helen was a horrible wife, horrible mother, and undoubtedly, and overall horrible person. Did you think that I...that I could or would ever treat you the same? Frankly, if you painted me with the same brush as that...creature, I don't think my pride would ever recover."

"No! I don't think that at all. I've *never* considered that. It's only that Mom made me consider that my tragic, one and only long-term relationship, scared or, I don't know, scarred me enough that I became a fucking coward."

"You don't know the meaning of cowardice, Hugh, and I never want to hear you say that about yourself." Rowan knew some of the shit his ex-wife had put Hugh and his sons through but hearing Hugh speak of it wrecked her inner calm and made her want to find that bitch Helen and push her off a cliff.

"There isn't a man or woman with a modicum of intelligence that wouldn't hesitate at entering into another commitment, especially if they'd endured *that* reptile's coldness. I appreciate how hard it was to talk about that time in your life. I'm grateful for the insight. I'm very grateful to know you better. I'm very, *very* grateful your problem with me wasn't *all* to do with our ages," she smiled.

"Whatever comes of this, you and me, I need you to know I'm not ready to jump all the way in."

"I understand. As long as I have a chance. Are you," he paused, appearing unsure of his next words, "still going to see Will while we're figuring things out?"

Hugh's stormy expression was fierce. Rowan knew who owned her heart, but that didn't mean she wasn't scared. This was the first time Hugh had discussed what a toll his ex-wife had taken. It didn't mean those hurts and wounds and reactions had magically disappeared.

Rowan also wasn't the type of woman to lead someone on. Will was amazing, but until things were resolved one way or another with her and Hugh, she would need to end things. "I'll call William tomorrow and pause things with us."

Hugh's jaw flexed. He hadn't liked the word 'pause,' probably preferring 'end.' "Good. Then I'll have my people *pause* their investigation on the Stantons."

Rowan felt her jaw drop, aghast. "Tell me you didn't start an investigation on Will! Do you know what boundaries are? You should, you cross them all the damn time." Hugh didn't respond. Shaking her head...out of all the men in the world, she had to fall in love with the most annoying one. God, but his arrogant stare was sexy.

Closing the distance between their mouths, Rowan whispered against Hugh's lips, "Is there anything else you need to tell me?" She felt his body tense beneath her.

"No."

"You've never kissed me. Do you want to?" Rowan knew her teasing was about to gain her exactly what she wanted. Hugh out of control. For her.

"Desperately," he admitted.

Between one breath to the next, Hugh's mouth was covering hers, and oh God, it was everything. At first, they stayed soft, each of them testing and tasting the shape and feel of the other. When Hugh used one hand to cradle the back of her head and neck, the kiss intensified. Once he slanted her head opposite to his angle, nothing soft remained. They were in some sort of mad frenzy—tongues, teeth, groans, and whimpers.

Rowan's chest was smashed against Hugh's, his hardened length pressed insistently against her stomach. His other hand palmed her ass, grinding her center against him over and over. Rowan's hands weren't idle. She touched him everywhere she could reach, running her fingers over all the hard plains and muscles she'd dreamt about for months and months.

If they kept this up, Rowan knew they'd both be naked in a matter of minutes and use the couch to share far more than a first kiss. She already felt her core tightening at the continued rocking and friction.

Rowan gentled against his lips. "Hugh, we—"

"Jesus, Row, I'm on fucking fire for you. Keep rocking on me, baby, I want you to come apart." He took her mouth, breathing his fire down her throat.. further still.

Rowan was whimpering and shaking, her hips jerking. Hugh was expertly guiding her seam up and down his rigid sex. His pants were so thin, Rowan could feel every ridge and vein of him swelling further between her legs.

"If I come, you come," Rowan demanded.

"Fuck," Hugh groaned. He instantly had her suspended above his lap with one hand and used the other to free his erection. She'd seen him before, but holy cow, he was huge. He ripped his shirt off next before pulling her back to his mouth.

Rowan broke the kiss to stand with her feet on either side of Hugh's thighs so she could strip her shorts. The panties were staying on, but they were white silk and would feel so good for both of them. Hugh locked onto her center and watched as she sunk back onto his lap. The moment her heat made contact with his naked flesh, he practically roared in pleasure.

"This isn't going to take long, baby." Hugh grabbed her ass, his long, thick fingers locked on, moving her up and down his length.

Rowan leaned back so she could watch their bodies. Watching the two of them, the erotic sensations were intense. It took only moments before she felt her body start to pulse. "I'm close, Hugh."

"I'm there, Row. Give me your mouth, baby."

He continued to move their bodies together as he took her mouth. His kiss was sexual. Intimate. Her lips felt swollen, but oh Lord, she wanted to kiss this man for days. Her body reached its peak, and Rowan finally had to break the kiss as she came apart.

"I CAN FEEL YOUR ORGASM. God, Row, I wish I was inside you." Hugh increased their slide and grind—he was close. "You want to see me come, baby?"

"God, yes, Hugh. Do it. Now! I can't take much more," she moaned.

Hugh picked Rowan off his lap. A yelp of surprise slipped past her lips before he had her back against the couch. He leaned over her body so he could slide against her a few more times while their tongues tangled. He pulled back, and with a hoarse cry, he took himself in hand, pumping a few more strokes before his body seized.

Watching ropes of his cum decorate her skin where her shirt had ridden up had his balls tightening even more. He couldn't help himself, and before his intentions fully registered, he swiped his thumb over the head of his dick to gather the last of his seed. Rowan's eyes widened as he brought his thumb closer to her mouth. Her mouth was open and panting as he slipped his thumb between her lips.

When she sucked, Hugh didn't think he'd ever seen anything so erotic in his life. "Jesus, Rowan. I'm going to be hard for days. Seeing you taste me...Christ." She smiled as he removed his thumb from her mouth. Hugh pulled his pants up and grabbed his shirt to clean her stomach. She sat up then and looked for her shorts, finding them on the floor, she stood and slipped them on.

"I should go." He never wanted her to go. "I didn't mean for things to go so far." He wanted things to go a lot further and several times a day—but she was looking unsure, and he hated that.

"You're it for me. Whatever you're willing to allow me...give me, I'm honored." He stood before her then, taking her into his arms. She put her arms around his middle and looked up to meet his eyes.

"I do trust you. Maybe not with my heart yet, but my body? Yes."

15

Rowan led the way back to the foyer. She'd really let things go further than she should have so soon after their first serious talk. Her body disagreed, of course. It felt boneless, well-loved, and ready for more. "I need some time to think. I appreciate that you finally opened up to me. I hope that by speaking about your first marriage, you might find some real healing. But—" she paused.

"But?"

"You're a runner, Hugh. You've been running from true intimacy, I believe, long before we met. If we agree to...us, I want to make sure I'm willing to take the chance of you pushing me away again. River once told me that Patrick had destroyed her with what he'd done. I was furious she would even consider herself destroyed. I told her that Pat had hurt her terribly, but he could never destroy her because she was stronger than that.

"If we were together, really together, and you left or decided you weren't ready for that level of commitment...if someone told me I was too strong to be destroyed...I wonder if I would believe them because I think if you pushed me away one more time...I think it would destroy me.

"When you left me in that hospital room, my heart, my love, was in my outstretched palm. You walked away from it. I felt pretty destroyed then." Rowan didn't realize she'd started to cry until Hugh grabbed a towel from the bar counter and pulled her against his chest, using the towel to blot her tears.

"I destroyed myself that day." She could feel his body shudder as he held her close, rubbing her back in comfort. "Rowan, while you think things through, will you promise to consider something?" At her nod, he made her a vow. "I promise, with all the love I hold for my father and mother, for my boys, that I will never run from you again. I humbly accept your love and offer you mine. I don't care how long it takes. I *will* prove myself to you."

Oh God, Hugh was going to kill her with all this overflow of emotion. He wouldn't go back on the promise he'd just made. He had too much honor for that. He might regret making the promise, though. She still needed to think.

Placing her hands over his chest, Rowan leaned toward Hugh's warm body, tilting her head up so he would lean down. She placed a soft, almost reverent kiss on his lips before stepping back. "I love you, Hugh. Give me a little time to sort through everything, and I need to talk to my sisters and Nan."

Hugh took one step forward, his fists clenched. "Fine. I'm playing golf again tomorrow. Is a day long enough to decide?"

"Hugh," Rowan admonished.

"Your eyes are smiling. I'll take that as a maybe."

"You're impossible." And if she had to stare at Hugh's naked chest one more minute, she'd say screw thinking things over and drag him to the nearest bed.

"I don't want to let you go, but I will. I love you, Row. Even though I don't deserve it, at least call or text me while you're thinking things over."

Rowan smiled as she opened the front door. "I will." Giving Hugh an impish smile, she added, "I might even send a picture."

It was seven in the morning when Hugh used his phone app to turn his mother's alarm system off. He knew Rowan needed time to think and talk to her family, but he couldn't *not* see her all day. He'd been deprived of not seeing her and hearing her voice for weeks before coming to Oklahoma, and now that he had those pleasures back, he couldn't resist.

Admittedly, he could resist if he had to...but after tasting her mouth last night, his brain wasn't driving the decision making. He felt zero guilt as he opened Rowan's bedroom door to sneak inside, closing it quietly behind him.

Through the light slipping around the window blind's edges, he could easily see Rowan sleeping. She was on her back, arms raised, creating a circle around her head, and all that glorious black hair spread about her. It looked like dark rivulets of water enveloped her body.

A sheet covered her from the waist down. Her full breasts pushed against a white tank top on full display. He slowly pulled the sheet off, revealing white cotton panties with purple flowers. He tossed the sheet to the side and shucked his shoes before bending over her body. He placed a soft kiss on her mouth. Her eyes sprang open and then widened when she recognized him.

"Hugh! What in the hell are you doing here?" She quietly hissed. Probably not wanting to wake his mom any more than he did.

"You didn't send me a picture last night. I wouldn't have had anything to look at while I golfed today. So, I came to take one myself."

Shaking off her surprise, Rowan raised her brows in question. "Is that the only thing you came for?"

"A kiss," he admitted as he climbed onto the bed to straddle her legs. "You're so tiny."

"I imagine most women appear small when they lay underneath you," Rowan countered. "You'll be in so much trouble if your mom catches you in my room again," she huffed a laugh, probably imagining it—and imagining retelling the story to her sisters.

"She sleeps in every chance she gets. I'll be long gone before she steps foot out of her room," Hugh assured. "So, do I get my kiss and picture?"

"Since you went through the trouble of breaking and entering, I suppose you can."

"There was no breaking, only entering," Hugh countered. Looking over her body, he let his eyes touch every part before asking, "Where do you want your kiss?" Hugh heard her quick intake of breath. "Here?" He ran his thumb over her lips before running the same thumb over one of her pebbled nipples. "Or here?" Leaning back on his heels, he gently ran his thumb over her cotton-clad mound. "Perhaps here?"

He was breathing heavier than Rowan. The image of his broad shoulders spreading her thighs wide made him hard as stone. Making sure Rowan was watching, Hugh adjusted his growing erection.

"You're playing dirty, Mr. O'Faolain."

Hugh could see Rowan's body no longer lay still. She was subtly arching her back and squeezing her thighs together. "I should tell you that wherever you choose to have my mouth, you have to take a picture while I'm kissing you."

She propped herself up on her elbows in outrage. "No way, Hugh!"

"You owe me a picture, and you agreed to let me have a kiss.

Consider this multitasking," he growled, hardly able to look away from the barely covered breasts on display. Her current position made them impossible to ignore.

"Where do you want my kiss, Rowan. We're running out of time. Where?"

Rowan studied him a moment longer. "Take your shirt off. I want your bare skin in the picture," she ordered huskily.

As Hugh obeyed, pulling his golf tee over his head, Rowan sat up and pulled her tank off. She'd chosen breasts then. "Fuck, baby, I've dreamed of having those in my mouth."

She lay flat, palming both of her breasts in her hands before pinching her nipples. "Have you," she asked.

Hugh almost came in his pants. "Get your phone ready." As she stretched toward her side table, he took advantage of her position and pinched both her nipples. Rowan screeched and then giggled. Her phone dropped on her head before she could grab it again. They were laughing as Hugh bent to kiss her, sweeping his tongue inside her mouth. When she moaned inside his mouth, he deepened the kiss and began to massage her breasts.

Hugh reluctantly ended the kiss and watched Rowan's eyes flutter open. Her dazed expression, along with the phone hanging limply from her left hand, gave Hugh immense satisfaction.

Smirking, Hugh said, "Whoops, I kissed the wrong body part." Watching her eyes widen was a sweet victory over the vixen.

"You ass! *That* was your kiss. Now get the hell out of my room and go golf!"

She slapped his chest in a teasing way, but her hand never lifted. Instead, Rowan let her fingers trail over his chest, her palm settling over his abs. She looked *very* interested. Hugh couldn't help but feel some masculine pride over that.

Hugh didn't give Rowan any warning before he leaned forward and sucked one of her nipples deep into his mouth.

"Hugh, God." Rowan gasped, arching her chest, offering him a feast.

He spent several minutes worshipping her breasts and under, her scar. She could have died that day. He would happily love that scar because it meant Rowan was still alive, still here with him.

Hugh felt her hands on his scalp, anchoring his mouth exactly where she wanted it. Her hips were rocking against his stomach where he'd flattened his body over hers. He licked, sucked, and bit his way over both breasts. His sex ached and throbbed with every moan.

He'd been a second away from freeing himself when someone knocked on Rowan's door. They both froze, one of her nipples deep inside his mouth.

"Hugh Darcy O'Faolain. I am walking back into my room to get dressed. You had better be outside of Rowan's bedroom before I'm done. Is that clear?"

Jesus. Hugh was positive he was too old to get scolded over being in a woman's room. He slowly let Rowan's breast slide from his lips. He gave one last kiss to her wet, distended nipple before answering his mom.

"Very clear, Mom." Rowan's shoulders were shaking, and when Hugh shifted his body off hers, she was laughing so hard tears were silently streaking from her eyes. "Do not say a word, and if this moment reaches my sons' or your sisters' ears, there *will* be payback."

Wiping her eyes, she swallowed back her mirth enough to choke out, "I wouldn't dream of it, Hugh." Since Rowan was still topless, he was distracted, but he didn't miss her sarcasm. "You better get dressed before you get in *big* trouble."

· · ·

"Perfect timing, Row. We just finished lunch. Pat and I did a Mexican spread. My sweet boy, Jonathan, was quite satisfied with the effort. He's *always* hungry. Rave and Bran are almost finished clean—" River gasped and stopped talking.

There'd been a ton of racket in the background when Rowan had called River, now it was pin drop quiet. It finally clicked. "Oh my God, Riv! I love the name Jonathan for my sweet nephew." Rowan knew Matilda would cry her eyes out.

"What the hell, River?" Patrick complained in the background. "You said we had to wait to tell, and you just spewed it to everyone." At River's whispered apology, Patrick must have moved closer because his voice was louder when he added, "No, babe, I'm glad everyone knows. I've been dying to tell! I get to tell the middle name, though," he teased.

Everyone was laughing now. Raven must have been talking to River's belly because she heard her say, *Auntie Rave loves you, Jonathan.* "Hey, put the phone by your belly, River. I want to say hello too." After Rowan got in her hellos, she got to say hello to a wide-eyed Daniel. "Auntie Row can't wait to get home and see her sweet boy." It was missing these types of events that made Rowan super homesick.

"I can't wait to come home," Rowan admitted. "So, Patrick, what's the full name to be?"

"His full name is Jonathan Sean O'Faolain, named for both great-grandfathers," Pat announced proudly.

Bran and Raven, and Rowan exclaimed how perfect it was. "I still think we should wait to tell Nanand Tilly. I promise to not let pregnancy brain or food comas let me tell them," River laughed at herself.

"Are you going to tell Hugh?" Rowan would love to hang knowing the name of his newest grandson over his head.

"Yeah, I will. Bran and I were about to call him anyway

before he heads to the Club. They'll be playing all day with the lunch breaks and cocktails, I'm sure."

"Oh, he left about fifteen minutes ago. You might want to try him pretty quick." When neither Patrick nor Bran responded, Rowan thought maybe she'd lost the connection. "Did I lose you guys?"

"No, no, we're here," Raven assured.

River snorted, "We were just taken by surprise that you're admitting Hugh was in your bedroom."

"With the door closed, I heard," Raven added.

Rowan could feel embarrassment burning her cheeks. Obviously, she'd planned on talking things through with her sisters—but not everything, and certainly not in front of Hugh's sons. "H-h...how...who said that?" she finally asked.

"Gran called me." Rowan could hear the smirk in Bran's voice.

Raven butted in then. "Your grandma called my phone when I was in the shower. You answered it and wheedled it out of her." Rowan could hear the exasperation in her sister's voice.

"That's what I meant, babe." Bran had the nerve to chuckle. "Gran said she wasn't sure what you to were 'getting up to,' Gran's words, but it wasn't knitting, she said."

"Was Dad installing a new shoe rack for you, Row? Is that why he was in your room?" Patrick was quite the comedian this morning.

Rowan knew exactly how to shut both boys up. "He wasn't, but I imagine he would be an amazing carpenter. I've learned his hands are quite...handy."

"Jesus Christ! I'm leaving, River. Tell your sister to stop being disgusting." Patrick's mantrum was priceless.

"For fuck's sake. Tell your sister to never speak of naked things or...Dad's...whatever," Bran whined.

As soon as Rowan heard the front door thud shut, all three

sisters began to laugh. Men were all big talk until a mom or dad was mentioned.

"Oh my God, Row, I ate way, way, way too much to be laughing this hard, but damn, did you ever put our husbands in their place," River chortled in glee.

"The disgust on Bran's face was—oh God, priceless," Raven finally got out between bursts of giggles.

"They deserved it," Rowan said after her laughter ran its course.

"So, tell us about last night."

"And this morning," River added.

Rowan told them about Hugh finally opening up and some of his revelations. Not everything, though. Some of the stuff to do with his ex-wife was too personal. Raven and River had dealt with Bran and Patrick's own shit where that woman was concerned, so they would understand what a big step that was for Hugh without needing details.

"I'm so happy—happy for both of you. It's been really hard watching you two hurt and be so lonely. I'm relieved," Raven admitted. "Whatever happens, I hope Hugh is finally able to properly heal. No matter if you guys stay together or not, which you better, he needs closure from his past."

"She and Hugh *will* be together. Right, Row?" River demanded.

Rowan hesitated, wanting to choose her words carefully. "I want that. More than anything, but you know Hugh. He's complicated. He wants a relationship with me. He made that clear. Will he talk himself out of it next week? The answer is, I don't know."

"Does he love you? Did he admit it?" River asked.

"Yes, and yes. I love him too, and I told him."

"I understand that you're afraid, and rightly so. He's broken your heart before. Of course, you would hesitate. I only know this, River and I had to make tough decisions for the men we loved. We had to take a chance that they meant it when they promised us forever.

"If Hugh comes to you and offers you forever, then I think you should be all in. He's your person. Your other half."

"I agree with Raven. Last time I checked, my youngest sister didn't shy away from a challenge. You've been locking horns with that growly grump since the moment you laid eyes on the man. Don't give up now," River encouraged.

Rowan took several deep breaths. Her sisters had laid some pretty big truth bombs on her head this morning. "If he wants forever, I'll give him forever." Her sisters were instantly whooping and clapping and prematurely congratulating her. Rowan loved them for it.

"Not to put a damper on this moment, but William said he'd be in meetings all day. He's having some issue at work but said he will call me tomorrow and discuss his jet picking me up Friday afternoon for a weekend in Houston. I'll have to tell him about Hugh when he calls. God, I feel like such an asshole!"

"You couldn't have foreseen Hugh storming your castle. Don't be so hard on yourself," River encouraged.

"If William's half the man you thought him to be, even though he isn't the love of your life, I believe he'll understand," Raven reminded.

"Thanks, you guys, and thank you so much for all the support. I'm going to hang up so I can call Nan and fill her in on the Hugh Havoc. You guys know she'd never forgive me if I didn't keep her in the loop, and for some reason, she has a sweet spot for all the O'Faolain men."

Five more minutes of goodbyes and three minutes of promises to give them more of her and Hugh's sexual exploits, she was finally able to hang up and call Nan.

"How's my sweet girl?"

That's how Rowan's grandma always answered the phone. "You call all of us your sweet girl, Nan," Rowan laughed.

"Because you are," Nan defended. "River is more like my sweet and salty girl, but I'll deny that if you choose to tattle."

This was why everyone in the world should have a Nan, Rowan thought. "Is Devlen there? Tell him hello if he is." Rowan absolutely loved her grandma's new husband. He may be a man of few words, but he fiercely loved his wife. He had Rowan and her sisters' loyalty forever for that.

"Dev says hello. He planned a picnic by the lake for us today. We were just about to leave so I'm glad you called when you did."

Rowan could hear love in her grandma's voice. So much love. "Well, I won't keep you, but I thought you might want to know that Hugh came to Oklahoma, and he told me he loves me, Nan. What do you think of that?"

"It's about damn time! Oh, that sweet boy. Finally."

And that was that.

16

———————

Rowan was going to pay for that video. Hugh had been on the eighth hole, bantering with six other men, drinking and enjoying the sunshine, when his phone dinged. As soon as he saw it was Rowan, he fumbled his club, almost dropped his drink, and literally tripped over his own damn feet as he quickly moved a distance away from the group.

When he saw it was a video, he started to sweat. He found his golf cart, thankfully the furthest cart away, and leaned on its side. Before he pressed play, he turned the volume up.

"Christ," Hugh cursed. She'd teased him about forgetting to take a picture for him this morning. She hadn't lied. She'd taken a video. Hugh was mesmerized, watching himself work over her breasts, sucking and kneading and biting.

"Oh God," Hugh muttered, feeling his shorts become uncomfortably tight. She was moaning and calling his name. The hand not holding her phone was pressing the back of his head tighter against her chest, her nails scratching his scalp. The camera tilted just enough once to catch Rowan, her head thrown back. "So good, Hugh," she'd moaned.

He heard himself tell Rowan he could play with her tits all

day and her replying, "God, babe, I want you too." He would be fifty-four this year, and he knew, with absolute certainty, that there was no other woman who could make him feel the level of intensity that Rowan Byrne inspired.

He watched it four more times. A mistake. It was almost his turn to tee off, and there would be no mistaking his conceal and carry erection. He had to think of something else. Any fucking thing else. He sent a quick text to Rowan.

You won't know when, you won't know how, but I will pay you back.

Don't put too much thought into it. We all can't be winners. Plus, I'm having dinner with your mom and Diana again tonight. XOXO

Maybe I should join you for dinner. I can think of a lot of things a person can do under a table.

I would love for you to make me come...I mean, I'd love for you to come. Diana would enjoy catching up too.

You're playing with fire.

I hope I don't get burned. My nipples are already soooooo sensitive.

Hugh groaned. He knew when he was beaten. For now. Damn that woman! He quickly pulled up his national news app, which thankfully had the intended effect of shrinking certain appendages so he could finish the rest of the holes. He'd lost all interest in golfing, and unfortunately, they'd be at it several more hours.

Hugh smiled as he rejoined the group while mentally reviewing his best options to torture Rowan later. She shouldn't have told him about her dinner plans tonight. He might not want to sit down with Diana Gaines—Rowan knew very well he wouldn't volunteer himself to endure the creature's bad attitude

—but he wouldn't mind checking in. After all, Hugh was capable of making a video too.

IT WAS MONDAY MORNING, and Rowan had just finished meeting with the boutique's main contractor, Fern Rogers. Fern was a powerhouse in Oklahoma known for being honest and hard-working. Her crew was top-notch. The work they'd gotten done over the weekend was crazy, and she planned on recommending them for any future Tulsa clients. Fern had taken Rowan's sketches and vision and could run with them with little supervision.

Rowan was sitting at the temporary desk she'd set up in the store. It was easier to have a dedicated space on-site to keep track of orders and scheduling. Her fingers kept hovering over the keyboard. After fifteen minutes of staring at the screen, her to-do list had nothing but a number one. Damn, Hugh!

His payback for sending him that video had come back to bite her in the ass. Dinner with Diana and Matilda had been a true test of patience last night. She'd only sat down at the table, and Diana's chef had placed a beautiful garden salad in front of her when her phone had dinged. Rowan silenced it quickly. Ringing phones at the dinner table was a no-no with both older women. She'd seen Hugh's name as she was sitting it back down and couldn't resist clicking on it.

I just watched your video again. Going to need another shower.

Since Diana had been engaged in a lengthy story about her inept dry cleaner, Rowan sent a reply. **Three words. Carpal tunnel syndrome.** Smirking, she'd dropped the phone in her lap.

Dinner was delicious as usual: Tuscan butter salmon with a side of grilled Brussels sprouts and broccoli—one of Rowan's favorite meals. She'd just taken her first spoonful of lemon mousse when her phone vibrated in her lap. In what Rowan hoped had been a casual move, she'd propped the phone against the heavy crystal dish of mousse where the two older women couldn't see it before she opened the text.

It was a video. Sweat started prickling her brow as she'd debated on whether or not to push play. She'd at least had the forethought to turn her volume off. And oh God, just remembering Hugh stepping out of his shower, rubbing his big body with a fluffy white towel had Rowan panting. Thank goodness her desk was tucked away in a back corner.

The towel had been irritatingly large and long, covering the X-rated bits as he'd dried his body, muscles twisting and flexing. Rowan sipped her morning lemon water, her throat suddenly parched. A text had come in just as the video ended. **Have you decided where you want your next kiss?**

Purposefully misunderstanding, Rowan had replied, **Stop by the boutique tomorrow, you can kiss me there.**

The boutique's owner was due to arrive in an hour, and Rowan believed she would flip out when she saw how close her shop was to being completed. Soon, she could start having her stock delivered. The coffee bar was going to be installed tomorrow. She was definitely checking more off than adding to her new checklist. She'd met with the lighting contractor as soon as she'd gotten in this morning before Fern. Mr. Craig's people had also worked the weekend and only had one chandelier to hang that morning.

Rowan finally engaged her brain again and got her work done. It was satisfying that her client's reaction to the progress was just as ecstatic as Rowan knew it'd be. It was after lunch when she and Angela finished going over the week's schedule.

"Is the cleaning crew still scheduled for tomorrow?"

"Yes. I got the confirmation email last night."

"Perfect. Then, when all the furniture arrives on Wednesday, we can have the delivery crew place it exactly where it goes. That's one of my favorite parts." Rowan clapped her hands once in excitement.

"I know! I can't wait. It will be heaven to finally have a desk and chair that don't fold up. Oh, I almost forgot. I hired a barista for the café. Laura's a college student, but her classes are online or at night. I told her during her downtime upstairs that she was welcome to study. She worked at Starbucks for three years."

"Sounds like a perfect arrangement for both of you, Angela." Rowan was about to ask Angela if she'd gone over her assistant's duties yet when the bell on the back door chimed. Hugh O'Faolain made an entrance. Today, he wore khaki jeans that looked like a high-end version of work pants, a white button-up with the sleeves rolled—she got stuck on how good his muscular forearms looked for a moment—and brown leather tennis shoes. The man always looked dangerously delicious.

"Oh, hey," she said, standing to greet him. "Good morning." Rowan was flustered. She hadn't considered introductions when she told him to come to the store.

Angela stood as well, looking at Rowan and smiling before walking to Hugh. "I've been dying to meet you. I'm Angela Carvey. You must be Rowan's William."

Oh shit. Angela hadn't noticed that Hugh had turned to stone.

"I won't get after you for sending Rowan back to work so often looking well-kissed and starry-eyed," she laughed sweetly, "because she's the most talented designer I've ever worked with. I already told my husband I want her to completely redecorate our condo in Florida. Also, I was young once," she laughed.

Thank you, baby Jesus, Angela's phone started to ring. "Oh, it's Julie. I've got to take this! My new assistant...I'm so nervous," she admitted absently, already walking away from the burning building exploding behind her. "So glad we got to meet, Will." *Christ, have mercy.*

Rowan grabbed her purse and silently led the way out of the store's back entrance. She would rather take her chances swimming off the coast of New Zealand in Great White infested waters than attempt placating Hugh at that moment—and honestly, Rowan had not one damn thing to feel bad about. Hugh threw her away, and she dated. End of story—or it would have been if her phone hadn't started ringing as they stepped outside.

"Oh no," Rowan whispered under her breath. "I need to take this call. I'll only be a minute if you want to wait under the pergola." She turned and took several steps in the opposite direction. Answering the call, Rowan attempted a lighthearted, "Hey, Will. Did you find anything helpful in your meetings yesterday?" Keep it about work, not personal. *Please.*

"Nothing yet. Dad and I are getting ready to grab some lunch, and I wanted to call you while I had a minute. I miss you, Rowan. Please tell me you'll come to stay with me this weekend. If you can't, I'll try to come to you, even if it's only for a day. I need to have my arms wrapped around you again."

No, no, no, no, no, no. Rowan had every intention of letting Will know her change of heart today but not while Hugh was around. "This weekend," she repeated as quietly as possible, taking a peek over her shoulder to make sure Hugh was out of earshot. He was standing directly behind her.

If Doomsday were a man...and named Hugh...

Turning completely to stare at the eavesdropping ass, Rowan began to make her excuses to Will, "Hey Will, right now isn't a great time. Can I call—"

. . .

Hugh recognized he was out of control. He didn't care. The man who'd so recently had his hands on Rowan, his Rowan, wanted her to spend the weekend with him. Not a snowball's chance in fucking hell was that happening.

His jealous rage in the driver's seat, Hugh grabbed Rowan's phone from her hand, ignoring her outraged gasp. "William Stanton. Hugh O'Faolain." Silence greeted him before Stanton recovered his composure.

"Hugh. It's been a while. Is everything okay with Rowan?"

"Yes." Fuck him for asking.

"Okay," William paused, clearly confused. Hugh didn't care. "Please put Rowan back on the phone so she can tell me herself that everything is okay."

Hugh was mildly impressed with Stanton's resolve. Rowan was yanking on his arm, attempting to get to her phone. Not happening. Rowan never needed to talk to William again.

This was not smart. Hugh obviously knew he was screwing up. He'd just gotten her to consider giving him another chance. He wouldn't back down now, though. Like he'd done twenty-five years ago. Helen liked to flirt with other men to embarrass Hugh. She'd flirted with William at the Club one evening, and he'd flirted back.

That night, Hugh had wanted to punch the man over a woman that he despised. He wanted to destroy the man now.

"I'm saving you from the prolonged misconception that you and Rowan will ever be seeing each other again. She's mine. She's been mine for a year. I suggest you lose her number."

"She sure didn't taste like she was yours, O'Faolain. I think you might be mistaken. Give the phone back to Rowan. I'd hear it from her."

Red-hot, blinding rage. He'd only felt rage like that a few times in his life, and they were all connected to Helen's treatment of his sons.

"Let me assure you, when I made her come, the day after you left town, it was my name she was screaming. Not yours. Final warning, Stanton. Don't come after me or mine. The consequences might be more than you're willing to pay."

Hugh hung up with such force he was surprised the phone didn't buckle, collapsing from the strain. He found Rowan leaning against the boutique's brick exterior. The hurt on her face was a bucket of ice water over his head, flushing the anger from his body so fast it left him shaky. He took several steps toward her but stopped when she shook her head.

"Give me my phone and leave."

A gunshot through the heart would have had less impact. Hugh felt crushing alarm. His brain had evidently come back online. He didn't want to know the consequences of what he'd just done.

"Row—"

Rowan cut him off. "Give me my phone and leave. Right. Now."

He gave her the phone and left.

17

————

"So, basically, you're in the middle of a shitstorm. Your sisters are in Dublin, and I'm in Zürich helping Mom with the spa. You love Hugh, but he ruined it. You started dating a man you like, William, but Hugh had a change of heart. You decided to drop the boyfriend and find out if sex with Hugh is as good as the dry humping's been. Hugh goes all alpha wolf on Will, hurting Will's feelings and embarrassing the hell out of you, which leaves you to plan Hugh's murder all by yourself," Jo succinctly summed up Rowan's current situation.

Once Rowan had calmed herself enough to go back into the boutique, finish her notes, and check on the backordered bathroom mirror, she had called Jo. Even though it was nine hours later in Switzerland, Rowan knew her friend would be up late working.

Jo had quickly shut down any discussion involving Thomas MacGregor. Jo had become increasingly cagey in her responses the past few weeks. Rowan agreed to drop it but warned her that a Byrne reckoning was on the near horizon. Rowan made a mental note to get MacGregor's number. Perhaps it was time to see what the Scottish giant had to say for himself.

"The problem, Jo, is I don't even want to kill him. I don't...I would like to understand why he did it. He had no right!"

"We're talking about Hugh O'Faolain, Row. He believed he had every right. Don't give me an ounce of bullshit like you weren't aware of your man's personality. He isn't known as a wolf for no reason. You know this. Our families have known each other for years. My father would wax on about Hugh's business savvy. Dad said that there were tales of men crying during meetings, and all Hugh would do was stare at them.

"My point is, Hugh didn't allow his people to make excuses for failure, and I believe he wouldn't make an excuse for his own."

Rowan sighed. "I'm sure he wouldn't, but the fact remains that what he did was disrespectful to myself and William." Hours later, and Rowan was still in a state of petrified mortification.

"Did he explain?"

"No. I told him to leave." Rowan refused to dwell on how crushed he'd looked. Damn him. He didn't deserve a grain of sand's worth of sympathy.

"I get that he was highhanded. I get the frustration of a high-handed man, trust me, but...I don't know...was it that bad what Hugh said?"

"Umm, I don't know, Jo. You tell me. He told Will that the day after he returned to Houston, he made me come, and I was screaming Hugh's name, not his." Jo's gasp, followed by silence, meant probably meant her 'surely it wasn't that bad' attitude took a hike.

Finally, Jo was back into damage control versus a kiss and make up mode. "Tell Matilda her son needs a time out for bad behavior. Hugh's her son. She'll get it. Pack a bag and head to my parents. I'll call the housekeeper and tell her you'll be there in an hour."

"No, Jo. I'm only venting. Staying at your home isn't necessary." Hugh wouldn't just go away. Rowan knew he was planning how to corner her at this very moment, but that didn't mean she needed to hide.

"Hugh needs to think about his actions and why he did them. You need to calm down and remember the reasons why you were willing to dump William for him. Your trust was new, and he fucked that up in the first hour. Give yourself a moment to breathe."

Jo was right. She just needed time to order her thoughts and feelings. "Okay. I'll pack now."

"You do know that even though he made an ass out of himself, you need to give him a chance to explain. Right?"

"Right."

Rowan packed a weekend bag, only planning to stay at Jo's for a couple of days. She threw in her best running shoes, planning on taking advantage of the gorgeous park near the O'Connor's home. She gave Matilda a very abbreviated version of Hugh's conversation with William, knowing she would need to be armed with some information if it came up between her and Diana.

It was late by the time she got situated at the O'Connor's. It had been an excruciatingly long day, and Rowan wanted nothing more than to shower and sleep. She'd spoken to William for an hour. He was furious at Hugh and furious at himself for his part in the conversation. Apparently, he'd said something Rowan wouldn't have appreciated that he refused to repeat.

Rowan admitted that she and Hugh had had something in the past, but when she'd agreed to date William, she was completely free to do so. Will had seemed so pensive and sad. It had crushed Rowan. She, of all people, knew what disappointment tasted like. Had Hugh not inserted himself into her private life, the breakup conversation with Will would have looked vastly different.

He admitted work was tense and it was probably best to focus on the company instead of his love life. He did make her promise to reach out if she ever decided to get rid of the "O'Faolain asshole." William told her that he really had felt like they could have had a future.

What a mess.

Hugh hadn't tried to contact her until ten minutes ago. Speaking with Will had drained her emotionally. She didn't want to deal with Hugh tonight but knew it couldn't be put off. Rowan slipped into the fragrant bath, rose essence slicking the water's surface and permeating the hot air of the room. She put on a new eclectic playlist River had sent her a few days ago that she hadn't had a chance to listen to yet.

Bleeding Love by Leona Lewis began playing. Christ, there were times when Rowan would swear she and her sisters had an otherworldly connection. She palmed her phone as Lewis crooned. *The lyrics certainly held an omniscient quality..*

Rowan sighed. She felt like she was bleeding, flayed. It was torture to be at odds with Hugh. She relaxed further into the bath and went to her text messages, tapping on his.

Please, Rowan. Talk to me.

I'm exhausted, Hugh. You might not care, but hurting William hurt me.

I care.

Then understand it's been a long day.

You're gone. Mom won't tell me where you are.

Goodnight, Hugh.

I love you. I'm sorry.

I love you.

. . .

Running was exactly what Rowan needed this morning. Seven o'clock and it was already a steamy eighty-two degrees and one hundred percent humidity. Welcome to an Oklahoma August morning.

Sweat waterfalled from her scalp to her ankles, detoxifying the negative energy from her body. A night of tossing and turning produced several truths. Yesterday's fiasco had in no way shaken her faith and love for Hugh—and...He would explain his actions. No ifs, ands, or buts. He wasn't hiding his feelings. Not from her. Rowan had chosen Hugh. She was his and he was hers. That meant no secrets.

She had stopped trying to understand her strong connection to Hugh a year ago. Some things just were—fate, destiny—whatever the label, it began and ended with that man.

She veered toward a lesser run path, but one she knew had more trees and flowers. Rowan flew by blankets of gorgeous Blue Violets, startling a squirrel who chittered furiously at the interruption. Grinning, she pelted down a steep ravine and leaped up a rock incline.

She was about to meet the main path again. Ten more strides, and she'd be out of the rougher, more natural path. Rowan was about to burst through the shaded haven when a shadow startled her. She yelped and stumbled over a loose rock. She would swear she'd seen a man move behind one of the large, older oaks fifteen or twenty feet off the path.

Her heart pounded out of her chest, the ghost of Samuel Delton raising its ugly head momentarily discombobulating her run. Frustration burned that she'd allowed herself to get spooked. Delton was dead. May he rest in Hell.

Being shot by Delton produced occasional random fissures of fear, but honestly, it had started long before the shooting. The discovery that he had taken pictures of her and put them on his dark web rape page. That he'd planned on kidnapping and violating her. Videoing the crime for his followers to rent and view.

Imagining that had left her feeling exposed. Vulnerable. Jumpy. Everyone had been heavily guarded. The difference was that Rowan's sisters and Jo had Bran, Patrick, and MacGregor to share their innermost fears. Allowing another to share the burden lessened the hold. Delton was dead and couldn't follow through with his threat, but sometimes, her brain didn't care. The dreaded what-ifs.

Rowan had promised her sisters before leaving Dublin that she'd get a therapist, and she was thankful she had. Dr. Sehoy was a Native Creek therapist and had been helping her tremendously over the past several weeks. She was learning what might trigger her anxiety and coping methods. Still, it was frustrating that she allowed negative thoughts to intrude during her run.

Shaking off her unproductive thoughts, she regained her easy stride, maneuvering onto the main trail and smiling at a few other runners. Rowan finished her run and quickly showered. She was treating herself to a few spa treatments this morning. The cleaning crew would be there most of the day, so she decided to take advantage of the time off.

Rowan was in the middle of getting her calves massaged, pure heaven, during her pedicure when her phone dinged. Groaning at the interruption, she checked her messages regardless. It might be a family thing.

Please let me see you tonight.

Rowan was about to reply when she noticed Angela walk-running across the spa heading toward her chair. One look at her frantic, tearstained face and Rowan's heart dropped. "What happened?"

"Oh God, Rowan, I'm so sorry to interrupt your pedicure like a lunatic, but oh, God, you mentioned your appointment," she wailed, gaining the other customer's attention as she slipped into the empty chair next to Rowans. "The furniture company called me. The delivery truck, with all my furniture, was in a traffic accident and the truck caught on fire. Fire, Rowan! No one was hurt, thank God—only my furniture. All of it."

"Oh Lord, no." Angela's dramatics were well-founded. Most of the pieces they'd picked had taken weeks to get in.

"They said they can reorder, but it will take four to six weeks, and some of the pieces are backordered. I'll have to put my grand opening off. I already had all the mailings made. The article for the newspaper is set to run this weekend," Angela recited the nightmare list in panic.

The boutique owner looked a minute away from hyperventilating. Shit! *Think, Rowan think.* "We'll figure this out, Angela." Glancing down at her pedicurist, she asked, "Would you mind just drying me off? I'm sorry, but I have to leave."

Angela and Rowan walked into a small bakery on the same block as the spa. "Would you order me an iced green tea? I'll grab a table. I need to return a few texts before we figure out some amazing plan for your furniture." She nodded and smiled, looking slightly relieved.

There's been a problem at the boutique. Furniture order delay. I should know in an hour what my schedule will look like. Meeting with Angela now.

But will you see me?

Will you explain?

Yes.

Then, I'll see you.

Thank fuck, call me when you know. I love you.

I love you.

God, she loved every gorgeous, infuriating bit of that man.

Angela sat, handing Rowan her tea and placed a plate of... three pastries and two cookies. "Don't judge. I could lie and say

I'm stress eating, but I won't bother. I eat donuts for dinner on the regular."

They both laughed. It looked like the extreme panic from earlier had passed. "I'd like to preface my solution with one demand. You have to send me new stock pics every season and ship anything I buy to Dublin free of charge."

Angela grinned, "Done. What's your solution?"

"Is Mr. Peterson the salesman who called you?"

"Yes. He felt terrible."

"Okay. Call Mr. Peterson. Tell him we'll meet him first thing in the morning at his store. You and I will leave this afternoon as soon as we can pack a bag. It'll take a little under four hours to get to The Colony, Texas. We'll check into a hotel close to the store and spend Wednesday picking out every single item, no matter how long it takes.

"That means we can only pick in-stock items, but you'll remember, Nebraska Furniture Mart is a city unto itself. We will find everything. I understand you might feel bummed out that it won't be your first pick, but there is always a chance you'll like some of the things even better. After all, it will all be purchased in person. A lot of your pieces were chosen from pictures and websites." When Angela just sat there blinking, an orange-glazed scone dangling from her fingertips, Rowan assured, "If you want to wait and simply reorder, I'd totally understand. I will stick around and help you reschedule your opening, no problem."

Bursting into tears, Angela dropped the scone to grab Rowan's hand. "I may not have to put off the opening. Oh my God, you aren't just the most amazing designer but the most wonderful friend. I know I've been so extra about the opening, but it's just...I really, really wanted to prove to myself that I can do something...do this. I want to show my husband that I'm not just a rich housewife. I'm a badass businesswoman.

"My husband does love me, but there have been times over the past few years that I've felt I'm no longer enough, just being me, you know."

"Oh, Angela, whether this store is a success or a total failure, you need to understand that you are enough. Just you. I imagine your husband would agree. After all, you might not have noticed him staring at you in absolute devotion every time he dropped by, but I sure as hell did." Angela's eyes flared with hope. "So, does that mean we're going with my road trip plan?"

"Hell yes, it does! Text me your address, and I'll pick you up in," she paused to consult her watch, "two hours. And thank you, Rowan. Really. Thank you."

"I should thank you. Your store is going to be so amazing. I'll probably get a ton of work because of it," Rowan grinned, both women laughing as they left the bakery.

Rain check? I'm on my way to Jo's to pack my things and then to your moms to pack a new bag. Total catastrophe with Angela's furniture. Going to a furniture store in The Colony, Texas, to rebuy everything. Should be home by Thursday afternoon.

Let me know when you get to Moms. I'll come.

You don't have to do that.

Let me see you, Row.

Okay.

Hugh let himself into his mother's home. Mom and Tina were in the living room watching a World War II documentary. He paused just outside the room. "Tina. Mom."

"Oh, good to see you, Hugh." Tina smiled, eyes twinkling. She probably knew everything there was to know about his personal life.

"Son," his mother acknowledged, eyebrows raised in question.

"I'm here to see Rowan before she leaves town."

If his mother was surprised, she didn't show it. "I'm glad. I wish she didn't have to drive."

"Yes." And before he chickened out, he asked, "Would you be available to run an errand with me Thursday morning? I'll take you to Wolves for lunch after." Hugh had an appointment with a jeweler. Christ, he started sweating at the thought. He was looking at stones for a ring. For Rowan. An engagement ring. He wanted his mom's opinion. Jesus, he barely recognized himself these past weeks.

Mom gave him a shrewd look. She couldn't possibly know what he was up to, but maybe she did. Parents had superpowers where their children were concerned. Hugh had always been able to sniff out any subterfuge his boys attempted from ten miles away.

"I would love to."

"Fine," Hugh replied stiffly before heading back to Rowan's room, where soft music could be heard through the closed door. He recognized *Just a Dream* by Nelly. He shook his head. Mozart was probably queued next. Rowan was unpredictable. That made him smile as he tapped on her door softly, aware his mother had purposefully turned the television volume down to make sure she didn't miss anything.

When Rowan pulled the door in, his heart hammered at seeing her again. It was the first time since he'd taken her phone and made an ass out of himself. She opened the door wider, a silent invitation to enter. He knew Rowan loved him. She'd never lie, but he had hurt her and embarrassed her, and he was still unsure of where they currently stood.

Had Rowan called William later to smooth things over? That was not a thought he should ponder if he hoped to work things out with her.

He saw that she was mostly packed, her bag open at the foot of the bed. He heard the door click behind him and turned to see Rowan leaning against the closed door regarding him.

"Don't go." He hadn't meant to say that, damn it.

"I have to help Angela."

She wore a white linen blouse tucked into soft white linen shorts. It was simple and sophisticated and completely Rowan. Her bare feet made him ache to kiss each of her delicate toes. Hugh closed the distance between them and, without a moment's hesitation, lifted Rowan under her arms and brought her body against his own.

She wrapped her legs around his waist as he placed one hand on her ass for support and backed her against the wall. She didn't say a word. She watched him intently, most of her long, silky hair trapped behind her with a few strands draping her front and touching his chest. He used his free hand to cup her jaw and angle her mouth where he needed it.

Hugh brought his mouth close, sharing Rowan's breath. Her hands flexed against his shoulder and neck. "I don't like you being gone from me."

"I don't like it either," she admitted.

"When you get home Thursday, I want you with me always."

"We still have things to work out. To discuss."

Fucking William. "I'll talk. I swear," Hugh conceded. He'd promise the moon to keep her. "Thursday."

"Thursday. Fine."

"Then you'll stay with me after?" Hugh really needed her to commit. Otherwise, letting her out of his sight—again—would be impossible.

"If we can work through things. I've always wanted forever," she finished tenderly.

Hugh wanted so badly to have forever. He dug his fingers into her ass, pulling her as tight together as he could get their bodies. He bent to kiss her neck, speaking against her skin. "I know we still have to talk about yesterday, but will you kiss me goodbye?"

Rowan cupped his jaw this time, lifting his head so that she could place small kisses at the corners of his mouth. "I want to kiss you hello and goodbye. I want to kiss you good morning and goodnight. I want to kiss you for no reason other than because I want to. So yes, Hugh, you can kiss me."

Hugh felt his legs quiver, and his eyes—damn his eyes—he felt Rowan's words like a building pressure behind his lids. She was fierce. She'd known all along that it would always end with *Hugh and Rowan.*

He heard her phone ding and knew she had to leave. He took her lips gently, moving atop her seam until she gasped, allowing him to slowly deepen the kiss. He tried to put all his love into that kiss. Rowan palmed the back of his head pulling him in deeper, the slow tangle of their tongues wrung moans from them both.

Rowan pulled back...slowly. "I have to go. God, I wish I didn't," Rowan spoke between small kisses and nips to his lips.

"Thursday, I'll talk. I'll explain, and when you forgive me, I'll make you promise me forever."

"Give it your best effort, babe. I'm not averse to hearing you beg," she chuckled, giving him one last kiss before wiggling out of his arms. She checked her phone. "Angela's waiting outside the hotel. I've got to run." She quickly threw one more small tote in her suitcase and zipped it closed.

Hugh grabbed Rowan's suitcase and followed her to the door. Rowan kissed his mom on the cheek and hugged Tina goodbye. "I'm walking Row to her car, Mom. I'll talk to you tomorrow."

Angela was waiting outside a Mercedes Sprinter van. "My husband got a driver and this van thing for the trip. I filled it with all sorts of drinks and snacks. Oh, hi, Will! Thanks for letting me have Rowan for a few days."

Hugh clenched his jaw so that he wouldn't make a scene, only dipping his head in acknowledgment. Angela climbed inside while Hugh placed Rowan's bag in the back. She was waiting for him when he turned. She placed her hands against his chest. "I'll make sure Angela knows exactly who you are and what you are to me. Okay?"

"Fine," Hugh replied stiffly. Rowan just watched him and waited. Hugh sighed, bending so that he could kiss her once more. "And what am I to you?"

"Mine."

. . .

HUGH WAS JUST PULLING BACK into Tulsa. He'd gone to the Muskogee compound as soon as Rowan had left. Even though he had a company that he paid to oversee the property and homes, he wanted to go over the place himself. Plus, he'd always loved his house there, and Sara, his housekeeper, wanted to see him before she and her husband left for a two month holiday to visit family.

Hugh had never minded solitude. Quiet allowed him to center his mind. He could look at any new deal or problem and formulate a plan that would yield the best results. Silence was his friend. People referred to him as a wolf in the business world. They weren't wrong. Hugh could be cunning and fierce when he needed to be. He'd always expected the best from his people, and in return, he was loyal.

He never needed to be the loudest in the room, everyone's best friend, or the life of the party. He enjoyed company, but he knew there was always a...separateness. His sons ignored his wall and climbed all over it like he was their own personal jungle gym—and he was grateful for their irreverence. Bran and Patrick were the two people in his life that were easy to show affection.

And then the Byrne sisters. Raven and River were daughters by marriage, and he couldn't love them more had they been his own. Rowan, though...he'd never thought of her as anything but...his. Hugh had only been at the compound from Tuesday night until Thursday morning, but it had been enough time to realize solitude wasn't the balm it used to be.

He tried sitting by the pond, watching a game in the outdoor bar, sitting on the patio, reading in the library...lying in bed. He admitted he missed his boys, he missed their wives, he missed his grandson, and he missed Rowan.

He packed up early that morning and headed back to town. He'd barely spoken to Rowan since she'd left. She'd been busy working and had spent hours at the furniture store yesterday and still had one more item to find this morning. Angela thought it was a great idea to share a room, which meant they'd mostly texted. Hugh grinned as he pulled into the hotel's parking garage—some of their text strands had gotten hot.

Are you asleep?

No.

Angela's asleep. I'm in bed, but I can't sleep.

Is it work related?

No.

What then?

Before I tell you, I wondered if when you snooped in my bedroom, if you actually looked in my nightstand drawer.

Why?

Did you?

No. Tell me what I would have seen.

There are two things.

#1?

I didn't just buy Rave sex toys from that party last year.

Christ. #2?

I have an entire book of charcoal and pencil drawings.

Of?

You. You and me with the family. You and me having sex in every position I've ever read about.

Did you get off to the pictures?

Yes.

Fuck me.

I want to.

Jesus.

When we have sex the first time, I was wondering if we would be so crazy to do it that we wouldn't do any...before stuff. I've dreamed of taking you in my mouth.

For fuck's sake, Row. I've literally been hard for days and then you say something like that...

Still, I wondered about it. If I tell you a secret, one that even my sisters don't know, will you promise not to tell?

Of course.

I'm not a virgin. My sisters were you know. I had sex once in college. In the back of a truck at a party. A totally disgusting cliché, I know. Anyway, alcohol had been involved and I was barely keeping myself together after my parents died. It hurt and it was awful in case you're wondering. Completely cured me of wanting a repeat. I pretty much ignored all men after that. Until you, of course.

I'm not a virgin either. So, we have that in common. I'll give you a secret of mine. I've told two women in my life, who weren't my mother, that I loved them. I lied to the first.

You're my only too.

Goodnight, Rowan. Take a nap on the way back to Tulsa—you're going to need it.

One word. Condoms. BC made me puke my guts up for weeks. Oh! Do they come in fun colors?

I'm not a room. You aren't decorating my dick. (If I were ever to break your trust and tell your sisters a story, it would be this condom one) Goodnight.

Rowan texted Hugh this morning to let him know that it

would probably be closer to three before she was back in town. That worked perfectly for him. He had an appointment with a jeweler.

Hugh held the door to Wolves for his mother to pass. He was trying his best not to smile, but it was a difficult ask. Hugh had told the jeweler when he made the appointment that he only wanted to see yellow diamonds, and he'd made sure there were several stones to choose from. Yellow was Rowan's favorite color, and he wanted the ring to make her smile when she saw it on her finger.

The jeweler had thought Hugh should choose a white gold or platinum band, but Hugh really loved the gold. It made the yellow diamond shine brighter. Mom had agreed and helped with the band design and setting. He couldn't wait to see it done. If they were already back in Dublin, the store's owner assured Hugh that everything could be shipped.

He and his mom decided to sit at a table near his father's memorial. He loved being able to glance around and see so many wonderful pictures and special mementos. Rowan had outdone herself with the space.

Once their waters were on the table, his mom said, "Oh, Hugh. That will be one of the most beautiful rings when it's finished. I'm so glad you went ahead and had earrings and a bracelet made to match."

He loved the bracelet. Hugh had chosen a linked gold chain. A yellow diamond would be encased in gold and soldered to the chain. He could picture how beautiful it would look wrapped around her delicate wrist. He had the jeweler add tiny gold H and R charms.

"I thought she could add charms to the bracelet over time."

Hugh felt his cheeks heat and knew his mom had caught the blush.

"I'm so very happy for you, Son. So happy. Your father would have adored Rowan," she added, dabbing her eyes with a napkin. "I think this calls for a celebratory drink. Don't you?"

"I do." Hugh did feel celebratory. He wanted to call the boys but decided against it. They would tell their wives who would start texting him proposal ideas.

"I'll take a tall vodka and Sprite with a splash of grapefruit. Make sure it's Absolut Elyx. Rowan got me started on Elyx. She said it is the best and she was right."

Mom was grinning, clearly excited by the visit to the jewelers. When he picked her up and told her his plans to pick out an engagement ring, she squealed in delight, gave his arm a squeeze, and told him to hurry up. Hugh knew his mother enjoyed her life and friends here in Tulsa, but he had thought about asking her if she might consider living part of her time in Dublin. She would be able to watch her great-grandchildren grow. He knew she also missed seeing Bran and Patrick. She and Bébhinn really enjoyed each other, and Ireland was closer to all the holiday spots she and Diana enjoyed visiting.

Hugh gave the waitress their drink orders, a double of Redbreast for him, and was about to ask his mom what appetizers she wanted when he heard someone address him. The last voice he ever wanted to hear again in his life.

"Hugh, how wonderful to see you."

Without an invitation, which she would never have received, Helen, her white hair in a perfect shoulder-length bob, and her perfectly made-up ice-cold face, sat in the open seat at their table. He despised absolutely everything about this cold bitch of a woman and really regretted sitting at a three-person table.

When Hugh didn't respond or acknowledge her presence, she turned to Mom. "Lovely to see you, Matilda."

"Mrs. O'Faolain. We aren't friends or family."

Hugh watched in satisfaction as Helen's lips pinched in anger. That's right, Helen, you can't yell and scream and break things. No public spectacles today. She surely had several of her old Country Club girlfriends near, watching the show.

"I didn't realize this was your little place, Hugh, when Sheryl set up the lunch date. I'm in town for her daughter's wedding this weekend."

"Have you had a chance to look at the appetizers, Mom?" His mom looked up from her phone. She'd been texting or pretending to text someone.

"I rarely eat appetizers. Why don't you order several so I can try a bite of each," she suggested.

"Such a rustic restaurant, but then, it suits you, Hugh. You've always been rough around the edges. At least our children didn't inherit your lumberjack personality."

Hugh felt his face flush. She'd always told him he was embarrassingly big with no conversational skills. Helen had always done her best to undermine his confidence. It had hurt, but he'd taken it. He'd taken her malice and her coldness and her cheating.

He saw his mother's eyes were getting glassy. She didn't like Helen speaking to him this way. Hugh was about to throw Helen out on the sidewalk when another woman addressed him.

"Hugh! I'm so happy you haven't eaten yet. I got back earlier than expected, and I can join you and Tilly for lunch." Smiling brightly, Rowan walked over to their table, standing between him and Helen. Hugh felt the momentary paralysis of absolute mortification stiffen his limbs. He didn't want Rowan to be anywhere near that white-headed viper. She made him feel...less, unworthy. He never wanted her poisonous fangs to sink into the woman he loved.

19

————

Rowan had practically been dancing in her seat during the last hour and a half of their trip. Angela had teased her about it. "I wonder if I ever was as excited to see Steve as you are to see Hugh." She groaned, covering her eyes, "I still can't believe I called Hugh O'Faolain, Will! I'll blame you forever for that embarrassment."

Rowan belly laughed. She couldn't help it. Remembering Angela's face when she'd explained the situation had been priceless. "I'm still pissed I didn't video your reaction to send to my sisters and Jo. Speaking of Jo, Josephine O'Connor, she can't wait to check out your store when she and her mom get back from Zürich. They plan on coming in."

Angela started fanning her face. "Lord, Rowan, do you have any idea how many important people you're connected to in this town?"

"Well, if Jo makes you fan your face, I wonder if I should tell you who else will be stopping by."

"Seriously, how did I get so lucky to meet you? Honestly. Stantons, O'Connors, O'Faolains...Okay, I'm chill, tell me."

"Did I ever tell you who Matilda's best friend is and who I eat dinner with once or twice a week?"

"You have not."

"Diana Gaines."

Angela fell sideways on the plush couch in the Sprinter. "Shockwaves just blew me down. I...I can't even...I'm—"

Rowan cut off her stumbling. "My suggestion. If you see Diana walk through your doors, take her coffee order, and let her drink on the floor. She may or may not acknowledge you. Don't be offended. I redecorated her condo a few years ago, and it was an excruciating lesson in humility. She is honest but fair.

"I believe in your taste, your store, and your business acumen. You will be successful, Angela. I truly believe that."

Angela gave Rowan a hug. "You have made me believe in myself and that's worth more than any future success," she confessed, sniffing back tears.

Their mad ten hours of shopping had been a success, and Rowan felt she'd helped create a boutique that would have Tulsa, and hopefully much further afield, talking.

After a quick goodbye at the hotel, Rowan flew through the lobby and up the elevator to Matilda's. Dropped her bag and changed into a gorgeous butter-yellow wrap dress. It hugged her breasts perfectly, no bra needed. She brushed her hair until it fell in a thick wave down her back, dotted her nude rose perfume behind her ears and, at the last minute, slipped her panties off.

If this was going to be her and Hugh's first day of forever, she felt like paying homage to the first day she'd met him. She slipped nude flats with delicate muted gold straps on her feet and sprinted back down to the lobby to catch her Uber.

One minute from her destination, Wolves Irish Pub & Eatery, she received a text from Matilda.

Do not come to Wolves, sweetheart. That devil

Helen is here and sitting with us now. Saying mean things to Hugh. He wouldn't want you to be anywhere near her. I'm sorry. I'll text when we finish here.

Oh, hell to the no, was that evil woman spewing anymore of her trashy venom. Not toward Hugh. She entered Wolves and ordered a shot of Slane and tall water to be delivered to Mr. O'Faolain's table before zeroing in on where they were sitting. The memorial area, of course.

It was a three-chair table. Better and better. "Hugh! I'm so happy you haven't eaten yet. I got back earlier than expected. I can join you and Tilly for lunch." Hugh looked miserable, and Matilda looked close to tears.

Purposefully, Rowan positioned herself between that… that…no, Rowan wouldn't even utter the 'c' word in her head, but she wanted to, and Hugh. Smiling at a stunned Matilda before bending to kiss Hugh, she finally turned to the unwelcome interloper for introductions.

"Oh my," Rowan's slight Irish accent was much more pronounced, thickening along with her anger, "you must be Helen. Your lovely hair gives you away." Before the woman could preen at the compliment, Rowan added, "I imagine you have to pay your colorist a mint to keep it that shade these days, right?" Smiling as if she'd just delivered a compliment, Rowan continued with, "I had no idea you would be able to join us today. I'm so thankful my business trip ended early."

A waitress brought over Rowan's drinks, and she thanked her as they were set on the table next to Hugh's. "Oh no, Helen, don't get up on my account," Rowan waved her back as if the woman were standing to give up her chair, which she absolutely hadn't been, and sat in Hugh's lap instead. "Hugh's lap is my favorite seat in the world." Hugh automatically adjusted her, his long fingers wrapping around her waist. Helen was turning a very unbecoming shade of beet.

She kept up the one-sided commentary, as it seemed Hugh and his mother were still speechless at Rowan's obnoxious behavior. Snuggling her behind more comfortably against Hugh, which caused his fingers to flex deliciously, she continued to drop the hammer on the White Witch.

"It's good that you sit whenever the opportunity presents itself. My grandma told me what a nightmare swelling becomes as women get older. Yikes, not looking forward to that. Of course, that's literally decades away for me, thank God." Annnnnd...that was all she wrote. Helen stood so quickly that her chair threatened to tip over.

"Glad we got to catch up. I must get back to my table." Helen was stiff and clearly beaten, but that wasn't good enough for a woman so rotten.

Rowan stood, adjusting her skirt before stepping toward the older woman. She leaned close so no nearby tables could over-hear. "You had Hugh and two amazing sons, and you threw them away. You disgust me. Do not ever approach Hugh again. He is mine, and you won't like the consequences if you do it again. I will make sure to ruin you so publicly that you will never be able to show your face outside again without being shamed for your behavior.

"You aren't going to join your friends. You are going to leave and never step foot in this establishment again. Have I made myself perfectly clear?"

Helen was breathing like a freight train. Her shaking hands gripped her Berkin against her diaphragm. "Perfectly."

Rowan stayed standing a beat longer, making sure Helen made her way to the exit. She did. She turned to Hugh, who still looked shell-shocked. She took one of his hands into her own. "Do you care what Helen thinks of you or what I think?"

Hugh blinked several times, clearly coming out of his stasis. He moved their hands to his lips and kissed her fingers. "Only you."

"Then let's enjoy our lunch. Your mom knew I was going to get here early so I could surprise you. Surprise," Rowan added, grinning as she moved Helen's abandoned chair next to Hugh's before she sat down.

Matilda chuckled. "If only someone had gotten that whole...that spectacle on video. Tina and I would have watched it on repeat for months. Too bad you didn't have Rowan back when you had to deal with recalcitrant business partners."

"She is a force," Hugh agreed. He looked at Rowan then with an intensity that she felt from her head to her toes.

Matilda excused herself from the table to use the restroom. "Order some food, Hugh. I'm starving after all that." As Matilda passed Rowan, she leaned down to kiss her cheek. "Thank you for loving my son."

Once Rowan swallowed her emotional response, she forced herself to turn and face Hugh. "Are you angry?"

"What?" Hugh truly looked confused.

"I was mean. I'm normally never mean. It's just...I don't know, when your mom texted me not to come, that Helen was here and she was saying not nice things—I lost it, I guess."

"Because I'm yours?"

"You are."

"The fact that you stood up for me, protected my feelings— Christ, Row, I'll never forget that moment." Hugh pulled her chair until it sat flush with his. He grasped her jaw and, uncaring that they were in the middle of his pub, took her mouth in a kiss that left them breathless and wishing they were alone.

Smiling against his mouth, Rowan asked, "Do you know

that I'm wearing the same thing under this dress that I wore when we first met?" Hugh's eyes widened in comprehension.

His hand instantly dropped to her knee, sliding her dress upwards. Rowan placed her hand over his wandering one even though she wanted nothing more than to allow his fingers to finish their journey. "Your mother is on her way back."

"Tonight," He grumbled against her mouth.

"Talk first," Rowan reminded.

"Fine."

She grinned at his martyred tone.

Hugh walked Mom and Rowan to his mother's door. After Mom stepped inside, Rowan told Hugh, "I'll come to your place in just a bit. I need to go over some stuff with your mom and change.

He pulled her close to his chest and fisted his hand in her hair to angle her face toward him. "Don't change. The first day we met, you left me aching when I found out you were bare under a pretty yellow dress. Not this time," he whispered in her ear.

Grinning, she agreed. "I won't change."

Hugh stuck his head in the door and hollered goodbye to his mother. "Don't be long," he said to Rowan as he walked away.

He let himself into his place. His mind felt chaotic. They were so close to a resolution. So close to being...together. It had seemed impossible for so long, but now that it was in front of him, Hugh felt uneasy. He could still screw this all to hell. Say the wrong thing. Push Rowan away with his...personality. He knew he infuriated most people. Even his children.

She might come to think he was too much work. But then, he *had* been better. Rowan made him smile. Hell, she made him laugh. Bran and Patrick wouldn't even recognize their father.

He went to the bar and poured a drink, contemplating the honey amber color.

He pounded a fist on the bar top. "I will get this right," he promised himself.

He called Bran, taking a chance that Pat would be close by. Normally, he would have something to discuss with one or both of them, but tonight, he realized he just needed the familiarity of their voices. Once he and Rowan talked some things through tonight, he planned on getting some long-term promises out of her.

"Hey, Dad," Bran answered. "What's up? You want on speaker? Pat and the girls are here. We just got back from having dinner with Dom."

He hesitated. Shit. He had wanted a moment with his sons, but that was selfish. He enjoyed listening to the banter between them and their wives too. "I—" He took too long to reply. Bran noticed and cut him off.

In a quieter voice, Bran asked, "Should I step out of the room?"

Hugh sighed. He was really doing a shit job of this conversation so far. "No, put me on speaker. It's fine. I had a few minutes and thought I'd check in." Bran was silent for moment like, he didn't quite believe the excuse for calling but was not willing to push. Hugh appreciated the restraint.

"You're on speaker now. Hey Pat, come here. Dad's on the phone. Hopefully, he isn't going to discuss his recent sexcapades."

Bran laughed, knowing it would irritate him. It had. The reason he'd been missing the boys currently escaped him. Hugh went to his bedroom and changed into a t-shirt and shorts.

"Hey, Dad. When are you coming home?" Patrick asked. "I'm dying for you to look over the preliminary drawings that the architect and Tim have been working on. Very preliminary, but Bran and I think they have promise."

"Email what you have. I'll look over them tomorrow. I'm not sure when I'll be back in Dublin.

"How've you been, Hugh?" Raven asked.

"Fine." Talk to one, talk to them all, he thought, shaking his head.

"Is Row with you?" River asked.

"No." River's voice sounded smug. Hugh did not kid himself into thinking Rowan didn't share what had been happening between them. She probably shared more than Hugh was comfortable with, but he also knew it was a package deal when involved with a Byrne. He'd heard the boys complain more than once that the girls discussed their sex lives with each other. Surely, they didn't discuss *everything*.

Hugh felt his cheeks flush. Damn, that would be awkward since Raven and River were his daughters-in-law.

Christ. This family..."How's Daniel?"

"Oh my, Hugh. You won't believe how big he's getting. He's already down for the night, or I'd let him talk to Grandpa O. I swear he's almost ready for his first haircut too," Raven gushed.

She was an amazing wife, but an even more amazing mother. "Grandpa O?" Since the whole family used O equally for O'Faolain and orgasm, he wasn't sure he could hear Grandpa O come out of his grandson's mouth without cringing.

"Bran and I are trying it on for size. What do you think?"

If he'd been having this conversation with River, he would understand she was being ornery. However, this was Raven. "I'd prefer Papa or Pop if you wouldn't mind. It's what I called my grandfathers."

"Oh, Hugh, I love it. River, which do you prefer, because our kids will both need to use the same name."

"Papa. Definitely."

"That's settled." Raven laughed in delight.

"Fine." He wouldn't admit it to anyone, but he was thrilled. He loved seeing his children having children, and he loved that he would get to see them grow up. He would really love hearing them call him Papa.

Bran and Patrick were discussing what the kids would call their uncles when someone knocked on his front door. He swore his muscles swelled. He opened the door to see the most crave-able woman alive standing in the hall. Still wearing the yellow dress.

He forgot he was on the phone, letting it drop by his side. As Rowan walked beside him, River decided to ask, "So, what does Rowan call you?" Hugh could have done without the sexual innuendo. He looked toward Rowan who was pouring Glenmorangie 18 into a lowball glass. Her shoulders were shaking, amused at her sister's antics.

Hugh stood opposite her at the bar. She smiled, her dimples so damn sexy he forgot again about the phone in his hand until she reached over and took it.

"I call him Daddy but only when I've been naughty."

As Rowan ended the call, he heard his sons cussing about their wives being disgusting. "Daddy, huh?" Her laughter made him grin.

"Bran and Patrick are so easy to rile up. Seriously, they're both prudes at heart," she admitted, grinning.

They stood another moment just watching the other. "My grandpa name is Papa. The motion was put forward and seconded."

Rowan smiled sweetly at the news. "It suits you. You'll be the best Papa ever born."

Her smile turned pensive before smoothing itself out. This was it then. They were going to talk, and she was going to accept him or not.

"You made it clear to me, on more than one occasion, that we weren't ever going to date. So, when I started seeing William, I was free to do so. Why did you react the way you did when he called? I had made up my mind to end things. You didn't trust me."

THIS WAS a conversation that Hugh had clearly been dreading, but trust was everything in a relationship, and he hadn't trusted her to be honorable.

Hugh placed his hands flat on the bar and took a deep breath. She knew he hated getting this open with his feelings and she wanted desperately to lay her hands on top of his and tell him he didn't need to talk about it. However, that wouldn't serve either of them well.

"I've never been jealous. Ever. I have mutually satisfying hookups. Jesus," he groaned, "I sound like Patrick. Anyway, my point is that I never think of a woman beyond that moment. I haven't touched another woman since the day we met because I considered you mine. When a man would talk or touch you...a woman that I had claimed in my mind...Jesus, this is embarrassing."

"It isn't embarrassing at all. Listen, Hugh. If another woman touched you...if you allowed a woman to touch you when I couldn't, I would have wanted to destroy her. I get where you're coming from. I've loved you for so long and wanted you longer, but you refused to commit. I was always committed. You knew I'd be yours if you had wanted it.

"You know why I agreed to date Will. I've explained my reasons already, but when you got to Oklahoma this time and admitted that you loved me—I knew there would never be room in my life for another. Why didn't you trust me with William?"

Hugh pinched the bridge of his nose as if he had a

headache. He certainly ached. "Helen cheated on me. She enjoyed making me watch her flirt and flaunt her body for my friends and peers at the Club. I didn't love her, but it did make me feel...feel, I don't know...less of a man. It was what she wanted. She wanted me to feel like an uncouth giant. Not a man with a smooth tongue and manners.

"When she was feeling particularly vicious, she would take one of the men and screw him in a back room at the Club, knowing I knew and the man's wife as well. She managed to make me feel like I wasn't good enough, and I hated her, but I hated myself more for allowing her that power over me.

"I pretended indifference. I learned to swallow the humiliation and the hate for my...for Helen."

"I'm sorry that you had to go through that." Rowan was frantically blinking. She didn't want to cry and interrupt Hugh, who was sharing his deepest traumas.

"William was one of them. We were in our twenties and just taking over our family businesses. We were brash and didn't care fuckall if we hurt someone's feelings. Everyone knew Helen was lose with her favors. It appeared to our group that I didn't care what she did. I don't believe William ever slept with her. I had the feeling it was just for show, on his part, at least. I think he truly loved his wife, Katy.

"When I found out you were seeing each other...Christ, Row, I know my reaction was terrible. I know I was out of line, but it was you, Rowan. *You.* It took me back, and I'm ashamed that I embarrassed you. I'm drowning here, Row. I need an absolute commitment from you. I need the words to feel secure."

"What words do you need besides I love you?"

"I want you with me always. I want us to live together. Here in Oklahoma and in Ireland. Wherever we find ourselves, I want it to be you and me."

"Will you acknowledge our relationship? To any and every one we're around? Will you call me your girlfriend?"

"No. I'll call you mine. My everything."

"What words then, besides I love you, do you need?" she asked again.

"Forever."

"Forever then." Rowan could feel tears spring to her eyes again.

She walked around the counter where she could take his hands in her own. "I'm glad that's settled, babe." She couldn't help the giggle that escaped. Giddy didn't begin to encompass the joy flooding her body. Rowan climbed up on the tall barstools, swiveling the seat so that she could grab Hugh's hands and pull him between her legs.

"I vow to never give you any reason to doubt my commitment to you. Do you accept?"

"Yes. God yes, Row. I vow the same to you. I will never give you any reason to doubt me, either. Ever."

"Good, because I wasn't going to let you run again. I would chase you to the ends of the earth if I needed to. When you look at me like you are now..." Rowan shook her head, unsure how to describe Hugh's strength, the thrill she felt when he looked at her with his grave, dark eyes.

"What do you see?"

"I see a wolf in wolf's clothing," she smiled, hooking one foot around his calf. "What do you see?"

Grinning, he leaned down so his eyes were in line with her own. "Dinner."

20

———————

"Dinner, huh?" Rowan teased as she leaned against the back of her stool, putting a bit of distance between them. "Do you still want to look under my dress, Daddy?" Hugh's hands paused on the hem of her dress, a look of horror rounding his eyes.

"Please, God, never call me Daddy again. Our family's going to get enough looks as it is when we show up together."

"Fine," she laughed, but does this mean you won't call me your good little girl?"

"Never."

Hugh was barely paying any mind to her words. His focus was trained on her dress slipping further up her thighs. Her voice sounded breathier than a moment before when she asked, "Even if you spank me, and I'm brave and don't cry?"

"Even then, but Christ, stop putting thoughts like those into my head," he growled. "I've been praying for hours that I don't come the moment I touch her soft skin."

She leaned as far back as she could, arching her back and opening her legs just that tiny bit more as he finally got all the soft linen of her dress bunched at her waist. Hugh exhaled deeply as he looked his fill.

"For all we've done in front of one another, and on my couch and in your bed, we've never touched each other," he paused to grasp her inner thighs, placing her thumbs to either side of her sex, "here."

She felt a pulse between her legs at his words. "No, we haven't. I dreamed of touching you." Hugh looked away from her sex to meet her eyes. "For our first time," Rowan felt her cheeks heat but continued, "I want to be in your bed. I want both of us naked. I want to feel your body as you feel mine."

"Anything. Everything."

Hugh swung her into his arms and walked them to his bedroom. She took a moment to appreciate all the beautiful whites. Her eyes landed on a lovely, crocheted blanket. Hugh set her down. She touched the blanket draped over the foot of his bed. It was the palest of yellows and very soft.

"Yellow is my favorite color."

"I know," he replied, heat touching his cheeks.

He'd had something on his bed that reminded him of her. She slipped her sandals off and took a step toward where Hugh stood as still as a statue. She slipped her hands under his shirt. "Take this off." He ripped it from his body so fast a breeze ruffled her hair. She let her hands trace his body; his chest, nipples, ribs, and abs. She might have drooled, tracing his V-line.

He groaned as her fingers ran lightly across the waistband of his shorts. One fingertip dipped underneath. "Take these off too," she demanded. He slid his shorts and briefs off together. Now, it was her turn to moan. His sex bobbed free, engorged, and wet with precum. Rowan didn't know if every man's penis was as mesmerizing, but Hugh's hypnotized.

"Surely, there is no man that compares to you," she whispered. It was his turn to close the distance. His hands went to the bow at her waist and slowly tugged the ends, unraveling the tie until the simple wrap dress fell open.

"Fuck me," he groaned. "I can't believe that bit of material was the only thing between me and your body."

"Remember that in the future."

He finished slipping it from her shoulders before answering. "Oh, I will."

No sooner had her dress hit the floor than she found herself picked up and wrapped around his massive body. All his hot, hard muscles pressed against her skin, his length snug between her legs. His mouth took hers almost frantically.

Breaking the kiss, Rowan demanded, "Bed." She couldn't stop the squeak of surprise when her body went airborne, only to land in a nest of blankets, a fluffy down comforter, and down pillows. Hugh still stood next to the bed, the bedroom's surround lights highlighting his body perfectly. He had fisted his length, pumping twice, slowly.

"I've dreamed of you in my bed, just like you are right now, naked and waiting for me. Christ, Row. You texted me when you were in Texas that you wondered what our first time would be like. How do you see it now? Before stuff," he grinned wolfishly, "or straight to me inside you? We'll do it all, trust me, but in what order is the question."

"You. Inside me. Before stuff, after. I've dreamed about you sliding into me too many times only to wake up empty and wanting." He slid open the drawer of his nightstand, taking out a box of condoms. Rowan started to pant as he ripped the foil packet open and started rolling it on.

"You remembered to get them."

"As soon as you told me, I texted housekeeping to get some." At her shocked look, he asked, "What, should I have left my mother in the car on the way to lunch to run in and buy prophy-lactics?"

As he kneeled on the bed and crawled his way over to straddle her body, she kept giving his sex side-eye. He was... large, and she was...not. "Umm, Hugh, I know having sex one time doesn't make me an expert on...size, but—"

"It doesn't."

He distracted her for a moment by kissing a path to her breasts.

"But...I've fooled around before and—"

"Can we agree to never discuss anything that you've done with a man who isn't me? We'll fit together perfectly. Trust me."

"Fine. Since we're discussing do's and don'ts—you will never say the words woman and hookup if they aren't referring to me." She raised her eyebrows in question.

"Noted. Now relax and let me touch you," he demanded.

He touched her everywhere until she begged him to take her. "Please, Hugh, please." He took her mouth again, their tongues savagely using the other. She stretched her legs around his hips, opening herself for what was next. He was rubbing his sex over her own, creating friction that had her hips lifting before fitted himself at her entrance and slowly began to push.

"I love you," he whispered against her mouth.

He went a few inches deeper, stopping when he felt her stiffen. It felt tight. Scorching. Impossible.

"Rowan, baby, look at me."

When she opened her eyes, wondering when she'd even closed them, it was to find Hugh looking at her with such raw need his body shook with it.

"Take a few deep breaths, my love. Calm, deep breaths. Let me love you. Trust me with your body."

She could feel his tightly leashed strength cradling her body. His tenderness and patience washed away her anxiety.

She reached behind his head and pulled him down to her mouth. She undulated her tongue against his, mimicking the movement they both wanted where they joined. He started to move again, short in and out thrusts.

"Fuck, Row, you're taking more of me now." He leaned back, giving them both a better view. "You can take more. Will you?"

His voice was rough, gritty, and harsh. He liked touching her. He really liked being inside her. She liked him there too. When he took her hand and placed it where they joined, she cried out, lust making her hips jerk and him sink deeper.

"Make yourself come, baby. I've dreamed of you touching yourself while I'm buried deep in your body."

There was no timidity between them. No more doubts about what would fit where. They had always craved each other and definitely craved watching one another touch themselves. She circled her nub with increasing speed, barely registering that he was fully seating himself over and over except to acknowledge how good it felt. He held her hips in a viselike grip as he pounded into her.

When her movements became uncoordinated, jerking, she moaned deep. "So close, so close, babe," she wailed. As her body exploded, her orgasm squeezing and pulsing around Hugh, he slammed into her a final time before stilling. His whole body seemed to swell, including the part inside her—his sex became wider before pulsing, and his orgasm drew out her own, wringing a keening wail from her throat.

Hugh was shaken. His body felt wrung out but energized at the same time. He bent to kiss Rowan, who was looking a little befuddled. He smiled, satisfied. She took his mouth, deepening the kiss and making him almost forget himself. "Shit!" he exclaimed, "I almost forgot." He slowly pulled out, careful to hold the condom in place until he could get it off. He was already getting hard again, which made the process difficult.

"I made an appointment with my gynecologist. I'm going to try an IUD. Maybe my system will like that better than the pill," she smiled sheepishly. "I desperately want to feel you inside me without anything between us."

"God, I love how open you are talking about what you want. I always want you to tell me what you need from me." Once the condom was tied and set aside, he rolled to his back, bringing Rowan's body on top of his. "I'll take you any way I can get you, condom or no," he grinned, adjusting her body so he could take her mouth in a kiss.

"I feel like I just jumped from the sexual novice class and went straight to pro," she laughed against his throat, where she was currently kissing and sucking his neck, taking his dick from half-mast to full attention. "I do have a few more holes in my education," she said as she moved back to his mouth, moving her lower body against his erection.

"What holes?" Hugh moaned, distracted by her body moving over his sensitive flesh.

"I'm ready for the before stuff," she admitted, pulling back to swipe her tongue over his lips, earning a moan from him.

She started to scoot down his body, obviously intent on furthering her education. He stopped her by grasping her hips and pulling her higher instead. "I'm afraid you've landed your-self a man who plans on living out every single fantasy I've ever had about you—and there are hundreds," he finished speaking as he pulled her close enough that his warm breath touched her core.

He expected some resistance to the position—her knees on either side of his ears, her center suspended above his face, but she only looked at him with intense interest. Rowan was intrepid. Bold and adventurous. He always felt her quiet calm hid something else...edgy and real. It had called to him. He imagined it always would.

"Grab the headboard, baby. I'll do the rest." As soon as he eliminated the space between them, he worked his mouth over her sex until she was begging for release. He dug his fingers into her ass cheeks so she couldn't move away, forcing her to ride him until she was screaming her release.

She moaned a holy shit before she slid back down his body to lay boneless and content beside him. She maneuvered her arm to support her head so she could see his face. She leisurely kissed and stroked her tongue over his mouth.

"I made a mess of your beard."

She wasn't apologizing. "I planned on shaving it off before tonight, but you mentioned wanting to know what it felt like against your skin. Would you be upset if I got rid of it?"

"Of course not, babe. You'll be the sexiest man I know, with or without it. When did you grow it out?" she asked curiously.

Hugh tried not to stiffen, but he felt her go still. She'd noticed his unease. "Right after I got married."

Her hand patted his chest, making circles over his stomach. "Helen hated beards, huh?"

Hugh huffed out a laugh. Row was a smart woman. "Correct," he admitted. "Let me know when you get hungry. I'll order room service." Rowan used the hand pressed to his chest to lever herself up. Smiling mischievously, she announced she was ready for more before stuff. He could order food later.

As she moved down his body, he thought he might die from the anticipation alone. When she knelt between his legs and took his aching arousal between her hands, stroking just the way he liked—like she'd seen him do to himself—he came close to orgasming. When her mouth came into play, he almost lost his mind.

He gathered her hair in his fist so his view was unimpeded, doing his level best not to push her head down and slide further in. Watching himself disappear over and over into her mouth had his balls tightening. He was close.

Before she took him over the edge, he gently eased her head back until he fully slid from her mouth, causing them both to moan. "Come here, baby. I want to be inside you again."

"And *I* wanted you to finish," she teased.

Hugh got out of bed and put another condom on. "Come here, Row." She raised her eyebrows in question but crawled to him without comment. She kneeled in front of him, running her hands down his chest and reaching around to massage his ass.

"Mmm, I've spent hours studying your ass. My imagination is good, but not as good as this."

"Turn around and get on your hands and knees." Her easy capitulation and look of interest, made his abs contract in anticipation.

"Raven told me that when Bran takes her from behind, it goes way deeper, and River said Pat almost gave her whiplash once, so she puts her head on the bed now. I'll try both ways," Rowan announced.

She spun around and got into position. Thankfully, the sight of her lush body bent before him helped mute the horror of listening to her casually discussing her sisters and his sons' sex lives.

Bending, he kissed the tattoo on her ass before massaging the round globes, only letting his long fingers graze her sex and between her cheeks. She was panting and squirming in minutes with his teasing. He let two fingers enter her core. "Christ, baby. You're so wet. Are you ready to take me again?"

"So ready, please," she begged.

He placed himself at her entrance and slowly slid in. He

couldn't help the shout that left his mouth at how damn exquisite they fit together.

He kept slow constant strokes. Rowan was already close to orgasming, panting, and begging for release. Seating himself fully, he turned her to her back. She was so tiny he was able to grab her hips and lift them high enough to put him at the perfect angle to hit her G-spot.

"There, Hugh, there. Right there. Don't stop, please don't stop," she pleaded.

He went harder and faster, pistoning like a machine. Her mouth opened in a silent scream as she came. His climax followed, a feeling similar to freefalling—a heart-pounding, breath-stealing, muscle-seizing moment.

He had to keep reminding himself that this wasn't a dream. Rowan was actually beneath him—currently collapsed with him laid over her front—both sawing in deep breaths, sweaty skin slick between them.

"My vagina is calling a truce for at least a couple of hours. I love you, Hugh, but I'm not a Timex watch," she snorted in amusement.

Hugh pulled out and disposed of the condom. "A Timex?" he asked while picking her up to move her to a more comfortable position on the bed.

She laughed outright then. "Don't you remember the old Timex slogan? 'It takes a licking and keeps on ticking.' My dad would use it all the time. A pen, an old car...my mother. My sisters and I finally caught on in high school to what Dad meant when he said it about Mom, and Mom would blush."

He sat down on the bed, running his fingers through Rowan's miles of black silky hair. "Give me a few minutes in the bathroom, and then I'll run us a bath. I don't want you to stop ticking too soon," he winked, making her laugh.

"I love you."

"I love you beyond reason," Hugh easily admitted. "Can you do me a small favor?"

"Of course."

She sat up, her expression suddenly solemn as if whatever favor he needed she would take seriously, but watching the sway of her breasts momentarily interrupted his request.

Clearing his throat, he asked, "Do you think you might...not share our sex life with your sisters or, God forbid, Bébhinn?" Bran and Patrick would live to give him a hard time if their wives enlightened them of their father's bedroom activities—anywhere activities if Hugh had his way.

Rowan looked taken aback like he'd asked her to shave her eyebrows off or stop drinking Slane.

"How precious, babe. You're shy," she smirked.

"I am not shy, and you know it."

"We like to put our experiences in, I don't know, like an information bank. Like when you held me over your face...Bran and Patrick may not have done that to them, but when I tell them how amazing it was, they would suggest it to their husbands. See?" she asked, speaking slowly as if he were a simpleton who didn't understand why privacy was a silly concept. "Don't worry. We never tell everything, but did you know that River and Patrick had a video sex call once, and Pat totally ruined his keyboard with the mess?"

"Jesus, God. I don't want to know anything you find out from your sisters. Ever." Sighing, he'd known this was a battle he wouldn't win, but damn, he could have lived happy the rest of his life without that visual. His boys endured the Byrne share fest, so he would too. Maybe.

21

———

Rowan was grinning like a lunatic while changing into her running gear. She felt different, light, and ridiculously happy. Mom always said that the best things in life were unexpected. Hugh was *definitely* unexpected.

Speaking of unexpected—Hugh had a big surprise waiting in the bathroom when he finally called her in. She could hear bathwater running and assumed he was getting things ready to soak in his huge clawfoot tub. She grabbed his t-shirt from the floor to throw on and pulled off the black band she wore around her wrist to put her hair in a bun before walking into the huge open bath.

She looked at her reflection in the floor-to-ceiling mirror—totally rocking the fresh from sweaty sex cardio class look. Out of the corner of her eye, she saw a giant naked man standing to her left. She barely swallowed a scream—a clean-shaven Hugh O'Faolain was a shock to the system.

"Good Lord! You scared the heck out of me," she gasped as she turned to fully face him, and then gasped again, almost tripping on her own feet when she really took him in. His beard had been sexy. Manly. A statement.

Beardless? She practically had to manually close her mouth...holy cow, the man would cause traffic accidents if he walked down a sidewalk without a mask. He was that gorgeous. His skin was smooth, flawless. His lips were soft and full without a trace of femininity. The beard had done a spectacular job of disguising his lean face, chiseled jaw, and...Jesus...cheek-bones that were so sharp, hollows contoured below them.

Striking. He had been silently watching her with his dark eyes, waiting for the verdict. Putting her arms around his waist, she kissed his chest. "I loved your beard—like really, really loved it." She kissed his chest again, running her hands across his wide shoulders before tracing the muscles down his arms. "Never grow one again."

He chuckled at that, finally wrapping his arms around her. He lifted her then so she could wrap her legs around his waist— his preferred way of holding her, probably so he didn't have to constantly bend to get to her level, she thought, smiling.

"I take it you like my face." He grinned.

That grin, good Lord, as if he needed the added sex appeal. "You'll need to work on not smiling in public, babe. Otherwise, you'll need to hire some of Macgregor's guards back. Women will be throwing themselves at you."

He kissed her in between pulling his shirt over her head. They spent an hour soaking in the tub, talking and touching, discussing what their lives might look like going forward together. Hugh made the transition sound as easy as breath-ing. She would move her things from Matilda's and bring them to his place. His home on the Muskogee compound was now their home. His Dublin flat was now their flat. Easy-peasy.

She had wondered aloud that they didn't have to rush things. They could, in fact, try dating.

"We've sort of been dating for over a year," he countered.

"Is that what you'd call that? Dysfunctional dating, maybe," she snorted in humor.

"You were always mine. In my head. You *are* mine now," he argued, "and I want you with me always."

"Fine. We'll do it your way...Daddy," she added, grinning when he looked at her sharply. He really hated her calling him that, even in jest.

She screamed when he stood suddenly and grabbed her out of the tub. He threw a fluffy white towel on the bathroom counter and set her down on it, ripping a condom packet open that he had forethought to grab earlier and rolled it down his length.

He'd taken her on the counter. The mirrors everywhere had given them both several erotic angles with which to watch themselves. When she'd thrown her head back as a climax ripped through her body, Hugh palmed the back of her head as he brought his mouth crashing down to hers. He plundered her mouth as wildly as his sex thrust in and out of her body.

After they caught their breath and dressed, they ordered a late dinner and snuggled on the couch. Hugh showed her the initial plans for the distillery in Ireland. They each added notes, and he asked her to add some of her drawings to the margins for the architect and Tim.

Before they went to bed, she texted Matilda goodnight and let her know she was staying at her son's. Matilda texted back a wink emoji, which made her laugh.

In the early morning hours, snuggly-spooned by Hugh's body, she woke to him palming her breast and stroking his erection against her ass and lower back. She pushed her body back into the cradle of his thighs, eliciting a moan. He moved his hand from her breast and ran it down the length of her body, grasping her top leg and pulling it over his hips, opening her thighs to his fingers and shaft.

They made love soft and slow, a gradual burn building until they'd both burst into flames. Neither spoke a word, both drifting back to sleep, connected physically and mentally.

It wasn't until she'd slipped out of bed and tiptoed into the bathroom to dress that she felt the stickiness between her legs. She froze, her mirrored reflection looking like a deer in headlights. No condom. Christ, have mercy.

She took a deep breath, shaking her head and sluffing off her freakout. It was one time. She was going to the doctor soon. She would talk to Hugh about it. He would probably have his own freakout, and then they would come up with a plan. Nothing to do about it now. She grabbed a bar of soap and did a quick washup in the cold bathwater that neither of them had bothered to drain last night. It was freezing, but her lady parts felt better for it.

She went through the process of putting on last night's dress, braiding her hair, and splashing water on her face. She'd take a shower at Matilda's after her run. All her things were there. She needed to check in with Angela after that, and then she planned on honoring the "Where I live, you live" edict by moving her stuff into Hugh's place. Before she left, she found paper and a pen behind the bar and left a note for when the sleeping giant rolled out of bed.

So here she was, practically bouncing on her toes as she entered the hotel's lobby. Ready for her run, her day, and life with Hugh. Her perma-grin was beginning to hurt her cheeks. Stepping off the elevator, she hit send, sending the message she'd written to her sisters in their group text.

We did it! For hours and in a million different ways. How in the hell did I ever live without Hugh's D in my life? I just snuck out of his suite—he deserves to sleep in. 😉 I'm going to change at Tillys and go for a run. Sore muscles. I'll call you

both after. PS. I hate condoms. PPS. We decided on Forever.

Exiting the hotel, she held on to the brick façade to finish stretching before taking off down the sidewalk. At this time of morning there were quite a few people out running or power walking in groups. It was already hot and sunny. Oklahoma summers were brutal, but she didn't feel the humidity or the sweat already making a trail down her spine and between her breasts—she felt Hugh, felt his touch, his breath, his mouth.

She stopped at a light only a quarter mile into her run. She was getting closer to the River Park trails, where, hopefully, the tree-lined paths would provide shade and drop the temperature by a few degrees. She was preparing to walk as the signal turned when she caught a glimpse of someone. She would swear it was the same man she'd seen outside the hotel when she was stretching. He quickly looked away when she made eye contact.

A zing of fear wound through her body, but she shook off the unease, knowing she was being paranoid. Delton was dead. For the love of God, how many times would she have to keep reminding herself? Stalkers weren't a buy-one-get-one half-off deal. Delton was dead, and she refused to allow a *dead* psycho to make her see bad guys on every street corner.

One more stoplight later, Rowan jogged through the River Park parking lot and finally entered one of the many shaded trails. Her muscles already felt loose, so she veered off into a less traveled, rockier path. She smiled as Wheatus' *Teenage Dirtbad* started rocking through her earbuds.

She felt her phone buzz in the side pocket of her joggers. Normally, she wouldn't look at her phone until after her run, but it might be Hugh. Stopping by a decent sized boulder she took her phone out and used the big rock to stretch her calves while she opened her texts.

Why aren't you in my bed?

I went for a run. I left you a note.

Why aren't you in my bed?

"Stubborn man," she said out loud, grinning at his grumpy antics.

I'll work on that.

Do that. I finished cardio. About to start weights.

You're up. So you did see my note.

I wanted you in my bed.

Rowan snorted in amusement. **Work those V-lines extra hard. They frame something delicious.**

Why you should be in my bed. Right now. Lunch?

She was in the middle of replying that he could help her move her stuff in, and then they could eat when someone grabbed her from behind and wrapped their hand tight across her mouth. Their other arm wrapped tight around her middle, pulling her body tight against a large frame.

Shock immobilized her until finally, her fight or flight kicked in. There would be no flight. Whoever held her was strong and much larger than she was. Fight then. She went from petrified to a rabid animal. Twisting and jerking and drumming her shoes against the person's shins. Her backward headbutt was rewarded with a grunt.

She felt her phone slip from her hand. Not good.

"Fucking shoot her up already," the man demanded. His deep voice telling her that it was definitely a male holding her.

Oh God, she thought, they were going to inject her with something. She kept struggling, but the man's grip was crushing.

"Listen, lady, this will all be over soon enough if your boyfriend Stanton gives my boss what they want. If he doesn't...well then, I imagine you'll be an early holiday bonus for me."

Rowan went completely still, stunned. Was this man insinuating he'd keep her if Will didn't do what this guy's boss asked? Was this truly happening because of William? What the hell had he gotten himself involved in? How would these people even known the two had dated? Moaning against her kidnapper's hand as the 'how' came to her. The newspaper article.

Her body was shaking now as she realized she wasn't getting out of this one on her own. Oh God, her sisters would panic. And Hugh...tears pricked her eyes at the same moment she felt a sting at her neck. The shot.

"Find a smaller trail back to the parking lot, G. No one can see me carrying a woman out of here. She'll be knocked out in a few minutes."

Less than that, she thought, as her body went limp.

ROWAN CAME to disoriented and very thirsty. She was hot and sweaty and had a hellacious headache, and...oh God, she'd been kidnapped. A moan escaped her taped mouth. She yanked at her tied hands and wiggled her bound feet.

Panic fully set in as she took in her surroundings. She was in the back of a van. There was no carpet beneath her cheek, just chipped paint. A work van? The windows were tinted, so it was hard to gauge the time of day. There were dim interior lights that, once her eyes adjusted, she could decently see. It was dark, but it could be evening or early morning, for all she knew.

She was able to squirm slightly sideways to see more of the front of the vehicle. The front proved fruitless. A metal divider was the only thing to see. There were a few plastic totes with hinged yellow lids and a folded extension ladder. There was no way of knowing how many people were upfront. Surely, not more than two if the cab was the normal two-seater work van most of the contractors she'd met drove. She then wiggled a bit more to get a better angle of the back, and if her mouth hadn't been taped, she would have screamed.

There was another woman bound and lying limp amongst paint-splattered canvases and tarps. Her eyes were closed, but Rowan could see that her chest was moving...she was sleeping, or drugged like she'd been. She didn't recognize the woman, but it was apparent from what Rowan could make out in the dim interior that her clothes were designer.

It was hard to tell her hair color, but it appeared to be shoulder length. Light brown, maybe. Her age was also something she couldn't determine with black masking tape covering half of her face. She desperately wanted the woman to wake up, not that they could communicate, but so that Rowan wouldn't feel so alone.

She could feel tears wanting to bead and fall. She ruthlessly shut them down. Tears would do nothing for her. Panic wouldn't serve her. She had to stay alert and focused. She decided to mentally flip through the few things she did know. The man she'd seen outside the hotel and at the stoplight had definitely been one of her kidnappers. He'd been wearing khaki cargo pants, military-style boots, and a black t-shirt.

He was a big guy, which meant he was most likely the man who'd grabbed and held her. Military? Ex-military? A mercenary? From the millisecond they'd locked eyes, Rowan could definitively say he had a dark flattop. If there was a second man, she hadn't noticed, but then she'd been busy poo-pooing her "overactive imagination."

One of the men was called G. Short for George? Guy? Gregory? Gregor? Unimportant for the moment. The most important bit of information she had was why she'd been taken. Not the whole story, of course, but a partial explanation. The men's boss believed she was William's girlfriend, and that's why she was taken. She was blackmail and insurance all rolled into one. Give them what they wanted, or he wouldn't get her back. The other woman must be someone important to Will too.

Thinking back to the night of the Philbrook Museum event, William had been distracted and mentioned he was having an issue at work. A security breach...It had to be connected. It was clear she was a mistake. Not that that knowledge would help her now.

Hugh would be looking for her. He *would* find her. He was the fiercest man she knew. He wouldn't rest until she was back in his arms. She blinked back more tears that wanted to fall, thinking of what her family must be going through. She'd been shot only a few months ago, but at least they'd known where she was.

The van hit a pothole in the road, bouncing both women's bodies against the hard floor. The other woman's eyes flew open, and terror-filled eyes met Rowan's.

22

Hugh thought he'd felt real fear before. He'd hydroplaned on an interstate with both his young sons in the back-seat. Nine-year-old Bran fell out of a tree he wasn't supposed to climb, dislocating his shoulder and suffering a concussion. Patrick and his friends were robbed at gunpoint during his high school senior Spring Break. Mom calling to tell him his father was having chest pains, and they were on their way to the hospi-tal. Rowan getting shot.

There had been fear—this was terror. Blind, frantic terror. Rowan was missing. Gone.

She never texted him back about meeting for lunch even though his phone showed she was texting, the bubbles just bubbled. He didn't think much of it then. She'd been jogging. He assumed she thought she'd hit send and put her phone away. An hour later, when he hadn't heard anything, he called.

No answer.

Agitated but far from panicking, he phoned his mom.

She assumed Rowan went straight to his place after her run.

He called Raven.

"Hey, Hugh."

Hugh heard Daniel cooing in the background. He wanted to enjoy the sweet sound but..."Have you spoken to Rowan today? Or has River?" He was trying not to sound freaked out, but he was definitely getting to that point.

"No, she texted us both, oh, let me think, probably around six-thirty or seven your time. She was going for a run. She said she would call us when she finished. Why? What's going on?"

Raven wasn't dumb. There was no disguising his concern. "She never came back to the hotel. She isn't answering her phone or texts. Who's by you?"

"Bran. Bran," she hollered. "Come here quick, please!"

Raven had put him on speaker, so he heard his son's heavy feet run into whatever room his wife and son were in. "Have Bran call Rowan. I'll stay on the phone. Text River and ask if she's heard from her." He could feel his heart pounding harder and harder. His chest felt close to exploding.

He heard Bran's phone ringing and ringing, and then Rowan's voicemail picked up. Fuck. "River?"

"She just texted. Nothing since our group text. Oh God, what the hell?"

Bran wondered, "Maybe she twisted her ankle or...or her phone is dead."

"She stayed at your place, Hugh. Did she charge her phone?"

There was no room for embarrassment that they knew he and her sister had slept together. "Yes." He took a deep breath, attempting to engage his brain, shoving his panic to the side. "Do you know what route she takes since she's been staying at Mom's?"

"Oh God, Oh God, Oh God. Shit! Let me think."

There were tears in her voice, her own panic a twin to his.

"Take a deep breath, Rave. Dad will find her. Just breathe and try to remember if she ever mentioned anything. I texted Pat. They're coming up. River might know something."

"Wait, wait, wait," Raven sounded breathless. She mentioned trails by the river were shady. That would be River Park, but there are a million trails," she wailed, clearly losing the modicum of calm she'd been clinging to.

Hugh grabbed his truck keys from the counter and ran out his door, rushing toward the parking garage. "Okay, that's good. That's southwest of where we are, I think. Bran," he barked, "pull up Google Maps around the hotel. See if you can figure out her route from the hotel lobby to where the trails might start. I'm getting my truck now."

"On it," Bran replied.

Hugh heard Patrick and River's voices. "River. Call Rowan's phone." She immediately dialed without saying a word. It rang three times, and then, "Hello?" A woman answered. A woman who wasn't Rowan.

"Hey, this is Darcy. I just found this phone on one of the back trails. I'm so glad you called when you did. The phone was under some leaves. I never would have seen it. Can I drop it somewhere?"

And that's when he discovered the difference between panic and terror. He had River put her phone by Raven's phone. He proceeded to tell the woman, Darcy, to please wait where she was. She needed to show him and the police exactly where she'd found the phone.

He had to hang up with Raven, promising to call her back after he called the police. Hugh called the Tulsa detective who had been instrumental in helping the FBI collect enough information on Samuel Delton. He explained to the detective that there was no doubt that something bad had happened to

Rowan. It had killed him to admit that she was definitely missing. She would never put everyone who loved her through this kind of worry without a good reason. Detective Jeffreys said he would call two police officers who had also helped with the Delton case.

He called Raven back as promised the minute he'd parked in the trailhead's parking lot. Jeffreys and the two officers pulled in behind him.

Bran asked what everyone had to be fearing at this point. "Could this be someone from Delton's group?"

Hugh could hear stifled moans from Rowan's sisters. Considering what those men did to women, he prayed not. Choosing not to answer—because he couldn't even voice the possibility—he said, "I'm at the park. Jeffreys is pulling in behind me."

He saw a woman in running clothes near the large map directory of the trail system. It had to be Darcy. She was nervously bouncing from foot to foot.

"I'll keep my phone on speaker so you can hear what the police and Darcy have to say." Hearing Raven and River's barely contained whimpers threatened to undermine his thin thread of control. He wanted to destroy everything his eyes landed on until Rowan was found, but he had to stay levelheaded. She needed him stone-cold and clearheaded.

As Jeffreys rounded the hood of his black sedan, he didn't waste time with pleasantries. "Officers are already combing through the CCTV footage from the intersections between here and the hotel. This parking lot has a camera. It's older but should give us something. Some of the newer cameras downtown have facial recognition. I sent them Miss Byrne's photo, which we still have on file from the Delton case."

As the three men walked over to Darcy, Hugh asked, "Will they have something soon?"

"They were instructed to forward everything to me immediately. It shouldn't take long since we have a good timeline. An officer is heading to the hotel now to review their footage, too."

Jeffries introduced himself to Darcy, who immediately handed Rowan's phone over to a gloved officer.

"I studied this map while I waited," Darcy said, pointing to a spot on one of the several red lines running across the board. "This is an offshoot trail. Less traveled. Rockier terrain. I can take you there now."

"Thank you, ma'am," one of the officers remarked. "We'll need to mark that part of the trail off. Once we do that, we'll take down your information, and you'll be free to go. Your cooperation is very appreciated."

The officer holding Rowan's phone asked if Hugh knew the password. Raven answered him. "113070." His birthday. The officer typed in the password. It opened to reveal his and Rowan's text thread. **Help me move my things into your place and**...That was it. She'd been texting him back.

They were almost at the spot where Darcy found the phone when he heard through his speaker a phone ringing on Raven's side. He tensed. Patrick announced, "It's Gran." He didn't ask what his mom wanted, not wanting to speak or interrupt the officers as they looked around the scene. Mom knew what was happening. He made a quick call on his way to the park.

"Dad, Jesus," Pat sounded breathless. "Gran said Diana just called her. Her brother Owen called to let her know that William's ex-wife, Katy, is missing. I know this might sound far-fetched, but is it possible this is connected? Row was just all over the internet as Will Stanton's new girlfriend," Patrick trailed off, probably realizing that it did, in fact, sound like he was grasping at straws.

Except...well, Hugh might be grasping at those same straws. Jeffreys stopped taking pictures of where the phone had been found and walked close to Hugh, so he could hear Patrick. "They know nothing of Rowan?"

"Nothing," Bran answered. "Dad...maybe...what are the odds that two women connected to William Stanton are missing?"

Jeffreys was frowning, considering. There was no idea, however unlikely, that Hugh wouldn't follow. "Boys," he barked, his emotions fraying by the second, "call MacGregor. Tell him I need every man he has close to us and even those that aren't. Give him our attorney's contact information. I had him hire private investigators to look into William Stanton. Tell Don that I want the case completely turned over to MacGregor's team."

Silence. They were probably shocked that he'd gone there. He had considered at the time that he was overstepping, and that it might come back to bite him in the ass. He was fresh out of fucks now.

"Patrick's calling him now, Dad. We'll do anything and everything for you and Row. Will Jeffreys work with MacGregor?"

The detective answered for himself. "Yes. Hugh, call this William Stanton. Tell him I want to talk to him. Now. He knows something. Or he doesn't know that he knows something. Either way, get him here."

THE LAST SIX hours had been a test of impotence. Despite the manpower and dedication to finding Rowan, helplessness crushed Hugh. He needed his sons like he needed Rowan—desperately.

MacGregor had pulled eight of his crew to work here and remotely. Jeffreys had the CCTV feeds showing Rowan outside the hotel and at each stoplight leading to the park. There was a man watching her at two of the locations. He was big, wearing a suit, and clearly looking for opportunity. There was one frame that showed Rowan's head turn and look directly at the man. She must have felt his eyes on her.

Damn her for not turning back. Damn her for leaving his arms empty and his heart bleeding. He couldn't think of how she was feeling. If he went there...if he considered how scared she must be...if he pictured her hurt...No. Sanity did not lie in that direction.

"They found the car from the park's parking lot camera. It was dumped on a country road outside Indianapolis. No cameras, obviously. Plates match. The car was stolen in Houston." Hugh was in Jeffreys' office. William had just walked in, red-eyed and pale.

"Stanton?" the detective asked. At his nod, he continued his report. "I was just going over the latest intel with O'Faolain. They found the car seen on CCTV outside Mrs. Stanton's Houston address and here in Tulsa. It was dumped in Indiana. Countryside. No cameras," he continued succinctly.

"A local unit found where another vehicle had been parked for a while. Heavy rain showed deep ruts where a truck or van sat. The car has been towed to a forensics facility. They recovered long black hair and wavy red hair from the trunk," he finished that last bit grim-faced, jaw clenched.

Will stared at the wall in front of him, devoid of expression. He looked like a corpse. Hugh felt like one. Rowan. Rowan. Rowan. She'd been shoved in the trunk of a car for who knew how many hours.

"So, we don't know what vehicle to look for now," Hugh stated flatly.

"Correct. However, MacGregor pulled his best man away from his honeymoon. Fleet is working on a timeline and triangulating possible routes they might have taken after changing rides. Tulsa put out an APB on the kidnapping. If he can get a direction or catch a break on their new transportation, we'll alert the appropriate authorities.

"Once Fleet figures out approximately when they dropped the vehicle, he'll have a timeframe for the PD in surrounding towns on when to check their CCTVs. However, most small towns don't have them. Still, it's worth pursuing. Because the area of the drop is mostly rural, if we get lucky and find one of those small towns with cameras, it will be that much easier to check tags and identification of the owners."

Hugh nodded, swallowing thickly. Attempting to come to terms with the fact that this nightmare wasn't ending tonight.

"Hugh's investigators and Thomas MacGregor's security firm have several leads they're working on, some of which you might be able to shed some light on."

"I'll answer any question," Will gritted out, clearly struggling.

"The only link between the two women is you. Katy is your ex-wife, but reports show that you and Mrs. Stanton are seen quite regularly in each other's company. True?"

"Yes. We attend some family events for our children and attend all of our granddaughter's dance recitals. We don't go together, but we are seen together at them."

"It has been reported that you and Miss Byrne are dating. Is that accurate?

"We were," Will's hands fisted in his lap. He looked at Hugh then, clearly still pissed about their last conversation. "Until this asshole decided to reinsert himself in her life."

"She was never yours, Stanton," Hugh answered quietly. He was a hairsbreadth away from yanking the jackass out of his chair and beating the hell out of him. "If you'd been a better husband, you wouldn't have needed to try to poach on another man's girlfriend," he added, giving into his fury that William had touched Rowan. It was a great diversion from the kidnapping.

"What the fuck is that supposed to mean, O'Faolain? You don't know shit about my marriage," Will shot back, sitting straighter in his chair like he, too, was jonesing for a fight as well.

"Enough, gentlemen," Jeffreys tried to interrupt.

Hugh ignored the detective to deliver another blow. "My men uncovered that Katy never cheated. She hired that society journalist to take a picture of her kissing that man. The kiss wasn't even real." William was reeling. "My guy spoke with the reporter. She said that Katy admitted to her that she was only doing it to get your attention. And it worked. Without allowing her to explain, you kicked her out and divorced her.

"I've been an asshole to Rowan for over a year and finally pulled my head out of my ass. When we find the women, I suggest you pull yours out." By the look of horror on Stanton's face, he'd never considered his wife to be innocent. Pride led to brutal consequences. Hugh would know better than most.

Sighing, Hugh realized he had let his emotions cloud his judgment again where this man was concerned. He slapped Will's back before squeezing his shoulder. "I shouldn't have spoken about your marriage."

Will shook his head, looking grim but more determined than he had when he'd first walked into the room.

"I'm glad you did. I should have realized...I should have known...Katy...it was so out of character. Christ," he said, shaking his head again. "Sorry about that, Detective. Finish asking your questions."

For three hours, they reviewed the information gathered thus far and pounced on every report coming into the detective. William admitted the security breaches to his company were still a mystery, and because one of Stanton's biggest money-makers dealt with blocking hackers, the fact that they'd been hacked had been incredibly worrisome. One of MaGregor's guys joined them to go over Will's company, the hacking, and Stanton Industries' hundreds of employees.

There was also a Canadian tech company that has been aggressively trying to partner with Stanton, but they had been turned away. Will said the company was known for some shady deals and they were toeing the edge of bankruptcy.

Dean, MacGregor's guy, sent the company information out to the team and told them to make BlackOut, the Toronto based firm a priority. Dean said by tomorrow they should have a better picture. "We'll find out about BlackOut's key players, their financials, their friends and family, and hopefully any suspicious or abnormal activity. We'll eventually start seeing connecting strands as we gather more pieces of intel."

His determined confidence was welcome. Jeffreys' phone dinged. After a minute of scanning the newest report, he announced, "Facial recognition software found a match for the man following Miss Byrne. Shane Reynolds. Ex-military. Special Forces. Flagged for anger issues. He left the military eight years ago."

Dean was reading the report over the detective's shoulder. "He became a ghost. Totally off-grid. Until now."

"Sloppy for someone with his background and training," Jeffreys said.

Dean agreed. "However, the article on Stanton and Miss Byrne mentioned her family lived in Ireland, and her business was there. Fewer people to worry about her going missing in Tulsa. Stanton lives in Texas. Reynolds was much more careful with covering his face in Houston."

"It could be that whoever is paying him doesn't know what in the hell they're doing. Maybe Reynolds is used to being the muscle, not the brains. If BlackOut is behind this, desperation might have made them careless." Hugh was by no means a detective, but with both women taken by the same man, all fingers pointed to Stanton as the common denominator.

"All true," Jeffreys agreed. "O'Faolain, Stanton, go home. You'll be notified if anything changes. Hugh, you're paying MacGregor for his services, so you'll probably know before me anyway."

Dean told Hugh he'd call with a full report by eight in the morning. He and Will left the detectives office and headed to the precinct parking lot. Hugh looked at Will. "Do you need a place to stay?"

"I'm staying at Aunt Diana's."

The elevator ride to the lobby was strained. He and William were both lost in thought. Mom's assistant Tina texted earlier to let him know that his mother and she were sleeping in his spare bedroom. She wanted to be close to her son. William wouldn't be alone, though Hugh shuddered at the thought of sleeping in that Dragon's lair.

When they stepped out of the elevator, Hugh took a deep breath and apologized again. "I should not have spoken about Katy. I should have just given you my investigator's file. When you and Row are brought up, I lose my mind."

Will stopped once they walked outside. He sat on the steps outside the building, his body deflating. Hugh understood the feeling. They were both trapped in hell.

"I put my goddamn job before my wife. She gave me everything. I loved her, just not enough. For the past few hours, I've had to live with the fact that Katy and Rowan wouldn't have been taken if I'd been a better fucking man years ago."

"We will find them. I will never stop looking. We can't look back, Stanton. If I hadn't been such a colossal cocksucker to Row, she wouldn't have run to Oklahoma. We are both to blame for this—and whoever the hell is behind their abduction." Will nodded, accepting Hugh's peace offering. "I'll have my people email me the file on Katy and send it to you tomorrow."

"Appreciated." Will hung his head for a moment, massaging the back of his neck, deep in thought. "I know you hired MacGregor's services to find Katy and Rowan, which I plan on paying for, but why did you already have investigators looking at me?"

Hugh wondered when he'd ask. "If Rowan didn't choose me over you, I planned on finding something to ruin you. I believed that Katy was never like Helen and that the divorce had to be on you, so I hired people to find out what happened. I won't apologize. Rowan is everything to me."

William huffed out a laugh. "I guess you being an overbearing asshole has served me well. I might have a chance of getting my wife back when all of this is over. When we find them safe," he added softly.

"We will find them," Hugh answered as he sat down on the steps next to the man, up until a few hours ago, he'd hated with a single-minded intensity.

"Helen was horrible. I hope you don't mind me saying."

"Worse than you even know. She flirted with you once, her one-thousandth attempt to make me jealous, at the Club," Hugh admitted, wanting William to know where some of his animosity stemmed from. You didn't shut her down even though your wife was in attendance. Even though I was standing right there. I hated you for that."

William reeled back at the admission. Blanching at the honesty. He swallowed several times, looked forward, and then turned to Hugh once again. "I was young, dumb, and clearly full of myself. Christ, Hugh, I don't blame you for not liking me. I want you to know I never touched your wife. I wouldn't have done that to you and certainly not to my own wife. Even though allowing her the leeway to speak to me in a flirtatious way disrespected you both. Forgive me."

He could tell William was sincere. He couldn't have known how bad things were for Hugh back then. He didn't want anyone to know. He'd probably appeared uninterested in his wife's infidelity. "Forgiven." Will stood and offered Hugh a hand up. "We *will* find them."

"We will," William agreed.

23

―――――

Raven

Raven just got off the phone with Nan. Difficult didn't even begin to describe that conversation. River grasped her hand and squeezed. Tears shone against her sister's red-rimmed eyes. She and Bran and River and Patrick had been absolutely paralyzed with fear. They hadn't slept, all of them sitting in Raven's living room, holding their phones—waiting for a miracle. They hadn't gotten one.

Around three that morning, Hugh had given them a rundown of what intelligence had been gathered so far. Raven almost fainted when he told them that forensics had found hair matching Rowan's and William Stanton's ex-wife, Katy, in the trunk of the car. The kidnapper changed vehicles, and the police were working on what they were being transported in now.

She and River hadn't been able to speak, shock freezing their tongues. She looked at her husband, her eyes pleading for him to do something, anything, which was wholly unfair, but Raven was long past caring about fair.

Her sister was gone, and she wanted her back!

"I called our pilot, Bobby, Rave," Bran cupped her face in his palms, forcing her to look at him. "We'll go to Oklahoma and not leave until we have Row back. I promise, baby."

Raven twisted her head to kiss his palm before she looked at her sister. "River?"

"We're coming. Right, Pat?" She turned pleading eyes to her own husband.

River was almost seven months along and Raven knew Patrick would prefer to keep her from flying especially when she was so distraught. He also knew keeping her from going would place even more stress on his wife's shoulders. So, he agreed. "Of course."

Raven looked at Bre, her assistant, and Daniel's part-time nanny and asked if she would come with them.

"Of course. I'll run home and pack now." Organized as ever, Bre told Raven to "Go ahead and pack your bag. As soon as I get back, I'll help you pack Daniel's things. I'll bring the travel crib from my house," and with that, Bre flew out the door.

Raven looked back to River. "Would you email Dom now so he'll know what's happening first thing in the morning? Tell him to cancel our calendar for the foreseeable future. He'll know which clients want to meet Josh for his metalwork sculptures, and those appointments can stay. Tell him we won't be coming back without Rowan."

There wasn't a business manager in the world that could top Dom's skill. Raven and River wouldn't have to spare Triskelion a thought, which was a blessing since there wasn't a thought left that wasn't focused on Rowan.

"I'll text Jo that we'll call her once we land in Oklahoma. I hope she takes our advice to stay and finish the Zurich job with her mom. Maybe by then, we'll be back in Ireland with Rowan, and she can come straight here," Raven finished, rubbing her eyes in exhaustion. Jo was frantic, and she loved her friend for it, but there was no reason not to finish her current job. Jo admitted they'd be done in two days.

"When I spoke with MacGregor, he told me that he is working closely with his team on deep diving into BlackOut's IT infrastructure. He said if there were links to be found between the company and the kidnapper, they should know in the next twelve to twenty-four hours. Since he is currently in Scotland, I asked him if he would make sure Jo knew everything we know in case the time difference screws us once we're in Oklahoma," Patrick explained.

"I'm sure that wasn't a problem. He probably talks to Jo constantly," Bran said as he scooped Daniel out of Raven's lap and grasped her hand to pull her up.

"Turns out, it was a problem," Pat raised his brows, clearly still surprised. "He said he and Jo were currently not in touch."

River started to cry. Hormones.

"No worries, Riv. Once we have our sister back, we'll find out what the hell Thomas did to hurt Jo. Now, dry your eyes, Riv, and go pack. Hugh will get Rowan back."

24

Rowan woke up groggy, sore, dry-mouthed, and...handcuffed. It was the last that shot panic streaking through her body, stinging her fingers and toes, ears and scalp. Her chest felt constricted, and her breathing was rapid, panting, and shallow.

Her situation came screaming back. She'd been kidnapped. Drugged. Tied and transported in the back of a van. Her reality didn't produce even a sprinkle of calm. How much time had passed, she wondered. When the van finally stopped, she and the other woman looked at each other. Fear was swimming in her eyes. Rowan knew her eyes reflected the same.

The back of the van door swung open, almost dumping the woman to the ground. Without a word, a smaller man wearing a ski mask produced two syringes and efficiently stuck them both in the necks with a fresh round of drugs. Without saying a word, the man climbed out the back and shut the door. It was the last thing Rowan remembered until waking up for the second time.

They weren't in the van. The cold metal floor had been replaced with a cold floor, definitely not metal. Concrete maybe.

When she and the other woman had been awake in the van, they hadn't been able to communicate. Their captors never removed the thick tape covering their mouths. There was no tape now.

It was dark in this new place, pitch black, so she couldn't be sure if she was alone or not. She tried to take stock of what she could feel. One wrist was cuffed to what felt like a thick pipe. With her free hand, she was able to trace the pipe, thick and solid and never-ending. The scaly texture could have been peeling paint or corrosion. No light, industrial type pipes, concrete floor...a basement?

She felt her ankles. Plastic ties secured them together. Painfully tight. Her running shoes and socks were gone. Taking several deep breaths, she ran her shaking hand over her body, and a small moan escaped. Her fear ramped up tenfold as she felt bare legs, bare midriff. They'd stripped her exercise pants and tank top off, leaving her in her bra and panties.

She pulled her knees up, wrapped her free arm around them, and rested her forehead. She was shivering almost violently. Probably a combination of shock, the temperature, and whatever drugs they'd injected her with.

Deciding to risk making noise, she whispered, "Is anyone with me?" There was a noise to her left, a shaky inhalation. "Are you the woman from the van?"

In a scratchy voice, the woman whispered back. "Yes. I just woke up. Are we alone?" she asked frantically.

"I think so. We're maybe in a basement. Are you handcuffed to a pole?"

"Yes. Feet are tied too."

Rowan heard the woman's breathing escalate, and heard her cuff rattle against the metal of a pipe. She wasn't cuffed to the same one as Rowan, but she wasn't too far away either. Probably far enough that they wouldn't be able to touch.

"They took my clothes," she whimpered.

"Mine too, except for my bra and underwear."

"Same," the woman answered, voice wavering. "Are you from Houston?"

"Tulsa. Who are you? They mentioned William Stanton when they took me."

"Oh God. I'm Katy Stanton. Will's ex-wife. Do you know Will?"

"I'm Rowan Byrne. My sisters and I own an interior design business in Ireland. We are originally from Oklahoma and split our time between the two places. I've been in Tulsa for several weeks working on a job," she whispered back. Rowan paused, not wanting to fully admit how well she knew her ex-husband. She decided on, "I'm well-acquainted with his aunt, Diana Gaines."

Silence greeted her words. More sniffling. "Don't lose hope, Katy. We will get out of here. My family will never give up looking for me."

"You are Will's girlfriend."

It wasn't a question. *Shit*. There was no time for subterfuge. The more information they knew, the better chance they had of figuring out what in the hell was going on. "We went on a few dates, yes, but...well, the man I love came back into my life. We are completely committed. My...sisters are married to his two sons." She choked on the last part. It was hard to think of what her sisters were going through right now.

"I saw pictures of you and Will kissing. You both looked so happy...and in love."

Katy said the last so low, that Rowan almost didn't catch it. She was obviously still very much in love with her ex. If the situation was reversed, Rowan would be equally devastated. "We were never in love. My heart has always been Hugh's. I am sorry, Katy. I won't lie to you. We did kiss a few times. Only kiss.

I believed Hugh and I would never be together. I came to Tulsa for a job, yes, but also to nurse a broken heart and attempt to move on.

"William was my attempt at moving on. When Hugh showed up, I called Will and let him know that I would no longer be seeing him and why." Katy's cuff clinked. She must be adjusting her position.

"Thank you for being honest. It's been a tough couple of years. Suffice it to say, I made a huge mistake, just not the one he thinks I made. I've tried to stay hopeful. When I saw those pictures," she paused, "I thought…I believed I might need to finally let go."

"Don't give up. If he thinks you did something that you didn't do, then explain it to him."

"He refuses to speak to me. Even at family things, he won't even meet my eye."

"Stubborn men. We must have chosen the two most stubborn men alive to love. When we get out of this mess, don't allow him to have a say. Force him to listen."

"Who are you seeing?"

"Hugh O'Faolain. I imagine you know him. William does." A sharp intake of breath followed her admission.

"I'm glad he found a woman who loves him. He deserves it. I knew Helen. I…oh God, as if it matters, we're handcuffed in a basement, but I think Will cheated on me with her."

Rowan winced. Helen certainly enjoyed hurting others. "Only Will can answer that, but I can tell you that Hugh believes they only flirted and that it went no further."

"You know, I'm beginning to see that my marriage might have been much different if I'd spoken up. If I'd demanded answers and demanded respect, but enough of that. It's nice to meet you, Rowan, though I wish it was under different circumstances. Let's figure out what's going on."

"Did the people who took you say anything?"

"No. I walked outside to water my roses, and a man grabbed me from behind. I didn't know at the time, but the pinch in my neck was them giving me a shot. I woke up in the trunk of a car. A man with a mask on took the tape off my mouth and had me drink some water, gave me another shot, and shut the trunk lid over my head.

"Before I passed out again, I truly thought I was being taken somewhere to be killed. The next time I woke, it was in the van with you."

Rowan swallowed several times before she could go over her experience. He throat was so dry between the drugs and no water. "I got up early Friday to go for a run. I saw a man twice downtown watching me. He wasn't wearing a mask. He is very large, dark hair, flattop. I was too far away to make out more than that. I thought I was being paranoid."

Rowan briefly considered that the man was somehow connected to Delton's dark web filth and had tracked her from the site. The possibility had paralyzed her for a moment. She'd been able to shake it off thanks to her weekly online therapy sessions. Dr. Sehoy said it was perfectly normal to feel fear. The doctor encouraged her to acknowledge that the fears were valid but to recognize that Rowan could control how they affected her.

"So," Rowan continued, "I kept jogging toward the River Park trails. Do you know where that is?"

"It's been years, but yes."

"I stopped on one of the trails to answer a text and was grabbed from behind. I realize now, it was the man I'd seen following me. There was another man on the trail, too. The big guy called him G and told him to give me a shot. The man holding me said that if my boyfriend William gave his boss what they wanted then they would let me go. If William didn't, he would get to keep me." Rowan still shuddered at his words.

"So, you were taken because they still believed you were seeing each other, and I was probably taken because Will would be honor-bound to free the mother of his children. Good Lord, what a mess. Stanton Industries designs new tech and security programs. I suppose someone, somewhere, wants to steal a design."

"William would never do anything shady?"

"Never. Absolutely never. Our children work in the business. He would never jeopardize their safety, and of course, he wouldn't do anything that would hurt Owen, his father."

"Then there's really nothing to do but wait. Surely, whoever had us taken has already contacted Will. I'm not sure how much time has passed. I'm worried that they gave us more shots than we know of. It might have been less than a day or days for all we know."

"I did get a little water once. You weren't in the trunk with me then. I was taken Thursday night. You were taken at least twelve hours later. You're right though, we don't have any idea how long we've been drugged."

"We definitely haven't eaten in quite some time. My stomach feels like it's caving in on itself and—" Rowan abruptly cut off her whisper, stiffening at the squeak of stairs. She wanted answers, but she also didn't want the men who had stripped her clothes from her unconscious body to come anywhere near her.

Light blinded her when a door on the opposite side of the room swung open. She could just make out two blurry images crowding into what was definitely a basement. Windowless as far as she could tell. As her eyes adjusted, she quickly glanced to her left, about six feet away, Katy sat, leaning against the metal pole that her wrist was cuffed to. They shared a look before focusing on their kidnappers.

Rowan was relieved to see they each were carrying a bottle of water. Her throat was painfully dry. The biggest man sauntered toward Rowan while G went to Katy, handing her the water bottle and what looked like a protein bar. Her stomach let out a low rumble causing the big one to smirk. Only G was wearing a mask. Big guy hadn't bothered—that scared her more than anything had so far.

Why would a criminal let their victim see their face? Did he not expect them to be released? He stopped right in front of her knees and bent to clasp the back of her head in a painful grip, positioning her face toward his.

"Thirsty, Miss Byrne?" His voice sounded low and smokey.

Rowan swallowed, fear making her already parched throat burn. "Yes." He took the bottle and rubbed it slowly across her lips. She didn't dare breathe, praying this monster would stop touching her.

He kneeled on the floor, his legs touching hers. "I bet Stanton only needs one of you back. What does he need two women for? Would you like to stay with me instead," he bent to whisper the last in her ear.

Even though her body was quaking in fear, the thought of what this man was suggesting…"I would rather be dead." Instead of becoming angry, he looked amused.

"I like my women feisty. I bet you'll be hell to break in bed. You should know—I'm extraordinarily patient." Standing and addressing she and Katy both, he announced, "In case you're under the impression that this will be over soon, you should know that my boss isn't even going to send a ransom until you've enjoyed my company for seven whole days," he chuckled at our gasps. "Four more to go, ladies."

He finally dropped the water and protein bar next to her feet, backing up a few steps. My God, they'd been drugged for three days already. Her sisters, Nan and Hugh, had been frantic for seventy-two hours.

"Are we still in Oklahoma?" Rowan dared to ask.

He grinned, the scar on his cheek pulling his skin at odd angles. "While you ladies napped for three days, we've crossed into seven different states. I don't want to be found, which means I won't be. If I were to take you, no one would ever find us again. I'm very good at disappearing." He and G moved to the door. He stilled with his hand on the doorknob. "We'll be back in a couple of hours to help you ladies to the bathroom. You'll have to be watched closely, of course."

"I won't need to go." Rowan was sickened by the delighted grin on his face.

"No need for modesty. G and I helped you two take a piss yesterday. You both were so doped up you didn't mind flashing us the good stuff. See you soon, well, maybe not too soon. G and I decided to spend a little money at the strip club around the corner. All those naked ladies will probably make us eager to see you."

Nausea dipped fear tightened her stomach. He grinned after that parting threat. Once he flipped the lights off and shut the door, Katy and she were in complete darkness again, blacker than before after the bright light.

It felt like being trapped in Hell. If Hell was cold and colorless.

She heard Katy whimper. Rowan laid down on the cold, hard floor, curling her body into a ball, the bottle of water and protein bar forgotten. That man didn't plan on letting her go. Worse was considering what might happen in a few hours.

25

"What do you mean?" Hugh demanded. Dean was updating Detective Jeffreys, Stanton, Hugh, his sons, and Rowan's sisters about the intel on BlackOut, the tech company in Canada suspected of being behind the kidnapping.

"We did not find anything that would indicate that this company or any of their people are behind the kidnapping. They are months away from bankruptcy, and they've made many foolish investments, but they are not involved in this case. They were also not responsible for Stanton's breach of security. MacGregor agrees, and he's spent probably more hours combing through every single email, text, phone record, and bank statement." Dean sat back, clearly disappointed they were no closer to an answer.

"We've already pivoted our efforts. All my people are now invested in a deep dive into Stanton Industries. If this problem isn't a result of outside influence, it has to be internal, Stanton," MacGregor boomed. The Scottish security firm owner was on speaker. "I am pairing you with Ethan Jones and Sara Deter. You are going to help them go through every division of your company, who has access to sensitive information, and who might be willing to turn on the company and take your loved ones down at the same time.

"Ethan and Sara are expert profilers. If someone working for you raises even the most infinitesimal of red flags, they'll find them. Stanton, I have already sent you their contact information. I want you to give them full access to the names of those who are working on your newest Government project—especially the names of those who wanted to work on it but weren't chosen. The rest of the team will start with phone and email records, specifically overseas and, of course, relating to Shane Reynolds."

"I don't understand why they haven't contacted William, Thomas," River questioned, her hands covering her face, trying to cover the tears that hadn't ceased flowing.

Patrick murmured in her ear and rubbed her back, but Raven and River were inconsolable. They'd moved into the hotel, in his boys' separate small apartments, and attended every meeting, no matter the time of day. All of them looked haggard. None of them had slept more than a handful of hours since Rowan's abduction.

When he got her back—and he would—she was never leaving his sight again.

"It's a very common tactic, River," MacGregor answered. "Fear. They want Stanton to be so out of his mind with fear that he'll agree to any and everything."

"In cases like this one, six to seven days is not unusual," Jeffreys' concurred. "Whoever planned this has been working on it for a while. They probably feel confident. They'll ask for the projects files to be sent to an untraceable email address, then once it's been verified, they'll give up the location of the women. They may already be in another country, leaving their hired men to complete the trade."

"They may think they're smart, but I can assure you,"

MacGregor's voice rumbled over the line, "they are not smarter than my team. Between us and Jeffreys, we'll find a thread and then pull that sonofabitch until it's completely unraveled."

The meeting broke up. Everyone silently walked out of the precinct conference room. The mood was eighty leagues below somber. He walked because he had to move from one point to another. He breathed because he was no good to Rowan dead. He no longer cried himself to sleep because his body was numb. Empty.

He chose to walk back to the hotel. He needed the quiet. He loved his family, but seeing their tortured faces increased his barely capped horror, and he selfishly wanted a moment to himself to just picture Rowan the last time he'd seen her. His favorite memory to examine was her leaning on his chest in bed, grinning with her precious dimples on full display, telling him... *I love you.*

He pulled out his phone and clicked on Raven's text messages. She'd sent him Rowan's last message that she'd sent to her sisters. Less than an hour before she'd been taken.

We did it! For hours and in a million different ways. How in the hell did I ever live without Hugh's D in my life? I just snuck out of his suite—he deserves to sleep in. 😴 *I'm going to change at Tilly's and go for a run. Sore muscles. I'll call you both after. PS. I hate condoms. PPS. We decided on Forever.*

We decided on Forever. They were forever, damn it. He read it again and again as he walked, smiling at the massive over-share. Shaking his head, he realized he didn't give a single goddamn if she gave her sisters a play-by-play of every one of their moments. He just needed her back.

Tomorrow had to be the day the kidnappers contacted Will. It must. Stanton was struggling with his guilt. His company might have been the impetus, but he couldn't have foreseen or prevented what was happening. He was thankful the man's father and children had come to Tulsa. It was important for them to comfort one another.

As he exited the hotel elevator and opened up his front door, he stared at how empty it felt. He felt empty. He walked to the bar and poured three fingers of Slane. Taking a sip, he remembered the first time Rowan had been to his Muskogee home. She and her sisters had been invited for a weekend after he and his sons had hired their design business.

The six of them, plus James O'Connor, had been enjoying the bar Hugh had built next to the pond when he heard Rowan tell James she would have asked for Slane Irish whiskey over the Scottish Glenmorangie, but there wasn't any on the shelves. It had infuriated him that he hadn't had something that Rowan had wanted. He became even more frustrated that he even gave a shit.

Slane had been stocked in every bar he owned from that day on. Such was his need to make her happy and see her smile...see her taken care of and loved.

He took another deep pull of whiskey, his gaze landing on three jewelry boxes. Oh God. It was Rowan's wedding jewelry. His mom picked it up earlier today. She'd texted him. He forgot. The boxes were made of beautiful, soft, butter-colored leather. He'd had the jewelry store find a set of handcrafted boxes for the set.

He nudged the two bigger boxes asides, touching the smaller ring one. He almost picked it up. He wanted to see the ring that he prayed would eventually encircle Rowan's finger. He shoved it aside with the others. He would look at it when he had Rowan back. He only wanted joy associated with the ring. Not sorrow and despair.

Hugh picked up the crystal lowball of Slane and walked slowly to his bedroom. He didn't look at the mussed sheets or the pillows still on the floor. He'd canceled housekeeping, not wanting the last place he'd felt her in his arms to change. Still, he couldn't look, walking on into the bathroom.

A hot shower and whiskey. Maybe he'd catch a few hours of sleep on the couch. He learned to try to nap in the afternoon. Darkness was where nightmares ruled.

Day seven was still several hours away.

Rowan. Rowan. Rowan.

It was four in the morning when his phone buzzed with a notification. His hands shook when he saw it was a group text from MacGregor. With suddenly clumsy fingers, he opened the short, heart-stopping message.

Found the person behind Stanton breach and kidnapping. Apprehended trying to board plane-Houston airport. Meet at precinct. Now. Dean will take you to a conference room. Jeffreys waiting.

Hugh had been working on the Irish distillery project, tweaking the architect's design and creating a business plan for the property to send to Bran and Patrick. He stood so quickly that his office chair crashed to the floor. He was already dressed and only had to slip his feet into shoes on the way to the door. His phone dinged again as he stepped into the hallway.

Another message from MacGregor. To William and Hugh only.

Have your pilots on standby. Will need to be in the air as soon as suspect gives up women's location.

Hugh flew to the elevator, calling Bobby as he got in, barking instructions. His pilot knew what was happening and didn't waste time with questions.

"Understood, Sir. Notify me immediately with the destination. I'll have everything in order."

Hugh disconnected and called his mother. She'd only moved back to her apartment two days ago. He knew she and Tina were prepared for calls no matter the time. She answered on the first ring.

"Hugh," Mom answered breathlessly.

"They arrested the person behind all of this. Everyone is on their way to the police station. They're going to work on getting Rowan and Katy's location. I'll call you when I know something. Bobby's on standby." He heard his mother choke off a cry before yelling to Tina to grab her purse.

"I'm not waiting. I'll meet you there. Diana is calling me now. I love you, Son. We're getting our precious girl back."

Mom didn't sign off, just hung up, as determined as everyone in their family to see Rowan returned.

Lucy Pérez. A forty-five-year-old MIT graduate and disgruntled Stanton Industries employee was behind everything. The hacking, the kidnapping, and attempted extortion. MacGregor's team found one text, made eight months ago, sent from her phone to a person called Guilermo. Guilermo Pérez was her brother. Ex-military. He had gone on three missions with Shane Reynolds.

That single text was the nail in her coffin.

After six hours of interrogation, where the Stanton and O'Faolain families sat in tense silence in the police conference room, the woman finally confessed to her fury at being excluded from the team picked to work on the newest Government military project. Mrs. Stanton was supposed to be the only target, but then pictures of Stanton and Miss Byrne began circulating. She decided to hedge her bets and take them both.

The technology was so classified, William did not receive clearance to divulge any specifics to the police. The case did not hinge on the disclosure of the project. It was neither here nor there.

Hugh understood the secrecy of Stanton's project, and because that intel wouldn't help them find Rowan, he brushed it off. MacGregor, being a special forces vet, had no problem with the omission.

Lucy had hacked Stanton's system on three separate occasions with help from her Chinese conspirators.

Pérez used her vacation days right after she hacked into the system the final time to clean out her apartment. She sold or trashed her belongings, planning to take only what would fit in two checked bags and a carry-on.

Her deal with a Stanton Chinese competitor promised them the new tech in exchange for ten million dollars. She had overseas accounts set up to receive the tech files, a new bank account to route in her millions, and fake identities for herself and her brother. She planned on never stepping foot on American soil again.

She admitted that she'd planned on messaging Stanton Friday morning, this morning, with her demands. Her brother and Reynolds had driven cross country. They were supposed to have rented a house in Alabama and await instructions.

She hadn't been able to contact her brother for four days.

MacGregor cautioned patience. He was handling it with faster results than the police force could produce. His people went after the brother's IP address and found an address in Alabama that it had pinged at several times four days ago.

The day he went radio silent.

They were in the air an hour and a half later. Bre and Daniel were already onboard when, he, Bran, Patrick, Raven, River, Mom, Tina, and Detective Jeffreys boarded the O'Faolain jet headed to Huntsville, Alabama. Jeffreys was working with the Huntsville SWAT team who were currently moving people into the area surrounding the block and the house where they believed Rowan and Katy were being held.

The team would monitor the area and look for movement in the house and anyone coming or going before moving in. Pérez and Reynolds were dangerous and assumed armed. Hugh sat in his seat, looking at nothing. Not speaking, barely breathing. Rowan could easily be hurt if there was a standoff. If she wasn't already....

Rowan. Rowan. Rowan.

26

―――――

Rowan existed in daydreams and dread. She and Katy did their best to distract one another. They each drank their water and ate the protein bar. Slowly.

It felt like hours had passed since the men left. She used the pole to lean against. Her body was sore from lying flat on the concrete. She told Katy about her sisters and Nan and even Jo and Thomas. The Honey Bunny stories made them both laugh. She told her about Triskelion, about Dublin, and about her parents.

She explained that her sisters were married to Bran and Patrick O'Faolain and how they bought a four-story building next to their shop.

Katy snorted, a smile in her voice when she said, "And you're dating Hugh. Wow, you six must get some looks when you all go out together," she laughed. "Those boys were precious towheads with the sweetest smiles when they were little. I would see Hugh and the boys at the Club on occasion. He was a very proud father."

"He still is. My sisters and I are very lucky to have them in our lives."

Katy told Rowan about her children. What an amazing blessing being a mother was. That being a grandma was even better. "My granddaughter, Samantha, is a wonder. My son and his wife were only sophomores in college when they found out they were going to be parents.

"Good thing Ben takes after his father. He wrote out a life plan, from buying a ring to investigating the best high yield savings accounts for the baby. My daughter works for her dad too, but she's a gamer at heart," Katy chuckled. "World of Warcraft. WoW. Evelyn's team did well during the finals, and they'll be competing at the Arena World Championship. It's televised," Katy added proudly.

"Oh my God, Patrick will die when I tell him. He games once in a while with friends. I imagine when River has the baby, his gaming will diminish." Rowan shifted her back against the pole. Silence descended. Sharing fun stories and talking about their families had helped to lift some of the terrifying shroud.

Unfortunately, panic was a dirty film covering her body.

They couldn't pretend anymore. This situation was so much worse than just being held for ransom or whatever they wanted from William in exchange for giving them back. The possibility of not being given back, even if Will did do what they ask, was something she tried not to dwell on. The possibility of being physically hurt...raped...she couldn't set those thoughts aside. *My fears are valid, but* I *control them.* Her new mantra.

"I feel like it's been hours and hours. Surely even a strip club isn't open all night."

"The passage of time is damn hard to grasp when it's always dark. It does seem like they should have been back a long time ago."

"I was thinking that maybe they aren't coming back. Maybe the people looking for us figured out who they were. Maybe they knew they were about to be caught and ran," Rowan felt foolish for how hopeful she sounded, knowing it was likely not true.

Katy remained silent, perhaps thinking over her own wild speculations. "This Thomas MacGregor you told me about. You mentioned his security firm is the best. They even work closely with the FBI. Surely Hugh would have called him as soon as he found out you'd been taken. And since he was with your family for so many months because of that stalker, he'd be familiar with your family.

"He would take the case if Hugh asked. Right?" Katy asked. Hope creeping in her voice.

"No question." There was no way her family and the Stanton family, especially Diana Gaines, wouldn't throw every one of their resources into finding them.

"Our situation is dire, Katy, but never hopeless. Not with our families."

"Agreed."

She heard Katy's cuff clink. She must be trying for a more comfortable position. The cuff was digging into her wrist. It felt raw. The zip ties around her ankles were worse. Her skin felt swollen around the plastic strips. She'd worked her ankles more than once trying to ease the discomfort, the ties only bit into her skin worse.

"Once we're rescued, I bet William will be so thankful you're okay that he actually pulls his head out of his ass and listens to you."

Katy chuckled. "I won't hold my breath."

She'd told Rowan about her plan to make William jealous. How William only cared about his work. How she felt like a dummy when he spoke tech with his colleagues. She'd never felt like she was enough. After this, she knew Katy was one of the strongest and best of women. Perhaps William wasn't good enough for her if he didn't relook at their marriage after this.

"I have to pee," Katy whispered.

"Me too, damn it. Let's lay down and try to sleep. If they haven't come back by then, we'll have to...I don't know...figure out how to pee where we aren't sitting in it."

THE KIDNAPPERS NEVER CAME BACK. Days had to have passed. It felt like years. Rowan would cry, but her body was too dehydrated to waste any fluid on self-pity. She'd peed only once since the beginning of this nightmare. She and Katy slept, no guess as to how long, waking with bursting bladders and few choices of disposal at hand.

"I think we should scoot as far as the handcuff will let us toward the door where they came in. We only have underwear to pull down, thanks to those perverted bastards. We pee and scoot back to the pole as quick as we can."

At least they'd been too busy with the logistics of not peeing on themselves to be embarrassed.

Rowan was laying half around the pole, giving her cuff the most slack. Her wrist was painful and crusty. She'd felt liquid oozing around the metal bracelet a few times. It could be blood from broken scabs, or it could be puss from an infection. There was a three-inch swath of skin around her wrist that was hot and painful to touch. Most likely infection.

There were also the zip ties. Her lower calves were a never-ending cycle of discomfort. Okay, she knew she was lying to herself. It was way more than discomfort. Throbbing excruciating pain was a way more accurate description.

Katy moaned occasionally. Rowan heard them even though the other woman tried to muffle the sound.

"Shared pain lessens the burden. At least, that's what Nan

used to say. Though right now, I call bullshit. If I thought sharing would make me feel...less, I'd scream at the top of my lungs." Katy snorted in tired amusement. They'd tried the screaming bit, hoping someone might hear.

It managed to make their throats dryer and dishearten them further. It felt like they were in the belly of a soundproofed beast. The concrete floor would eventually soak up every last drop of their humanity until someday, someone would find nothing but bones and her frayed thong.

Rowan would have laughed at her morbid grossness if she had the energy. "I don't think it's been as long as we think, Kat." They'd picked the nickname for Katy after Rowan explained that she and her sisters shortened their names.

"I'm sure you're right. I know you're right," she amended. "I keep telling myself that no matter how long it's been, Will and Hugh will find us. I know they will."

Another round of silence. Rowan found silence held the perfect ingredient for negative thoughts to grow. She'd already daydreamed that Daniel was grown up and looking at pictures of his Auntie Row. Who he never knew. Not a road to stroll for long.

"I haven't seen much of it, but your hair is stunning. I've always thought redheads won the beauty lottery."

Katy chuckled, appreciating the distraction. "My father had red hair, which is funny because I was adopted."

"I bet you your parents saw your red fuzzy head and fell in love."

"Parent. It's always been just Dad. He never wanted a wife. That would have cut down on his traveling and affairs," she fondly mused. "My father is from old money, excuse the snobbery but since we're currently handcuffed in a basement, and I'm almost positive I have urine dried on my feet, I'm not retracting the Society reference."

"Instead of people talking dirty, we're dirty people talking," Rowan quipped.

"Exactly. So, my father was wonderful, well, technically, he's still wonderful, and I visit him often. He has advanced dementia and lives in a great assisted living community with the best care. He remembers me sometimes. Those are the best days.

"He doesn't know William and I are divorced. Will still visits Dad every week," Katy added with a slight catch in her voice. "Anyway, his hair is silver with hints of strawberry these days. I hope I haven't missed one of his good days. I think that would devastate me more than peeing on myself."

"You know, when we get out of here, I'm going to insist that you come to Dublin for a visit. My sister, River, is due with her first child on October 25th. Maybe you would consider bringing your family and celebrating Thanksgiving with the O'Faolains and the Byrnes. You'd be able to meet River's new baby and Raven's son, Daniel."

When Katy didn't answer right away, Rowan figured she was mulling over the offer, but when she heard the soft hiccupping cries, she dragged herself up into a sitting position—not that elevation helped her see the other woman.

"Tell me what's wrong."

"Forgive me. I'm a middle-aged emotional wreck. It's only your invitation to visit. To spend Thanksgiving...oh my...I mean, I would love it. The last couple of years since we divorced, well, the holidays have been really, really hard. I'm always invited to family things, but going from a wife to a guest is—"

"—worse than pissing down your leg," Rowan finished.

"Oh yes. Much worse. Last Thanksgiving, I forgot myself and started to cut the pies. William told me the chef would take care of it. If a person could get third-degree burns from blushing and humiliation, I would have spent the afternoon in the emergency room."

"I understand why you didn't force William to hear your truth...then, but now, after this...Surely, you're strong enough to demand your due. I believe that once he hears you, he'll be begging for your forgiveness." Because if he wasn't begging, Rowan thought, if that man didn't grovel at this woman's feet after this, Rowan would be paying that blockheaded imbecile a visit.

Silence cocooned the basement...lost in dreary thoughts again. Damn. "Let's take a nap. If we wake up to the same shit show, I'm going to work on getting my wrist free. If I can get free, I won't need my feet to scoot."

"You can't. If your cuff is as tight as mine, it's impossible."

"Not impossible. Freedom is the perfect motivation. Sleep for now. I'll keep my wrist flush to the floor to help numb it a bit." Katy didn't answer. Clearly not in agreement but accepting she had no better ideas.

Rowan was only able to sleep fitfully. Her feet were throbbing. She no longer ran her free hand over the ties. The bloated skin and...wet...stirred panic. It was time to try and get her hand free. She had to try while she still had the energy.

The kidnappers were MIA—a blessing and a curse. She had to try. She didn't need her feet, only her hands.

She began by twisting her wrist over and over again, trying to muffle her moans so she didn't wake Katy. She assumed it was blood and puss wetting the cold metal and her hot skin. She spun on her back and braced her feet against the post for leverage.

She didn't give herself time to second guess. She grabbed the cuff with her free hand, aligning her bound hand and then she pushed herself backward with her feet. An involuntary scream rent the dark.

She felt her skin tearing. The pain would be worth it if she got free. Katy's voice screaming at her to stop registered between her own screams. When her back dropped to the floor in a spine-bruising collapse, Rowan cried. Bawled. Wailed. It wasn't from the pain. It was from the failure.

"It didn't work. Oh, God," Rowan cried. "It didn't work."

27

Hugh's phone dinged a message from MacGregor as they descended toward the runway.

Call.

As he dialed, he looked to Raven and River, who were both staring at him with identical looks of fear and put the call on speaker. MacGregor answered on the first ring.

"I sent an address to Jeffreys. The hospital where Rowan and Mrs. Stanton will be transported." The detective looked at his phone and nodded. "Less than an hour ago, Pérez and Reynolds' names popped up. They were in a fatal drunk driving accident Sunday night, killing themselves and the man driving the other car."

Hugh wanted to ask a thousand questions. He refused to interrupt.

"Jeffreys," MacGregor continued, "I spoke to your partner at the department, and she notified Huntsville's SWAT unit that the house should be clear of threat but to still proceed as though it's hot. They moved on the house minutes ago. Dean is speaking with Stanton now." He hesitated.

MacGregor doesn't hesitate. Hugh looked at his sons, both deathly white. Raven and River swayed in their seats. "Tina, please go tell Bobby that we need this plane landed now, and my goddamn cars better be waiting." She took off like a fired bullet. He glanced at his mom. She had a death grip on her chair. "What else, MacGregor?"

"I received an update minutes ago. They are waiting for bolt cutters to be delivered. Rowan and Mrs. Stanton are cuffed to metal poles in the basement. Rowan tried to pull her hand free. She has torn her skin down to the bone in several places, and the wounds are infected. They are dehydrated but awake and able to answer questions." He hesitated again.

"They were stripped to their bras and underwear and held in a completely blacked-out basement. They were drugged several times. Their feet are bound in several zip ties. The plastic has dug into their flesh. They won't remove them until they reach the hospital so they can numb the area."

Stunned silence filled the plane. Raven and River got out of their seats, shaking their husband's hands away and knelt at Hugh's feet.

Raven grabbed Hugh's wrist and brought the phone close. "Thomas," she whimpered, "Thomas. Tell me...was she...was our sister—"

"Hurt in any...other way?" River finished.

"Unless she didn't want to say, lass, she said no," MacGregor answered in a gentle Scottish brogue. "She's terrified and hurting...but, no, not that way I think. She told an officer on the scene that the big guy, she meant Reynolds, told her that he wasn't giving her back. James told me that Jo's pilot rerouted her plane to Huntsville."

The landing gear hit the tarmac. Hugh ended the call without a goodbye. He couldn't speak. His throat was too tight.

It was a matter of ticking things off in his mind to ignore the rage begging to be unleashed—to hold in the scream.

He stared again at nothing. He looked at no one. He spoke to no one. He didn't even have his beard to hide behind.

He clasped his hands together so the urge to destroy the plane's interior couldn't manifest. He just kept repeating the steps required to reach her.

Land. Disembark. SUV. Hospital. Rowan.
Land. Disembark. SUV. Hospital. Rowan.
Land. Disembark. SUV. Hospital. Rowan.

THEY GOT to the hospital before Rowan. Jeffreys was on the phone with Huntsville police, but everyone else, Stanton's family, a subdued Diana Gaines included, was standing outside the emergency room entrance waiting for the ambulances to arrive.

No one spoke. Bran and Patrick flanked his sides. Raven and River stood slightly apart, holding hands, tears rolling steadily down their cheeks. He imagined his sons wanted to comfort their wives. They understood that neither would find comfort until they laid eyes on their sister.

Someone behind him gasped, jerking Hugh's head up to scan his surroundings. Two ambulances, lights on but sirens off, were pulling into the emergency vehicle-only drive. No siren was good. Sirens meant emergency. He felt a hand land on his shoulder. Whichever boy it was thought he needed the support. They were right. He needed it. Badly.

He couldn't rush her. He knew she would need her sisters more than him right now. He understood. He would wait.

The ambulances parked side by side, the first door opened, and a bed was wheeled out. Cries of Mom were shouted. Katy looked weary and drawn. A wobbly smile brushed her lips.

"Oh, my babies," she cried.

The EMTs rolling her gurney slowed as her children ran to give their mom light kisses on her cheeks. They were probably afraid of touching her somewhere tender and hurting her. He glanced at Stanton, who stood still as a statue. He looked relieved and devastated at once. He didn't approach his ex-wife. It was clear he desperately wanted to.

And then the second ambulance finally opened. Hugh crossed his arms over his chest, locking his joints so he didn't fall to his knees. There she was, looking so tiny. A light sheet covered her body. Her bare arms rested on top of the sheet. An IV ran from one, and light gauze wrapped the opposite hand...a metal chain snaked its way between the wrapping. A bastardized version of freedom.

He held still as Raven and River ran to her side, causing her EMTs to stop just as Katy's had. He, Bran, and Patrick watched the women they loved reunite. It was beautiful and painful in the same breath.

None of them spoke. They just looked at each other. Rowan was the first to move. She touched her fingers to Raven's cheek, then lifted the hand wrapped in gauze—the one still sporting her handcuff and touched River's. Her wince at moving her obviously wounded hand had Hugh taking a step forward, ready to intervene.

Bran and Pat grabbed his arms.

"Wait," Bran demanded.

"They need this," Patrick added.

He exhaled and shook his boys' hands off. He would wait.

Raven touched Rowan's cheek. River did the same. They were a triumvirate of absolute, pure love. After a moment, Rowan let her hands rest back by her sides, giving her sisters a small nod.

"I love you. I'll see you soon," Rowan assured them.

"I love you."

"I love you."

They backed away from Rowen, and the gurney started its forward momentum toward the motion-activated glass doors leading into the hospital. He couldn't see Rowan's face. An EMT was blocking her upper body. She was speaking…arguing? He heard his name spoken in an urgent whisper.

Before his brain fully comprehended what his body intended, he lunged toward the gurney, startling the EMTs and causing them to stop once more.

He stared at her. She stared at him. He expected her to look broken. She looked fierce. Brave. Strong.

"Row," he managed to choke out.

Her breath hitched. They both were crying silent tears at seeing each other again. "I love you, baby. Go now, and let the doctors make you better. I'll be waiting."

She only nodded, a tear dripping from her jaw. He bent and placed a soft kiss on her lips, one of his tears dropping to her cheek.

She moved her mouth to his ear and whispered, "There was not one second of one moment that I didn't hold your love close and take comfort from it. Don't be a bear while I'm getting fixed and tell my sisters I want them to give me a shower."

He could only nod in affirmation. If she wanted it, she would have it. He stepped back and let the EMTs take her away. He wrapped his arm around his mother's shoulders when she came to stand next to him.

She squeezed his waist tightly, her small body shivering with strong emotion. "What can I do?"

He knew his mother, and she would feel better if she had a job, so he gave her one. "Find Diana. I want both women moved to an offsite care facility with round-the-clock nurses and room for the families until they're well enough to go home. Surely, there are plastic surgery recovery facilities for the wealthy in a city this size. The doctors will insist they stay in the hospital. Insist otherwise."

Mom straightened from leaning against her son, ran her hand down her navy silk blouse, and buttoned her white blazer. A woman on a mission. Hugh suppressed a smile.

"Girls," Mom turned to Raven and River, who looked as deflated as twenty-day-old birthday balloons. "I need you both." Hugh was pleased to see some life come back to his daughters-in-law. They straightened from leaning against each other and their husbands.

"River, my sweet girl, I need you to research the best, the very best recovery facilities with 24-hour nursing care. Rowan isn't going to have one more night of being uncomfortable." At River's raised brow, Mom added, "Hugh suggested a posh plastic surgery facility."

River's eyes brightened instantly, pulling her phone from her purse. "On it."

"There needs to be plenty of room for family. We'll want rooms for Bre and Daniel."

River barely nodded as she grabbed Patrick's hand and walked them over to an outside bench. "As soon as Pat and I lock down the location, I'll send the details in a group message."

"While River works on that, Raven, you and I need to find Diana. She'll help us convince the hospital of the necessary change of address."

Raven quickly kissed Bran, dropping his hand, which she had previously been holding like a lifeline, and walked to Hugh's mother. "This will be right up your best friend's alley, Tilly. Let's go." She turned to look at Hugh before disappearing inside the hospital. "Send a car back to the plane, please. Riv and I packed up all of Rowan's things from your mom's. She'll feel better for having the bag Mom made her. It has all her personal items and makeup."

His mother wasn't the only one who appreciated having a helpful task. "Consider it done."

"Oh, and Hugh," Raven got his attention again. Sharing a smile with River. The first smile he'd seen from them in days. "The brown leather tote has the stuff from Row's nightstand."

Hugh raised an eyebrow at her announcement. He would look, of course.

"Tina packed those boxes sitting on your bar," the jewelry for Rowan, "and your five boxes of condoms," his mother added helpfully.

Hugh's arm froze in the act of calling Bobby, their pilot. Embarrassment burned up his neck and into his cheeks. He refused to acknowledge the comment.

Rowan was back. Everything else was white noise, there but easily ignored. He'd take sex jokes from Diana Gaines without batting an eye at this point.

Mom, Raven, and River came through...and Diana, damn it. She acted like it was all her idea. River found a rehabilitating facility that was fully staffed with medical personnel, which was why the hospital released her. It had long-term family lodging. Stanton was extremely thankful.

Tina and Bre, after the assistant/nanny handed Daniel back into his mother's arms, took charge of designating rooms and making sure the luggage was distributed accordingly. Josephine O'Connor arrived a few hours before Rowan was released to the rehab facility.

Jo, Raven, River, and Rowan cried and laughed, hugged, and kissed, and generally made a spectacle. Without a beard,

Hugh didn't have a chance in hell of hiding how much joy the scene gave him.

Rowan had damaged her hand pretty severely trying to slide the cuff off. Hugh didn't want to consider the desperation she must have felt to do something like that to herself. The wounds had been treated and dressed. The doctor liberally numbed her lower legs before cutting off the zip ties. Again, those wounds were cleaned and dressed. The nurses at the after-care facility were given care instructions and had schedules to change her dressings and administer pain medicine as needed.

It was now eight in the evening. He gave Rowan space to talk with everyone and to call Bébhinn. Her grandmother had been sick with worry. Now, she was closed in with Katy. Katy's nurse had rolled her wheelchair into Rowan's room forty-five minutes ago. Their legs were too tender to hold weight just yet, which crushed him to even think about. He and William were pacing outside the door.

"Becky, my nurse told me that with the antibiotic cream and leg massages, I'll still be sore, but I should be able to walk by tomorrow without too much discomfort. The swelling is almost gone. What did they tell you?" Rowan asked.

"Almost the same. I'm still pretty swollen, but that's probably due to my age. It was so good to hug and kiss my children, Row. I can't even describe it. Ben held my hand like he used to when he was a little boy. Evelyn wouldn't stop crying until I told her how I peed on one of my legs and feet," she snorted in amusement.

"Then the three of us were laughing. I told them no more tears. The percentage of people getting kidnapped twice was extremely low." In a change of subject, she asked, "How is Hugh holding up. He never struck me as a particularly patient man. I'm surprised he isn't in here."

Rowan was still giggling about the pee. "It was almost a blessing we were dehydrated. I couldn't imagine experiencing that again," she admitted, shaking her head. "He's grumpily perfect, isn't he? Trust me, he'll be the next person through that door and the last until morning if I have anything to say about it."

"Oh, I almost forgot, your sisters came to see me. Did you tell them about what happened between William and me?"

Katy didn't seem angry, just curious.

"They asked if you knew about us going on a few dates. I told them you knew everything. I did *not* tell them anything personal you shared with me. I promise. But," Rowan couldn't help but smirk, "I did tell them that William must be the dumbest man alive to have let you go."

She snorted at that, a blush tinting her pale cheeks. "When Raven and River came to my room, my kids were there, and I believe Will was still lurking outside the door. They told Ben and Evelyn that you said I was doing Thanksgiving in Dublin this year with your family, and they would love it if they would come too.

"I will preface their reaction by reiterating how devastating the last couple of years have been, enduring the holidays as the *ex*-wife. They didn't mean to, but they acted differently. I guess they were unsure. I felt out of place and...unnecessary. So, I was thrilled when both kids immediately said they'd be thrilled to join.

"There was a loud crash in the hallway. I think William may have thrown a chair," she huffed in amazement. "The kids acted like they didn't hear it. I feel ashamed to have thought this of my children, but...I never believed they would pick me over William. It meant everything."

Rowan reached over and took Katy's hand between her own, squeezing in understanding. "I'm glad they know what a treasure you are. Will's directed your path for long enough. It's time to take charge of your life. You should never feel second best, Kat. Plus, you promised to bring me samples of your woven wool table mats.

"Our customers want custom everything. Bring me product, and I'll bring you customers," Rowan assured. One of the gazillion topics she and Katy had discussed when they were in the basement was her dream of starting a small business, starting with her woven table mats.

"I know I spoke with your sisters, but how are they doing now that you're back? They seemed great, but they were united in making William squirm, so it could have been false cheer," she grinned, letting Rowan know she'd enjoyed her sisters' antics immensely. "I know you are very close."

"Raven and River...they...we," she paused, trying to explain in a way that would make sense to Katy, "love one another so deeply, we're so damn close that sometimes it feels like we're the same person. When one of us is hurting, we all hurt.

"We do our own things and have our own relationships, but our cores, I guess, are inseparable. Raven is a new mother, and Riv is seven months pregnant. Emotions are running high in the Byrne circle," she snorted and rolled her eyes.

"Mentally, I feel pretty good. I'm tired and sore, but we're safe and with family, and I don't care if I sound like a princess, but I'm damn happy to be sleeping in an actual bed tonight."

"Well, you are old money, dear," Rowan teased, and Katy pretended to swat her leg. "I almost cried when Raven washed my hair, so yeah, no judgment zone here. Change of subject, but have you spoken with Will? At all?"

Katy twisted her shoulder-length red hair several times around her finger before blowing out a deep breath, and her head dropped back to the top of her wheelchair. She let out a moan and admitted, "Not one word. Nothing. Flipping nothing!"

"Jesus! What a jackass, and yet...he's stalking you like a tiger with his first boner."

Katy's head was still tilted back, and when she laughed, it turned into a choke and coughing fit. She was now bent forward, her forehead touching Rowan's mattress, wheezing in laughter.

"I'm not wrong. My sisters are nothing if not informative, and I have it on good authority that Auntie Diana called William a twat when he wouldn't go into your room."

They giggled uncontrollably at that tidbit. Once their mirth receded, they looked at one another, no words, just simple contemplation with their partner in terror. It's funny how shared fear can bind. Rowan understood that she and Katy were inexplicably connected. Humans can't survive such a harrowing experience together without creating an unbreakable bond.

"I wonder if I should tell Hugh that those men took us to the restroom while we were drugged. That I'm worried they touched us. That I'm worried they did more." Rowan swallowed the lump lodged in her throat. "I woke up once, and my bra was below my breasts. I didn't remember that until a few hours ago."

"Between the drugs and our fear, I imagine our brain is trying to blur the edges of what happened." Katy leaned her head back once more, contemplating the ceiling in all its white wonder before continuing. "If William and I were together, I would tell him. Your fears are yours to share and his to bear, and vice versa. Let him take those fears and crush them. No matter what, Row, never forget those cowardly pieces of shit are dead. They can't hurt us or anyone else ever again."

Rowan felt fat tears slip down her cheeks. All truth. It was strange to feel so shaky and out of sorts now that she was safe.

"Here, help me up," Katy said as she leaned forward and held her hand out for her to grab. "I'm tired of being in this chair. Let me lay by you for a few minutes before I go find my own bed."

Rowan was already sitting up in bed, so she scooched over and fluffed two pillows for Katy to lean against.

"Ahhh, much better. My bony ass is going to be bruised forever from sitting on that darn concrete floor."

Rowan knew Katy was trying to give her comfort and ease her moment of anxiety. She knew that imagining scenarios that may or may not have happened wasn't going to help her heal mentally or physically.

She would give her fears to Hugh, and he *would* burn them to the ground. With that decision made, Rowan felt her heart slow and peace settle more easily on her shoulders. At least the police took their statements while they were still at the hospital, and they said they didn't believe they would need anything further. No trial meant no testimonies. *Thank God.*

"Plus," she added, patting Rowan's leg, "it feels nice to have a snuggle bunny after one of those dratted kidnappings."

She laughed. Laughing was so much better than crying. With Katy's wacky sense of humor and Jo's irreverence, she knew those two would become fast friends once they met tomorrow.

"Oh, I plan on having a snuggle partner tonight. I wouldn't call Hugh a bunny, though."

"Badger?" Katy suggested.

"Grizzly. He's all big paws and growls." She grinned at Katy's sputtering laugh. "Have you considered a broody, tech-obsessed dingleberry to snuggle with?"

"Did you just liken William to a dingleberry? Oh my God, I wish someone had recorded that so I could listen to it every time he ignores me. Seriously though, I doubt snuggling is in the cards. He hasn't looked me in the eyes for two years," she sighed.

Rowan sighed too. "Life would be so much easier if men were as relationship savvy as women."

"I have to pee," Katy whined.

"Oh God, me too. Do you think if we leaned on each other, we could hobble to the bathroom?"

"Here's a better idea. I slide back into the wheelchair, and you sit on my lap, and I *wheel* us to the bathroom."

"Ahh, the brains of this group, I see. Fine. Hurry though, all those IV fluids at the hospital have made this a 911 situation." With a bit of rolling and twisting, Katy settled in the chair. Rowan had just placed her hands on the chair's armrest and was pushing off the bed when they both realized at the same time that the chair brake wasn't engaged.

As the chair made an abrupt reverse, Rowan was dragged partially off the bed. Unfortunately, Katy sat forward to grab onto Rowan's shoulders, which tipped the chair forward. Katy fell to the ground, pulling Rowan the rest of the way off the bed and onto the floor beside her.

They looked at each other from their now prone positions and burst out laughing. "So help me God, if I pee on myself again, I will never forgive you," Katy gasped out between hysterical shrieks.

The door burst open, and Hugh and William looked like they were fighting each other over who got to go through the door first, cursing and elbowing. Hugh won. They stopped abruptly when they saw her and Katy lying on the floor with giant smiles on their faces.

Katy broke the silence. "I see a Grizzly."

"I see a DG." At the reminder of the whole dingleberry comment, a fresh round of giggles assailed the two floor huggers.

"Row?" Hugh's concern instantly sobered her.

"I'm fine, babe. Honest. We needed to go to the bathroom and decided to try to make it on our own. We fell off the bed—"

"You. *You* fell off the bed," Katy interrupted.

"Since you and I are both on the floor, your correction is noted and discarded. Hugh, please help us up." He looked grim-faced. His go-to look when he was feeling...well, anything. She was about to put his mind at ease when her Becky rushed in.

28

___

5 MINUTES EARLIER

"**K**aty should already be in bed," Stanton repeated for maybe the fifteenth time.

"Maybe she and Rowan needed to talk some things out. Have you fucking thought of that?" Hugh was on edge himself. He needed to hold Rowan against his chest and feel their hearts beat against one another. He needed the reminder that she was safe.

"Yes, I have, actually, asshole. I just...she hasn't...Jesus, she hasn't spoken one word to me," he admitted, looking crushed.

"Think about it from her end. I understand you didn't know she hadn't truly cheated on you, but you admitted you divorced her without ever talking to her. You never asked her *why*. She knew she hadn't really cheated, but she also knows you didn't love her enough to find out why she might have."

Stanton took Hugh's words and swallowed them. He didn't deny them or make excuses. He sat heavily on one of the chairs in the hallway outside Rowan's room, where they'd been camped out for a while now.

"I know you're right. Until this whole kidnapping thing

happened, and because of my fucking work, I didn't realize, or I didn't let myself realize, how badly I took her for granted. She was someone I loved and that I always felt would be there. Had she really cheated, there would have been no one to blame but myself.

"And yet, even after the divorce, I still felt like she was my wife, and even though I threw her away, I still wanted her to acknowledge that she's mine. She never dated after the divorce. Not that I know of, anyway. Christ, what if she did? Rowan was the first woman I was serious about, but even then—"

Hugh cut him off. "Don't." He couldn't elaborate more. His jaw was on lockdown, and his fists were clenched. Another man casually discussing dating Rowan didn't work for him. Between Delton shooting her and this kidnapping, Hugh was feeling on edge, unbalanced, and volatile.

"Right," William grimaced. "I just wish I knew if I had a chance of getting her back."

"Have you considered talking to her instead of skulking outside her room? Yes, before you ask, everyone has noticed. My boys told me she accepted an invitation to Dublin for the holidays, and your kids did, too."

"I heard that," he groaned, tipping his head back to rest against a wall.

"Are you going to do anything about it? Rowan could have died twice this year. If I had lost her...I would have had to live with knowing she'd died thinking I didn't love her...what would my pride have gotten me? I'll tell you where—alone and full of regrets."

Stanton rubbed his hands over his face several times. "Do you know I'm considered a genius in some circles? But look at me...I'm a complete idiot. Katy is—"

His epiphany was cut short by a loud thud and groans

coming from inside Rowan's room. Both men lunged for the door, the handle slipped through Hugh's grasp as Stanton plowed into him from behind. He finally got the handle turned, shoving the other man against the door jamb.

"Move, you moron."

"Screw you, O'Faolain."

Stanton elbowed him hard in the side as Hugh slipped through the door first, only to see Rowan giggling on the floor.

Both men came to a sliding stop. The women they loved looked to be enjoying themselves. Immensely. Flat on their backs with a wheelchair tipped over beside them.

"Row?" He hated to interrupt the two women having fun. After what they'd survived together, they needed to decompress, but they were...on the floor. She was supposed to be recuperating and relaxing.

One of Rowan's nurses rushed in. Hugh was relieved to have someone with medical authority join what was clearly the opposite of rehabilitation going on.

"Miss Byrne," the nurse gasped, "what happened? Are you hurt?"

"No Becky, please don't worry yourself. Both Mrs. Stan—or rather, Ms. Blake and I needed to use the restroom and had a small tumble. Kat is embarrassingly clumsy," Rowan grimaced in faux concern.

"Ms. Blake?" Stanton asked.

Offended Without a Cause, Hugh inwardly sighed.

"*I'm* clumsy? Really?"

"Can we admit that peeing 'in the wild' isn't your strong suit?"

Rowan air quoted 'in the wild,' causing Katy to gasp and lightly kick Rowan in the shin. Katy must have forgotten they were still injured because, even though the teasing kick was meant as a joke, it hurt them both. Each woman sucked in a pain-filled breath. The nurse tried to get to them, but he and Stanton had the women scooped up and off the floor before Nurse Becky could take a knee.

The nurse righted the wheelchair and smoothed her uniform, attempting to bring order to the chaos. She told Rowan she would help her to the restroom.

"I also want to change the dressing on your wrist and work on your lower legs." Turning to Katy, she told her that her nurse should be coming for her in a moment.

"Please put me in the chair, William. Tammy can take me to my room."

"You don't need the chair, Kate." His ex-wife raised her brows in surprise at her old, but still beloved, nickname. "I can take you myself."

Hugh noted that Rowan didn't say anything to help Katy out of the awkward situation. She surely had her reasons, so he decided to stay silent as well.

"The chair. Now."

Becky's eyes were wide as saucers, but she was clearly a professional. "Mr. O'Faolain, if you could take Miss Byrne to the en-suite bath and set her on the bench closest to the, uh, toilet, that would be a great help. I will let you know when we're finished, and you can carry her back to bed."

Hugh shifted Rowan in his arms so he could look directly into her face. He quietly asked, "Will you let me stay with you?"

She cupped his face with her uninjured hand, leaning in enough to place her lips to his. "Only you," she promised.

Hugh tightened his hold. "I love you." As he straightened to follow the nurse into the bathroom, he was surprised to see William and Katy watching them. Honestly, he forgot they were still there.

"Do you need me?" Rowan asked Katy.

Katy was about to answer when her nurse walked in. "Oh, Tammy. Thank you for coming. If you could take me back to my room, I would appreciate it."

"Of course, Ms. Blake. I want to try a different massage tonight and see if we can get rid of the last of that pesky swelling. I've requested that Dr. Davidson stop by in the morning. I hope you don't mind, but some of the cuts above your ankles are quite deep. I don't want to take any chances of infection."

"Of course. I appreciate you being so diligent. I'm ready to go to my room."

Hugh was pretty sure she'd said that already, but the jackass Stanton was still holding her tight to his chest.

"I'm carrying you. I already said I would."

Did Hugh make this big of an ass of himself over Rowan? *Probably.*

"Since I'm quite used to you treating me like an unwanted guest for the past two years, you'll forgive me if I tell you that I don't give a *shit* about what you want anymore."

Hugh walked at a snail's pace so Rowan wouldn't miss any of Stanton verbally hitting himself in the face.

Shocking the room, William angrily retorted, "You don't have to give a shit, Kate, but I do. *I* give a shit. About you. About us. I'm not going to leave you alone."

"Your attention will wander like it always has. You'll forget about me the moment something more interesting crosses in front of you. I've always been an afterthought. What I've been through the past few days made me realize that I deserve better." Katy sighed and looked at Rowan. "Please, go let Becky take care of your hand and legs, Row. I'll see you tomorrow."

William ignored everyone in the room except for the woman in his arms. Hugh could appreciate that.

"You're right. I've been a selfish idiot, and that's why I

quit. I told Dad and the kids yesterday. I have a few projects to sign off on, then I'm done. We have more than enough competent employees to run Stanton Industries. I plan on putting you first, which is what I should have been doing all these years."

Katy's eyes rounded at the news. "What do you mean you quit? It's *your* company."

"Technically, it's Dad's. Having you taken, kidnapped, stuffed into the trunk of a car, starved, and scared..." he swallowed thickly, "changed how I think. Now, I plan on carrying you to your room. You can kick me out then if you wish." He looked at Nurse Tammy before he walked out and added, "Please bring *Mrs. Stanton's* wheelchair."

With that mic drop, the Stantons and their nurse left. One more to go until he was alone with Rowan. Thank God.

Rowan was flagging. By the time Becky poked her head out of the bathroom to help carry Rowan to bed, another hour had passed. She was always small, but this past week had taken a heavy toll. She looked fragile, and of all the Byrne sisters, Rowan was the least fragile of the bunch.

Once she was tucked in, he dimmed the lights as low as they would go and pulled a chair up next to her side of the bed. She'd done nothing but watch him so far. Now, as he settled himself on the chair, his thigh lengthwise to the mattress, he watched her watching him.

"I thought you wanted to stay with me tonight. Just us. Did you change your mind?"

"I'm not leaving you." He watched Rowan pick at her blanket, fidgeting in a way that was not usual for this levelheaded Byrne. "Are you feeling okay? Do you need Becky?"

"No. I...no."

"Rowan," he growled. She was keeping something from him. "Tell me."

"Take your clothes off and get in bed first," she countered.

"I don't want to take the chance of hurting you, baby." He took her hand and brought it to his mouth, kissing her palm.

Her answer was to sit up and pull her t-shirt off, leaving her bare-breasted and in simple, white cotton panties. He gripped his knees to stop himself from touching what he shouldn't.

"Clothes off. Lights off. In bed." At his frown, she added, "Please."

When he stood, towering over her, he could tell by the way her eyes tracked over his body that she wanted more from him tonight than comfort. He felt his dick twitch, remembering their last night together. Their only night together.

He pressed his palm against the seam of his jeans, causing him to hiss in the pleasure and pain of having her eyes boldly watching. She restlessly pulled the sheet from the rest of her legs, and that's when he got his first full view of her lower legs.

His body's wants were forgotten. He gently took one of her feet and lifted her leg. Up until now, they'd been lightly wrapped. He swallowed the lump in his throat. He didn't want her to have to deal with his emotions on top of healing her own. But Christ, starting below her ankles to halfway up her shins were circular welts and thin new scabs. Every bit was bruised, all purples and deep blues.

He took immense satisfaction knowing the men responsible for this were dead.

"How badly are you hurting?" he asked, gently replacing her leg on the bed.

Rowan watched him for a beat before answering. "It looks much worse than it feels. Can you help me with something?"

"Anything." He should have known what was coming by the look in her eyes. "Take my panties off." She held up her bandaged hand. "This thing makes getting undressed such a chore."

"Does it?"

"Yes. You'll help an injured woman out, surely?"

If she didn't want to dwell on her injuries, then he would make sure she had something else to focus on.

29

Thank goodness Hugh finally realized that just doing as she wanted was the easiest path, the only path really, to making her happy tonight. The lights were very dim. She'd thought of having him turn them completely off before he got in bed, but having spent days in a pitch-black basement, the soft lights were soothing. An added bonus was being able to see Hugh.

A well-dressed Hugh was delicious. A naked Hugh was perfection. "I've changed my mind about the lights. They can stay on." He'd just hooked his thumbs into her panties when she added her light preference addendum. He paused, his body leaning partially over hers, and met her eyes.

Her stomach flipped at the almost brutal beauty of his face. She still wasn't used to seeing him this way. The beardless, smooth planes of his face took her breath. His sharp, defined cheekbones and sensual lips were stunning. His dark eyes had always smoldered. They scared most people shitless. When they were trained on her, like they were now, her body was at his beck and call.

Without a word, he resumed gliding her panties down her

hips and thighs, taking extra care around her bruises before slipping them free.

Naked, she settled back on the pillow, purposefully arching her back in invitation. "You're still dressed. I would help but..." she shrugged, all 'what's a gal to do', holding up her wrapped hand again. "Looks like I get to enjoy a striptease."

"Looks like it," he said, his hard stare only wavering when he slowly pulled the soft tan t-shirt over his head before toeing off his shoes and socks.

Rowan sucked in a breath at the sculpted upper body now revealed. Honestly, it still felt impossible that she could not only look her fill but *touch* him as she pleased. It was a heady, powerful feeling. He was back to watching her, serious and quiet.

She knew that he liked how much she loved his body. He worked hard for his powerful physique. It would be a sin not to worship it. She lifted her head and leaned back on her elbows. A much better position to watch Hugh unbutton his jeans.

They were loose on his hips, and once the zipper started to slide down, his jeans slipped low. She had to swallow a moan as his boxer briefs barely contained his hardened length. He let the jeans drop to the floor, stepping out of the denim. She took in his powerful thighs and calves. Even his feet were sexy.

Rowan raised her brow, letting him know he wasn't quite finished. He didn't perform the unspoken request. Instead, he moved closer to her side, and before she realized his intent, he scooped her up, cradling her to his chest before sitting on the edge of the bed.

"I want you to tell me what's been bothering you besides the obvious. You've avoided being alone with me. You've seemed happy, but there are times when you look...pensive, for lack of a better word. Tell me, Row."

Raven and River had asked her if she needed to talk about

anything with them. They were gentle and didn't push, but they could tell Rowan might have omitted a few things about the kidnapping. And in all honesty, some of those things were only now surfacing. She wished they wouldn't.

She sighed and leaned her head against Hugh's solid chest. "Katy told me that my fears are mine to share and yours to bear and vice versa. She told me to give them to you and let you crush them." The palm of his hand cupped the back of her head and tilted her face to match his. He gave her the sweetest kiss.

"Give them to me," he quietly demanded.

So, she did. She told him about the big man's threats, her terror, her helplessness, her fear that they wouldn't be found. She told him that the man never planned on letting her go, even if William gave his boss what they wanted, and Katy was returned. She admitted that she'd remembered a few things this afternoon that made her sick.

After telling him about her bra being down, she admitted, "My nipples felt tender but...but one explanation could be that I was dirty and had been lying on a concrete floor. Another explanation could be that I was still sensitive from you, from the night before I was taken. The truth is, I won't ever know everything. I really hate thinking that another man may have touched me. A man that wasn't you."

"God, baby," he whispered against her head, "you're so brave. Christ, Row, I'm humbled by how brave you are."

"Katy and I chose to get rape tests at the hospital, though they said anything over two days wasn't that accurate. However, during the examination, they said I didn't appear...hurt." Hugh's body shuddered beneath hers. "In all honesty, I never felt that I had been touched down there. More than likely, he didn't even touch my breasts other than pulling my top down.

"I think it was to make me fear what was coming. The last time we saw them, he said they were going to a strip club, and would get ideas for what they would want to do to us when they got back. He was very calculating in what he said and did to keep us scared." Even though she knew it had been hard for Hugh to hear, that it had burdened him too, Katy was right, she did feel better.

"You know, even though this past week was horrible, Katy and I found ways to make each other laugh—even when she got some pee on her leg. It's amazing how something as simple as a laugh can give someone hope. We talked about everything and nothing. I wanted you to know that it wasn't all terror. I did have someone. I was never alone. It helped me to know that, so I figured it would help you to know that too.

"When they never came back, our fear became less about what they might do to us and more about whether we'd be found in time. We knew you and William would never stop looking. It just became a matter of...well, time."

"I would never have stopped. I refused to ever let myself think that you might not be found. What life would be like without you in it."

"Do you wish I wouldn't have told you the stuff about the men?"

"Never. We both share your fears and doubts now. When you need me, I'll know why, and I will always be there for you. I'm glad that you were examined and that your mind was at least put at ease as much as it can be. With the timeline Jeffreys and MacGregor put together from Lucy Pérez's confession, we know the route they took before reaching Huntsville.

"That information, coupled with knowing the exact day and time of Reynolds and Pérez's time of death, they believe there wasn't time for any stops other than refueling. When you woke in the basement, you couldn't have been there long, which is good. It isn't likely they had much interaction with you or Katy before they moved you out of the van. They wouldn't have risked you being seen."

The hand splayed across her back was rubbing soothing circles, slipping higher to massage her neck and scalp, successfully bleeding all the tension from her. "I believe those men didn't have much of a chance to do more than transport you. I hope that gives you some peace of mind, but no matter what, your fears are valid, and I will always be available to talk to you about them."

She sniffed back her tears. He'd known exactly what she needed. An ear to listen and strong arms to hold her. The truth was, she was flooded with peace. Rowan had called Dr. Sehoy before leaving the hospital, and they agreed that they should speak twice a week for now. It was a relief to have the therapist, but it had felt even more cathartic opening up to Hugh.

Rowan would heal. She had her friends and family, and she finally had Hugh right where she'd been wanting him since the day they first met.

"If those men were still alive, I would make them wish they weren't," he rumbled.

Rowan admitted to herself that she'd felt immense relief that the kidnappers were dead. She tilted her head back so she could be in a better position before making her request. "Are you going to kiss me now?"

She didn't have to ask twice. He took her mouth before she was done asking for it. What started out slow and simmering became desperate when Hugh escalated the pace. He kneaded her breasts, plucking her nipples until she was writhing in his lap.

He broke away suddenly, leaving Rowan bereft of his heat. She tried to pull him back to her mouth, but he wouldn't budge.

"We can't, baby. You're hurt, and this isn't helping, damn it."

He sounded so miserable, she had to laugh. "I'm not asking you to let me run a marathon! Lay me back on this bed and have your wicked way with me," she taunted. "Becky told me that my legs were doing great, and that I wouldn't hurt them by using them. The cream softens the scabs, so they don't pull. I just need to use good judgement."

"And did Becky give the okay for sex?" He raised his brows in doubt.

"She wasn't that specific, you jackass, but I can ring her and ask if that would make you feel better." She tried to distract him by massaging his chest. Her fingers dragged lightly over his nipples, causing goosebumps to prickle his skin.

"Fine, you win. Lay me down, and I'll take care of myself." It was her turn to raise her brows in challenge. "Or" she quickly added when her offer got more interest from him than she wanted, "you could lay me down gently and cover my body with yours and be oh so gentle." Rowan's voice grew husky as she described the many ways he could make love to her.

He was waffling. She just had to bring it home now. "I'm only tender a few places, babe. Surely, as strong as you are, you could lift me by my hips where we could come together easily. Right?" She moved her bottom against his erection, causing him to close his eyes and groan.

"You aren't playing fair."

"You're right." She gasped as he stood up, still cradling her in his arms only to swivel and gently place her on the bed. She watched him walk over to one of his bags sitting on the couch. When he walked back, he was holding a box of——

"Condoms?" Even in the low light, she saw his cheeks pinken and was hard-pressed not to tease him.

"Mom took great joy in telling me that Tina packed them. Christ, you'd think she's reminding her fifteen-year-old boy to make better safe sex choices," he growled. "You and your sisters have been a bad influence on those two."

Precious. "How many did she pack?" She asked with barely a giggle, but Hugh caught it and gave her a death stare.

"Five boxes."

"Hmm. We might have time to use all of them before I get an IUD."

"We can try," he grinned at her as he walked back to her side, tossing the box on her bare stomach before casually debriefing himself.

When he gripped his length and lightly pumped himself, her mouth was instantly dry. The man was ridiculously gorgeous.

"Come here, Hugh." She reached her hand out until he laced their fingers together so she could pull him slowly toward her. "Enough talk. Enough emotional baggage. Let it just be Hugh and Rowan in this bed."

"Me and you," he said as he gently laid his body atop her own.

He braced his upper body up with his arms so that he could kiss her sweetly.

"God, you feel good underneath me."

She rolled her hips against his body, rubbing her core against his strength. He took her mouth again, her arms went under his so she could trace the flexing muscles on his back and sides, lightly scratching her nails over his beautiful golden skin, the contrast against her own pale body fascinated her.

Hugh moved down her body, unhurried and thorough. Her breasts were always sensitive. He knew and was paying them lavish amounts of attention. She watched his mouth and tongue worship her body. He made her feel languid and, at the same time, impatient for him to drive his body into hers.

She moaned and writhed faster as he sucked one of her

nipples deep in his mouth. She placed her hands on each side of his face and lightly tugged upward. He let her nipple slide from his mouth and crawled back up her body until his mouth was once more on hers.

Breathless, she ended the kiss by pulling back. "I want you to change places with me." He only looked at her for a moment, probably calculating whether or not the position would hurt her. "My weight will all be on you, babe."

The mattress was a queen, so he slowly rolled to the side until he was on his back, propped against several pillows. Rowan followed, lifting her right leg to straddle his middle. He groaned as soon as her hot center made contact.

"Christ, baby, you're so wet for me, aren't you?"

Leaning forward, she licked and sucked his neck and whispered, "Always," in his ear. He'd already grabbed her hips, moving her against his erection at a breath-stealing rhythm.

Rowan used her position to trace, rub, suck, and kiss every bit of his exposed flesh until he was begging her to take him into her body.

"Condom, baby, please," he begged.

She grabbed a box of condoms, and while watching his expression, she ripped the foil packet open with her teeth and proceeded to roll the rubber down his sex. His chest was pumping with his aggressive pants, turning her on even more.

He was tired of waiting and lifted her body with one hand, positioning his dick with the other, allowing her to sink slowly down. "Jesus, Hugh, you feel so good." He filled her body to an almost uncomfortable fullness, but God, she didn't mind the pain for the pleasure.

She leaned forward, where they could feel their hearts pounding against each other's chests. She let him make all the effort, working her body over his, setting a pace that took her breath and thoughts.

"Come for me," he demanded.

He thrust up hard and pulled down on her harder, sealing their bodies together. He shouted, she cried, and they both pulsed against one another with an intensity that she would have claimed impossible if she wasn't currently experiencing it.

As she slumped against his body, she whispered against his neck. "Forever, Hugh."

"Forever, Row," he whispered back against her hair

30

———

*I*t *was time to go home, and...Hugh was definitely avoiding her.*

That morning when she woke, he was already gone from her bed. A quick glance around the room showed his bags were gone, too. Becky came early to get in one more massage treatment and stretching. Except for several scabs and bruising on her shins and a bandage around her left wrist, she felt back to normal.

She got dressed and Becky helped pack her things. Everyone was gathered in the facilities open living room. She spotted Hugh, whose eyes were trained on her the moment she stepped through her door. She started in his direction but was intercepted by Jo and her sisters who surrounded her.

Raven handed Daniel to Jo. She moved Rowan further away from everyone, obviously wanting a private moment, and hugged her sister tight, whispering, "We're going home, Row. There was one point that I lost faith I'd ever see you again," she whispered softly against her neck. "I didn't even tell Bran or River, but I wondered...I wondered if I might not see you again.

In this life," she sniffed quietly. "I wondered how I'd make it without you. I'm so glad I didn't have to find out."

River, who was hugging her baby bump into Rowan's other side, must have heard what Raven said.

"We would have gone on, Rave, even without Rowan. We're Byrnes, after all, but I would have missed you every moment of every day had we not found you." She briefly touched her cheek before smiling at Raven and her. "I would have confiscated all your clothes and put them in my closet. I couldn't let your lovely wardrobe go to waste. Oh," she grinned, pinching Rowan's side, "I also would have told Raven you lost your virginity in college and didn't tell us."

Raven gasped, and Rowan choked on an inhalation. She and Raven surely wore identical looks of horror. "What the hell, Riv? You total and complete bitch," Rowan hissed. Trying to keep any unwanted attention off their conversation.

"You had sex and didn't tell me?" Raven asked through gritted teeth.

"How in the hell did you find out? I didn't tell anyone!"

"You told Nan, and I listened in on the conversation," River admitted, completely remorseless.

"You listened to one of my private conversations? Are you flipping kidding me?" Rowan ground out, using her hip at the same time to bump her sister off her. "That was a dick move, Riv."

River only shrugged. "You were acting weird, and I thought it was more than Mom and Dad. When I heard you crying on the phone, I listened. Nan straightened your ass up, and you weren't sulky anymore, so I never said anything."

"Rowan, I can't believe you didn't tell us, and River, that *was* a total dick move," Raven finished, shaking her head in exasperation.

"I would have regrets, but now Rowan can regale us on the plane about her first time in all its romantic detail," she smirked before her face turned serious. "Gross college sex stories are still way better than kidnapping stories," she finished quietly, blinking back tears.

Rowan realized that River only brought up the embarrassing story to lighten the mood. They were all deeply affected by what had happened to Rowan, and the relief of being together continued to wash over them. Instead of changing the subject like a normal person, River chose the 'go big or go home' route.

"It was one time. One gross mistake." Rowan smirked at her sisters, willing to go along with River's segue. "Hugh knows the whole story." She dragged out 'whole' just to rub it in their faces that they didn't know everything about their little sister.

The O'Faolain men had moved closer to the sisters while they chatted, probably concerned when they saw tears. O'Faolains disliked Byrne tears. When her sisters looked at Hugh with angry scowls he froze, then scowled back.

Rowan laughed at her sisters before walking to where Jo stood, cooing at Daniel in her arms and speaking with Katy. "You're going to Tulsa for a while, Jo?" she asked. Her good friend was continuing to be evasive about what had happened between her and Thomas.

She knew from her family what an integral role Thomas and his team played in figuring out who was behind the abduction. She couldn't wait to give the giant Scotsman a hug and then punch him in the balls, because there was no way Jo would have walked away from him without a good reason.

"I am," Jo said, handing Daniel back to his mom. "Dad has some project he wants James and me to work on together. Jane quit her marketing job and started her own small company. This will be the first time James and I will be working with his wife on a project. I'm looking forward to the fireworks. You know how dramatic my brother can be," she laughed and rolled her eyes.

Jo and her brother James loved and fought each other with equal enthusiasm. Rowan gave Jo a swift hug, not wanting to get emotional before they went their separate ways, but also not wanting to let her off the hook. Jo had been a next-level dodger during Rowan's ordeal, managing to change the subject with ninja skills when MacGregor's name was mentioned.

"Your time of subterfuge, Josephine O'Connor, ends sooner rather than later. I don't care what "special" job your father has in store for you. You'll tell me what in the hell is going on, or my sisters and I will make a trip to Scotland and find out for ourselves. The choice is yours. I'm giving you three weeks to spill your guts. I won't play nice or fair after that." Rowan looked deep into her friend's eyes. "Your final warning."

Jo blew out a frustrated breath at being cornered. Yeah, Rowan could understand the pain...hello...Raven and River.

"Fine. I love you."

"Three weeks or sooner," Rowan reiterated. Jo huffed in exasperation but hugged her again before giving everyone in the room a wave goodbye and walking out to catch her Uber to the airport.

That only left Ms. Katy Blake—Mrs. Katy Stanton if Will could win her back—the woman who was handcuffed in a basement beside her for days.

Rowan kissed Katy on the cheek and hugged her tight. William was hovering close by, his eyes never leaving his ex-wife. She whispered in Katy's ear, "Looks like WS might not be as big of a DB as we believed."

Katy pulled back, her eyes bright with laughter and grinning. "Perhaps," she admitted mischievously.

They took one another's hands, holding them between their

bodies. "So, one more day here for you?" Katy's legs had swollen more than Rowan's, causing her to have more uncomfortable scabbing.

"Yes. We'll fly to Houston tomorrow morning. The kids and Owen are leaving this morning. Samantha misses her daddy."

Matilda and Diana had flown home yesterday afternoon. Both women planned on traveling to Dublin for the birth of River and Patrick's baby in October and staying through Thanksgiving.

"I imagine her daddy misses her more."

"Definitely. Grandma misses her, too," she added, speaking of herself.

"You're still coming to Dublin for Thanksgiving?" Rowan asked.

"I wouldn't miss it. Everyone is excited. The kids and I can't wait to see the new O'Faolain distillery. Bran and Patrick showed us all sorts of pictures and plans. I imagine in the three months until Thanksgiving, there will be a bunch of changes." She hugged her one more time. "You better get going, Row. Call me. Anytime," she added.

"Same goes for you. We'll all expect updates," she teased, raising her eyebrows several times.

Hugh was still avoiding her as the family left the facility.

So now, here they were, loaded in SUVs. No hug. No kiss. Only his trademark scowl to send her on her way. Yes, they were going to the same place, but...well, damn it, she wanted to be chatting with her man about what they would be doing once they were home like her sisters and their husbands were.

Perhaps she was being too sensitive. Just because Hugh was demonstrative when they were alone didn't mean he would be the same in public, except in this case, the public was her sisters and his sons.

Why are you avoiding me?

Rowan was forced to text Hugh since he wasn't currently in the same vehicle with her. She was in the SUV packed with her family on the way to the airport. *He* was in another smaller SUV with everyone's luggage.

Bobby, the O'Faolain pilot, was waiting for them. They were flying to Dublin today after spending two days at the rehabilitation facility. She'd been given the option of returning to Tulsa, but really, other than a wish to visit Hugh's Muskogee property, returning to Oklahoma held little appeal.

She'd spoken to Angela, who'd left several lovely messages throughout her ordeal after Jeffreys brought her phone to the hospital. She'd gotten emotional reading the heartfelt messages from her boutique client. She'd responded that she was doing very well but needed some time with all of her family in Dublin. Angela was completely understanding and promised to send her updates. She even remembered to send 'after' pictures of the shop so River could put the makeover on their website.

She felt good. Not a hundred percent, but close. She and Hugh had made quite a dent in his condom stash and still managed to talk for hours. They spoke about the new distillery. He couldn't wait for her to see the place. Raven and River had sent her some of the initial design concepts. She couldn't wait to start on that project.

They spoke about her painting. He thought she should pursue it as a career. She didn't. Her favorite color was pale yellow. He knew that. His favorite color was black. She knew that. They told each other about bucket list vacations. Traveling Norway was the united winner.

They spoke of children. She wanted *one*. He was...vague.

He was attentive and loving at night. He was aloof and distant during the day. She barely saw him between the hours of seven in the morning to eight or nine in the evening. He never left the facility, he just wasn't...there. He would stand across the room from her, have conversations with his family, her sisters, or William and Owen Stanton. He would stand like a brooding fallen angel for hours, never coming close enough to touch.

Rowan had tried to tell herself all day yesterday that he was giving her time with her sisters, Jo, Katy, and Matilda—that it wasn't personal...that there was nothing to be concerned about. After all, he came to her room the minute it was time for bed, spending the night giving her multiple orgasms and whispering promises of love.

A week and a half ago, he'd told her that he wanted them to live together. He hadn't mentioned it since. She told herself that he assumed it was a given and wasn't bringing it up again because the conversation would be redundant. But now...the distance he was putting between them—suspect.

He was texting her back. She anxiously watched the bubbles wave across the screen.

I'm not.

Ahh...She refused to take the bait. He could try to hide his feelings from her. It wouldn't do him any good.

I love you.

She grinned when she hit send. Take that, Hugh the Resistant.

I love you more.

Exactly. She knew he could never not say it back. Now to make him regret even attempting to give her the cold shoulder.

If we were the only ones on the plane, would you let me jack you off under a blanket if I promised to not be obvious? The point is moot, of course. Just curious.

Rowan.

What if you held me in your lap? And we were naked from the waist down?

Christ. Stop. The driver will think I really like him.

Switching gears while he was warmed up, she went for the throat.

Are you embarrassed for our families to see us together? As a couple?

His reply was immediate.

I could never be embarrassed of you.

Then???

Bubbles waved off and on for several minutes. Starting and stopping again. What was he really struggling with?

Then finally.

I'm not embarrassed. Of you.

Her heart squeezed at that. Was he embarrassed at dating a younger woman? Still? What were all his declarations back in Tulsa about then? She started and erased several replies. Her sisters, at one point, gave her side-eye. She smiled and pretended she wasn't picturing ways of murdering Hugh.

I see.

She didn't really, but she would try since she loved him desperately—even if he could drive a sane woman crazy.

Do you?

She could almost feel his irritation through text. That made her smile. He may be quite a few years her senior, and she may be quite naïve about men, but he had a lot to learn about being in a relationship.

???

Hugh's impatience was showing. She grinned. He wouldn't like the truth bomb she was about to send his way, but he would have to get over his hangups for them to truly be happy—and they would be happy. Rowan wanted him to figure his shit out. Now. A swift kick in the butt was called for.

You need space from me. You aren't ready to be with me. You need time to decide if you're all in...I guess I need time, too, to decide if dealing with your mantrums is worth my time as well. PS. I'm turning my phone off.

31

"*Goddammit*," Hugh growled. He tried calling her phone to see if she'd actually shut it off. It went straight to voicemail.

Damn. Damn. Damn.

He knew he'd been screwing things up with Rowan, but damn it all to hell, he hadn't meant to build any type of barrier between them. He lived for her. She knew that! He had wanted Rowan from the sidelines for months. It still shocked him that she was finally his. Watching and doing were two vastly different actions.

Where he would normally watch her interact with her sisters and his sons, he was now expected to jump right in the middle of them. The five of them were a group, one he knew he could join, and did on occasion, but also one that he didn't feel he quite fit.

He loved his sons. He loved their wives. He loved Rowan. They were all of an age. He belonged to a way older demographic.

The day before Rowan had been taken had been one of the best of his life. He thought then that as long as they were together, he could handle getting out of his comfort zone. She and her sisters told each other everything. He told himself he didn't care. He could laugh it off like his sons did—and if that were the only thing, he could and would endure the ribbing.

The truth was, all of those things were true, but not the real problem. He fucking hated he was so much older than Rowan. He hated that she was the youngest out of the whole family besides his grandson, Daniel.

While they were at the rehabilitation center, he could tell she didn't understand why he was standoffish during the day. He was hoping she wouldn't address it.

The thought of having everyone there know he was in an intimate relationship with someone almost thirty years his junior was...Jesus, he couldn't even describe how much he despised anyone knowing his private business, especially if they had an opinion about it. And they would...have opinions, that is.

It shouldn't matter. He knew it shouldn't matter. He was never letting her go. She would be forever his. They'd made a commitment to each other, for fuck's sake.

He needed more time to get used to things. Public things. Forgetting his age.

After that last text, time didn't seem to be on his side. He'd hurt her feelings, and she wasn't happy, which meant he was fucking furious with himself. He stared ahead, watching the SUV in front of them, ignoring the driver's two attempts at conversation. He needed to fix this, but they wouldn't have any private time on the plane.

Hugh leaned his head against the headrest, resisting the urge to slam his skull repeatedly against it. They would work this out. They would always work things out. There was no other course. Rowan was busting his balls because he deserved it, but she'd always known their path would be rocky. His stomach clenched at the coming confrontation.

Perhaps he should lighten the mood by bringing up her sketchbook. He barely suppressed a moan as he remembered the turn of each erotic page—the driver had been eyeing him suspiciously and was probably one weird noise away from dumping his ass on the side of the road—but that book... Rowan's drawings were so lifelike, so detailed, Christ Almighty, he'd even blushed at some of the positions. They would reenact them all.

His untimely sexual fantasies paused as they took the exit ramp toward the private airfield. He texted Bobby before putting his phone away. There was no point in waiting for a text from Rowan.

THE DRIVER PARKED NEXT to his family. Bre had already exited the front passenger seat, a diaper bag over her shoulder. Bran was helping Raven out, who was holding their son to her chest. She smiled sweetly at Bran, who then kissed his wife.

Patrick climbed out next. Hugh shook his head in wonder. His boys' similar looks and striking white hair always made him smile. The fact that they were also affectionate, funny, and intelligent...those things spiked his pride. Pat turned to help River down. Before she took the final step, he bent to kiss her stomach, which was quite rounded with their first child. River smiled and kissed her husband when he stood straight.

And then it was Rowan stepping down. Hugh stood there dumbly, suitcases and bags weighing down both arms as he watched the most beautiful woman he'd ever known peek her head out. He inwardly groaned. He should have been there to help her down, to have her smile at him, her dimples giving away her mischievous nature.

He should have given her a kiss. Instead, Patrick helped her down too, making sure she was steady on her legs. She laughed at something his son said before following her sisters to the plane.

She'd wrapped her silky, black hair into a messy bun. Some of the long strands had escaped, draping around her shoulders and chest. She probably put it up for the long flight.

Rowan wore a yellow and white striped summer dress. It had small straps and a full skirt. She reminded him of a vibrant painting come to life. Canvas to blood and bone.

Yellow made her happy. It made him happy seeing her wear it. He wished the yellow diamond ring wasn't in his bag but on her finger already. He really wished she'd look at him.

She stopped halfway to the plane and turned, searching the lot. For him? Their eyes met and held before she turned back. How in the hell could he fix this?

Raven and River turned at the jet's stairs, waiting for their sister. They were clearly looking at him, and they weren't happy. Jesus, he'd swear they were mind readers. He watched helplessly as Raven took one hand while River the other and walked up the stairs hand in hand.

"Jesus, Dad, what did you do now?" Bran swore behind him.

"When one of them is upset, they're all upset, and I was hoping to talk River into joining the Mile High club this trip," Patrick joked. "She'll hover over Row and ignore me now," he sighed, slapping his dad's shoulder.

"Seriously, let me help you help yourself," Bran added.

"Fuck you both," Hugh groused. "Stay out of my business," he warned. Used to their father's bad attitude, they only shrugged.

"I'll stay out of it as long as it doesn't affect my wife," Patrick doubled down.

"Agreed," seconded Bran.

Traitors. Hugh's face was burning. Christ, he was unprepared for this level of...sharing...intrusiveness. He was getting more embarrassed and more furious by the moment. He looked like an old fool chasing a woman way too young for him, which was exactly what he was.

He refused to put up with this bullshit. He was a private man. An older, private man. He didn't respond. He only stared at them both. His expression must have conveyed his immense displeasure. The boys picked up the remaining suitcases.

"Sorry," Bran looked so abashed that Hugh almost let him off the hook. Almost.

"Understood, Dad," Patrick added solemnly.

THE GIRLS MUST HAVE PICKED up on the tension between him and the boys. The first couple of hours were uncomfortable, to say the least. Rowan hadn't looked at him after her initial look of disappointment. When her eyes got glassy, he would have gladly allowed himself to be tossed from the plane.

He could now say he knew what spiraling looked like. He was making one bad decision after another.

Everyone had taken turns entertaining Daniel, which thankfully meant his sons weren't casting leery looks his way, and the Byrne sisters weren't casting him metaphorical middle fingers.

Raven just put Daniel down for a nap in the bed that was set behind a partition in the back. She was back and Bre was going to lay down with the sleeping baby, claiming she was just as tired as he was. She was probably tired of the tension in the cabin. He sure as hell was.

The sisters sat opposite him and his boys. Raven and River sitting on either side of Rowan. He noticed they touched her leg or hand or arm often. Losing their little sister for a week, not knowing if she was okay or suffering had taken a toll, and they probably needed the continued reassurance of contact.

Once Raven was back, talk turned to Saoirse Kennedy and Timothy Daniels' wedding.

"I get that Americans are the only ones who celebrate Thanksgiving, but come on, I can't believe Saoirse picked that weekend to get married!" River complained.

"Well," Rowan countered, "just think, everyone from our side will already be in Dublin, including Jo. It's kind of perfect timing, really. I plan on talking Katy into going. She'd love a good Irish wedding."

Raven was nodding her agreement. "I wonder if William will be joining his family," she mused. "But consider the wedding date like this. Thanksgiving is on Thursday, so there will be a ton of extra hands available to help with the wedding setup. Tilly and Nan will be on hand to help with Daniel and your little one, Riv. We'll have all day Friday and Saturday morning to finalize. Friday night's rehearsal is going to be very casual. Finger foods only."

"That's true," River grudgingly admitted. "It just seems un-American to plan an event on a holiday."

"She's Irish, sooooo," Rowan bumped her sister teasingly. "I'm stoked she chose Murphy's. Tim wanted something lowkey and fun for everyone. Saoirse must have paid the Murphy brothers an ungodly amount of money to close the bar to the public for two days."

"Nah," Raven corrected. "Saoirse, Cormac, and Ciaran have known each other since primary school. It was their wedding present."

Rowan looked surprised. "That was incredibly kind."

Hugh gritted his teeth. He fucking hated Ciaran Murphy. That man wanted Rowan and made no effort to hide the fact. He'd shoved his flirtatious bullshit in Hugh's face on more than one occasion. He'd considered, several times, if he were honest, ruining the Murphys financially.

Whether it meant buying up the real estate surrounding the bar or screwing with their suppliers. He'd lain in bed many a night contemplating taking them down. The only thing that stayed his hand was the fact that if Rowan ever found out, she'd never forgive him. He still fantasized about their downfall. He was yanked out of his contemplations when Raven spoke.

"River already got the invitations out two months ago, so we're good there. RSVPs have been coming in steadily. The cut-off date for responding is six weeks before, with plenty of time to adjust the headcount for food and seating.

"As River will be needing to take it easy in another few weeks, her tasks will be confirming hotel rooms for out-of-town guests, scheduling pictures, and" Raven smirked at River, "since she's pregnant and starving 24/7, she gets to join Saoirse and Tim at the cake tasting. We already reserved the bakery, but the flavors have got to be finalized."

"No fair," Rowan frowned teasingly at her sister, "I wish I was pregnant. I love cake!"

Everyone laughed—Hugh broke out in a cold sweat. He'd avoided that discussion with Rowan so far. He hoped to avoid it a while longer.

Patrick stood and plucked River out of her chair and sat back down, settling his wife in his lap. She was laughing until his son kissed her into silence. Hugh quickly looked away. Voyeurism held no appeal, especially when it was family. What would his sons think if he took Rowan into his lap and kissed her for an indecently long time in front of them?

Probably clap.

He caught Rowan looking at him, a wistful look gracing her delicate features. Damn. He didn't want her to be disappointed she chose him. Her earlier text aside, she had chosen him, and she would never change her mind. His brain understood that. His self-consciousness was a 'him problem.'

He tried to convey his regret and remorse, but she turned away, adjusting the dividers between her and Raven's chairs now that River had moved. She twisted sideways, propping her head on the side of her chair and swinging her feet into her sister's lap.

"Okay, Rave, give me my marching orders," she laughed as she placed her tiny feet on Raven's thighs.

Hugh watched Raven flinch as her hands touched the red crisscrosses covering Rowan's lower legs. He saw tears gather in Raven's eyes before she glanced desperately at Bran. Rowan must have felt her sister tense up and tensed herself.

Thankfully, Hugh had raised extremely smart sons. Patrick started to discuss the Mile High club and all the benefits it came with to River in a mock whisper.

"Jesus, Pat. River's pregnant. We all get it—your dick works," Bran joked. "So, babe," he turned to Raven, "you're working with Cormac on table arranging and turning the band stage into a temporary wedding sanctuary. I assume you're working with Riv's ex because Patrick won't let her near Cormac."

"We never dated, you douche canoe," River snarked.

"My wife doesn't need to work with a man who used to look at her like she was a...woman," Patrick ended on a wheeze when his wife elbowed his stomach.

"Perhaps you've forgotten, Mr. Mile High, but I am a woman," River shook her head and rolled her eyes. "Raven is taking that job because it will require dragging those heavy-ass wooden tables around, and Raven is super anal about 'room flow,'" she air quoted the last, smiling at her sister.

Raven was smiling again, gently rubbing Rowan's legs. Her tears were gone, which he supposed was the whole point of the current ridiculous conversation. He was even amused by the kids' bullshit until Raven told Rowan her part in the wedding.

"Row, you and Ciaran are responsible for the rehearsal and wedding menus. Saoirse has given you two free reign. You'll need to find out how many menu items Ciaran and his staff can easily handle for whatever the guest tally ends up being."

Hugh saw red. Fucking red. He stiffened, straightened in his chair, and looked at Rowan, mentally imploring her to turn and look at him. She had to know he wouldn't want her anywhere that close to Murphy—that she shouldn't even be speaking to the son of a bitch.

From his peripheral, he saw both Patrick and Bran look his way. Nervous about his reaction. They knew he'd be furious, and better than that, they would both understand it. No good would come of him voicing his opinion now. Though Hugh reasoned, Rowan's sisters didn't seem to mind when their husbands voiced their opinions. Still, after his idiocy at the rehabilitation center and her texts on the way here, he didn't think it was the right time.

She would tell Raven no. Surely.

"Sounds great, Rave."

Thirty minutes of uncomfortable silence later, Bran asked Raven to move by him, sharing his seat, and suggested they rest their eyes while their son slept. Rowan sat up and stretched, studiously avoiding eye contact with Hugh.

She could feel his eyes watching her as she excused herself to the bathroom, thankfully, roomy and beautifully appointed— the exact opposite of the gross, smelly cramped affairs on commercial planes. She was definitely becoming spoiled.

She knew he watched her walk from the main cabin. He hadn't liked them discussing the Murphy brothers. He really didn't like finding out Raven had assigned her to work with Ciaran directly on the menu. She might have listened to his thoughts on the matter if they were openly dating. If he was going to go back on his word, then she wouldn't take his feelings into consideration.

She'd allowed him to get by with way too much in the past. She was done trying to soothe his ruffled feathers.

She needed to soothe him, though. *Damn, his stubborn ass!* She desperately wanted to sit next to him and at least hold his hand. She wasn't going to push him any further than she had already, but she wasn't going to let him get by with hiding how he felt about her for much longer.

She didn't really have to pee. She just needed a moment away from Hugh's aggressive silence. After locking herself in, she stood looking in the mirror. Sighing, she pulled the scrunchie from her hair, the messy bun tumbled down her back and shoulders. She used her fingers to massage her scalp, blowing out a frustrated breath. Hugh made her crazy. He'd always driven her half mad with his broody looks and silence.

He could be as antisocial as he pleased as long as he was hers. She thought he knew that. With a defeated sigh, she put her hair back in a messy bun and unlocked the door, only to have the panel pushed in and the man of her turbulent thoughts standing there with his hand fisting the handle, blocking her exit.

He crowded her until she moved back enough for him to enter and close the door behind him. When he turned the lock, her pulse started to race. She knew he had to be furious that she'd agreed to work with Ciaran Murphy, knowing they'd had a mild flirtation. He didn't know that the two had kissed one evening when Hugh had infuriated her. She would have told Raven to switch jobs with her. After all, if Hugh wanted to work closely with a woman that he had flirted with or kissed...no way.

She walked back to the marble countertop attached to the wall next to the sink and leaned her back against it. Crossing her arms over her chest, she watched as Hugh followed and stood before her. She thought she'd seen all of his severe looks. Apparently, not. If he was attempting to intimidate, it was working—if intimidation felt like a giant turn-on.

He crossed his arms over his chest, matching her stance. He was pissed, well, so was she.

"I don't want space. I am ready to be with you. I *am* all in."

No beating about the bush…good. "It hurts me when you treat me like you do my sisters. It kills me that you want to pretend we are nothing more than relatives when we're *with our relatives*! Everyone out there," she jabbed her finger at the door, "knows we've had sex, Hugh! They know I love you, and you love me. You do understand that, don't you?"

His jaw was clenched as he released his arms to hang stiffly at his sides.

"I do know that, yes," he admitted.

He looked so pained at the admission that she wanted so badly to wrap her arms around his waist and reassure him, but they needed to get this monster between them dragged out of the closet.

"You don't have to joke and laugh with everyone. You don't have to say silly things like Bran and Patrick do just to make us roll our eyes. You don't have to smile when my sisters and I are goofy or groan when we tell each other private things. You only have to love me. Hold my hand. Claim me as yours."

She felt tears pooling in her eyes and desperately tried to blink them back.

Hugh's chin dropped to his chest, a deep sigh escaping his mouth. He looked as miserable as she felt. When he straightened, he stepped close enough to grasp her waist and sit her on the tall counter.

She couldn't help but spread her legs wide enough for him to step between them. She kept her hands firmly on the cold marble, careful of her left. Nurse Becky had taken the larger wrap off that morning, allowing her to wear bandages over the deepest wounds. It was healing quickly with no infection.

She wanted to place her hands on his chest or around the back of his neck so she could pull him to her mouth. It was a distraction they didn't need. Yet.

"I'm just...I'm an idiot who needs more time to adjust to this new version of us. I need grace, Row. Forgive me when I fuck up. Love me anyway," he begged, his voice low and raspy with emotion.

"I would never not love you. You just...I don't expect...geez, I mean, you never need to change yourself for me. You can frown and growl all day long, but when you walk by, whether it's when we're alone or in a crowded room, you better stop to at least kiss my cheek."

She finally let herself touch him, placing her hands carefully against his neck, her thumbs tracing his strong jaw. "I want everyone to know I'm your girlfriend. Tell me I'm not asking for too much. Tell me you understand."

He covered her right hand with his own, leaning down to kiss her lips. Once. Twice. Three times.

"You aren't asking too much. You aren't asking nearly enough. I swear," he closed his eyes and rested their foreheads together, "that I am devoted...completely to you. You have my promise to be better."

Their mouths fused once more. This time, the kiss was free of reserve. It was tongues and teeth, moans, and biting. She felt him hot and hard between her thighs and wrapped her legs around his waist to trap them together, whimpering at the delicious friction their bodies made when they ground against one another.

She broke the kiss and breathlessly reiterated, "Just so we're straight, I won't let your lapses of supposed indifference faze me because I know you love me, and you'll remind yourself that the age difference is a *you* problem. A problem I don't share, and you'll endeavor to get over it. Sound right?"

"Correct," he agreed right before taking her mouth again.

"In accordance, you will make an effort to show everyone that I'm yours. Yes?"

"I will," he growled before taking her mouth again.

"We have a few more minutes before they send out a search party," she panted between Hugh's tongue working hers over. He got the message and pulled her sundress over her head, his eyes widening at her bare breasts, then widening further at her sheer, pale yellow panties.

"Christ," Hugh moaned. "Had I known what you had under your dress, my dick would have been hard before we boarded the plane."

"I have warned you to expect it." Her grin turned into a moan when he ran his fingers over the silk between her legs before stepping back so he could pull the panties from her body.

"Always so wet for me, baby. I wish we had more time," his deep voice rumbled, eyes never straying from her center.

He stepped back between her legs, his jean-clad bulge pressing firmly against her heat, pulling a moan from them both. Then they were frantically kissing, and he was trying to unzip his pants. Finally, his body was free. "Yes," Rowan whispered as her hand found his length, stroking him between their bodies.

He told her to hold on as he scooped her off the counter. Her back landed against a small space of wall that was free of counters or mirrors. He was frantic, using the wall for support and his hands to grip her ass, steadying her as he moved between her legs, sliding his hardness through her wetness.

"I hate when you're upset with me. It makes me crazy," he admitted between biting and licking her neck.

Rowan ran her hands over his broad back, digging her

fingers deep in the grooves of flesh and muscle. "You make me crazy, babe. Please, don't make me wait," she begged, wanting him inside her desperately.

Their relationship was old and new. It felt unbreakable and fragile at the same time. The two of them had been through a lot of emotional upheaval together. After even a few hours of not being in sync, she badly needed the closeness.

"Oh shit, the condoms are packed. Christ, no," he groaned.

Hugh paused mid-grind, a look of intense pain on his face. She felt the loss of movement like forced paralysis. They needed to move, to continue on their journey to euphoria, but...birth control...

"Pull out," Rowan hissed. A breath rushed out of his lungs in relief at the solution.

He lined up with her passage before slowly breaching her depths. The fullness always drew a moan of pleasure from her throat.

"Fuck, baby...so tight," his fingers clenched her ass tight, holding her perfectly to take his deep thrusts. "Your body's going to strangle me until I come."

Hugh O'Faolain may not embrace a demonstrative lifestyle, but the man had his moments. He took one of his hands from her ass to pinch her nipples as he deepened their kiss. She wanted to beg him to go harder and faster, but the steady pace, the measured in and out motion, had her body quaking and chasing release.

"I'm close, baby," he panted against her mouth before reaching between their bodies and pinching the sensitive bundle of nerves at her apex.

"God, yes! Right there!" She had to bite her lip to stop a scream from escaping when her orgasm hit. The intensity bowed her back and had her clenching her knees around his hips.

"Want to feel you tighten around me," he growled, "just... for...ahh," he growled when he pulled out and pumped his seed on her stomach.

Rowan wrapped her hands around his neck to lean forward and kiss her lover tenderly. They were both breathless and satisfied.

"That was close," he admitted. "I almost didn't pull out in time. You felt too good."

He looked at her with a solemn expression as he set her gently on her feet. He grabbed a couple of hand towels out of the stationary basket by the sink. Wetting them before cleaning her up first and then himself.

His shaft was beginning to soften—the process fascinated her. Everything about him fascinated her, but his sex, yeah...

"If you keep looking at it like that, we're never going to leave this bathroom."

His teasing tone, combined with his serious expression, made her stomach flutter. She sighed, knowing they needed to get dressed and rejoin the family. "Fine," she conceded, retrieving her dress and panties and dressing.

Before he unlocked the door, he bent down to kiss her one more time, his thumb running over the reddened marks along the crook of her neck where he'd lightly sucked and bitten.

She'd seen the red marks in the mirror while fixing her hair and took the scrunchie out again. Leaving it down seemed to be the best course of action. She didn't want her sisters to tease Hugh about them.

"I can't wait for you to be back on birth control," he confessed. "It was too close this time."

She stiffened at his words. After their talk about children, or her talk rather, since he hadn't added any of his own thoughts on the subject, he was clearly letting her know he didn't want to take chances again like they'd just done.

"You do remember you came inside me our first night together, right?" His eyes widened in shock and fear.

"We used condoms," he denied.

"Not that one time in the middle of the night when you woke me up by slipping into me from behind." His normally golden skin tone paled. "When I got up that morning, I felt it between my legs," she finished steadily. Annoyed.

"I'm sorry. I...this...there's no excuse for being that reckless."

He was obviously beating himself up, which she had no intention of allowing to continue. "We both have responsibility for what happens in our bed, babe. Stop acting like you forced me to have sex without protection. It was only once. Don't worry."

"Did they do blood work at the hospital?"

"They did, but even blood tests usually require the woman to be pregnant for at least a week to show up positive. Seriously, it was once. Let it go. I'm not going to try to get pregnant when you clearly don't want me to be."

When his shoulders stiffened, and he didn't offer any rebuttal, she sighed and unlocked the door herself before walking forward to the cabin. She sat opposite her sisters and their... *doting* husbands. She squeezed her eyes tight, refusing to allow herself to feel anything but pure joy for her sisters.

The brooding man at her back may not be everyone's ideal boyfriend, but he sure as hell was hers, and she was willing to give him grace as he'd asked for and trust that they'd eventually find themselves in a mutually satisfying relationship.

When they got back to the main cabin, they sat where Rowan had before. In the same row of seats, not quite touching. Four sets of eyes were watching his and Rowan's every move. He ignored them.

Rowan cleared her throat, earning Hugh's attention. She wouldn't meet his eyes.

"I was thinking, Rave, that I would be better suited to set up the tables with Cormac if you don't mind switching jobs."

Hugh couldn't believe what he was hearing. She was doing this for him. Totally for him. She'd known it would bother him and was trying to rectify the situation. He'd planned on trying to speak to her about it later. He'd been such a giant, jealous ass about that Murphy piece of shit in the past, he hadn't been looking forward to broaching the subject.

"No problem. You've always been the Feng Shui guru of the three of us, and I love planning dinner menus. I should have put you on that in the first place. I'm not sure how I overlooked that."

Hugh looked at Raven then, something in her tone caught his attention. She smirked at him with a 'call me out if you're brave enough' look. Clearly his devious daughter-in-law had planned to goad him from the beginning with her job assignments. He narrowed his eyes at her, briefly acknowledging that her scheming had worked.

"Oh, well, thank you," Rowan answered after sending a quick glance his way.

"Are you still planning on going to Nan's apartment when we land?" River asked. "I want to go with you."

"Me too," Raven immediately chimed in.

It was obvious to him and the boys that the girls were going to have a hard time letting Rowan do things on her own for a while.

"You know, all of your stuff is still there," Raven continued.

Hugh was watching Rowan intently, so he saw her glance in his direction quickly before answering.

"Oh, that's perfect. I plan on staying there for a bit longer anyway."

Like hell. She was moving into *their* apartment in the O Building. Immediately. He wanted to say something, but damn him, he couldn't bring himself to address the living situation in front of everyone.

He took a deep breath as things deteriorated further. Raven and River sat up and looked at their sister like she'd just told them she was shaving her head and moving to Timbuktu. Bran and Patrick could tell their wives were becoming distressed, and they didn't like it.

"Oh," Raven half-whispered, fluttering her hand in front of her uncertainly. "Well then, I—"

River cut her off. "We'll stay with you, of course."

"Exactly. Great idea, Riv," Raven smiled, clearly relieved. "Nan will think it's so much fun to have us all to herself. Daniel will come, too, or else she won't let us in," Raven laughed softly.

Patrick and Bran were looking at him with identical looks of alarm. Hugh looked to his left wondering what Rowan thought of her sisters' clinginess. She looked uncomfortable, but Hugh knew she wouldn't tell them no.

She probably needed them with her. She just wouldn't have asked. If they needed her, she most definitely needed them, and he wasn't about to let the woman he loved be distressed after the trial she'd endured.

"No." Everyone stopped talking since Hugh had managed next to no conversation on the flight so far.

"No, what?" Rowan asked.

"You aren't staying at Bébhinn's." Her eyebrows shot up at the announcement.

"Oh, really," she said, her eyes round with surprise. "Why is that exactly?"

He gritted his teeth. She was going to make him say something or back down. She would let him retract his statement and not say a word. She wouldn't make him feel bad. She'd only just agreed to give him grace, and he knew she wouldn't go back on her word. He was the only asshole here.

In this, he wouldn't back down. "You already agreed we'd live together. Did you change your mind?" His face was burning. He refused to look at the peanut galley across the aisle and stayed focused on Rowan, who was looking flushed herself now.

"You're right...memory lapse," she fluttered her hand self-consciously. "I didn't change my mind."

The look of absolute wonder in her eyes wouldn't let him feel a single ounce of regret at speaking up. He gave her a nod and turned to look at the others. He crossed his arms over his chest and stared at them.

"It still freaks me out to see you without a beard," Patrick admitted, chuckling at Hugh's scowl. "I knew you, but my brain kept telling me I didn't."

"Your brain tells you a lot of irrelevant things," Hugh countered.

"When I was a kid, and you used to stare at me like that when I did something bad—"

"Which was all the time," Hugh interrupted Bran.

Bran smirked back. "Anyway, when you had a beard, I could pretend you might be smiling, and it didn't seem so bad."

"Your point?" Hugh asked.

"His point is that now we know you were probably never hiding a smile," Patrick laughed. "Your hairless face has ruined one of our best childhood fantasies. Now we know you were actually pissed."

"Of course, I was pissed, you little shits. You and Patrick were a trial. You should be thankful I didn't sell you at one of those weekend farmer's markets."

"You loved us too much to give us up," Patrick chimed in.

"I did," was Hugh's only reply.

THE LAST OF the flight was uneventful, everyone taking turns napping or reading. They'd landed early in the morning at Dublin's airport and were about to disembark. Their bags were already being loaded into a waiting SUV.

"Let me take Daniel," Hugh offered, holding his hands out to Bran. He hadn't gotten much alone time with his grandson in recent weeks, and he missed him.

"Sure," Bran yawned, handing his son over. "He just woke up. We're hoping it isn't a nightmare to get him back on Dublin time."

Hugh held him in the crook of his arm. He took Daniel's tiny hand in his own and rubbed it against his beardless face. "Do you like Papa's face without his beard? Not so scratchy now, but I think you'll miss tugging on it, won't you?" Daniel smiled, his baby laugh pulling a chuckle of his own in response.

"Aunt Row loves Papa's face with or without a beard," she said as she walked up to his side, kissing Daniel on his head.

Hugh felt his face flush, pleasure and embarrassment warring for dominance when he heard his sons chuckle behind him. Luckily, Rowan went to grab the rest of her carry-on bags and started to walk off of the plane. Her sisters filed out next, then Hugh, with Bran and Patrick bringing up the rear.

The sisters had stopped, waiting for their men to join them by the SUV. He gave Rowan a small smile to remind her that he loved her. She knew, but he'd promised to try more in public.

"So, Row likes your baby face, Dad?" Patrick joked.

Hugh shifted Daniel to his shoulder, ignoring the jibe.

"I like it when Dad holds Daniel. He can't tackle us when we make him mad," Bran laughed.

They were almost to the women. *Ignore them*, Hugh chanted in his head.

Bran continued speaking. He obviously was in need of an ass-kicking from his father. "Is that why you were in the bathroom so long? Were you and Row talking about beards?"

And that was all he could take. Running a hand down Daniel's back, he canted his head toward the baby and said, "Did you know Papa is the only member of the Mile High club here? Your Daddy and Uncle Patty have no game."

At that announcement, he enjoyed watching Raven and River's mouths drop open. He really enjoyed Rowan's blush and sparkling, wide eyes when she met his trademark blank face, huffing a laugh when he winked. The best, however, was hearing Bran mutter, "Damn," and Patrick's angry, "What the hell? That was my idea!"

33

After showering and changing, they went to see Nan, who they knew would be anxious to lay eyes on Rowan.

Nan had filled three tables full of food. She'd made the girls' favorites—*all* of their favorites—some of their parents' favorites. The O'Faolains had a table just for them, Devlen had a spread, and her grandma even did Jo's favorite apricot jam-filled sandwich cookies and Scottish shortbread for MacGregor in thanks for all his help in finding Rowan. Kitchen therapy.

Raven, River, and Rowan, because they could be childish when the need arose, took a picture of them each grinning around a whole sandwich cookie shoved in their mouths and sent it to Jo. She took a picture of her flipping them off with a 'Paybacks' caption.

Nan had hugged her for at least an hour, rocking Rowan in her lap and crying over her head, sniffling, and patting her and her sisters at five-minute intervals. It had taken a lot of talking and reassurances, but finally, she'd settled into grandma and great-grandma mode.

Nan insisted on seeing each of Rowan's scrapes, bruises, and scabs, gently kissing the worst of them. When she teared up, they all did, but it was cleansing.

Hugh, Bran, Patrick, and Devlen moved her things out of the apartment while the women visited and caught up. Hugh wanted her things moved to his flat, or *their* flat as he insisted on calling it, immediately.

With every pass through the living room carrying her things to the waiting truck below, he would make eye contact. She felt her stomach flutter with every box and rack of clothes that went out the door.

She and Hugh were going to be living together. Every day and every night. It still seemed impossible. While River was in the middle of telling Nan about her last doctor visit, Rowan slid her phone from her pocket and pulled up her text messages.

You're so handsome you take my breath away.

Bubbles appeared...

You're biased.

Women embarrass themselves daily drooling over you. Why can't I?

Untrue.

Always so modest, Rowan thought.

What would you like to do tonight...that includes my mouth specifically?

Rowan had just hit send when the apartment door opened again. Hugh looked at his phone and must have seen her last text because the look he gave her was all angry smolder.

Her favorite.

Patrick announced that they had everything loaded and were going to head back to the O Building. Bran walked to Raven and kissed his wife and son. Patrick walked to River, kissing her—far longer than was appropriate, of course—and cupped her stomach, grinning like a maniac. Hugh thanked

Devlen for his help, accepted a to-go treat box from Nan, and stared at Rowan from the doorway.

He didn't even say goodbye.

Breathe. She told herself. She knew he wouldn't become demonstrative in an afternoon. He loved her, and she loved him. It was more than enough.

His huge paw of a hand flexed on the door's frame as he stared at her one more time, his jaw flexing with emotion before he firmly shut the heavy door behind him.

Thirty seconds later.

You. On your knees. Specifically.

"Is your Daddy texting you something naughty?" River poked Rowan's thigh with her bare toes.

Rowan felt her face flame. If they only knew. With Nan's keen eye laser-focused on what River was talking about, Rowan knew a change of subject was needed.

"We're going out to dinner tomorrow night with Tim and Saoirse, Nan. The guys want to go over the plans for the distillery, and we just want to talk to Saoirse about her wedding dress," she chuckled.

Nan showed them the dress she was thinking about wearing to the wedding and what she'd picked out for Devlen. Thanksgiving lists were made, and tasks were divvied up. They discussed possible scenarios about Jo and Thomas breaking up. Unanimously, they agreed it had to have been something the grumpy Scot had done.

The rest of the afternoon was wonderful and relaxing—sprinkled with hundreds of random inappropriate thoughts about her boyfriend. Smothering her random grins was the only trial.

. . .

"I ORDERED French onion soup earlier and garden salads from that bakery down the block that you like, *Bácús*. Would you like me to heat some up for dinner? It's early yet, I know, but just in case you're hungry..." Hugh let his voice trail off, inwardly groaning at his awkwardness. Rowan was standing in his kitchen, the soft, butter-yellow appliances the perfect backdrop to her causal lean.

It's too bad he sounded like a nervous waiter on his first day on the job. Was he about to ask what she'd like to drink? He fidgeted with the barstools before toying with the blown glass sculpture Rowan must have picked out. It was all the colors of the sun, deep red, fire orange, and too many yellows to count all swirled together. He wouldn't have picked it, but he could admit it looked perfect on the kitchen island.

And what was Rowan doing while he did his best to not look like a squirrely, clueless teenager? She just leaned there. Her back against the counter, elbows resting atop the barstools on either side of her.

Unruffled, casual, and, if he wasn't mistaken, calculating... something.

"I'm not hungry for that," she finally managed to speak.

Hugh grimaced. Damn, he'd thought that was one of her favorite meals. "I have eggs and cheese. I can make a simple omelet...though Pat is the best cook. I could call h—"

Rowan interrupted. "I'm not hungry. For food."

He swallowed thickly at the blatant innuendo of what she *was* hungry for. So, that was her game. His body instantly responded, forcing him to adjust himself, which he didn't bother to hide.

Her eyes followed the movement. He didn't say another word, just waited and watched, leaning against the counter himself now. Watching her watch him.

She would cave eventually.

She didn't cave. She just took what she wanted.

Rowan pushed off the counter, moving left to sidle up in front of him before laying her hands flat on the marble, either side of his body.

"Take your shirt off," she demanded.

Fuuuuckkkk. He almost got whiplash. He ripped the offending garment off his head so fast. When she ran her nails over his chest, leaning forward to kiss and lick his nipples, his legs threatened to buckle

Clearing his throat, he said, "Please, be careful of your hand." She'd told him it felt fine. Most of the damage had been around her wrist and above her thumb. Still...

When her fingers paused at his waistband, he placed his hands around her tiny waist and pulled her tight against his body. She stood on top of his shoes, giving her a few extra inches. He leaned closer to her upturned face.

Instead of kissing him, she whispered, "Get your phone out and read the last text from you to me."

He felt fire race up his spine. He knew exactly what his last text had been. "I don't need my phone." *You. On your knees. Specifically.*

"Well?" She whispered against his lips.

His answer was to scoop her up and sprint to their bedroom.

Two hours and a shower later, he and Rowan settled in the living room, wolfing down French onion soup and crusty baguettes on their cream-colored leather couch, watching the first season of Great British Bake Off. Apparently, he had to see the original judges, Paul Hollywood and Mary Berry, to fully appreciate the later seasons.

His body temperature was still running warm from coming twice, but he felt insatiable where Rowan was concerned. In fact, he was having trouble concentrating on the difference between a stodgy cake and a claggy one—who in the hell cared? Rowan.

He was in the middle of dunking a bite of bread in his soup and pondering why the contestants were made to use, surely, the smallest ovens in the world, when his attention was snagged again by the woman sitting next to him. Rowan had slipped the silver spoon between her lips and sucked off the broth, licking the stray drops from the metal. Christ, have mercy.

Her mouth had been doing something similar to his body not long ago. He gritted his teeth as he felt himself swell against his pajama pants. He really should be satisfied, but where wanting her was concerned, he had little control.

Rowan looked away from the television, glancing his way, probably feeling his gaze.

"Do you like the soup?" she asked.

"Yes."

"You aren't eating it."

"I'd rather eat you." Her faced flamed with rosy heat. Her pale skin had no chance of camouflaging her reactions. This flush wasn't from embarrassment but from need. He could tell by her eyes that she wanted him.

They set their trays on the side tables. She crawled over the couch and straddled his lap, kissing him once before sliding his t-shirt over his head. He took hers off, too, palming her breasts the minute they were free. She was wearing tiny sleep shorts that allowed her to feel the thick ridge rocking between her legs.

"Condom?" she asked between kisses.

"Pocket."

"Prepared." She nipped his lip and rocked faster.

"Always," he moaned.

"Want you inside me now," she panted, dropping her head back to give him better access to suck her nipples into his mouth.

He'd just hooked his thumbs into the waistband of his pajama pants when someone—he would gladly kill—pounded their fist on the front door.

"Ignore it," Hugh demanded, continuing to take his pants down when the pounding started up again, and he heard, "Dad, I know your home. Open up."

He and Rowan both groaned at the interruption. Her hands had already fisted around his sex. "He'll go away," he reasoned.

She was already backing off his lap, pulling her hands from his body. "It's Pat. It might be about River."

"She would have called you," he groused, standing and pulling his pants up. He attempted to find a position for his dick where it wouldn't pop out.

"God, I love your body, babe," she said, stepping forward once more, smashing her chest against his abs.

He wrapped her up and was about to lift her against his body when Pat had the nerve to bang on the door. Again. "Dad! I need something!" Pat whined.

He grabbed up his shirt and slid it over her body before storming toward the apartment's entrance.

As he yanked the door open, Patrick's fist was raised, presumably in preparation to beat on his door for a third time. His son smirked as he took in Hugh's appearance—raging hard-on and shirtless.

"Jesus, Dad, you'll poke my eye out with that thing. I would have called, but I forgot my phone downstairs."

Hugh gritted his teeth against the teasing, wanting desperately to tackle his son and beat the smartass out of him. He heard Rowan snort in amusement behind them. She must have moved into the kitchen.

"What in the fuck do you want?" Thankfully his erection was powering down. He only had to get rid of the jackass at his door, and he'd be hard again and sinking into Rowan's heat.

Patrick pushed past his dad and went straight to Rowan. Over his shoulder, he said, "Riv wants one of those German garlic pickles, and I'm out. I saw you had a case in your pantry the other day."

Deep breath in. Deep breath out. Deep breath in. Deep breath out.

He disappeared into the walk-in pantry and got out two jars for River, shoving the heavy glass jars into Pat's chest, causing the nuisance to make a satisfying grunt. He propped his hip on the center island near Rowan and crossed his arms over his chest.

"Leave." Patrick ignored him.

"Hey Sister, Dad's shirt looks better on you than him." He grinned at her blush. "It'd probably be more comfortable if it wasn't on backwards."

With that parting shot, the swaggering shit let himself out. Hugh was congratulating himself that he'd managed not to cringe when his son called Rowan, Sister. He promised her to lighten up, and he was pretty sure he'd nailed it.

"He's gone. You can stop clenching your jaw in embarrassment," she giggled, poking him in the stomach.

So, he *hadn't* nailed it. Shit.

"Let's pick up the food in the living room, and then you can take me to bed," she smiled, pressing a kiss to his chest.

He walked to the TV and shut it down. She'd remembered to pause it so they wouldn't miss the 'Showstopper bake,' she'd explained. *Grrrreat.*

Rowan's phone pinged with a notification. She was carrying her food tray to the kitchen while she looked at her phone. When she snorted in amusement, he girded his loins.

She handed it to him. It was a text from River, of course.

Jesus, Row. Give Daddy's D a break. He promised to help Pat put the baby's crib together

tomorrow, and he won't be able to if he's all chafed…down there…

He handed the phone back, suppressing a shudder. Rowan took the phone back and rapidly typed out a reply before handing the phone back to him.

Tell Patrick to stop watching you eat your pickle. It's creepy.

She grinned at him. He couldn't help but grin back.

34

"Mmm," River moaned as she took a huge bite from her double cheese, double pineapple pizza.

She, Hugh, her sisters, and their men met Saoirse, Tim, her sister, Sadhbh, and Josh at Bonobo in Smithfield. A pizza joint that had the best pies as far as Rowan was concerned. They got two tables outside and put them together so everyone could talk to one another. It was a gorgeous evening, and the outdoor patio had fun twinkle lights, and music.

"You sound and look like a pregnant porn star," Saoirse teased River.

"A damn good combination, as far as I'm concerned," Patrick quipped. "Speaking of porn stars, Bran, I went to Dad's last night and—"

Hugh threw a quick jab to Patrick's side, who had the misfortune of sitting by his dad, efficiently cutting off whatever his son was about to relate to the group. Everyone chuckled and begged Pat to tell them. He only grinned and shook his head, rubbing his side to let everyone know he wouldn't chance another bruise.

Rowan sighed, the group might have been amused, but Hugh's still form, and grim expression screamed the opposite. She looked around the table and noticed that all the couples were touching or leaning into one another—except for her and Hugh.

She leaned toward his side so he could hear her over the chatter and asked quietly if everything was alright.

He barely spared her a glance, replying with, "Yes."

She slowly straightened. Disappointment blanketed her mood. She tried to shake it off, reminding herself that he had moments of fun and teasing, but it certainly wasn't often. It didn't mean he didn't enjoy himself or love her. Grace. Grace. Grace. They promised each other to give one another grace.

Except...earlier, when the group was walking into the Bonobo, he hadn't held her hand or even placed his hand on her back. She had asked him for a few small signs of affection when they were out.

Raven, who sat across from her, must have seen the short exchange with Hugh and gave her a questioning look. Rowan shook her head. They could talk about it tomorrow.

"I'm going to run over to Nan's in the morning to say good-bye. I have a doctor's appointment and a few errands to run if you need me to do anything while I'm out." She'd called her gynecologist that morning for an appointment. Dr. Daley had a cancellation the following morning. Thank God, no more condoms. "I also want to hug Devlen, as well, since it makes the straight-faced Irishman uncomfortable," she laughed.

"Devlen is a great man, but I admit, I love seeing him squirm on occasion," Patrick confided. "When I first met the man, I swear my balls disappeared!"

"Damn, Pat, did you meet Devlen in high school?" Bran asked, totally straight-faced.

"Fuck you. I was a freshman, for Christ's sake. I was a late bloomer," Patrick defended. "Why in the hell were you looking anyway?"

"It was Dad's fault. He made us share one of those damn Jack and Jill bathrooms. Do you know how many times I would be trying to use the bathroom, and you would get out of the shower naked?" Bran complained.

The whole table was dying laughing at this point. Hugh even managed a small smile when Rowan glanced his way.

"First, people don't get out of the shower fully dressed. Second, you did your level best to take a shit every time I took a shower," Patrick glowered at his brother. "You were always such a dick."

Bran smirked, "At least I covered mine up."

"Enough, boys," Hugh grumbled. "And you weren't covering it up when I caught you measuring yourself...with your Gran's ruler."

"Burn," Patrick choked on his drink.

Tim and Josh had tears running down their cheeks, and the Kennedy sisters and River weren't even making any noise, they were laughing so hard.

"You actually measured your penis?" Raven asked, giggling. "Tell me Hugh is lying!"

"How else is a man to know where he stands, babe?" Bran asked his wife.

"Greek sculptures," Josh suggested. "Everybody's dick is bigger than that."

"Porn," Tim added.

"Timothy Daniels!" Saoirse gasped. "You've been holding out on me," she teased.

To which Tim gave his fiancé a lovely, smacking kiss. The table cheered. Tim had certainly come out of his shell this past year.

The waiter came by with another round of drinks, placing

Rowan's shot of Slane on the table last. He told her that a gentleman paid for hers.

Oh shit! The table went silent. She felt Hugh stiffen next to her, and just when she was about to tell the waiter thank you, another man approached her end of the table.

He was tall with a sandy blonde mohawk, brow piercings, and his muscular arms sported full tattoo sleeves. What could be seen of his legs beneath his shorts were fully tatted, as well... and he was smiling wide enough to show off his dimples.

Davey. The man who'd tattooed her ass. She knew she must look like a deer in headlights as Davey took the place of the waiter.

She had to say something..."Davey, wow, what a surprise." Lame and awkward AF.

"Hey, Rowan. I've been watching your table for a bit," he admitted with a laugh. "I was sure it was you. Since you seem to be the only one in your group not on a date, I thought I'd take a chance you might want to hang out tonight."

There wasn't enough damage control in all of Europe to dampen this shit show fire.

Davey looked sheepish but committed. She gave him props for being so bold. She could never have approached a table full of people to ask someone out, but oh God, the worst was when he said she was the only one not on a date. *Damn it, Hugh!*

Before she could come up with a brilliant reply—a thank you and have a good evening, I'm going home soon—Davey addressed the group.

"Hey all, I'm Davey Paxton. I met Rowan at my shop a few months ago."

Raven, bless her, tried to fill the silence. "Oh, that's cool. I'm Raven, her sister. What kind of store is it?"

"I'm a tattoo artist. I own Grey's off Cow's Lane."

Rowan mentally began the Act of Contrition. *O my God, I am heartily sorry for having offended thee and I detest all my sins, because I*...let this man tattoo my bare ass, and now Hugh knows his name, knows his face, and where he works.

She heard River's quiet, "Oh, *fuck*."

Preach.

When she heard the scratch of Hugh's chair over the cobbled patio, signaling he might be about to make a move, she knew she had to end this.

"Thank you for the drink, Davey—very thoughtful." She fluttered her hands, a gross abuse of gratuitous gestures. "However, I am on a date. I apologize if you thought otherwise." She blindly reached her hand back to lay her palm on the top of Hugh's thigh. His muscles were stiff enough to bounce her hand off.

Davey's smile faltered. "Damn, sorry. I would have never... that is, I thought he was someone's da—"

She cut him off before more damage could be done. "Haha," she cringed at how robotic she sounded. "It was so good to see you. Thank you again for the drink."

River tried to help too. "You did a killer job on Row's tat. If I ever decide to get another one, I'll give you a call."

"Yeah, Davey, "Raven added. "It was great to meet you, and we'll definitely remember Grey's."

Davey gave Rowan a pointed look as she slipped her hand from Hugh to fully face the tattoo artist. "Enjoy the rest of your evening," she finished with a stiff smile.

"I will, thank you. If you change your mind, find me. If you went out on a date with me, love, everyone would know we were together." With that mic drop, he waved goodbye to the table and left.

Needless to say, the jovial atmosphere of pre-Davey never

made a second appearance. Her sisters and friends tried their best, but Hugh never spoke another word. Not one.

By the time they got home, he still hadn't spoken. Grace only went so far. His lethal silence and clenched jaw had pushed her past pissed off.

She wanted to confront his behavior, but honestly, she wasn't sure she could stay level-headed. The worried looks that her sisters had kept sending her on the drive home only made her more pissed at Hugh. He promised he would try. If this was trying, she'd hate to see what their relationship would look like if he gave up.

Hugh watched Rowan silently walk to the refrigerator and grab a bottle of water. She didn't turn back around but stayed facing the opposite direction from where he stood. She took a few sips, probably hoping he would leave the room.

He wanted to. He wanted to avoid discussing the evening, but not at the expense of her feelings.

"Rowan." Her shoulders stiffened. She didn't acknowledge him or turn around. "Please, talk to me." She placed the bottle down on the counter before slowly turning. Her eyes were red-rimmed like she was barely keeping herself from crying. He kept hurting her, and it was killing him.

"You managed silence quite well most of the evening. Why break it now?"

"I did try to join in more. I did enjoy tonight." He sounded pathetic, but he had enjoyed everyone laughing and enjoying themselves. She didn't say anything else.

"I fucked up by not...from the beginning, I should have... held your hand. Like you asked. I'm sorry."

She shook her head and sighed. "You didn't just treat me like a stranger. You were actually unkind to me at the table. If I leaned too far into your personal space, you looked like you wanted to run. I let it go because I said I'd be patient."

He could only nod. Everything she said was true, except if he'd run, it would have been with her over his shoulder so they could be alone.

"You did start to enjoy yourself, I agree, but after Davey stopped by, you were...horrible, for lack of a better word."

Even hearing that man's name again sent sharp jealousy stinging through his chest.

"I explained that I was, in fact, on a date. You should have let it go," she blew out an exasperated breath.

"Your very young, very attractive tattoo artist that touched your *bare* ass and thought I was your *dad*!" he roared the last. He was livid. Not at Rowan—only at himself.

"The same man who bought me a drink and asked me out because he didn't have a clue I was on a date. How could he have known? How could anyone have known we were together?" she yelled back. "And you shouldn't care what anyone else thinks of us being together. You," she stopped to jab her finger in his direction, "should only care what *I* think about it!"

He leaned on the center island, palms flat on the cool surface, facing Rowan's disappointment. His goddamned hang-ups were going to lose him everything if he didn't step up. He started to tell her that he wouldn't screw up as bad as he had tonight ever again, but she shook her head and raised her hand to stop him.

"I'm sleeping in the guest bedroom. I'm too emotional tonight to be rational, and I'm exhausted. Give me tonight. I want to be rested when I see Nan off in the morning, and I have an early doctor's appointment. I'll talk to you tomorrow when we've both cooled down."

He didn't want to wait. He wanted this resolved. He needed

her forgiveness...again, but he also wanted to give her what she needed, so he nodded okay.

She went to their bedroom, grabbed some clothes and toiletries, and walked silently down the hall to the spare room, quietly shutting the door.

It sounded as loud as thunder.

35

───────

"Thank you again for coming," Rowan sniffled, embracing her sisters in Nan's old house—their house now after Patrick bought it from their grandma.

"What in the hell is going on, Row? Seriously, your text scared the shit out of me, and I know Pat's going to skin me alive when I get home," River grimaced. "I texted him halfway here to tell him the three of us had to run to Boyle today and would explain everything this evening."

"I told Bran that you needed River and me. I packed clothes and stuffed them into Daniel's diaper bag before running out the door." Raven didn't look any happier about leaving her husband without an explanation. "To say he was pissed when he got my text an hour later saying we had to go to Nan's is putting it mildly. I did admit that you were upset about something and needed us. He still wasn't happy, but he understood. River and I both asked Bran and Pat not to tell Hugh for now like you asked us to." Daniel was still sleeping in his car seat but was starting to stretch and yawn.

Rowan dropped into one of the kitchen chairs surrounding

the huge wooden table, placing her forehead on the smooth but scarred surface. "I'm sorry. So, so sorry, guys. I panicked."

"No shit. Pat just made a big breakfast, and I only got one bite," River whined. "Eating for two isn't just a job. It's a privilege."

From Rowan's prone position, she saw River smile from her peripheral. River was trying to lighten the mood. She appreciated the gesture, but Rowan couldn't think of a single thing that would make her current reality smile-worthy.

"Tell us what's going on. When you texted us both that you hopped a ride with Nan and Devlen, I knew something had to be seriously wrong," Raven said, rubbing a hand over her sister's head, which was still on the table. "While you start, I'm going to heat a bottle up for Daniel."

Forcing herself to sit up, she gave them the abbreviated tale of the most recent shitshow episode of Hugh and Rowan. She hit the highlights of the past year, which they knew most of by now. Went on to describe their time in Tulsa. They knew some of that, too, but not everything.

"He wholly committed to me, you guys. Completely. You know how he is, though. He can be quite hilarious, at least in smaller groups, but by and large, he's reserved and...bad-tempered," Rowan huffed a laugh. Trying to describe that man's unpredictable moods was laborious at the best of times.

The Seven Deadly Moods of Hugh.

"Of course, we only had the one night together before I was kidnapped. Then, when we were reunited, you both saw how standoffish he was at the hospital. There but not.

"He didn't change at the rehabilitation center. No touching and barely any conversation during the day, and then affectionate the minute we were alone at night. We spent hours talking about everything. However, when I brought up my wanting to have a child, he shut down hard. No discussion.

"The morning we left to drive to the airport, he'd left my room before I was awake and took his bags with him. You guys might have noticed he chose to drive separately from me."

"I thought it was strange, but you should know, Rowan, that I don't judge how you and Hugh choose to live your lives," Raven explained as she picked Daniel up, who was awake and smiling. Once she settled at the big table again, she continued. "It will be a problem with me if you aren't happy, however."

"I knew it would take time for him to come to terms with showing you affection, but after last night..." River trailed off, a frown marring her face.

Continuing where she left off, Rowan explained that she'd texted him on the way to the plane. He knew she was upset, that his behavior wasn't going to work.

"Remember when he followed me to the bathroom?"

"Mile High Club," River smirked. "Yeah, we recall."

Raven cooed at her son. "Papa is naughty. Isn't that right, my sweet boy?"

Raven and River laughed at her blush. "I can't believe he said that. See! That proves that he's capable of being public about us. That wasn't what I was going to talk about, though, assholes," Rowan shook her head at their big grins.

"*Before* we had sex, we hashed everything out. My expectations, his reservations. I was willing to give him time as long as he tried to show me a few signs of affection in public. I want people to know he's mine, damn it," she burst out angrily. "Is that selfish?"

"Absolutely not."

"Hell no."

"And then last night happened. I get that Hugh is territorial over me, just as his sons are over you two." They nodded in understanding. The men weren't big sharers. They could happily stay in an O'Faolain bubble with their women—and after the hardships and trials the six of them had been through together, she understood the impulse.

"He was angry about Davey. I get that too. Hugh's biggest hangup is our age difference. He hated a man so much younger than him hitting on me. I get all of that. It wasn't what pissed me off last night. It's the fact that if he'd treated me like his girlfriend, Davey would have never approached me." She had to press her fingers to her eyes so the threatening tears wouldn't fall.

"I slept in the guest bedroom last night. Or tried to sleep. I hated we didn't resolve things. I was too emotional and too angry to make good decisions and...I wanted to punish him for embarrassing me," she ended quietly. "It was petty and mean, and I should have been better than that."

"Don't be so hard on yourself. Jesus, Row," River fumed, "you've been through a shitload of shit for weeks. Hugh rejecting you, the shooting, the fu—flipping kidnapping," she corrected herself, glancing at their nephew. "So you'd had enough last night. It's okay to have feelings."

"You had every right to be hurt," Raven agreed, "but you also knew going into this that Hugh is an extremely complex man with a difficult personality. However, he loves his family and *you* fiercely. I understand needing a break after last night to recalibrate, so to speak, but what is up with coming here? I get it's only two hours from Dublin, and the distance might clear your head faster, but I saw a large suitcase by the door. Are you planning on staying longer than a night?"

River gave her a sharp look. "You haven't told us everything."

No, she hadn't. "I'm working up to that," she admitted sheepishly. Before she could give them the rest of it, Nan hustled in, carrying a basket of, if her nose was still working after crying, freshly baked scones covered with an embroidered tea towel.

With a quick, "Hello, girls," she set the basket on the table and went to fill the kettle. "I left some breakfast tea here, and glad I did. You girls need to really keep some staples here."

She and her sisters smiled at Nan's no-nonsense attitude. Rowan was relieved to have her here. Nan hadn't questioned her this morning when she'd asked to bum a ride not forty-five minutes after leaving her apartment that morning. She didn't ask a single question on the drive to Boyle, even when she had to have heard her sniffing in the truck's back seat.

Nan would have known she wouldn't want to speak in front of Devlen. They dropped her at the front door, Devlen grabbed her suitcase, and Nan said she'd be back. And here she was. Thank God.

When she tried to help set the table, Nan shooed her back. Once she had plates, napkins, and four mugs of steaming tea, she joined them, but not before scooping Daniel up and cuddling him close.

"Now then, what's all this?" She waved a hand around the table, which presumably meant, why had Rowan run to Boyle and dragged her sisters with her.

Clearing her throat, Rowan explained some of the problems she and Hugh had been having. "Last night was particularly difficult," and she told Nan some of what happened there, as well.

"Hugh is Hugh. It's never stopped you from loving him, my girl."

"I love him still. Desperately. None of those things could ever change that," she assured.

"Then why have you run away? That isn't like you. What else is it?"

Nan wasn't buying her partial story any more than her

sisters. She took a deep breath before telling them the rest. "Okay, but let me get it all out. I found out at Dr. Daley's this morning that I'm pregnant." When they gasped and started to speak, she held her hand up for silence.

"The first night we were together—together together that is—"

Nan interrupted with a snort. "Together together...what in the world does—"

Rowan cut her off that time. "We didn't use a condom. Once. It was the middle of the night and...umm...kind of like surprise sex," she stumbled over discussing her sex life with Nan, but there was no getting out of it now.

"It was an accident on both our parts. Hugh was horrified when I told him during the flight home. He literally looked sick at the possibility of me being pregnant. This was after I'd tried to broach the topic of wanting a child with him. He shut me down every time, Nan. He one hundred percent does not want another child.

"And it's not like I don't understand his predicament. He has two grown sons. I do understand, but he should have at least talked it out with me." Rowan swiped her hand in front of her, setting that bit aside. "The truth is, even without the words, he made it abundantly clear that children weren't an option. And now look," she sniffed on her tears, "I'm pregnant anyway. He'll be furious. I don't know how to tell him. I don't *want* to tell him," she wailed.

Everyone was up and pulling Rowan into hugs. Daniel smiled at his auntie in the middle of the huddle.

"Well, I'll say this much for the O'Faolain brood. They're a potent lot," Nan said, shaking her head.

"Need we remind you of Mom and Dad, Nan?" River grinned, swiping tears from beneath both eyes.

Raven grabbed tissues and handed them out before telling

everyone to sit back down. "Okay, let's eat, drink our tea, and figure out our next move."

"You mean *my* next move," Rowan grimaced. They sat, doling out the warm lemon iced scones. She took a big bite and moaned at the sugary tartness on her tongue. Food did make most things better.

"No," Raven continued, "I meant what I said. You know as well as River knows that Bran and Patrick aren't going to give us much longer before they demand answers. I imagine they are brooding together already. I also imagine Hugh is with them. I expect we'll be hearing from the three of them before we finish these scones. We need to come up with a plan to make Hugh come around."

"He's all bark with you, Row," River smirked. "He would never see you upset or disappointed. Not if he could do something about it. You should have seen him when you were missing. He would have never given up looking for you."

River surreptitiously dabbed her eyes. Nan and Raven took drinks of their tea to settle their feelings. No one liked to think of that time.

"Exactly. He is never going to give you up. He'll adjust to having a baby," Raven finished.

Nan had stayed quiet, finishing her scone in thoughtful silence. "Did you know he called me twice a day when you were missing?"

That surprised Rowan, though it shouldn't have. Hugh was incredibly thoughtful. He knew how much Nan would be worrying. "I didn't know that."

"Your sisters called, of course, and Bran and Patrick did too. My point is that you six are a package deal. Do you honestly believe Hugh would walk away because he got you pregnant?"

"We both are responsible," Rowan was quick to add. "And no, I don't think he'd walk away, but that's what makes it even worse. He doesn't want another child. I would become an oblig-ation, and I don't want that," she finished quietly.

Nan looked at her sternly. "Well, he's damn well getting another child, no matter what his previous concerns were. That part is well and done. If you think that man would ever, even for a moment, consider you an obligation, then how do you girls put it...that's a *you* problem."

That broke the tension, each of them snorting in amuse-ment. Tears were dried, tea was imbibed, and focus was brought to the table.

"This isn't about Hugh having trouble expressing his emotions publicly. You need to admit that, sweetheart," Nan said kindly, taking her hand between her own. "That man loves you whether he shouts it to the masses or not. This is about the baby. Only about the baby. Yes?"

"It is. I'm scared, but I know between the four of us, we'll figure this out. Just like we did with Raven and Bran and River and Patrick." The funny thing was, once Rowan admitted that out loud, she did believe it. They would make this right. She believed in Hugh even when he questioned himself.

"This meeting of the Byrnes is officially in session," Rowan declared. "Let's plan." They didn't start for ten minutes. Her precious nephew decided to poop and stink the kitchen up to high heaven. Daniel's diaper changed, they reconvened in the sunroom, wanting to include their mom and dad in the process.

Rowan smiled fondly at her favorite snapshot in the memory armoire. It was of her parents looking into each other's eyes, laughing, and holding hands. She imagined they still did that same thing in Heaven.

River was just starting a list of ideas on her tablet when all three of their phones started pinging with notifications. They must have all gotten a touch of déjà vu from the last time they'd all sat together awaiting an O'Faolain message. The three sisters grinned as they opened their messages.

Hugh was livid. Bran and Patrick were being cagey when they met for lunch. Rowan hadn't come home before he'd left. She must not have finished her errands yet. He didn't text or call, afraid she was still angry. When he'd asked the boys where their wives were, they ho-hummed around and shrugged their shoulders like adolescents.

They took seats at Oliver St. John Gogarty's bar. It was one of Hugh's favorite pubs in the Temple Bar district. Gogarty's Boxty was good, but anything with potatoes was good in Hugh's book. After ordering drinks and appetizers, he spun on his stool and stared at the two towheaded miscreants he'd helped create.

Bran cleared his throat. Guiltily. "We need to meet Tay Withe at the distillery. I thought about taking Rave there on Friday and spending the night at a local B&B. She would love to get Daniel out of the city for a day."

Hugh didn't respond. The key to his sons was making them so uncomfortable they eventually gave up the information he wanted. He crossed his arms and continued to look between them. Even when the drinks were set in front of them and they pretended great interest and joy in a glass of water, he didn't relent.

Patrick cleared his throat next. Guilty AF. "River would like a short excursion too. Plus, now that Rowan's back, the three of them are supposed to be getting a design plan together."

He'd give it to them. They hadn't given up their wives' whereabouts yet—which meant they'd been asked by those same women not to tell him. This had to be about last night. Christ. He was starting to sweat. He didn't like that he and Rowan had gone to bed without working things out. He really didn't like not knowing where she was. He'd just gotten her back, and now this. He was barely holding his shit together. His sons would talk, or they would regret it.

Before the shit hit the fan last night, she'd said she was telling Bébhinn goodbye at eight. Her doctor's appointment was at eight forty-five. She only had a couple of errands after that. She should have been home for lunch.

The Byrne sisters were together. They had to be.

"Withe is a hell of a distiller. Good call on that, Dad," Bran rambled.

Hugh didn't even blink.

"For fuck's sake. What's your problem?" Patrick asked.

Finally.

"You're the one that fucked up last night, and now we're all paying for you being an asshole to Row," Bran gripped his shot glass in frustration.

"You hurt her feelings, Dad. It really upsets River when you do that," Patrick added.

Now they were getting somewhere. He gritted his teeth, pissed off that his sons knew how upset he'd made Rowan. He picked up his shot of Slane and took a healthy pull, hiding a slight grimace. He didn't really care for Slane. He kept his expression blank, continuing to wait for his sons to completely break.

The truth. His sons were strong-willed and intelligent. They wouldn't tell him if they truly didn't want him to know. Hugh could tell they were angry about last night. They didn't like their wives, or Rowan upset, or that their father was to blame.

Bran sighed, rubbing his eyes before looking at his father again. "Dad...Jesus, I know you hate talking about your personal life, but you've got to change, or you're going to lose Rowan.

The sisters' happiness is tied together. You can surely understand why Pat and I have a stake in you being a dick."

"Speaking of dicks, let's talk about yours. Spoiler alert, we know you have a dick. We know you use your dick—with Row. I've personally caught you mid-using your dick—again, with Row."

Bran butted in, "Say what now? You caught Dad—"

"Shut it, Pat," Hugh demanded. He had to keep repeating Endure, Endure, Endure, over and over and over again. He needed information about Rowan, but unfortunately, this travesty was the means.

"Later," Patrick told his brother.

"Anyway," Patrick began again. "We know you love our sister-in-law. Like, seriously, Dad, would it kill you to show her affection in front of us?" Patrick asked, clearly as fed up with him as he was with himself.

"Where are they?"

Bran met his gaze straight on. Looked like the preliminaries were finally over.

"Boyle," Bran admitted.

"They only told us that Rowan needed them and that they would call us later. I texted Devlen because I knew better than to question Nan. He said Rowan got a ride with them this morning. That's all I know," Patrick shared.

As if they were in a choreographed dance, the three of them pulled their phones out and began texting.

She left town because of him. He was having a hard time taking a full breath.

Please come home.

I'm not ready.

Forgive me. I love you.

It isn't enough this time. You really hurt my feelings last night. Like...really hurt me. You didn't

just treat me like a friend—you treated me like I didn't mean anything to you.

You mean everything to me. I keep fucking up. Hugh frantically wondered if there was anything he could say that would make a difference. It was unusual for Rowan to leave things unresolved.

I'll come back to Dublin in a day or two.

She said Dublin, not home. **Home?**

I'm not sure.

He glanced at his sons, who were both still busy texting. They looked up at the same time, their faces as grim as he felt. "When are Raven and River coming back?"

He texted back. **Please.**

I'm not chasing you anymore.

"Raven said not until Rowan does."

"Same," Patrick confirmed.

"You do realize," Bran began after taking a drink of water, "that fixing this is simple. It's always been simple."

Hugh could only look at his phone screen. *I'm not chasing you anymore.*

"How is any of this simple?" Hugh appeared unruffled from the outside as he sat sideways on his barstool. Inside, his heart was beginning a painful flatline. *I'm not chasing you anymore.*

"Make sure she never questions your feelings again," Bran explained, as if his dad was simple-minded.

"A grand gesture like they do in movies," Pat grinned, excited at the prospect. "I wrote River letters. Bran spent months growing that bread stuff for Raven."

"Sourdough starter, moron," Bran scoffed.

Hugh sat his phone on the scarred wooden bar and picked up his glass, shooting back the rest of the shot. His boys were looking at him expectantly. They believed he could be...this man Rowan needed.

"I have an engagement ring—for Rowan."

"Well, we didn't think you were going to propose to Diana Gaines," Patrick laughed at Hugh's glare.

"If I didn't have things to do, I'd enjoy beating the juvenile out of you."

"Nice. A proposal's a gesture for sure," Bran assured him, ignoring his brother as they were all wont to do.

"Fine. I'm going home to pack a bag and get the ring out of the safe." He frowned at their twin grins. "Do *not* tell your wives."

"We won't, but we're coming with you," Bran looked at his brother who nodded in agreement.

36

"The texts stopped," River announced.

They were still snuggled up in the sunroom nook, the rich scents of soil and green not as comforting as usual. They were palming their phones like the bits of flat metal were precious objects. Not Nan. She was cooing at her great-grandson.

She grinned at her granddaughters then, looking quite satisfied and not in the least concerned about the communication interruption.

"The men are planning. Raven and River were purposefully vague on what you were doing here and about how long you planned to stay. Bran and Pat wouldn't like that. Rowan," Nan continued, "you told Hugh, in not so many words that you might not live with him. You also told him you weren't going to chase him again."

"Nan's right," Raven agreed. "None of the O'Faolain men sit on their hands. They're much more prone to action. Me and Riv are married, so Bran and Patrick have security in that. Hugh doesn't have that insurance. He'll come to you," she predicted.

"I guarantee he's coming," River grinned.

Nan patted Daniel's back and stood, stretching her back and giving Daniel a smacking kiss, making the little boy grin. "Get off your lazy bums, girls, most likely we have two hours before that ornery boyfriend of yours arrives, Rowan. Let's all go to my house and get started on an early dinner feast."

She blushed sweetly when she told them she'd love for them to see the kitchen table Devlen had built her. "He knew how much I loved my old table here and wanted me to have one that he made with his own hands for all our new memories."

"Oh my," Rowan sniffed.

Raven smiled and kissed Nan on the cheek before lifting her son from her arms.

River dabbed her eyes. "You scored with that one, Nan."

"Why do we need to make so much food?" Raven asked as they made their way from the sunroom.

"You didn't seriously think Hugh would come alone? How absurd. Those three are as thick as you three."

Her sisters all grinned, anticipating seeing their men. Rowan tried to grin back. Her family was so sure Hugh would be overjoyed with a baby. She wasn't so sure. Ah well, it was too late to turn back now. The plan to draw Hugh to Boyle had already begun.

"Why does Bran always get to sit in front? It's bullshit," Patrick moaned from the back.

"The same reason it's always been, dumbass. I'm older."

"You're such a dick."

"I don't care what you call me. I'm in the front seat," Bran crowed.

"River told me that Raven said your bedroom game's gone downhill, bro. Have you considered vitamins?"

"The hell she said that!"

Before Bran could jump in the backseat and start a fight with his brother, Hugh warned them, "If I have to tell you boys to shut the fuck up one more time, I'll pull this car over and leave your asses on the side of the road." Hugh sighed when they both laughed. Did God truly never give someone more than they could bear? He'd pondered that over the years. Many, many times.

"Lighten up, Dad. You're just nervous," Bran offered yet more unsolicited opinions.

"She won't say no. Remember the rules," Patrick reminded. "Happy. Humble. Hugs. Happy. Humble. Hugs," he repeated.

Dickhead.

"Right," Bran chimed in. Again. "No growls, grimaces, or glares."

His boys must have decided today was the day for alliteration.

The truth was, he was too nervous to even yell at them again. His hands were white-knuckling the wheel. He'd be pulling into Bébhinn's in five minutes. Rowan didn't know he was coming. He didn't know if she would speak to him or be pissed that he came.

He'd taken the ring out of its fancy box and stuffed it down his front pants pocket.

He was going to do this. He was going to ask Rowan to marry him. In front of their family.

He was most comfortable with his sons and the Byrnes. This should not be a problem. It would *not* be a problem.

His first instinct was to ask Rowan to speak with him privately, but he knew this wasn't the time to hide his feelings. Everyone knew he loved Rowan. She was the only one who had doubts, and he was about to fix that, which was why he was currently sweating and having hot flashes like a menopausal woman.

Bran and Pat were still insulting each other when they pulled over the wooden bridge leading to the Byrne plot. As the trees thinned and the quaint Irish two-story surrounded by an explosion of flowers came into view, the vehicle became silent. He almost wished the boys had continued their inane chatter. Putting the car in park, he tried to breathe through the panic.

A hand came down hard on his shoulder. "Dad, Bran and I agree that Raven and River would have told us to keep you away if that's what Rowan had really wanted. They didn't. She wanted you to come here. There's no other explanation," Patrick encouraged.

"Our sister loves you, Dad," Bran thumped him in the arm, smirking as he hopped out of the car so Hugh wouldn't retaliate.

Sister. Jesus. Hugh got out of the car with a sigh. He wasn't ready, but if he waited any longer, he'd lose his nerve.

The house was empty. Used mugs in the sink and one of Daniel's blankets were the only thing to show they'd been there.

"I bet they're at Devlen and Nan's house," Pat offered.

Hugh grunted in response. They exited the house and walked to the abutting property.

"You're already forgetting the G's. No growls, grimaces, glares, *or* grunting," Bran reminded.

Hugh ignored the giant blonde mosquito buzzing in his ear and took long-legged strides to the neighboring house. As his feet hit Devlen's drive, his boys at his back, he spied Rowan and her sisters through the full-picture window facing them.

The three women froze at the sight. Eyes wide they placed hands on Rowan's shoulders almost simultaneously as his boys did the same. His heart actually struggled to produce its normal rhythm. She was breathtaking. Stunning. And she would be his wife.

. . .

"THEY'RE HERE," Rowan whispered. They'd been setting the table for dinner—and it *was* a lovely table, which she'd told Devlen, who'd blushed and left for the barn. It was then that she spied three gorgeous modern warriors striding across Dev's grounds. Good Lord, she forgot what a powerful image they made together. Her sisters obviously felt the same. Their eyes were glued to the trio.

"Get in the kitchen, girls, and do something besides trip over your slack jaws." Nan said, popping them lightly in their rears with a damp kitchen towel.

Three squeals later, they ran back to the kitchen, adjusted their aprons, and had just picked up three identical blue flowered mixing bowls when someone knocked at the front door. Nan gave them a *stay there* look before going to let their guests in.

This was it. Baby reveal time.

BÉBHINN OPENED THE DOOR, raised eyebrows and disapproval flattening her lips.

"Hugh, boys," she nodded and smiled, stepping aside to allow them to come in.

The smile was only for Bran and Patrick. Hugh tipped his head in thanks as he moved by the Byrne matriarch, his eyes scanning the open floor plan for any sign of Rowan. He barely repressed a smile at finding three sets of hazel eyes glued to him and his sons.

If he had his phone in hand, he would have loved to have had a picture to preserve this moment. Rowan, Raven, and River held mixing bowls in varying stages of spilling the contents—except the bowls were clearly empty. They wore matching aprons, one green, one blue, and one yellow, all with #1 Granddaughter embroidered on the chest.

They were so similar in appearance. It still startled him. Except he knew them all very well now. Raven's lips were fuller. River's eyes held a curious cat slant. Rowan, his Rowan, had deep dimples. Dimples he'd worshipped with his tongue more than once.

He felt his sons at his back, giving him the strength to move. He walked with purpose toward the one woman he couldn't live without. The girls each set their bowls on the counter before them. Sure enough...empty. They'd counted on them showing up. Raven and River weren't even pretending to be surprised.

Rowan looked...scared. That put him on high alert.

The kitchen was nice but by no means spacious. Seven people crowding around the narrow center island was putting the space at or past capacity.

Rowan finally met his eyes. His focus had never wavered, so he knew the moment she decided to look at him. He saw her breath shudder, her shoulders stiffen. He wanted her in his arms. He wanted every reservation she'd used to build this wall between them destroyed.

She cleared her throat and brushed her hands down the yellow ruffled skirt of her apron. "Hugh, would you step outside with me?"

Alarm bells went off. Her demeanor was screaming endings. He was only interested in beginnings. The five sets of eyes currently ping-ponging between him and Rowan was a test of endurance and one he planned on acing. He wasn't holding back. Not anymore.

"You can tell me whatever you need to in front of everyone. I have things to say to you too." Her eyes widened in surprise and then panic. Not good. When she looked at her sisters for help, and they shrugged, his nerves started blowing fuses.

"I would rather do it in private," she countered.

"I promised that I would try harder to show everyone in

public how much I love you. I screwed up last night. I'm not doing that today or any day from now on." She appeared shocked. Her mouth opened and closed several times. Nothing ever came out—yeah, he had definitely shocked the hell out of her. He crossed his arms and continued to watch her, waiting for her to realize he was dead serious.

"Okay...you're sure?" she asked. At his nod, she said, "I'm pregnant."

His mind took a nap. He could only stare and sway, sway and stare. Pregnant. "But...I don't understand." Even in his shocked state, he knew how dumb that sounded.

"One of the times we had sex the first night we were together—totally together—remember, we didn't use—"

A brief glance at Bébhinn had him cutting her off. "Okay, transparency doesn't have to mean full disclosure," he winced at the poorly covered cough-guffaws exploding around them.

He took a step closer to her. She was watching him closely, clearly trying to decipher how he felt about the news. If she discovered what that was, he hoped she would share her thoughts with him. He wanted to walk out of the kitchen and take some time to digest the news but knew to do that would hurt her. He would stay. Of course, he would stay. He and Rowan were going to have a child together. A zing of nerves pinched his chest, but so did excitement.

"Hey, Pat, do you remember all those safe sex talks Dad forced on us in high school?"

"Yeah, wear a condom, or I'll kill you. I guess practice what you preach doesn't mean what I thought."

"Boys," Bébhinn scolded. To the rest of the occupants, she said, "Let's give these two a moment."

Once everyone had filed out, he asked, "Why didn't you come home? Why did you run?" She blushed at that, clearly not impressed with her actions, but she didn't look embarrassed.

"I won't apologize. I got the news and panicked. I *panicked* because you made it clear more than once that you weren't interested in having any more children."

All true. He frowned, thinking about what an unbending ass he'd been. "You're right. I'm sorry." He stepped closer, close enough to take her hands into his own and hold them to his chest. He blew out a breath, not wishing to discuss what he knew he needed to.

"Helen was never kind to me. When she was pregnant, she was vicious. The results, the boys, was worth it, but it didn't make me want to repeat it," he explained. Rowan's eyes were glassy when he finished. She knew how much Helen had hurt him during their marriage. She was the one to close the last of the distance separating them.

"I will only ever love you, pregnant or not."

"I know that. This was all on me."

"I...I want the baby, Hugh. I wish we could have discussed it together and decided the right time. You know I would have worn you down, and you would have eventually agreed," she grinned up at him before sobering again, "but I do wish you'd had a choice."

Hugh pushed the empty bowls back the girls had been holding and lifted Rowan to sit on the counter, where he stepped between her legs. He bent and whispered against her lips. "I had a choice, baby, and it was to be balls deep in you without a condom. We made this child, and I sure as hell am not giving either of you up. Ever."

When her mouth parted on an exhale, he took advantage and kissed her. Something slow and sweet, a kiss that spoke of everything in his heart he wasn't poetic enough to speak. He broke away long enough to fish the engagement ring out of his front pocket. Her eyes were still dazed from the kiss, and it took her a moment to see what he held pinched between his fingers.

"I came here today to ask you to marry me, well, I would have apologized for last night first but...Rowan Clary Byrne, will you marry me?"

WILL YOU MARRY ME? Looking between Hugh's grim face and the ring, she felt her face flush with pleasure. Rowan was pretty good at reading his expressions, or lack thereof, and the blank one he was rocking in that moment was nervousness. As if he had any reason to doubt her answer.

"Yes, and it's about damn time, Mr. O'Faolain," she laughed as he slipped the—holy cow!—yellow diamond on her finger. *Oh my.* The cheers coming from the dining room made her smile and Hugh shake his head. His eyes were laughing, though.

"I picked it out in Tulsa after you agreed to give me another chance. I knew I couldn't let you get away again. I picked it because I know yellow's your favorite color, and I wanted you to smile whenever you saw it on your finger," he added quietly, his cheeks pinkened at the admission.

"I love you," she said, placing a kiss on the corner of his mouth.

"Christ, Row, I love you."

He was just about to kiss her when Nan and Devlen walked into the kitchen, followed by a grinning Bran and Raven and Patrick and River.

Nan hugged and kissed Rowan. Tears were swimming in both their eyes. Nan had known the longest how desperately in love she'd been with Hugh. Devlen gave her a brief hug and pat on the back—the man was finally getting the hang of hugs. He shook Hugh's hand in congratulations before stepping back, letting Nan hug...her fiancé.

"You're the best of men, Hugh. I couldn't have asked for a better match for my granddaughter. Rowan's grandfather, Sean, and her father, my son, Daniel, would have approved heartily. Her mama, Lily, would have loved you immediately because her daughter did."

"Thank you, Bébhinn," Hugh accepted the high praise solemnly.

With that, the rest of the family swarmed the newly engaged couple to give their own well wishes and hugs. Hugh pulled Rowan against his side and kept her there. It was one of the best moments of her life.

"We'd better call your mom, or we'll both be in trouble," Rowan suggested.

"And Jo," River reminded.

"Have you thought of wedding venues?" Raven asked.

Rowan cleared her throat and squeezed her arm tighter around Hugh's waist. "Is this a good time to let everyone know that I would like to get married at the courthouse and have a destination honeymoon with our family and friends?"

"The courthouse," Nan gasped.

"Really?" River wondered.

"Are you sure?" Raven asked.

"Sounds like a great idea to me," Bran said.

"Thank fu—" Patrick cut off the curse word at Nan's sharp look, "heavens," he continued. "I think we should all write down our honeymoon ideas and pick the best," Patrick grinned, patting his wife's behind. "Riv and I will have the best ones."

Hugh bent to whisper in her ear, placing his big palm over her flat stomach. "I'm praying the baby's a girl."

Rowan snorted in amusement.

Addressing the crowd, Hugh announced, "I knew you'd want that. You mentioned it once during Raven's wedding. In the hope you'd say yes, I called my attorney and had him start looking into the paperwork for an expedited wedding license.

We can get married as soon as you want and take our honey-moon next year once our baby is born. What do you think?"

"I think this is why I said yes." She stepped close, her body flush with his, and placed her palms against his broad chest. She melted even more when she felt the heavy thud of his heart. This man...*her* man had crushed his inhibitions and claimed her in front of everyone. Even if today was the only day for grand, public gestures, it was enough. Way more than enough. It was a story she would tell their child one day.

"Kiss me like you mean it, Mr. O'Faolain." His dark eyes shone brightly as he grasped her waist, pulling her into his body before claiming her mouth—thoroughly and irrevocably, like he'd already claimed her heart.

When he finally set her back on her feet, she was breathless. They smiled at each other, soft and secret. Let me have a moment alone. At his nod of understanding, and before she stepped away, she whispered, "You were always mine, and I'll always be yours."

"Until the end of forever," he whispered back.

Hugh released her waist as Rowan stepped away and went to take her sisters' hands. She noticed the men left the room, followed by Nan who blew her granddaughters a kiss as she passed.

Together, they formed a circle holding hands. Unbreakable. Never-ending.

"I love you," Rowan said, looking at the two most important women in her life.

"I love you," Raven echoed.

"I love you," River answered.

"We did it. We found our forever," Rowan grinned through her tears.

"We did."

"Hell yeah, we did."

Hand in hand in hand. Always.

EPILOGUE
MURPHY'S PUB, DUBLIN—KENNEDY-DANIELS
WEDDING

Diana Gaines

Normally, I avoid this type of event. Weddings are all well and good, but a wedding in an Irish pub...well, let's just say it wouldn't have made my top eight thousand things I might enjoy list. My best friend, Matilda O'Faolain, is admittedly not as uptight as I am. She was excited about the event, so here I am.

Tilly cheered as the new bride gave an impromptu dance on her new husband's lap. I cringed. They did look gloriously in love, and I am deep down, *way* deep down, a sentimental woman. I may have been a widow for almost twenty years, but I'm not dead. At seventy-two, I am still a fine-looking woman. My sleek silver bob is perfectly quaffed, shiny, and thick. My figure is, well, I'd never been some voluptuous Jessica Rabbit, but I *am* an average five foot six and trim.

I had been infertile—I wasn't infertile now, just old. When my late husband had brought up adoption, I'd eviscerated the suggestion. My set-down might have caused him internal bleeding. Adoption meant I'd failed. Diana Townshend Gaines didn't fail at anything. My marriage had certainly not been a great love story like my best friend's, but Tilly and Jon were exceptions to the rule.

I used to envy my dear friend, but Jonathan's passing had almost taken Matilda to the grave with her husband. When George had passed, it had been an inconvenience at best.

George and I were the rule. We were a match created between our two powerful families. We'd gotten on well enough. It had never been passion forward but rather duty, nothing more, nothing less.

I regretted my ignorant stance on adoption, but not until years later. Too many years later. A husband dead, no interest in replacing him, and at the time, I was fifty-five. An age that seemed too ancient to consider creating a family. Now, at seventy-two, I could admit that I'd stood on the wrong side of that argument. It happened rarely, but it did happen.

No matter. I had lived a full life and adored my brother Owen's children and my great-niece, Samantha. I also had my best friend Matilda, her son, and his children and their families. When Bran and Patrick had their own sons, I'd felt like a grandma too. One could have regrets. Wallowing in regrets, however, was a disgusting waste of time. Ignorant people wasted their time.

I have always been the antithesis of ignorance.

I moved to stand next to Tilly and my brother, who seemed to be glued to my best friend's side of late. I'd be pissed if Owen didn't look so damn happy.

Bran handed his son, Daniel, off to his wife, Raven. He and his brother had begun to hurl insults at each other while Hugh watched, shaking his head.

I was about to nudge Tilly's side and question her grand-sons' low behavior, but someone crowded my free side, the warmth of their arm irritating. I attempted to ignore the unwanted interloper. No eye contact assured no verbal communication. However, the Neanderthal, with no social intuition, cleared their distinctly male throat.

With an inner sigh, I glanced right and was surprised to see Bébhinn's husband, Devlen. Tilly adored the Irish woman and her new husband had seemed pleasant, but this behavior was about to earn the Irishman a set down.

He stuck his hand out to shake. "Evan Dunn," he introduced himself. To my obvious confusion, he added, "Devlen's twin. I'm an archeologist recently returned from a dig in Ecuador. Upano Valley," he clarified.

Christ, I should have realized Devlen Dunn would never have been half so obnoxious. I took his proffered hand and shook. Good manners held very few avenues except for the most courteous route. "Diana Gaines."

"I know. Bébhinn speaks highly of you."

That warmed my heart. Rarely did someone speak of me in any way other than hushed whispers with pinches of fear and submission. I didn't make the rules of society, but I did enjoy keeping the occasional aspiring socialite in check.

Bébhinn Byrne happened to be amazingly forthright and intelligent. Two attributes I admired, and so, I was pleased she felt similarly about me. Tilly had encouraged me to get to know the Irish woman, and her praise not unwarranted.

"I didn't know Devlen had a brother." Devlen and Evan were certainly handsome devils. I attempted to tamp down my girlish flush and maintain my infamous aloof, bordering on disdainful, stare.

"Devlen doesn't offer any information that isn't excruciatingly relevant."

"Mmhmm," I absently hummed.

"I'm not a man who cares much for ceremony. I'm educated, intelligent, and passionate about my work, so I'll cut to the chase. You're wealthy, and you like to travel. Would you sponsor my next dig?"

That took me aback. I have a weakness for direct confrontations, and I *have* been suffering from a touch of boredom the last few years, so I raised one imperious brow and waited for the rest.

"There have been other archeologists that believe a lost city exists near the Chandeleur Islands off the coast of New Orleans. I want to set up a base camp for myself and my team in the city with resources to travel to the islands. I want guaranteed funding for one year minimum."

"You're presumptuous."

"I'm fecking persistent." His Irish accent was flaring. "Presumptuous implies I don't know what I'm talking about. I can assure you, Diana, I do know. Your name would be listed as part of the team when we discover the ruins."

I watched the silver-headed fox's chiseled jaw clench. He was passionate, if nothing else...and I did love New Orleans. "Fine. Send me the details...at your convenience, of course," I barely held back a snarl. This man annoyed me. He also intrigued me. "I'll look over them and let you know if I'm interested." His deep exhale proved he wasn't nearly as confident as he'd tried to make her believe.

"Fine then. Good. Save me a dance," he demanded with enough cheek to fuel an adolescent for a week.

"I don't dance," I countered.

"You do now, though, right?" he asked and had the audacity to wink.

"We'll see," was as much answer as I was willing to give. He looked at me long enough to cause a slight warmth to flush my body before moving toward the bar. My goodness. He was inappropriate.

My attention was caught again by the O'Faolain men. They

were always highly amusing, though I tried desperately to hide how entertaining I found them.

Hugh looked amused as he told his sons to knock it off. Tilly's son had always been an unapologetic curmudgeon in my opinion, but since his marriage to the youngest Byrne, it was obvious that the man couldn't contain his emotions behind his semi-permanent stoic mask as often as he used to. It was a good change.

As I watched, Hugh grasped his wife's still trim waist, though she had to be close to three months along by now, and lifted her, holding her small body against his own massive one—that boy had always been...big. I know I just admitted that Hugh was more demonstrative, but witnessing him kissing his wife, passionately, in front of such a large crowd took me aback.

I glanced toward Tilly with pursed lips of disapproval for the public display. Her return grin meant my eyes must have given away my delight.

Not to be outdone by their father, Bran spun his wife, making her laugh before he, too, kissed his spouse. Patrick backed his wife, who'd just handed her son to Bébhinn, against the smooth wood of the bar behind them. River was the one to pull her husband's head to hers and give him a big smacking kiss, causing them both to grin like maniacs. Pat and River were definitely the cheekiest of the three couples.

"Mom," Hugh said, getting Tilly's attention, as well as several others. His deep voice was very distinctive. "Did Bran or Pat fess up to breaking one of the Lalique glasses you got me from that Christie's auction for my fiftieth birthday?"

I felt my brows wing up in surprise for two reasons. Hugh was being as ornery as his boys *and* because one of the crystal tumblers had been destroyed. I remember how excited Tilly had been when she'd won the auction.

"Dick move, Dad?" Bran complained.

Patrick walked back over to the group, River in tow, as soon as his dad spoke. Those three O'Faolain's were as close as the sisters they were married to. Magnets. Patrick's jaw dropped, "What the hell?"

Tilly gasped at hearing that one of the lovely glasses had been ruined. "I can't believe you boys would be so careless. Were you juggling them, for heaven's sake?"

"Sorry, Gran," Bran began. "Patrick was the one to drop it. I was just standing there," he tattled.

Patrick flashed him a pissed look before turning to his grandmother. "Sorry, Gran, it's true. It was me. I admit to it, but did Bran ever admit to what he used to use your fancy ruler—oomph," Patrick expelled a grunt when his brother punched him in the stomach.

Was I truly lamenting my lack of children only moments ago? I sure as hell did not want to know what Bran did with my friend's ruler. Christ, those boys. I bent to whisper a "Good luck" to Tilly before walking away.

I ordered another G&T and leaned against the bar, enjoying the revelry surrounding me. My gaze caught on Josephine O'Connor. Dean's daughter was a lovely young woman. She'd remained quite a mystery to me—never dating, just work, work, work. I was happy when the Byrne's befriended her. Josephine needed something besides her job.

It had come as quite a surprise when she had fallen so hard for her bodyguard. It surprised me more when the relationship ended abruptly, and according to Tilly, Josephine wasn't admitting to anyone the cause of the split.

I knew. I just wasn't doing anything with the information. Yet. The private investigator I'd hired created a file of his findings.

My eyes traveled the packed tavern until they landed on Thomas MacGregor across the way. The Scottish giant was attempting to hide his egregiously oversized body in the shadows, but really, the play of lights only reflected his intense focus. Josephine. The man had it bad. Unfortunately, he'd kept two colossal secrets tucked away in the Scottish Highlands.

Secrets rarely stayed secret. I hoped MacGregor would clean house. If he didn't, well, I was prepared to illuminate the error of his ways.

ABOUT THE AUTHOR

Anne Gregor is a Contemporary Romance writer and the author of *Raven*, the first book in The Irish Wolves trilogy. Anne loves using her master's degree in history to sprinkle a little of the past into a modern package. When she is not writing, reading, or book reviewing, she is obsessed with true crime documentaries and cooking challenge shows—a combination like fish and cheese—sometimes it works. An empty nester after her three children started adulting, she still loves getting together for family game nights. Quiet evenings are reserved for reading and peanut butter.

She lives in northeast Oklahoma on the Grand Lake O' the Cherokees and is passionate about all things Okie.

ALSO BY ANNE GREGOR

The Irish Wolves Trilogy

Raven

River

Rowan